S0-BNH-913

Final Approach

Spencer Dunmore was born in London and educated there and in
Yorkshire. He left Britain in the mid-1950s and now lives in
Hamilton, Ontario, where he is in charge of creative services for
one of Canada's largest advertisers. He has written for the
Canadian Broadcasting Corporation TV and Radio and for
various American and Canadian magazines. His first novel,
Bomb Run, was short-listed for the *Yorkshire Post* Best First Novel
Award of 1971. *Bomb Run*, and his more recent novels *The Last Hill*
and *Collision* are all published in Pan.

Previously published by
Spencer Dunmore in Pan Books

Bomb Run
The Last Hill
Collision

Spencer Dunmore

Final Approach

Pan Books London and Sydney

First published in Great Britain 1976 by Peter Davies Ltd
This edition published 1977 by Pan Books Ltd,
Cavaye Place, London SW10 9PG
© Spencer Dunmore 1976
ISBN 0 330 25206 2

Printed in Canada

to Jean

Prologue

I am ancient. A relic. Rheumy of eye and wobbly of limb, I observe the steady deterioration of the untidy bundle of pipes and bones, muscles and tissue that is me. I suffer from no specific ailment, simply a general wearing-down of everything. There can't be a great deal of time left. Does the knowledge sadden me or frighten me? I don't think so. I believe I can truthfully claim to accept the inevitability of my years with a certain tranquillity; even at times with some impatience.

My memory works better than anything else. Admittedly, I have been known to mix up my decades; occasionally, I have even managed to confuse my world wars. In the main, however, I remember it all with remarkable clarity. I have discovered an intense pleasure in memory. The human animal in decline seems to nourish itself on retrospection in much the same way that it fed on hope and ambition (and lust, I suppose) in its younger days.

I am ninety.

No applause, please. (Is anything more tedious than thunderous ovations for having survived eighty, ninety or a hundred years? There's nothing terribly clever about it. One simply continues to wake up each morning. The years add up by themselves.)

I live alone. I am told repeatedly that it is foolish of me to continue to live alone. Possibly. But I won't move. I've lived in this house since 1919. And all my memories are here. I know that I am an obstinate old blighter and a source of considerable concern to goodness knows how many estimable souls. Very well. I admit it. I am obstinate. Am I not to be allowed a vice at my age? I choose obstinacy. (I am, after all, incapable of most of the others.)

My daughter Georgina telephones every morning and evening. I reassure her: I am still breathing. (I like to say that my visa for the land-of-the-living expired some years ago but I am continuing to maintain an illegal residence. I have an uneasy feeling, however, that I may have made too much use of that particular epigram. These days I observe fewer and fewer smiles when I employ it. I must attempt to think up a new one.)

On fine days I walk. Or rather, I shuffle. I explore. I know every inch of the territory, yet still my ambling search goes on for one more clue.

I have every reason to believe that I am the world's leading authority on this place.

It is a fact that appears to be of practically no interest to anyone but me.

I don't care.

I am a familiar sight in the area. I am on nodding terms with a score of faces. The citizens who live here are decent enough folk, I am sure. They bring up their families in their overpriced modern houses that to these watery old eyes look garish, cramped, ugly and flimsy. So do their cars. Come to think of it, the comment might be applied to their society as a whole. It's a society that seems bent on squashing initiative and individuality and encouraging laziness and mediocrity; a society in which the majority are repeatedly blackmailed by minorities: a hand-out, something-for-nothing society. I don't pretend to understand it. I suppose it will work. I hope it does. But I suspect it will be discovered that one set of inequities has merely been exchanged for another.

What strikes me as odd is that so many of these foremen and shopkeepers, accountants and schoolteachers should reside here without being aware – or caring – that this is land on which history was once made.

One windy day my hat blew off. A fellow of about forty rescued it from the middle of the road. I thanked him and we agreed that the wind was unquestionably fresher than usual for the time of year. I asked him whether he lived in the neighbourhood.

'Just moved in,' he told me. 'Cody Drive.'

I asked him if he knew why the street was so named.

'Haven't the foggiest,' he said cheerfully.

And clearly he wasn't the least bit interested in knowing. I didn't pursue the matter. Nothing on earth is quite so tedious as an old man who insists on telling you something that you don't wish to know.

A week or two later a most friendly terrier came bounding up to me and jumped at my leg, tail a-twirl.

'Oscar! Don't do that! You'll mess up the gentleman's trousers!'

The speaker was a girl of perhaps fifteen. She was pretty in the straight-haired, carbon-copy way of today. I assured her that my trousers were so old and so shapeless that Oscar couldn't possibly do them any harm.

The girl said that she had often seen me out walking.

'We live in Dunne Street,' she told me.

I said that I knew it well. And, of course, I couldn't stop there. 'Nearly fifty years ago,' I declared, 'a man climbed into an aeroplane at a point very close to where your house is located; indeed your house may well be on the very spot, for all I know. The man took off in the hope of being the first man in the world to fly the Atlantic Ocean from east to west.'

She seemed genuinely interested in my morsel of information. (A bright, intelligent child, this; she is sure to go far.) She said, yes, she had heard someone say that there had once been an airport in the area.

'It was one of the very first in England,' I told her. 'And it was called Ashley Landing. Many famous airmen – and some airwomen – flew here. In fact, your street is named after a great pioneer of British aviation, a man by the name of John William Dunne.'

'That's super!' she exclaimed. 'What happened to the man who got in the plane and tried to fly the Atlantic?'

'He couldn't get off the ground. He had too much petrol on board.'

'Shame. Imagine our house being on an airport. I must tell Dad.'

I was about to explain that in those far-off days we used the term 'aerodrome', but she was already on her way, waving a cheery hand. She was one of the more charming representatives of her generation. I wished her a long and challenging life.

If you knew this place as intimately as I do, you would find it a simple matter to pick out the boundaries of the old Ashley Landing aerodrome (assuming of course that you have the slightest interest in so doing). The southern boundary was marked by the river, although airmen on the ground judged their distance by the row of stout oaks that stood on the far bank. Beyond these oaks once lay the ploughed fields of the Ashley Farm (the Ashley name persisted despite the fact that the place had been owned and run by the family named Morton for generations). Now there are a couple of factories on the property. One makes windscreen washer mechanisms, the other, meat pies. (Tasteless things; I tried one, once.) A Shell garage stands upon the spot formerly occupied by the Ashley farmhouse; it serves the traffic that dashes tirelessly along the London Road. That road was there in 1910 but it was narrower and safer; it was the field's eastern limit. To the west there is the cemetery and a street named, with monumental inappropriateness, Grand Avenue. To the north there is the High Street. Cross the High Street and you're in the old part of the district. There, the houses have that solid, proprietorial look acquired only by structures fifty or sixty years old. I live at number 47 Harvest Road. That house has been my home for well over half a century and I intend to live there until the march of time forces me to take up permanent residence elsewehere. Then, my son Martin and my daughter Georgina may have the property, with my blessing, to do with as they please.

I used to have an unimpeded view of the field from the windows of two of the bedrooms. I could see the brick hangar that Samuel Fenwick erected in 1910; beside it there was a flag pole from which, bold and proud, the Union Jack always fluttered. Mr Fenwick had purchased the two hundred and ten acres in 1909 with the avowed intention of making the site the greatest aerodrome in Europe. A man of means, Mr Fenwick engaged a staff of six to design and build an aeroplane for him. It flew. But in common with so many aircraft of the period, it was viciously unstable and hopelessly underpowered. After half a dozen wobbly, thoroughly dangerous journeys across his aerodrome, Mr Fenwick stalled and crashed into a pond on the Ashley Farm. Mr Fenwick survived but his ambitions as a pilot didn't. He decided that his future lay in providing facilities for other aeronautical hopefuls. He built a row of hangars.

In January of 1911 my brother Beresford and I set up shop in one of them. We spent a Saturday morning painting the legend MARSHALL BROTHERS AEROPLANES LTD in large red letters over the door. When we had finished someone pointed out our error: Beresford and I were not a limited company. But it seemed to be an unimportant technicality. We left the name as it was. We had far more important things to think about. We had a mission. In all things aeronautical, France and America led the world. Britain's designers – Roe, Handley Page, Sopwith, Graham-White – were just beginning to make their aerial mark. But in that year of the coronation of King George V (and of the hottest summer in living memory), the only British aeroplane of note was the Bristol Boxkite; and it was a frank copy of the French Farman. In all probability, if you wanted to purchase a reasonably reliable flying machine, you would travel to France to see the aforementioned Mr Farman or Mr Blériot, or to America to see the Wrights or Mr Curtiss. Beresford and I would change that. We would design and build the finest aeroplanes in the world. Britannia would rule the air. And we would make ourselves incredibly rich in the process. At Ashley Landing there were several other gentlemen with much the same thoughts in mind. Mr Wardle, whose workshop was next to ours, was convinced that the answer to stability in the air was to provide large numbers of tiny wings rather than one or two large ones. A ruddy-faced individual who wore farmer's leggings, he would talk endlessly on the subject, given the slightest encouragement. He eventually built a machine to test his theory. With its scores of little wings, all at different angles of dihedral, all joined by slender struts, it gave the impression of having just exploded. Although Mr Wardle clocked many miles in spirited dashes about Ashley Landings' acres, he never succeeded in taking to the air. Next to him, Messrs Glubb and Lyman worked assiduously on an aeroplane large enough to carry a dozen passengers in an enclosed cabin. Unhappily, they exhausted their limited funds upon the interior of the cabin long before tackling such components as wings and tail. One man built an aircraft with circular wings, another built one with aerial paddles; a third spent every waking hour on a primitive form of helicopter that enthusiastically beat itself to death early one Sunday morning in June.

I possess a fading photograph of Beresford and James Marshall. It was taken on a bright summer's day. The brothers stand in front of an aeroplane, arms folded, feet planted firmly in the grass; they squint against the sun that shines over the head of the photographer (Mr Wardle, the multi-wing enthusiast). It is an odd experience to look at oneself over a span of sixty-five years. I have to keep reminding myself that the young man named James is – or, rather, was – me. He wears aviator's garb: leather jacket, cap and goggles – and a rag tucked into his belt with which to wipe away oil during flight. He is dark-haired and has regular features. He looks serious; one might even say a little self-important. But perhaps he can be excused. This is, after all, an important day. James holds his head in the defiantly confident way of so many aviators of the era; there was an unspoken agreement between them all: never, by droop of lip or sag of shoulder, admit to even a modicum of trepidation when preparing to take to the air.

The family resemblance between the two brothers is striking. But Beresford, who is thirty-five, ten years James' senior, is a slightly more compact and considerably more intense version of his brother. There is greater determination in the set of the jaw, a more intellectual sweep to the brow. Beresford smiles in a slightly sardonic way as he peers into the camera. No doubt he is thinking of something other than the business at hand. As usual.

Beresford's right leg is artificial, although the fact is not discernible in the photograph. He lost the limb during early, totally unsuccessful, experiments with rocket propulsion. (Eleven months before this picture was taken, Beresford's wife, Marcia, ran off with a commercial traveller from Huddersfield. Beresford wrote the fellow a cordial letter of thanks.)

At the right-hand corner of the photograph, partly obscured, is Oliver Eggleton. He is older than the Marshalls, probably over forty. (He is unsure of his precise date of birth, since the tiny Essex parish in which he was born kept singularly sketchy records.) A sturdy peasant of a man, Eggleton wears a plain shirt *sans* collar and a dark, almost shapeless jacket that looks as if it has been in daily use since Dickens' day – as perhaps it had. Eggleton's garb never varies, no matter what the season. He is a mechanic and airframe constructor; he possesses remarkable talent but no formal education. He is the Marshalls' only employee. He earns twenty-five shillings per week on which he provides for a wife and four children.

Most of the aeroplane is visible in the photograph. It is a monoplane, a handsome machine of surprisingly modern appearance for 1911. Officially the aeroplane is known as the Marshall Model 21. (It was not our twenty-first design, however, but only our third. We named our first the Model 10, reasoning that prospective customers might be deterred from purchasing any manufacturer's products called the Model 1. We cannibalized the 10 to provide parts for the next machine, a biplane designated the Model 15. We completed that machine in March and had been working diligently ever since trying to find someone – anyone – who wanted to buy her.)

When Mr Wardle snapped the shutter, the Model 21 had undergone engine tests and taxiing trials. Now she was to take to the air on her first test flight.

Part One
Wednesday 7 July 1911

One

I gripped the rim of the cockpit and lowered myself into the narrow wicker seat. It was snug but comfortable. The view forward was obscured by the engine, but the fuselage was slim and during taxiing I could lean to either side to check on the path ahead. I fastened the quick-release belt across my lap (it was a device we added since seeing a man fall out of his aeroplane at Hendon one summer day). My feet had ample leverage on the rudder pedals; the control wheel was well positioned between my knees. The broad wings extended at shoulder height; to a remarkable extent they seemed to be an extension of myself. The wings' upper surfaces were scalloped between the wooden ribs; the doped fabric was taut and unmarred by a single wrinkle. Eggleton the perfectionist. I moved the controls. On the floor of the cockpit the bright steel wires shifted obediently, transmitting my commands to the wings and tail. This aeroplane felt *right*. And I was a part of it.

Beresford appeared. Typically, he looked bored with the proceedings. He glanced inside the cockpit.

'Everything all right?'

'Topping,' I replied.

'All right,' he said, 'we may as well see if the thing will fly.'

Eggleton ducked out of sight beneath a wing to reappear a moment later, his broad hands clutching the mahogany propeller blade.

'Try not to kill yourself,' said Beresford.

'Cheerio,' I said.

He gave me a brittle little smile as Eggleton swung the propeller. The 70 hp Gnome rotary caught and burst into clattering life, hurling back a pungent waft of castor oil. The control lever shivered impatiently. I checked the dials. Oil pressure up. Petrol pumping well. Glance to left and right. Beresford on one wing tip, Eggleton on the other. And behind, several score onlookers. Everyone came out when there was a new aeroplane to be tested.

I tugged the goggles down over my eyes. A nod to the wing men. A touch of power. The Model 21 rolled forward, her slim nose angled high, as if sniffing at the air.

I taxied for twenty minutes, increasing my speed gradually, getting a feel for the machine's response to the air that streamed over her wings and tail surfaces. She *was* well balanced; her looks hadn't lied.

But she deceived me when she took to the air. She didn't wait for me. I was taxiing a shade more rapidly, when suddenly, the rumbling of her wheels ceased. The earth was half a dozen feet below. And dropping.

Full power. Up she rose, eager, like the thoroughbred she unquestionably was. The earth tilted. I yelled, 'Whoopee!' or something of the sort. The aeroplane was a sensation! I had never flown anything that felt so stable and yet so manoeuvrable. Beresford had created the best aeroplane in the world. And I was flying it! All our troubles were over!

I zoomed across the field. The aeroplane's shadow bounded effortlessly over the grass and the sheds and the houses. Heads turned; eyes squinted against the early morning sun.

I remember carolling, 'She's a bloody miracle!'

Then I saw the smoke.

Something wrong with the fuel system. A broken pipe, perhaps, a faulty connection. No time to investigate. Black smoke billowed into the bottom of the cockpit and came through the edges of the instrument panel in tight streams. I felt it forcing its acrid way into my mouth and nose. I stared for an instant, hardly able to believe the evidence of my eyes. Fate couldn't be so bloody cruel!

I glanced quickly over the side. I had to get down. There wasn't an instant to waste. I thought I might be able to save the aeroplane. I hurled her into a side-slip, trying to keep the smoke and

16

flame from the cockpit. Down we went, crabbing, wallowing, staining the clear sky with our oily smear.

The starboard wing began to buckle. The fabric, blackened, glowing; the woodwork still white behind the dancing flames. Instinctively, I tried to turn. But it was hopeless. I had no control over her. The aeroplane had become so much burning timber and metal. She could no longer obtain support from the air. She tumbled, graceless, ugly. Below, the field turned as if on a pivot. Quite distinctly, I saw the sheds lined up beside the London Road, the pale wings of the aeroplanes parked on the grass, Mrs Braine's house, 43 Pogson Road, where Beresford and I had quarters . . . People, standing, staring, pointing . . .

My life failed to flash before my eyes. Only the moment mattered. And movements. Reaching forward into the smoke, snapping the ignition switch to the left. Pulling down on the petrol pump to cut the supply of fuel. Releasing the lap belt. Fighting the centrifugal force with every ounce of power in my body. Heaving myself out of the seat, tearing a handhold in the smooth fabric of the fuselage behind the cockpit. Dragging myself, inch by frantic inch out of the cockpit and towards the tail, to place myself as far from the inevitable point of contact as possible.

I felt myself spinning like a top. My innards crowded into my throat. Hold on, I told myself. It'll be over in a flash. Won't feel a thing.

But I did.

There was a thumping, cracking, splintering crash. I was weightless. Suspended. I thudded down on something. The impact snatched the breath from my body. I lost consciousness. I was cycling down Muswell Hill. I met my father. Beresford with a moustache. 'I've been looking for you,' he said. 'Come and have a pint; you're old enough to drink beer, aren't you?' And then I was awake, gasping for breath like a fish thrown up on the beach. I distinctly smelt horse. A moment later things snapped into focus and I perceived that my olfactory sense had not let me down. I saw a horse's foot. It was a yard or so away, beneath me. Therefore, I reasoned, I am slung across a horse, corpse-like. But presumably, because of the fact that I am observing the horse's foot so accurately, I am not a corpse – although, heaven knows, I certainly deserve to be one.

I slithered off the horse, and landed, quite painfully, on the road. It was at that moment that I saw the Model 21. It had crashed thirty feet away, into a field of tomatoes, and was burning furiously. I shook my head to clear it.

'All righ', mate?'

I said I thought so. My voice sounded peculiar; it seemed to be pitched a fraction higher than I remembered; and it possessed a curiously tinny quality. I wondered what I had damaged.

Then the world became a forest of hands: fingers reaching for me: some helping me to my feet, others pressing me, as voices exhorted me to remain where I lay. Someone declared in a gruff voice that I was a bleedin' lucky bleeder. I couldn't argue. I discovered that I had been tossed off the aeroplane moments before it hit the ground. Arms and legs flailing (according to one eye-witness), I had descended upon a Pickford's van that happened providentially to be passing by on its way to Purley. I was told, with considerable relish, that I had plunged through the roof, half-bounced, half-ricocheted out through the front, narrowly missing the driver, and had ended up across the nearside horse.

I apologized to the driver.

'S'all right with me, guv,' he said, 'but I got a feelin' you'll be 'earin' from the comp'ny abaht the way you buggered up me van and me load of bird cages!'

Beresford and the *Express* man went downstairs.

The room reeked of Turkish cigarettes.

Normally I detested the smell. Today, however, I found intense pleasure in being able to sniff the air and identify the odour. I kept wriggling my toes. I took deep breaths. I was keenly interested in sounds: those of the front door closing downstairs, the reporter's footsteps on the path outside, the clatter of a horse and cart, the high-pitched giggle of a child. A girl? A boy? It was a fascinating puzzle. Being alive was delectable. Never again, I vowed, would I take it for granted.

Two hours before, the doctor had examined me. Rather unnecessarily he informed me that I was a very lucky young man. The damage, he said, amounted to nothing more than a severe shaking and a few cuts and contusions. (My voice, thank God, had returned to normal.) I had a large bump on my forehead. I was instructed to spend two days in bed.

Beresford returned.

'I told him you were flying a Blériot,' Beresford said.

'Well done.'

'I think he swallowed it.'

He planted his lanky frame on a chair and leant back, balancing on its rear legs. They creaked piteously. He thrust his hands in his pockets. 'What did you think of him? Bit dubious, wasn't he? Never bend down in the presence of a man who smokes Turkish cigs. I think he minced a bit. And I fancy he rather liked the look of you, stretched out on your bed of pain.'

I thanked him for protecting my honour. 'Perhaps,' I said, 'they won't print the story.'

'They will. They love aeroplane crashes.'

It was true. The popular press delighted in blood-curdling accounts of the latest aerial disasters. The gorier the better. Even the more distinguished journals found the theme irresistible. Scarcely an issue of the *Illustrated London News* appeared without its half-tone of tangled wreckage flanked by suitably solemn onlookers. Sometimes an inset illustration of the late aviator was added for good measure. On the other hand, it had to be admitted that the press could have its value. Newspapers had made national heroes of Blériot when he flew the Channel, and Paulhan and Graham-White when they fought for the London-to-Manchester race . . .

I asked Beresford if there had been anything worth salvaging from the wreck.

'Not much,' he said. 'We might get a pound or two for scrap on what's left of the engine. That's all.'

He wasn't deceiving me with his what-the-hell attitude. He was as bitterly disappointed as I was; but he didn't have the satisfaction of personal survival to assuage the hurt.

I apologized for smashing up the aeroplane.

He shrugged. 'Not your fault, old man. Have you ever noticed anything odd about the second cow on the left?'

'I beg your pardon?'

He pointed to the picture which graced our wall: a remarkably

19

uninteresting study of Highland cattle. Mrs Braine valued the thing highly. She informed us that it had been in her family for generations.

'That bloody cow is cross-eyed.'

I looked. 'So it is.'

Beresford lit a cigarette and blew smoke at the ceiling. He studied it. 'You know,' he said, 'it occurs to me that we might be able to develop a fire-extinguishing system for aeroplanes, to avoid the sort of thing you had to face. One would have to work out some automatic method of smothering fires . . . triggered by smoke or heat, perhaps . . . have to give it some more thought . . . feasible, don't you think?'

'A splendid idea,' I said.

'It has possibilities,' he said. 'How are you feeling now?'

'A few aches, but that's about all.'

'Good. You really are a lucky sod. Not too bright but extraordinarily lucky. I was wondering if you were carrying your watch. I was rather hoping you might have left it behind when you went flying. I've had my eye on that watch for ages.'

I smiled. Typical Beresford, to ramble on about my watch. He avoided sentiment as a seminarist avoids temptation.

'Pity about the aeroplane, though. She seemed to be performing well until the plumbing let us down.'

I assured him that the Model 21 was a marvel, quite the best machine I had ever flown.

He nodded. 'Her landing characteristics seem to leave something to be desired. But we can work on that. If we get started immediately, we can have another Model 21 ready before the end of the season. With a bit of luck we'll still be ahead of the rest of the pack. What do you think?'

I cleared my throat. There was a problem, I told him.

He looked up, 'Money?'

'I'm afraid so. I had hoped that by now we would have sold the original Model 21 at a healthy profit and would have taken orders for fifty more . . .'

'How much do we have?'

'Two hundred and twelve pounds and something.'

Beresford sighed. 'One of the less attractive characteristics of a bank account is that if you continually withdraw and never deposit, the balance tends to diminish.'

'Eggleton's wages are due tomorrow. And Mrs Braine's rent on Monday.'

'And,' said Beresford, 'I fancy that we shall be hearing from Pickford's very shortly about the damage done to their van by our missile, to wit, your flying body. Thank God we didn't have to bury you. I understand funerals are bloody expensive these days.'

There was no doubt that we should try again to sell Bessy, the Model 15. She had been squatting in a corner of the hangar, unflown, for weeks. Surely, someone, somewhere, wanted her. We could arrange a bargain price. After all, she was no worse than the majority of aeroplanes then in daily use. Beresford loathed her for that very reason. 'All we've done,' he said, when Bessy first flew, 'is to make all the same mistakes that everyone else has been making. We've achieved strength by building a maze of struts and wires, but we've created a fantastic amount of resistance to the air which we can't overcome with the power that's available from the engines that are light enough for us to carry. It's a vicious circle. And the only way out of it is to *help* the air to flow over our aircraft's surfaces, not hinder it. That's why birds are shaped the way they are. But we haven't had the sense to see it.' Beresford would have scrapped Bessy if her parts had been of use to him. But they weren't; his head was full of new concepts and Bessy was forthwith relegated to the hangar. What a singular and thoroughly unpredictable character Beresford was. Industrious one day, bone lazy the next; gregarious in the morning, morose in the afternoon, positive and confident, then utterly negative. But it could all be excused because he was a genius. And one day, inevitably, the world would recognize the fact. Indeed, *today* should have been that day; by now the papers should have been full of our triumph, the aeronautical world should have been talking of nothing else. As it was, an obscure aviator had had a lucky escape at Ashley Landing.

The bump on my forehead was aching in earnest. I rubbed it – and succeeded only in aggravating the discomfort. Our problem, I reasoned, was largely one of anonymity. We had built the finest aeroplane in Britain – probably the world – but no one knew it. No one had heard of us.

What was the answer?

If we had plenty of money, we could of course advertise in the appropriate journals and exhibit our machines at Olympia. Presumably, then, the orders would come rolling in.

But we didn't have the funds to build another Model 21, let alone advertise it or exhibit it. Therefore it was necessary for us to obtain coverage by the press without paying for it. I told Beresford that we should build another Model 21 and do something remarkable with it.

'I thought your performance with this one was pretty remarkable.'

'No,' I said, 'what I mean is, something on the lines of flying the Channel or winning the London-to-Manchester race. Then the papers would write reams about it and it would make the aeroplane famous and us too, I suppose, and people would want to buy the aeroplane.'

'And all our troubles would be over.'

'More or less, yes.'

'Unfortunately the Channel has already been flown.'

'I know.'

'And the London-to-Manchester race is all over.'

I said that I knew that too. 'Therefore, we must find a new exploit, something to make the world sit up and take notice of us and our aeroplane. It's no use waiting to become famous; we've got to force the issue a bit.'

'Any ideas?'

I shook my head.

'The concept is sound,' he said.

'I think so.'

'Have to give it some thought,' he said. He stood up. 'I feel like going out for a little while, if you don't mind.'

'Not at all,' I told him. 'The doctor told me to rest.'

'I may even nip into Town.'

'I thought you might.'

Beresford had a habit of venturing into the West End from time to time. It was impossible to predict when he might return from such visits.

'Sure you don't mind?'

'No. I shall read. I have a new Conrad from Boots.'

'Good. I'd like to read it when you're finished.'

'Very well.'

He stood before the mirror and straightened his tie. Then he turned and patted his stomach. He was concerned about the onset of middle-age spread. He had little to worry about; he was extremely slim, almost skinny. He wore his clothes well yet he was careless about such details as buttoning jackets and keeping pocket flaps out. He wore his bowler hat square on his head but tipped forward in a manner that some conservative souls considered downright saucy.

'You're quite sure?'

'Positive.'

'See you later on.'

I told him to try not to catch anything.

I awoke. The room was in darkness, except for the glimmer of light from the lamp post at the corner of the High Street. I could just make out the corner of the dressing table and a faint reflection from the glass of the Highland cattle work.

'Beresford?'

I could hear nothing but the faint rumbling from the Southern Railway line. I started to drift back to sleep. Then my nose twitched. Alcohol.

'Beresford? What time is it?'

'Shhh. Don't want to wake Mrs B!'

Beresford sounded as if he had refreshed himself liberally.

'How are you, ol' man?'

I told him that I was well enough.

'Good. I brought you a li'l present. From the West End. Lisle Street, to be precise.'

I sat up. A present. How very good of Beresford. Who would ever have thought it of him . . .? I suggested that he turn on the light so that I could see the present.

'I think not,' he said. 'This present is better enjoyed in the dark.'

Giggle.

I heard it, quite distinctly. My mouth dropped open. I closed it.

'A li'l present,' said Beresford, 'for my baby brother.'

23

'You've got a . . . *woman* there!'

'I beg your pardon,' he replied. 'Not a woman. No. Definitely no.'

'You're potty!'

'Not a woman, but a mere girl, vibrant and fresh with youth . . .'

'You can't bring a woman in *here*!'

'Actually,' said Beresford, 'you can. And I did. Her name is Angela. Say how-do-you-do, Angela. This is my brother, the famous aviator.'

'Can I sit dahn?'

'Certainly, my dear. On the bed beside me, here.'

I stifled a croak of pain as something descended heavily upon my upturned foot.

'Angela has healing hands,' said Beresford. 'I brought her home to minister to you on your bed of pain.'

'Minister to me . . .'

'She's really awfully good at it,' he said. 'I thought I'd pop out for a smoke, for half an hour or so. Or an hour, if you'd prefer.'

'You idiot! Get her out of here!'

Angela said, 'Does that mean 'e don't want any?'

'It means nothing of the sort,' Beresford declared. 'My brother is a healthy young man, therefore he is in a state of almost continuous randiness. He is dying to avail himself of your services and experience the soothing balm of your touch; but his mind tends to run on conventional lines, he therefore follows the practice, so common in our hypocritical society, of not admitting to a perfectly normal biological urge . . .'

I hissed at him, 'For God's sake, shut up, Beresford. Mrs Braine will . . .'

'Have no fear,' declared Beresford in resounding tones. 'Angela is our cousin. From Southend. Is Southend all right with everyone? I can make it Worthing if you'd prefer; no trouble at all . . .'

A rap on the door. Righteous authority.

Mrs Braine's voice.

'Mr Marshall! What is going on in there?'

'In where?' said Beresford.

'I must ask you to open this door immediately, Mr Marshall.'

'I must remind you, Mrs Braine, that there is an invalid in this room!'

'Open this door at once, or I shall open it with my master key!'

'Don't you think,' said Beresford, 'that when a woman possesses a master key it should be known as a "mistress key"?'

'You have a woman in there, Mr Marshall!'

'In here? I don't see one. Do you see one, James?'

'Don't play games with me, Mr Marshall!'

'I wouldn't dream of it, Mrs Braine!'

Mrs Braine cried, 'I am entering! I have the key in the lock! I am turning it! I am opening the door!'

Two

We purchased two foldable metal cots and set them up in a corner of the hangar. From the local Sainsbury's, we obtained bread and butter, milk and jam, tea and sugar; we stowed these provisions beneath one of the benches, next to some piston rings and coils of wire.

I did my best to look on the positive side. We would save a good deal of money living in the hangar and we would be able to devote more time to producing the second Model 21.

And so we ordered the plywood, the spruce, poplar and hickory, the piano wire, the steel tubing, the Continental rubberized fabric. And we ordered the engine, a 100 hp Green this time, gambling that we would be able to sell the completed aeroplane before the Green Accounting Department became too persistent.

The work went well. Before the end of August the aeroplane had taken form; her structure was complete and was half covered with its skin of plywood and fabric.

On the evening of the 30th of August, a thunderstorm of unusual severity struck the Southern Counties. At times the winds generated by the storm reached speeds of ninety miles per hour. Scores of trees were uprooted; umpteen chimneys were blown down; a dozen light craft were sunk at their moorings; some buildings lost their roofs. One such building was the Marshall

Brothers Aeroplanes Ltd hangar at Ashley Landing aerodrome.

The roof broke in two as it tore away. One half, consisting of two iron girders and a couple of hundred square feet of sheet metal decking, tumbled into the hangar. The girders hit the Model 21 immediately behind the cockpit, instantly crushing the fuselage to matchwood. The decking fell across the port wing, snapping the main spar. Only the starboard wing and the tail unit were undamaged.

We were fortunate to escape without injury. Part of the roof crashed down half a dozen feet from Beresford's cot. Plaster and dirt showered upon us as we were shocked into wakefulness.

I opened my eyes to see the gaping roof and to feel the rain. I scrambled out of my cot and fell over Beresford.

'Are you all right?'

'Yes . . . What the hell happened?'

In moments, we had found out. Beresford hopped about obscenely, tearing at the girders, swearing at them for destroying his aeroplane.

I sat down on a box. I stared at the mess, blinking as the rain ran over my face. It was vile, unspeakably foul luck, and it wouldn't go away like any normal nightmare. It was reality. It had to be faced.

Beresford pointed to Bessy, secure and unscathed in her corner of the hangar. 'Look at the idiotic thing! For God's sake, why didn't the bloody building fall on *that*?'

The wind howled through the broken roof, scurrying around the walls of the hangar, nudging Bessy, making her rudder twitch.

'Oh, damn everything,' Beresford snapped. 'Damn the weather, damn the rotten roof, damn every stinking thing . . .'

Despair was a lump of lead, lodged somewhere deep within my intestines.

It was hopeless. We were finished.

Beresford sat on his cot, the rain beating on him, flattening his hair, soaking his pyjamas. He looked thin and defenceless. He clenched his fists, and beat one into the other. He wanted to fight, but there was no target.

The rain hit the taut fabric of Bessy's wings; the hollow thuds sounded like pennies falling on a drum. I found some sacking and threw it over her. The rain eased, then stopped. The wind faded. Nature had had her little game; now she was content to return conditions to normal.

I walked about the hangar, my bare feet slapping the cement floor. My legs trembled. I felt sick. Why us? What had we done to deserve such appalling luck?

I went outside. The sky was tranquil now. The storm had moved off to the east. Act of God. Wasn't that the term used by the insurance people? If so, it was a stupid, wasteful act . . . As for insurance, we had none.

A train clattered by, light coaches swaying. Oh, to be on the thing. Oh, to be anywhere but here . . . to be back earning a living at draughting table, drawing a semi-decent salary, living a sensible life . . . perhaps even married to some charming young lady who . . .

'Good God,' I said.

A thought had occurred to me. An intriguing thought. It had been lying there, simply pleading to be discovered.

I examined it warily, studying it from every angle to find its flaws. But it possessed none. It was sound.

'Good God,' I said again.

I returned to the hangar. Beresford was still sitting on his cot, his chin in cupped hands. For a moment I thought he was crying. But he was simply staring. Blankly. The picture of utter hopelessness.

'Something just occurred to me,' I began.

'Something just occurred to both of us,' he said flatly.

'Oddly enough,' I said, 'I was thinking of Angela.'

'Angela?'

'Yes, the girl you brought back to Mrs Braine's . . . I was thinking about being married and settled down . . . and suddenly I thought of Angela . . . she just popped into my mind and it set off a train of thought.'

He sighed. 'She has that effect.'

I drew up a chair before him. I wanted all his attention.

'Do you remember that earlier that day we talked about what a splendid thing it would be to fly the Channel because it would make our aeroplane famous?'

'I suppose I do,' he muttered, not very interested.

'We discussed the fact that the Channel has already been flown.'

'Did we?'

'Of course we did, Beresford. Please try to remember.'

'All right, I remember.'

He smeared his hands over his cheeks as if trying to warm them.

'We were wrong,' I said. 'The Model 21 must fly the Channel, Beresford.'

He frowned. 'We already agreed that it has been done.'

'Yes; I know . . .'

'Well then . . .'

'Who has flown the Channel, Beresford?'

'For God's sake, you know perfectly well.'

'Tell me, please.'

Beresford shrugged. 'Blériot did it in 1909. Several other people have done it since. Charlie Rolls flew it both ways last year, in June, if I remember correctly.'

'You do remember correctly.'

'Then what the hell . . .?'

Triumphantly, I said, 'Messrs Blériot and Rolls have more than one thing in common.'

'What on earth are you talking about?'

'They are men.'

'Of course they are men . . .' The penny dropped. At last. But the reaction was disappointing. Beresford nodded slowly, mechanically. 'You're quite right, of course. The Channel is still to be flown by a woman. But what has that to do with us?'

'Everything! Every damned thing! Don't you see – if the lady in question flies a Model 21, it will mean world-wide publicity for us . . .'

'I suggest we forget about it,' he said.

'No!' I clung to my notion with the desperation of a drowning man clinging to a lifebelt. If I let go, everything would be lost. 'Look, Beresford, it's a way of making our name known . . .'

'It's no use,' he said. He shrugged. 'We're finished. It was probably idiotic for us to start the thing in the first place. Well, we've learnt our lesson, haven't we?'

'Don't say that.' I could hear the pleading in my voice.

'Sorry, old man. But we've got to face facts. We tried. But we weren't bright enough or lucky enough, or both.'

'But, Beresford, a flight across the Channel . . .'

'How,' he said, 'do you propose to get in touch with the lady in question? And how do you propose to persuade her to fly a Marshall aeroplane instead of a Farman or a Bristol?'

Therein lay the snag. I knew of no female aviators who had their eyes on the Channel. In fact, I knew of no female aviators. I had heard reports that a Frenchwoman, a Hélène Dutrieu, had obtained her aviator's certificate. But this had to be an English-woman's flight. And so far Englishwomen seemed content to do their aviating as passengers.

'I'm sure there must be a suitable lady . . . or ladies. All we've got to do is find her . . . them.'

'Possibly we could run an advertisement in *The Times*,' Beresford suggested. 'LADIES, ARE YOU MAN ENOUGH TO TACKLE THE CHANNEL . . .'

'Please, Beresford, I'm serious.'

'So am I. I'm getting out of this ridiculous business before I lose my mind as well as everything else . . . Vickers have made me an offer that isn't totally unattractive.'

I held up a hand. Another idea was taking shape. 'We must get a newspaper or magazine to sponsor the whole thing.'

He gazed at me, pityingly.

'You don't give up easily, do you?'

'This *can* work, Beresford. Look, we must talk to the news-papers, of course, but I was thinking about those women's maga-zines. You know the ones I mean. The ones that are bleating all the time about women having the vote and society being unfair to them and paying them less than men, despite the fact that they can do anything a man can do . . . well, here's a perfect story for them: a woman flying the Channel just as well as any man.'

'You're wasting your time.'

'They'll jump at the idea,' I said.

He shook his head. 'No, they won't. Ideas like that stand a chance only if they are born at the top. Do you honestly think some cub reporter strolled up to Lord Northcliffe one day and suggested that the Mail put up ten thousand quid for the first man to fly from London to Manchester? Of course not. He'd have been booted out on his ear. It's always the same story in business organizations. If an idea comes up from the bottom it's harebrained and a shocking waste of the shareholders' money; but if the Chairman of the Board thinks of it, it's brilliant and totally feasible and it's implemented without a moment's delay.'

'You are a cynical sod.'

'Just realistic.' Wearily, Beresford reached for a towel and began to dry his head. 'Let's assume you manage to find a publisher who likes the idea and is prepared to put up the money for such a flight. Why in God's name should the man deal with us? We're unknown. And bloody unsuccessful.'

'We've got to try, Beresford, There's a chance . . .'

'There is also a chance,' said Beresford, 'that King George will pop his crown and run off to the South of France with a lady-in-waiting.'

The 8:50 to Victoria was packed. And hot. I shared a compartment with two elderly ladies, three businessmen, a sailor and two ugly schoolboys. I wore my only suit, the four-button clerical grey worsted that I had purchased from Whiteley's for nineteen shillings and elevenpence halfpenny three years earlier. I detested it. It fitted far too well. Its snugness evoked ancient memories of fat aunts who hugged one and would not let go until one was on the point of retaliating physically. To make matters worse, I had donned a stiff Castle collar (5/11d. the box of a dozen); it seemed to be cutting off part of my blood supply. If the train stopped suddenly my neck would probably snap over the wretched thing.

I carried two manilla envelopes. One contained photographs and plans of the Model 21; the other contained two cheese sandwiches: my lunch. In my pocket I had a sheet of paper bearing the names and addresses of twenty-three journals, prospects all. The local public library had provided these invaluable data, plus a map of the streets of the City of London by means of which I had charted my course. First on my list was Revell's *Weekly Journal* ("For the Young Lady of Taste and Distinction") for no other reason than that its editorial offices were located at 18 Andrew Street, a mere five-minutes' walk from Victoria. If Revell's happened to turn me down, I would not have far to stroll to 25 Juniper Street, headquarters of Bolton Publications Limited, publishers of *The Modern Maiden*, *The Modern Matron* and *The Modern Mother*. After half a dozen more women's magazines came the newspapers in Fleet Street.

I had been buoyant with confidence on boarding the train at Ashley Landing. I was eager for my mission, impatient to get to grips with the Fourth Estate. But the nearer the train drew to Victoria, the more rapidly my eagerness drained away. Now the train was slowing. Soon it would stop. I would have to vacate this secure little cell. I wished Beresford had accompanied me. I felt inadequate and rather frightened, an ill-dressed nobody venturing into a world where I wasn't known and in all probability wasn't wanted. The platform appeared, like a moving stage with its cast of doleful porters leaning on their barrows. It was, I decided ruefully, one thing to talk airily about magazines putting up hundreds of pounds to pay for cross-Channel flights, quite another to go and tackle them on the subject.

I stepped on to the platform, closing the carriage door behind me. I should have let it be. Damp, sticky soot caked my hand. I tried to rub the stuff off with my handkerchief. All I accomplished was to press soot into every pore. Now it was on my shirt cuff. A tide of earnest businessmen flowed on either side of me. How, I wondered, would that distinguished-looking chap react to my idea? Or that fellow with the floral waistcoat? Or the venerable gent with the beard? Every one of them looked singularly formidable, stern professionals with no time to spare for the fanciful schemes of aviators . . . I swallowed. It tasted bitter.

I paused before the W. H. Smith's bookstall. There in the centre of the display was the lastest issue of Revell's. A solid, sensible-looking publication. Thoroughly respectable, eminently worth-while. Packed with useful information about trousseaux and how to take care of the family silver. No sign on the cover of anything to do with aviation. My courage began to disintegrate. I could feel it falling apart somewhere deep within me. The whole idea was preposterous. What time was the next train back to Ashley?

I turned around. I thought again. I turned back. No. I couldn't go through with it. Again I turned.

Courage. Damn it all, I had to see it through. Didn't the idea possess merit last night? Wasn't I enthusiastic about it then? Didn't it promise to be the solution to our problems? I nodded. If it was a good idea last night, wasn't it still a good idea this morning? Again, I nodded.

I then observed one of the ugly schoolboys from the train. He was regarding me gravely, obviously fascinated to see how many more pirouettes I would perform for his benefit.

I asked him the time. He ran.

A bobby directed me to Andrew Street. By the time I arrived there I was hot and sticky. I longed for a cool drink, but there was none to be had in that austere street. It was narrow and housed the offices of solicitors and accountants, importers and exporters, printers and publishers. Frowning men and pale-faced boys hurried along the pavement. Evidently, business was maintained at a brisk pace in Andrew Street. I found number 18. A brass plate beside the door bore the legend: REVELL PUBLICATIONS COMPANY LIMITED.

I had vaguely expected a hive of activity: printing presses rolling, artists and authors striding about clutching illustrations and manuscripts. What I found was a narrow hall at the end of which was a small office. A remarkably plain girl sat at a desk and stared at me.

'Yes?' She had a cold in the nose.

I said that I would like to see the editor, if it wasn't too much trouble.

'Got an appointment, have you?'

I shook my head.

She sighed. 'Well then,' she said, with a sniff, 'what's the nature of your business?'

Nature? 'Well,' I said, 'it's a bit tricky to explain, but . . .'

'Editorial, production or advertising?'

'I beg your pardon?'

Another sigh, bewailing the world's ignorance. 'What I mean is, is your business to do with editorial matters or is it to do with printing or typesetting or engravings or is it to do with advertising? If it's editorial, it's Mr Fowler; if it's production, it's Mr Montague, and if it's advertising, it's Mr Beane. And he's in Scotland.'

I wished I was with Mr Beane in Scotland.

'My business is editorial in nature,' I told her with a confidence I didn't feel.

Another sniff. 'I dunno if Mr Fowler'll see you. Got a card, have you?'

A card? 'Oh, a business card? No; I'm awfully sorry; you see...'

A third sigh. 'Name?' A weary picking-up of an inch-and-half stub of pencil.

'Marshall. James Marshall.'

'Who d'you represent?'

Represent? What on earth did she mean? Then I understood. 'You mean, what company am I from?'

'S'right,' she said, tapping the pencil on her desk.

'I represent Marshall Brothers Aeroplanes,' I declared. It sounded quite impressive. 'Limited,' I added.

The girl scribbled something, frowning. 'Aeroplanes?'

'That's right.'

She shrugged, rose with yet another sigh and took the piece of paper into an inner office. She re-emerged a moment later.

'Mr Fowler'll see you.'

'Thank you...'

'But you'll have to wait.'

'How long?'

'I dunno. He's busy.'

Somehow her tone managed to convey the message that Mr Fowler was gainfully employed, doing a useful job of work and I was here for the express purpose of harassing him and wasting his valuable time. She indicated a chair, I sat down. I had to order myself not to jump up and head for the street with all possible haste. What lunacy had brought me here? Why didn't I have a normal job like everyone else? What, I wondered, would ever become of me?

I heard a muted giggle to the rear. Was that acetous little wretch telling her colleagues about the nincompoop coming to see Mr Fowler about *aeroplanes*? Chuckle, chuckle, ha bloody ha. What fun to brighten a dull day.

Were they peeping at me, smothering their laughter behind ink-stained fingers?

My stomach gurgled. I braced my abdominal muscles.

I touched my tie. Blast! It had slipped down. The collar stud must be visible for all the world to see. I gave the tie a tug. Damn! Now the thing slipped free of the collar at the back. To hell with it, I thought savagely. I studied my fingernails. Why hadn't it occurred to me that I might be kept waiting? Did I think all the editors in London would have put aside their work this morning on the off-chance that I might drop in? I should have brought a book. A copy of the current issue of Revell's lay on a table a dozen feet away. Just too far to reach without rising. I therefore rose. But I discovered that it wasn't a complete magazine, just a cover, for display purposes. I fancied I heard another giggle.

I sat down again, opened my envelope and studied the plans of the Model 21 for a quarter of an hour.

'Mr Fowler'll see you now.'

'What?' I promptly dropped my envelopes and scattered plans, photographs and cheese sandwiches over the floor.

'Cor,' said the girl. Yet another sigh. 'This way.'

Mr Fowler was plump and bald. He sat at a battered desk that was almost invisible beneath paper. He blinked with a chrono-metric regularity. The effect was hypnotic.

He wished me a rather vague good morning and indicated a chair.

'I understand you deal in . . . aeroplanes, Mr Marshall.'

'That's substantially correct.'

'Substantially?' Blink, blink.

'Well . . . actually, er, totally.'

I had to stop waiting for the next blink.

'Quite.' Blink, blink. 'I really do not wish to purchase an aero-plane, Mr Marshall. At the present time, I can think of nothing, absolutely nothing, that is further from my mind.' Blink, blink, blink.

'I'm not here to sell you an aeroplane, Mr Fowler.' I had memorized the speech. I plunged into it: 'These days, Mr Fowler, young women are becoming active in every pursuit. It seems to us that your magazine might be prepared to . . . er, assist in under-writing the . . . cost of a lady . . . to fly the Channel . . . the English Channel.'

34

God. Something went wrong as it was converted into words.

'Fly?' Mr Fowler blinked furiously, as if sending signals. 'The Channel? I don't think so, Mr Marshall.' More blinks. 'Simply not the kind of thing Revell's does. Too outlandish by far . . .'

I protested that there was nothing outlandish about flying. It was, I told him, the coming thing. The crowds at Hendon every weekend were proof enough of that.

'Quite so,' said Mr Fowler. 'But aviating is, without question, a masculine pursuit.' Blink, blink, blink. 'Revell's is, as is stated prominently upon our masthead, a journal for the young *lady* of taste and distinction; and that has been our guiding principle for many years. I hardly think that the typical Revell's reader is any more desirous of flying an aeroplane than building a bridge.' Blink, blink, 'Or going to war.'

'I think this might increase your circulation . . .'

'Do you really?' Blink. That blink said: And what, pray, do you know about building the circulation of a ladies' journal?

It was hopeless but I tottered on, telling him that he had an opportunity to capture the interest of the entire world, make an important contribution to the stature of British womankind – and sell more magazines at the same time. 'You will remember,' I said, 'how famous Monsieur Blériot became when he flew the English Channel and how much publicity was earned by the *Daily Mail* when they sponsored the London-to-Manchester race last year. Mr Fowler, your magazine could be instrumental in making history . . .'

A small vertical line had appeared between Mr Fowler's pale blue eyes. He had made up his mind. Now he wanted me to vacate the premises as rapidly as possible so that he could return to the business of editing his magazine. The blinks came fast and furious. It was nice of me to drop in but my idea wasn't quite up the Revell's street, if I knew what he meant, ha, ha, blink, blink.

I knew only too well.

I saw eight more editors that day. Some of them looked at me in the guarded way that people look at drunks, criminals and wild animals; if I had moved suddenly I might have caused more than one cardiac arrest.

It was a nightmarish day. By the end of it I was limp with fatigue

35

dazed by defeat. Would it be better tomorrow? It could scarcely be worse. At least I knew the form. I had gained a modicum of experience. I no longer hesitated when asked the nature of my business; I said 'editorial', adding that I represented Marshall Brothers Aeroplanes Ltd and that, regrettably, I had neglected to bring my supply of business cards with me that morning but I would jot down my name on this piece of paper that I happened to have in my pocket . . .

The next day I again travelled up to Town and spent seven hours and forty-two minutes trudging about in that world of noise and smell, dodging clattering horses and honking motor buses, elbowing my way through the entire human race, being exhorted by countless posters to buy everything from Eno's to holidays at Nice. I ate my cheese sandwiches in Green Park. I sweated freely into my clerical grey worsted but kept on smiling at disinterested or downright rude receptionists, and sat on hard chairs and waited. Some offices were large and splendid; others were tiny and shabby. A few editors told me candidly that my idea was insane and that I was wasting my time and theirs; a few more considered my idea most interesting – but, regretfully, it was not for them; *their* readers wanted only to read about breast-feeding and how to do original things with kippers. I became inured to failure. I absorbed rejections as a beaten boxer absorbs punches.

I caught the 5:24 back to Ashley Landing.

'It was a total flop,' I reported. 'Sorry. I wasted all that time and money and accomplished nothing.'

Beresford shrugged as if the matter had lost all import. He said that it had been worth a try, but I doubt that he believed it. He and Eggleton had spent the day nailing planks across the hole in the roof. The engine had arrived from Green's; the packing case stood in the corner of the hangar, next to Bessy.

I regarded it sourly. We would have to return it.

Dispirited, I went outside. It was late afternoon. The air was cool and calm. I took off my tie and undid that beastly collar at the front. It quivered as it came free, the ends sticking out on either side of my neck like starched antennae. A Farman buzzed over-head and settled on the grass. Mr Lyman emerged from his hangar and accorded me a guarded nod of greeting. He regarded Beresford and me as competitors.

What now? Accept defeat? Pack up shop? God, it was infuriating. We had the finest aeroplane in the country . . . yet we had to give up for the sake of a few paltry pounds. The banks were hopeless; we had nothing to offer as security. How could you make a bank manager believe that the lines on the blueprints represented something breathtakingly original, something that could bring orders from well-heeled sportsmen all over the country, indeed from all over the world?

Out of the hangars drifted smells of dope and oil, fabric and hot metal. Aeroplane smells. Heart-breaking smells.

The pilot of the Farman waved cheerfully as he taxied by. Blast him! He looked uncommonly pleased with himself. I raised a not-very-enthusiastic hand. Damn it, why did none of the other hangars suffer the slightest damage in the storm?

'Excuse me.'

I turned. A young lady confronted me. Smartly turned out, in dark blue with a white blouse and a bow tie. Business-like but feminine. On her light brown hair she wore a flat hat with a vaguely nautical air. A pretty girl, despite her large spectacles.

'I'm looking for Mr James Marshall. I was told I could find him at this end of the field.'

'I'm James Marshall.' Was she a lady bill collector?

'My name is Frances Gray.' She thrust a gloved hand in my direction. I shook it and found it small but firm. 'I believe you came to see us at Revell's the other day.'

'Revell's? Oh yes, the magazine.'

'I'm afraid I missed you. I was in Birmingham.'

'Oh, were you?' Why did I have to question her?

'You talked to Mr Fowler.'

'Ah, yes. The blinker.'

The words were out before I could stop them. But to my relief, Miss Gray laughed. She had an attractive, whole-hearted laugh. It was a pleasant change from the tinselly tinkles favoured by so many girls.

'I see you noticed our editor's little peculiarity, Mr Marshall. When I first met him, I found myself paying more attention to his

37

blinking than to what he was saying. But you get used to it after a little while.'

I said that I was relieved to hear it. Actually, I realized, she wasn't outstandingly pretty; her attractiveness had to be attributed to the animation in her features and the singular shapeliness of her cheekbones. The evening shadows found a cosy spot on either side of her mouth.

She told me that she was the assistant editor of Revell's.

I remarked that the position sounded very important.

'Do you think so? Yes: I suppose it does: I really hadn't thought of it.' She grinned. 'Anyway, I'm most enthusiastic about your idea, Mr Marshall.'

I stared. 'You are?'

'Very much so.'

'Good gracious!'

'When Mr Fowler told me about it, I immediately tried to reach you by telephone. But I couldn't find your telephone number.'

'Hardly surprising. We don't have one. We're a very small firm, Miss Gray.'

'I know,' she said. 'But you're a good one, according to a colleague of mine at the *Mail*. He told me that you had accomplished a great deal. And that you have experienced a lot of bad luck, in one form or another. She spoke directly, punctuating a point here and there with a tiny but emphatic finger. 'I told Mr Fowler that he was wrong to have turned you down. "You're a dear, L.G.," I said, "but sometimes you're out of step with the times. Today's woman is vitally interested in all aspects of her world. Of course she's still interested in babies and weddings, but she is also interested in exciting new developments, like flying!" I told him that if Revell's is going to maintain its position as the number one publication for the modern young woman, it's going to have to pull up its skirts a little and loosen its bustle!'

'Bravo!' I burbled.

'And, Mr Marshall, you're absolutely right when you say that our readers would like to read about a woman tackling the Channel. And, yes, Revell's *should* sponsor the flight. First-class, Mr Marshall!'

'Thank you. I thought the notion had possibilities . . .'

'It does indeed.'

'Thank you.' I cleared my throat. 'Does this mean, then, that Revell's is prepared to sponsor . . .'

'I think so,' she said.

'You think so.'

'Yes,' she said. 'But . . .'

'But?'

She shrugged apologetically. 'I haven't *quite* finished convincing Mr Fowler.'

My new-born hopes withered. All too good to be true. I might have known.

'Or Mr Duker, our publisher.'

'I see.'

'But,' she added quickly, 'I will convince them. There's not a shadow of doubt about that. I'm so sure of it that I'm prepared to wager my own money on it. Now, tell me, Mr Marshall,' – she had an odd habit of cocking her head at an angle when posing a question – 'how much will you charge to teach me to fly?'

'Teach *you*?'

'Yes. Is it so surprising that I should want to learn to fly?'

'No . . . no; of course not.'

'I wish to learn, Mr Marshall, so that I can be the woman to fly the Channel.'

She said it in a matter-of-fact way, as if saying that she wished to catch a Number 11 bus in order to get to Golders Green.

'Have you . . . ever flown an aeroplane?'

'No. I've not even been up in one. I'm looking forward to the experience with the keenest anticipation.'

I was unsure what to say. It had never occurred to me that we might have to teach someone to fly in order to produce a candidate for the Channel flight.

Miss Gray said:

'I shall pay for the lessons. And I shall write a series of articles about my experiences. A WOMAN TAKES TO THE AIR! Or perhaps YES, YOU TOO CAN BE AN AVIATOR! Revell's will publish the articles. And they will be a great success. I'm absolutely positive about that. I know what our readers want! They want to read about modern women doing modern things. It's a new century, a new era! And when Messrs Duker and Fowler see what a winner they've got, we won't have the slightest trouble getting them to sponsor the cross-Channel flight. By the way, how much will be needed?'

I told her that the aeroplane would cost twelve hundred pounds.

'Better add another eight hundred for incidentals. Say, two thousand.' She smiled. Her teeth were tiny and well shaped. 'Not much to pay for a marvellous story, is it?'

'No; not much . . .' I had no idea what marvellous stories cost.

She took a deep breath and held it as if savouring it. She exhaled with enthusiasm. 'To think that in a little while I will have learnt to pilot an aeroplane . . . and then I shall be the first woman in the *world* to fly the Channel!' She clutched my arm. 'Wouldn't it be awful if someone else is planning the same thing.'

'No one else seemed the least bit interested,' I told her.

'Good. Did you talk to many editors about the idea?'

I went through the list. She nodded knowingly at each name.

'And none of them liked it?'

'Not one.'

'Unfortunately there might be second thoughts by some of those individuals, particularly when our series gets into print. We must waste no time, Mr Marshall. When may I start my lessons?'

I thought rapidly. We didn't have a Model 21, but we did have Bessy. It would only take a day or two to fix a second seat on her lower wing and move the original seat so that both pupil and instructor would be able to reach the control levers. Thank the Lord Miss Gray was slim and light: another twenty or thirty pounds and Bessy might refuse point blank to leave the ground. A few hours to overhaul her structure and engine, repair her fabric where necessary, re-brace her wings and tail . . .

'Would next Monday be convenient?'

'Perfectly.'

'Would you mind very much coming at seven o'clock?'

'In the morning?'

'I'm afraid so. It's usually calm then, you see. Don't bother to come if it's windy. We won't be able to fly.'

'At seven, then.' She smiled and offered her hand again. Again I shook it. 'I am confident that this will be a most profitable enterprise, Mr Marshall. Revell's will be selling lots and lots of magazines and you will be selling lots of aeroplanes. And I shall be doing something that no other woman in the world has ever done before. And all because you had an idea. Aren't ideas quite the most thrilling things! Thank you so much for a most interesting discussion. I am looking forward to Monday. Good afternoon.'

Beresford reacted violently.

'You're bloody balmy!'

I tried to explain to him that it wouldn't be much of a job to convert Bessy to a two-seater . . .

'Who the hell is this woman?'

'The assistant editor; quite an important position.'

'Important? Don't be absurd! She's a bloody flunkey! Christ, man, it'll cost you more to convert that abortion to a two-seater than you'll get in fees from your precious pupil . . . *if* you get any fees. You're wasting money, not *making* it! That's not business, that's lunacy!'

I tried to explain that it should be regarded as an investment.

'Some bloody investment!'

'You see, she can't persuade her management to put up the money for the aeroplane until they see how successful the series of articles will be . . .'

'And how the blazes do you know they'll be successful?'

'Well, Miss Gray told me . . .'

'Oh she told you, did she?' His voice was heavy with scorn. 'Well, then we don't have a damned thing to worry about, do we? We have her assurance.'

'If you'd spoken to her, you'd feel differently . . . she's quite a remarkable young lady . . . very businesslike . . .'

'Which is more than we can say for you,' he snapped. 'No businessman in his right mind would get involved in an idiotic scheme like this. You don't even know if the wretched woman will come back on Monday. She probably doesn't have a sou to her name. She's laughing her empty head off at you.'

I squirmed as I told him how confident I was that Miss Gray would return on Monday, with her fee.

But Beresford had made up his mind. My heart sank as he said, 'We're not businessmen. We don't know the first thing about running a business.'

I tried to reason with him. I agreed that it was by no means a perfect arrangement, but it was the best I had been able to arrange.

'My point precisely,' he countered.

He said he was going out.

Which he did. And he didn't return that night. Or the next.

Three

Eggleton and I pushed Bessy out into the sunlight. She squeaked and creaked as her wheels encountered the scrubby, oil-soaked grass. Her wires buzzed, stirring themselves. The old girl resembled a bird-cage with wings but the nacelle helped. We had made it of plywood, painted it and installed it on Sunday evening. The paint was still tacky in places. It made Bessy look a little less like one of the Wright Brothers' early efforts; and it would provide some degree of protection for pupil and instructor against the early-morning chill.

I had flown Bessy the previous evening, carrying one hundred and ten pounds of ballast in the second seat and slightly less than half a tank of petrol. She had performed as well as could be expected of an aircraft that was so grossly underpowered and whose structure created such a burden of drag.

Promptly at seven, Miss Gray arrived. She wore a soft leather coat and a close-fitting cap.

'Is this suitable attire for aviating?'

I assured her that it was perfect.

'Isn't it an absolutely glorious day?'

'Also perfect,' I said. 'Meet Bessy.'

Miss Gray beamed and hugged herself with her folded arms. She told Bessy that it was a pleasure and an honour to make her acquaintance. Then she turned to me, head cocked. 'Is it considered proper to address an aeroplane as "she", like a ship?'

'I do,' I said.

'Then I shall too.' She examined Bessy from nose to tail, from wing tip to wing tip. 'Why do you call her Bessy?'

I said I had no idea. 'Officially, she's our Model 15, but for some reason we've always called her Bessy. This is Eggleton. He does all the work.'

'Good morning, Eggleton,' said Miss Gray.

''Mornin', miss.' Eggleton touched his forehead to signify that he classified her as a better. 'Good luck to ye.'

She thanked Eggleton, warmly; his cheeks coloured.

I spent ten minutes explaining Bessy's basic components and controls. Miss Gray made innumerable notes in a red book.

'Shall we have a flight now?'

'Love to!'

I assisted her through the maze of wires and struts and into the right-hand seat.

'Comfortable?'

'Perfectly.'

I told her to brace her feet against the spar and to place her hands – lightly – on the levers so that she could get an idea of what I had to do to control the aeroplane.

I took a deep breath, wondering what I would do if Miss Gray 'froze' on the control levers. Would I resort to a swift upper-cut? It was said that such measures were occasionally necessary; people had been known to react oddly to the sensation of being several hundred feet in the air and without visible means of support.

Eggleton swung the propeller. The engine clattered into life, emitting little snorts and puffs of oily smoke.

I taxied out into the field and turned into the almost non-existent wind.

'Ready?'

'Rather!'

Throttle wide open. Behind us the wooden propeller became a blur. Bessy lurched forward. She thumped across the grass, wings swaying, structure groaning. Then we were aloft, climbing laboriously through the gentle air. I was careful to keep Bessy heading straight. Turns could be fatal if attempted during a climb. A moment's lack of concentration and you could lose flying speed, drop a wing and be on your back in a deadly spin before you could do anything to prevent it. I glanced quickly at my pupil. She was grinning as the wind battered her. A stray curl pirouetted madly over one ear. An unusual young lady, Miss Gray.

At last we reached a safe altitude. I turned. Obediently, the fields tilted. I smiled as Miss Gray promptly leant away from the turn, forgetting that I had told her to lean into the turns as she did on her bicycle when going around a corner. I levelled the wings, then turned in the opposite direction. This time, laughing, Miss Gray leant correctly. I nodded my approval.

Twenty minutes later we landed.

I wondered what her reaction would be. She didn't leave me in doubt for long.

'That,' she declared, the moment the engine wheezed into silence, 'was quite the most remarkable experience of my life.'

'You liked it?' I wasn't sure.

'Liked it? I absolutely adored it!' She clutched my arm. 'Can we go up again? Now?'

I glanced at the Union Jack beside the gate. It stirred sluggishly. The wind was still harmless. I nodded.

'We'll go up again,' I told her. 'And this time I want you to handle the control levers for a little while. I want you to start getting the feel of them. It's quite easy, but you must remember to keep the aeroplane in the right attitude so that the air can pass over the wings fast enough. You see, the air going over the wings is the only thing that keeps us aloft. Think of a kite. The wind has to blow with sufficient force to keep the kite in the air. It's more or less the same with the aeroplane except that the aeroplane moves in order to make the wind do its stuff, whereas the kite stays still. Remember, as soon as the speed drops, so does the aeroplane. And so do its passengers.'

'I'll remember,' she promised.

But she didn't. A moment after she took the controls, Bessy reared like a startled carthorse. One wing dropped. Hastily I

44

grabbed the levers, thrusting the elevator lever forward and applying corrective rudder to swing the nose straight. Creaking, Bessy levelled off, having lost a couple of hundred feet.

The incident failed to dampen Miss Gray's enthusiasm.

'I know what I did incorrectly!' she bellowed.

'Glad to hear it!' I bellowed back.

'I pulled back on the lever. She rose and lost speed.'

'Correct!' I pointed ahead. 'Remember to keep your horizon in the same position in front of you. That will tell you that you're in the correct attitude!'

'I understand!'

But seconds later Bessy was again on the point of stalling. By now the earth was dangerously close. I landed.

I explained to my beaming pupil that an aeroplane must be kept in balance at all times, much like a bicycle.

'I see exactly what you mean.'

'We'll try again tomorrow.'

She looked disappointed. 'Can't we go up again now?'

I indicated the Union Jack. I lied a little. 'The wind's getting a spot too fresh for lessons. In any case, I think you've done enough for one day. You need time to absorb what you've learnt.'

And, I thought, I need time to recuperate.

Miss Gray's eyes sparkled. Head cocked. 'Same time tomorrow, Mr Marshall?'

'If the weather's good.'

It was. And punctually at seven each morning Frances Gray arrived for her lessons. On the fourth morning she encountered Beresford. It was a less than cordial meeting. Beresford said:

'So you're the woman!'

Whereupon he limped away.

I apologized for Beresford. I said that he hadn't been well (which was true, in a way). Miss Gray said:

'Your brother has injured his leg?'

I told her that he had lost it in a crash.

'I'm sorry,' she said. 'And I'm sorry he doesn't approve of our arrangement.'

She was an exceptionally keen student, totally absorbed in anything and everything to do with flying. She asked questions by

45

the dozen, dutifully writing the answers in leather-bound note-books. She was quite fearless; and her enormous enthusiasm seemed to leave no room for qualms. It may have occurred to her that aviating had its dangers; apparently, however, she considered herself immune. One morning we flew over the Surrey country-side for an hour. When we returned to Ashley we found a layer of mist blanketing the aerodrome. Roofs could be seen: roofs by the dozen. But without other references it was remarkably difficult to ascertain which roofs belonged to what buildings. I circled a couple of times.

'Picturesque, isn't it?'

I nodded numbly while she chortled about wishing she had brought her camera and how flying gave one such fascinatingly unexpected views of everything.

Damn the bloody mist! It wasn't budging. I twisted around in my seat. The glass tube beside the petrol tank told the unhappy story. Our modest fuel supply would soon be exhausted. I cursed the mist again. Still it didn't budge. I had two choices: fly away from the aerodrome and attempt a landing on some farmer's field – and risk smashing up the aeroplane in the process, or grope my way down through the muck – and risk smashing up the aeroplane in the process.

I made up my mind. Ashley it would be. Ashley had been immeasurably kind to me before; I had a feeling it would see me through again.

I climbed to give myself a wider view.

That, I decided, after much staring, is the farm.

It had to be.

Surely.

I reduced power and eased old Bessy earthward. I turned, gingerly, because the horizon was disappearing as we descended. I straightened. The prow of Bessy's nacelle pointed at what simply *had* to be open ground. Power off. The moment of truth. Bessy sank, rapidly, as if eager to be down. Her wing tips vanished momentarily. My innards palpitated. For one frightful moment, I was blind. Then, abruptly, the ground appeared. Colourless in the mist. But solid. And clear. With a thump, Bessy touched down.

'That was most interesting,' Miss Gray declared.

I said how glad I was that she had found it so.

She jotted. 'Coming down through the mist is rather like running downstairs in a strange house without a light.'

'Very apt,' I said, still savouring the solidity beneath me.

She snapped her notebook shut. 'This is going to make a most thrilling episode for the series.' She scrambled out of Bessy's clutches. 'Cheerio, Mr Marshall. See you tomorrow!'

Fearless Frances.

I helped Eggleton to put Bessy back into the hangar.

Beresford was sitting on his cot reading the new E. M. Forster novel, *Howards End*.

'So you got down in one piece.'

'Yes, thanks.'

They were the first words we had exchanged in eleven days.

'How is your student progressing?'

'Fairly well.'

'Only fairly?'

'She seems to find it difficult to coordinate the wing and rudder controls.'

'Most people do.'

'I suppose so.'

'Any further developments?'

It wasn't necessary for him to be more explicit.

'Not yet.'

'I see.'

He resumed his reading.

The following Friday Revell's carried the first of Miss Gray's articles on her aeronautical adventures. And an excellent job it was. She wrote with skill and verve. I squirmed a little when I found myself described as 'my athletic young instructor with the steely jaw and the skilled hands of a surgeon'; and I raised an eyebrow when she declared that Bessy was a 'powerful, purposeful craft that sped skyward to meet the early morning sun'. In the main, however, I found her work technically accurate. I was interested to note that she had quoted various of my 'hang-it-alls' and 'for-heaven's-sakes', presumably to show that even steely-jawed and athletic young flying instructors could display a modicum of irritation or anguish upon occasion.

The articles were an immediate success. Gleefully, Miss Gray reported the arrival of of 872 readers' letters the morning after the first episode appeared; well over one thousand arrived the following day. Not since the phenomenally popular series by the Prince of Wales's nanny had the magazine had such a winner. The Revell's management had already reimbursed Miss Gray for her flying lessons; now, she told us, they were seriously considering the Channel proposal.

Even Beresford was impressed.

'You're quite a talented journalist, Miss Gray.'

'Yes,' she said, eyes sparkling, 'I am.'

He smiled. The response appealed to him. 'We should become better acquainted.'

'Should we?'

'Most certainly. What say we have a bite to eat at Appenrodt's one evening? Afterwards we can pop along and see the show at the Hippodrome (they say it's rather fun); and then we can spend a few hours in scintillating intercourse.'

'Beresford . . .!' I blurted.

He was talking to me but his eyes were on Miss Gray. 'Tut, tut, dirty mind, young James. Intercourse is simply communication. Mind you, there are several types of intercourse. Some are more fun than others. I do think, Miss Gray, that I should warn you. I shall undoubtedly make indecent advances at every opportunity. I shall, in fact, do my very best to persuade you to spend the night with me at the Florence Hotel. I know the night porter there. Charming fellow. And have no concern about my injury. You may have heard that the body compensates when it loses part of itself. In my case it has compensated in a somewhat singular way . . .'

I squirmed. Blast him! He was so monstrously shameless. What a frightful impression to give Miss Gray . . .

But she was laughing.

Thank God, she was also shaking her head. No; she was already engaged for this evening. Perhaps another time . . .

My world slumped a little. I asked myself why. It wasn't as if I had any ambitions in Miss Gray's direction. Indeed, until this very instant the thought hadn't entered my mind. Wasn't it obvious that such a girl as Miss Gray would be bound to have a life outside Ashley Landing and Revell's? Most certainly. Why then did I suddenly and quite violently resent both Beresford and this cad she was to meet that evening?

I wasn't sure.

Four

After half a dozen bone-crunching landings, I switched off Bessy's motor. Miss Gray smiled. I cleared my throat. This was the moment I had been dreading. But it could be postponed no longer.

'I'm a bit concerned,' I told her. 'I feel I should tell you now, before we get too far along with everything.'

'What is it, Mr Marshall?'

'You're not making the progress I had hoped for.'

She nodded, absorbing this gravely. 'I had a feeling you might say something of the sort.'

'It's nothing to be ashamed of,' I added hastily. 'And it's not your fault; I mean, it's not that you haven't tried hard enough. The point is, some people seem to take to flying naturally. Some don't. I suppose it's either in you or it isn't. I'm sure you're an absolutely marvellous dancer,' I said. She admitted that she was rather good. 'There you are, you see. I can't dance at all. I just lumber about like an elephant. It simply isn't in me.'

'Are you telling me that the ability to fly isn't in me?'

'I'm not sure.'

She drummed her fingers on Bessy's wing. 'I *am* sure, Mr Marshall. I'm positive. You see, I want to do it so badly that I *must* be able to. Do you see what I mean?'

'Oh . . . rather.'

'Obviously I shall have to work much harder.'

'Then you wish to continue?'

'Yes, if you are willing to continue instructing me.'

'Yes, of course.'

'I shall work twice as hard as before. You'll see.'

And so we ploughed on into the Autumn: day after day: landings, take-offs, turns, climbs, glides. And gradually, by sheer brutal repetition, she managed to acquire a sort of skill. She learnt to position the controls to cope with a variety of situations. She absorbed her lessons. But still she lacked any instinct for what made Bessy fly. She was like a person who loves animals and yet is unthinkingly cruel to them. I kept wondering what would happen if she ever found herself in a situation that was totally new to her. How would she react? Would she take the correct action, automatically comprehending what was necessary? Or would she die or be horribly injured? I shivered. An instructor's responsibility was awesome.

One crisp morning in October, Miss Gray flew several reasonably good circuits of Ashley Landing. I sat in the left-hand seat, arms folded, no more than a passenger. The sun shone; the air was almost still. Ideal conditions. We landed.

I jumped down to the grass.

'Do you think you can manage her by yourself?'

Her eyes brightened. 'Yes, rather!'

'Topping.' I found that my voice had suddenly become a trifle husky. 'Why don't you do a circuit or two on your own . . .' I had to clear my throat. 'Er, you'll find her much lighter without my weight. She'll lift off the ground almost immediately.'

She nodded eagerly.

'But . . . be careful to put your nose down after you get off the ground . . . build up your speed before you start your climb.'

'I'll remember. I promise.'

'And keep your eyes on the horizon. Don't let your nose creep up.'

'I won't.'

My courage was beginning to fail. I told her that if she didn't feel ready to take the aeroplane up alone, she shouldn't be ashamed to say so; if she would like to take a few more spins first . . .

'I'm quite ready, Mr Marshall. Honestly.'

'All right . . . just take off and do one circuit of the field
land.'

'Yes, Mr Marshall.'

'One more thing: when you're landing, remember that without
my weight, she won't descend as rapidly as usual.'

'I'll allow for that, Mr Marshall.'

'Jolly good.'

I swung the propeller for her. The ignition caught. Old Bessy
shook in her palsied way. Miss Gray took a firm grip on the control levers. She gave me a quick smile, then she was rolling.

I turned and strolled back to the hangars in what I hoped was
an unconcerned manner.

Eggleton stood by the hangar, hands on hips.

'You're lettin' 'er try it by 'erself, are you?'

In my nervous state, I was instantly on the defensive.

'Yes; don't you think I should have?'

'Not for me to say, sir.'

He was quite right.

Bessy was about to commence her take-off run. I experienced an
almost overwhelming desire to go tearing out on to the field,
arms flailing, and order her out of the aeroplane immediately.
What right had I to risk that poor girl's life? She placed her trust
in me and this was how I responded! God, when one thought of
the countless things that could go wrong . . . ! If you weighed her
chances it seemed certain that she would be dead in minutes.

The sound of the little motor wafted across the field. Bessy
began to roll in earnest.

'Keep the wings level. Keep the nose down. Don't ever let your
speed drop off . . . watch the horizon . . .'

Bessy was aloft, swaying and dipping as she gathered speed. A
turn to the left. A little on the sudden side, but neat enough. One
had to make allowances for solo-day nerves. The bestrutted wings
came level. Up she went. The engine laboured; it sounded tinny
and uncertain. (Idiot! Why didn't I get Eggleton to give the thing
a complete overhaul before the flight? What would happen if it
cut out now? Would she react correctly? Or would she lose her
air-speed and spin into the ground? I winced at the thought.) The

figure of the pilot was diminutive now as Bessy came downwind, parallel to the London Road. What was Miss Gray thinking? Was she frightened, dreading the task of landing?

She turned again, the sun catching the fabric of her wings. A few minutes more . . . another turn . . . then the final approach . . .

Beresford emerged from the hangar. He yawned, looked at me, then up at Bessy.

'Ah, our heroine takes to the air alone!'

I turned on him. 'For God's sake, keep quiet?'

'Sorry,' he said. He smiled. 'I didn't know aviation instructors cared so much about the safety of their pupils.'

I apologized . . . 'I didn't mean to be rude.'

'Oh, but you did,' he said. 'I can see that I must watch what I say where Miss Gray is concerned.'

I started to protest but didn't get far. Miss Gray was approaching for her landing. Clearly she had taken to heart my remarks concerning the need to maintain her flying speed. Her engine was still clattering away merrily. I wondered if she would elect to go around again when she discovered what a difference the absence of my weight would make. She was over the hedge when she cut the engine. Pop-pop-pop. Silence. The propeller stopped. There would be no second chance at this landing.

Christ, I thought, she's going to run out of field.

'Down you go, miss.' It was Eggleton, his eyes riveted upon the little aeroplane as it swept past us, the wind singing through the wires and struts. Miss Gray was leaning forward, as if trying to persuade Bessy to settle. I turned my head as she passed. I saw the trees at the end of the field. God, she was going to go straight into the trees. She wouldn't make it.

But she did. Bessy hit the ground. Bounced. Bumped. Settled.

The three of us ran across the field to find Bessy within a dozen feet of the elms. Miss Gray had already clambered out. She greeted us with a rapturous smile.

'That was marvellous! I can't tell you how much I enjoyed it! There's nothing, absolutely nothing in the world quite as thrilling as flying all alone! Thank you so much for letting me fly alone, Mr Marshall! Just a jiff; I must jot down a couple of things before I forget them. Do forgive me.' Hastily, she scribbled something in her notebook. Then she looked up, head cocked at her questioning angle. 'I'm a real aviator now, aren't I? Oh, I know I still have lots of things to learn but I've taken that big step and I've actually handled an aeroplane all by myself. It will all be in next week's issue: GOING SOLO IS THE THRILL OF A LIFETIME.'

'For all of us,' said Beresford.

'So you're Mr James Marshall.'

F. S. Duker, Revell's Managing Director, looked me up and down. Then he waved a fleshy hand at the chairs drawn up in a neat line before his desk.

'Take a pew, Mr Marshall. Doesn't matter which one. All the same price.'

I sat down. Miss Gray and Mr Fowler sat beside me.

'Good of you to come up to Town to see us.'

It was evident from his 'coom', 'oop' and 'oos' that Mr Duker originated from somewhere in the vicinity of Manchester. His emphasis of these words suggested that he was fiercely proud of the fact. He spoke in rapid, abrupt bursts. He smoked as he talked; his cigarette wagged stiffly, in the manner of a terrier's tail. A stocky man, he wore a blue suit and a remarkably vicious-looking winged collar upon which his ample jowls reposed. His eyes were mobile yet heavy lidded. It was a disquieting combination. I had an uncomfortable feeling that he was about to fix me with a baleful gaze and tell me that I was a confidence trickster, or worse. The trouble was, I wasn't at all sure that I could deny the charge.

'Nice day.'

'Indeed,' I responded.

'Warm.'

'Rather.'

'Right,' said Mr Duker. Enough of the day had been wasted on the niceties. He looked at Mr Fowler. 'Brass-tack time, I think. Now, you tell me that the current series of articles by Miss Gray here' – he acknowledged her presence with an on-again-off-again smile – 'is meeting with some success.'

'That is correct, sir,' said Mr Fowler.

'Good.'

'Thank you, sir.' Mr Fowler's tone was softly deferential.

But Miss Gray's was not. 'I think "some success" hardly does it justice, Mr Duker. "Phenomenal success" would, I fancy, be a considerably more accurate term. Well over five thousand readers' letters to date . . . circulation up eleven per cent . . .!'

'Quite so,' said Mr Duker. Clearly Mr Duker did not consider this a propitious moment to mention such facts.

But Miss Gray continued. 'I want to make it clear, however, that the original idea was Mr Marshall's and his alone. He deserves all the credit.'

Mr Duker regarded Miss Gray without enthusiasm. His cigarette dropped momentarily. Half an inch of ash fell upon his desk top. He turned to me. 'You are suggesting, Mr Marshall, that Revell's put up the money to build an aeroplane so that Miss Gray can fly the English Channel. She will thereby become the first woman in the world to do so, a fact that should attract considerable attention. And the total cost you estimate at approximately two thousand pounds.'

''Er, yes.' I felt my cheeks burning. Why, for God's sake, did they burn? Why could I never discuss money without feeling guilty? I mumbled something about the advantages of such a venture for the magazine.

'We've never done anything like this before,' Mr Duker declared.

'Never,' affirmed Mr Fowler.

'Mind you, we do recognize that we do have certain responsibilities as the leading journal to encourage the participation by women in every phase of human endeavour . . .'

'Very true,' said Mr Fowler.

'Come now, gentlemen.' Miss Gray's small but sturdy finger was stabbing the air. 'Let's be frank. No one is suggesting that the magazine do anything the least bit altruistic. This is a business proposition pure and simple. And, I might add, an extremely attractive one. We have proof of the keen interest our readers have in hearing about women doing things like flying aeroplanes. When the news breaks about the Channel flight our circulation will take another jump. And so will our advertising revenue. It is a ripping opportunity, gentlemen, to make money! The magazine will also derive a great deal of prestige. This is an absolutely magnificent proposition, gentlemen!'

Mr Duker regarded her, then turned to me.

'Your Company, Mr Marshall, agrees to re-purchase the aeroplane at the conclusion of the flight . . . at ten per cent less than original selling price.'

Nods. 'Yes, that was our suggestion.'

'The outlay,' interjected Miss Gray, 'can only be described as nominal when the benefits are considered.'

'Two thousand pounds,' said Mr Duker, 'can never, under any circumstances whatsoever, be described as nominal.'

'Quite,' said Mr Fowler, blinking his agreement.

'Moreover,' said Mr Duker, looking at each of us in turn, and pausing to heighten the effect of his words, 'we have to face the melancholy fact that this flight may fail. Miss Gray might not reach the other side. I'm not saying that is what will happen; I am merely pointing it out as a very real possibility.'

'The flight will succeed,' said Miss Gray. 'Of that I am absolutely confident. But I have considered failure. And I have planned for it. I am working on a suitable story that the magazine can run in the event of my death. I shall have it on your desk by the end of the week. And you may rest assured that we shall take lots of photographs to illustrate it – pictures of the late Miss Gray enjoying breakfast only moments before her last take-off, getting into the aeroplane, waving farewell. I rather think, gentlemen, that you will sell more copies of the magazine if I fail than if I succeed. You simply can't lose.'

Mr Duker frowned. 'That is a matter of opinion . . .'

'On the contrary, it is a matter of fact,' declared Miss Gray, chin held high, her eyes bright. 'And I might add that there are plenty of other publishers only too eager to invest in a story of this calibre.'

I could have argued that point with her, but I thought better of it.

Mr Duker was racked by a paroxysm of coughing. Ash showered upon his desk; he glowed. I feared mortal damage. But, with a succession of gasps, he recovered. He stabbed his cigarette in the ash tray and promptly lit another. He informed Miss Gray that there was no need for that kind of talk.

'Quite,' said Mr Fowler.

'I disagree,' said Miss Gray, totally unabashed. 'There are times in life when one has to take a stand. For me, this is such a time. I have no wish to be rude but I must point out that the exceptionally good sales currently enjoyed by Revell's are due to a series of articles that you did not wish to run. I had to persuade you. It was hard work. I must also point out that I had to pay for the flying lessons in question! In other words, I took the gamble, not Revell's. But that is not important. What is important is that we have chanced upon a subject that is even more popular than I thought it would be. We must make the most of it! A cross-Channel flight will be an absolutely sensational climax to our series! Revell's will make history!'

I was awed by her performance. I wanted desperately to reinforce her with cogent arguments and dazzling barrages of telling phrases. But, try as I might, I could think of absolutely nothing to add. She was saying it all. Magnificently.

Mr Duker puffed furiously, his eyes darting about his desk as if he expected to find the answer there.

'And do you, Miss Gray, feel that you are capable of making such a flight?'

'Of course!' she replied. 'Have I not, Mr Marshall, flown the aeroplane all by myself on many occasions?'

'Yes . . . many times . . .'

'And are you not teaching me the basics of aerial navigation?'

Yes again.

Mr Duker's cigarette shifted abruptly from an angle of forty-five degrees – which presumably indicated indecision – to perfectly horizontal. His gaze fell upon me.

'How do we know that your aeroplane can fly all the way across the Channel? Has it ever done so?'

I had to admit that it hadn't. 'But it's perfectly capable of such a flight. I can assure you of that.'

'How can you assure me of that?'

It was a good question. I swallowed. Fortunately the swallowing made me cough. The coughing gave me a moment to think. I spluttered:

'Before you take delivery of the aeroplane we will guarantee to make a flight of equivalent distance, say, thirty miles non-stop.'

Mr Duker regarded the tip of his cigarette. He nodded. 'Fair enough, I'd say.'

Miss Gray gave me an approving grin.

Mr Fowler blinked.

Then Mr Duker leant back and blew smoke at the ceiling. It was the moment of decision. Silence reigned. From the outer office I heard voices: inquiries about deliveries to the printer and when the tea would be ready. My watch ticked loudly, impatiently.

'All right,' said Mr Duker. His chair squeaked as he leant forward. 'But not a ha'penny over two thousand. An aerial voyage of thirty miles to be made before we take over the aeroplane. And the whole thing is null and void if someone does it before us.'

It should have been my moment of triumph. I had conceived an idea and now it was about to become action. It could make our fortunes. Money was materializing, money with which to build our aeroplane. Soon that aeroplane would be famous the world over as the machine piloted by the first woman ever to fly the Channel. Orders for Marshall Model 21s would arrive with every post. Soon we would have to move to larger quarters to accommodate our production line. I had a great deal to celebrate. I should have gone to Piccadilly. With Frances. A slap-up dinner at the Café Royal. Front-row seats at the Duke of York's or the Criterion. Jollification unlimited.

Instead, agitated and depressed, I caught the first train back to Ashley Landing. I was haunted by the fear that we were all rushing headlong into disaster. Frances wasn't ready to make this flight – God knows whether she would ever be ready. She simply wasn't a good aviator. She would get lost, she would encounter fog and fly into the water, she would crash upon landing. The dangers were countless. Damn my idea. If it hadn't occurred to me her life wouldn't be in jeopardy . . .

I found Beresford lying on his cot. He had invested four precious shillings in a bottle of Black and White. He was mellow.

'If you bring glad tidings,' he said, 'then I have begun our celebration. If you bring sad tidings, the pain will be a little easier to bear.'

Flatly I told him: 'They bought it.'

He sat up. 'Good God. Really?'

'Really.'

'And they're going to part with hard cash?'

'Their legal people are drawing up the papers now.'

'Incredible. What a clever fellow you are, James . . . and how artfully you conceal the fact. I thought it was an utterly insane idea. I told you so if I remember correctly. Yes; I'm sure I did. But you were right, James old man, I have to admit it. You knew best.'

'Sometimes,' I said, 'a businessman has to take calculated risks.'

He was eager to start work on the new machine. He had been sketching a cleaner engine installation – as well as half a hundred other ideas. His table was littered with pieces of paper on which he had jotted what he called his 'passing fancies'. Most of them were notions that had to await their day; the world and its technology simply weren't ready. There were undercarriages that folded out of sight and out of the slipstream, wings whose shape could be altered mechanically during flight, fire-proof compartments for pilots and passengers that would separate from the parent aircraft in the event of trouble to drift safely down to earth beneath huge parachutes, multi-engined monsters that would be flying aerodromes for smaller aeroplanes . . .

'The sooner we get the aeroplane finished the sooner we get our money,' he chortled happily. 'So my proposition is that we work eighteen hours a day. We can have her ready in no time. Less, perhaps. I won't touch a drop during that period. Neither will I lust after women, loose or . . . er, tight. I promise.'

I said, 'Do you really think we should let this go any further?'

'What?'

I repeated my statement.

'The question is asinine,' he said. 'Therefore it's quite impossible to answer it sensibly.'

'The point is,' I said, 'Miss Gray could very easily get killed.'

'I know that. You know that. And she knows that.'

'Well, isn't that reason enough?'

He shook his head. 'She'll be all right, old son. She can point her nose in the right direction. She can't miss the whole continent of Europe.'

I stared at him. Sometimes it was hard to believe that he was my brother. He seemed able to consider a situation, allot it so much concern and not an atom more, then dismiss it from his mind.

He said, 'She knows there's a certain amount of danger. But the end justifies the risk. She wants to make her mark in the world. She wants to do something that no other woman has ever done. Perfectly understandable. She accepts the fact that there's a chance she could get killed in the process. She's made her mind up. She wants to try it. It's her decision, not ours.'

'I know all that. But if I hadn't gone into Revell's in the first place . . .'

'And if you hadn't fallen on that Pickford's van you wouldn't have been alive to go to Revell's. Don't for God's sake bore me with "what ifs". I may vomit. You've done your stuff. You've taught her to fly. You've taught her some navigation. You've told her all about the tricky weather in the Channel – sudden fogs and winds and everything. That's all you can do. And after it's all over and she's world famous she'll be eternally grateful to you and probably invite you to go to bed with her. Now let's drop it.'

Anger had me by the throat. I had to swallow before I could tell him that he was a bastard of the first water.

'I'm really not,' he responded mildly. 'I'm a realist. What is to be gained by worrying about a matter of this type? Every time Mr Webley sells a pistol does he worry that someone might hurt himself with it? Of course not. If we don't supply Miss Gray with an aeroplane someone else will. And if she skills herself in that aeroplane you will torment yourself for the rest of your days wondering whether she would have survived had she flown the Model 21.'

'Don't you give a damn about her?'

'My dear fellow, of course I do. She's a bright creature, attractive and intelligent . . . yes; I regard her highly . . . in fact, it is only her reluctance to surrender her all to me that . . .'

'Then how,' I blurted out, 'can you be so bloody unfeeling?'

He shook his head, in the manner of a teacher chiding a slow pupil. 'You disappoint me, James. I ask you, would you feel the same anguish, the same burning concern if it was a *Mister* Gray who was being prepared for this flight?'

'That's not the point . . .'

'But it is, James; it is precisely the point. As I have told you before, you don't spend enough time in bed with women. You don't get down to grips with them – metaphorically or literally. The result is that you are in the gravest danger of becoming a romanticist. You don't see in Miss Gray a doughty young lady with a craving for fame, you see the most precious, divine, untouchable creature that ever drew breath . . .'

'Don't be so bloody silly!' I retorted.

But he had described her perfectly.

The lessons ploughed on. Solo and dual, hour after hour, in sun and drizzle, sometimes in light snow. I taught my pupil to read the Clift magnetic compass that was bolted to a spar, down beside her feet in the depths of the nacelle. It was necessary to use the torch in order to read the thing. She learnt how to estimate the strength of a cross-wind by the crabbed angle that had to be assumed to fly in a straight line. We plotted courses and buzzed our way across endless fields that lost their colour as winter tightened its grip. It became colder. We huddled together in the plywood nacelle, trying to escape the worst of the wintry blasts. I found her proximity delightful; I hoped for ever chillier weather.

Revell's was now paying for Frances's flying time; she went up whenever the weather permitted. She worked like a Trojan – and at times it seemed that she had conquered her problems; she would handle the controls with authority; her judgement would be commendable. The next day, inevitably, she would be clumsy and inaccurate.

'I've always been a bit erratic,' she told me with an apologetic and quite exquisite smile. 'I'm like that in journalism as well as aviating. On some days the words flow marvellously and everything is succinct and logical; but sometimes I will be sluggish and stupid. But I do think my good aviating days are outnumbering my bad aviating days, don't you?'

'Oh, rather,' I said, not totally convinced.

'I know that I'll be at my very best when I tackle the Channel,' she said.

I began to acquire morsels of information about her and the Gray family. Her father ran a modestly prosperous timber business in Basingstoke. Her mother used to be an English teacher; now she wrote children's books and was consistently unsuccessful in finding anyone to publish them. There was a sister, married to a solicitor in Reading; and a brother, an engineer officer in the Merchant Marine.

Why didn't I ask Frances out? I wanted to. I thought about it endlessly. But I kept deferring the moment. Already she was a success, almost a celebrity. Soon she would be world-famous. At the moment I occupied a special place in her life: that of adviser and instructor in matters aeronautical. Our relationship, though strictly platonic, was warm and in many ways satisfying. It was a relationship that had become precious to me. But it was a fragile relationship that could easily be destroyed. I didn't want to risk it.

The articles in Revell's continued to be highly successful. And they had their effect upon the world of aviation. In several parts of the country, flying schools noted a marked increase in enrolments by female students. At Girton, it was reported that four young ladies were in the process of constructing a triplane; the newspaper quoted them as saying that there was no biological reason why women shouldn't build aeroplanes. Another story reported that a titled lady in Yorkshire had invested twenty-five thousand pounds in the design and construction of a ten-engined aeroplane that would fly the Atlantic – with an all-female crew.

Early in March Messrs Duker and Fowler paid us a visit. They examined the Model 21 and declared it to be a magnificent example of British workmanship. Frances flew Bessy on a couple of circuits to demonstrate the skill that Revell's cash had purchased. Fortunately she landed without bending anything. She taxied to the hangar and jumped down.

'In two weeks,' she said, 'it will be the first day of Spring. The aeroplane will be ready. And so will I. I shall make the flight as soon as we get a suitable day.'

'Bravo,' said Mr Duker.

I suggested that she wait until summer.

'As long as it's clear, I shall go. I don't care how cold it is.'

'That's the spirit,' declared Mr Duker.

I regarded him with loathing. To him, it was a business venture, an investment. The sooner he saw some return, the better.

'I've been thinking,' he said, 'that we could put together a very nice little booklet, all about the famous Miss Gray. And if we move a little sharply we could have it on sale the day after the flight. Sixpence a copy, say. Should be able to sell fifty thousand without any trouble whatsoever. And the beauty of it is, if we're smart we could use the same booklet whether she makes it across or not. I visualize a sort of biographical piece: childhood, family, all that sort of thing . . . should go like hot cakes.'

'That's . . . horrible,' I said.

They looked at me in surprise.

Frances smiled. 'It's really not horrible,' she said. 'It's simply good journalism. One must be prepared for any eventuality.'

'I still think it's horrible,' I muttered.

'Aye,' said Mr Duker, 'and I think it's horrible that I have to face a Board of Directors every quarter . . . and explain what I'm doing with the shareholders' brass.'

Five

The third Model 21 was nearly ready. At Revell's request the fuselage was painted royal blue and sported the Union Jack on either side of the nose.

'Let's put the flag under the wings too,' said Frances when she came to inspect the work. 'I want the French to know from the moment they set eyes on me that this is a British effort – a British aeroplane with a British pilot at the controls!'

'Perhaps,' suggested Beresford, 'you would like us to implant a flag pole behind the cockpit. You could run up your colours as you approach the coast.'

'You're hateful.'

'It's an essential ingredient of my charm. Shall we pop into Town tonight? My chum is still the night porter at the Florence.'

'I think not,' said Frances to my immense relief, 'but thank you just the same.'

We bolted the six-cylinder Green on to its mountings and slid the eight-foot diameter mahogany propeller along the shaft.

'She is without doubt the most beautiful aeroplane in the world,' breathed Frances with due solemnity. She made arrangements for a photographer to visit us the next morning. He was a watery-eyed individual who very nearly put paid to the third Model 21 when he lit a cigarette beside a tin of dope. He resented having the offending smoke whipped from his lips and stamped to death on the floor. He also resented being called a gibbering idiot by Beresford, an imbecile by me and a bloody stupid sod by Eggleton. His picture, which was published in the next issue of Revell's, depicted Eggleton tightening a bolt on the engine cowling (he had to hold the pose for four minutes until flash powder was successfully ignited). 'New Wonder Aeroplane Under Construction Near London: it is expected to be a World-Beater.' Somehow the accompanying article managed to suggest that the Model 21 was being built in hundreds.

'We haven't told the staff about the flight,' Frances said. 'But they know there's something big afoot. They can sense it. There are all sorts of rumours buzzing about; someone told me that the magazine is being sold to a big American publisher – William Randolph Hearst, or someone of the sort. The extraordinary thing is that no one seems to have thought about the Channel. Do you think anyone else has the same idea? I dread picking up a newspaper. I'm terrified that I'll read about some wretch of a woman having made a surprise flight across the Channel. I had a ghastly dream last night. I dreamt that a red-headed female from Ilford was going up on her first solo flight . . . but instead of going back to the aerodrome she flew straight across the Channel to France! And she got there, blast her! Good Lord, was I relieved when I woke up!'

'I imagine you were,' I said. What I wanted to say was: you are without doubt the most courageous and adorable of creatures and I urge you to give up any and all admirers instantly and come away with me because I love you totally and unreservedly and I shall devote the rest of my days to catering to your every whim . . .

I didn't say that because I lacked the courage. I was scared of her reaction. She might laugh. She might be repelled. She might say that it was nice of me to say such things but unfortunately her heart belonged to another . . . My hopes were too fragile. And too tiny. But having tiny, fragile hopes was better than having no hopes at all.

She plucked a curl from her forehead. A delicate, measured motion. No one else in the entire world would pluck a curl in quite that way. I had the most urgent of urges to wrap her in my arms and pepper her with kisses.

'Please,' I said, 'give up the Channel flight.'

Her eyes widened in surprise. 'Why ever should I do that?'

'Because . . . because it's dangerous . . . I think you should get someone else to do it . . .'

'But I want to do it.'

'I know . . . but I don't think you're ready . . . later perhaps but not now.'

'I will be ready,' she said. 'I know there are dangers. But the whole flight will take only about half an hour. Thirty minutes! And I'll have earned myself a tiny place in the history books. It's a thought that thrills me beyond belief! It's vanity, I suppose, and probably not very estimable. But I know how badly I want it; and I'm sorry for everyone else who doesn't have my oppportunity. I want to do something that no other woman in the entire world has done. It's my life,' she added, head cocked, 'so don't you think I have the right to select my own risks?'

No, I wanted to tell her. No; you don't have the right because someone else cares even more about your life than you do. I shrugged and looked out of the hangar window. It was raining; clouds hung low and dark over rows of identical houses. It was chilling to realize that Frances might soon be trying to fly through such clouds, groping her way blindly in an element totally without mercy. Millions would read about it in their morning papers.

They would shake their heads and say how sad. 'The poor girl didn't get across. Shame. They say the new ragtime show at the Hippodrome is ripping good fun.' Damn them! I found myself clenching my fists, whipping up anger at non-existent people. Already I was almost a mental case.

I told her that I didn't think the flight was worth the risk.

She smiled. Adorably. 'Why are you so surly about it?'

I apologized. 'I suppose it was because I meant what I said.'

'That's sweet of you, to worry about me. But there's no need.' She was inclining her head. I could have leant forward and kissed her. 'I've always been lucky,' she said. 'That's why I'm not worried now. I didn't worry when we found the fog over the aerodrome. I didn't worry when our engine conked out; do you remember? I knew we would get down safely. I feel the same about this flight. I know I'm not a good, natural aviator. But I can fly. I'll fumble my way across. I promise.'

A week later the third Model 21 was ready for the air. She looked magnificent; her nose was streamlined by a spinner fashioned from spun aluminium. It gave her the final touch, superb sleekness that no other aeroplane in the world possessed. Surely this was the new standard; from now on designers would rate their efforts against the Marshall Model 21.

I climbed aboard.

The inevitable onlookers gathered. Murmurs of admiration. Nods of approval. Heads drew together as comments and opinions were exchanged. Arms were folded, feet planted firmly apart. Much standing and waiting could be expected whenever new aeroplanes were to be tested.

Beresford stamped on the chilly grass, hands in pockets. His sole concession to the season was a thick woollen scarf which encircled his neck and dangled down the back of his suit jacket. He glared at the aeroplane from every angle, daring it to be wrong in any detail. He shrugged at me as if to say that everything appeared to be in passably good working order. We drained a few gills of petrol in case condensation had formed in the tank. I nodded to Eggleton.

The Green fired at the first swing. A puff of blue smoke sped back at me and vanished before it arrived. The fabric of the wing shivered. Oil pressure up. Fuel pumping correctly. Hearty sounds from up front. Beresford and Eggleton were sitting astride the rear fuselage. I ran up the motor. The roar was deafening. The entire structure of the aeroplane trembled around me; the instruments blurred.

I reduced the power. The propeller became visible once more. I nodded again. Eggleton darted under the wings, to reappear a moment later dragging the chocks.

A wave.

We began to roll, the 21 and I.

The Green's power was a tonic. The aeroplane yearned to go. But I restrained her for the moment. I had to test her behaviour on the ground. She consented. But her patience was limited.

Ten minutes later I took to the air. The grass of Ashley Landing dropped away. Rapidly. Lord, how she could climb! And how gloriously sensitive she was to every movement of the stick! I whooped with glee. All the misery and the worrying had been worth it! We had the world's greatest aeroplane! I was flying her!

We circled the field. The familiar rectangle of pale, scrubby green, the huddle of buildings alongside the road, the farm to the south. From up here you could easily trace the paths of tail skids and the oil-stained patches where aircraft had been parked. I banked. The field turned on edge for me. Was there anything in all the experience of mankind quite so stimulating as sliding effortlessly through the air, a thousand feet above the ground, your wing tip tracing your path between the poor earthbound souls far below who stare up at you, their hands shielding their eyes against the wintry sun?

Turns to the left; turns to the right. Climbs, descents; stalls, recoveries. Enough for the first flight. I turned over the farm and eased back the throttle. The ground slid nearer. A steam lorry trundled along the road. The driver was leaning out of his cab in an effort to keep his eyes on me. A girl in white stood on the pavement and watched my approach, her arms folded. A horse and cart. A man on a bicycle. Tiny, toy figures; they sped beneath me. The grass loomed, suddenly becoming a sea of separate blades. I eased back on the stick and cut the throttle. The engine backfired. There was a gentle rumble as the wheels touched.

Beresford waited at the hangar door, hands deep in pockets.

'It lands rather better than the first one.' His eyes quickly scanned her. 'How did it behave?'

'Beautifully,' I told him. 'She's the best aeroplane in the world.'

He nodded and scratched his chin. 'I think you could be right.'

The next few days were spent in familiarizing Frances with her new aeroplane. It was a nerve-racking business. She flew the Model 21 in the same Charge-Of-The-Light-Brigade fashion in which she handled Bessy. Turns were abrupt and sometimes almost violent changes of direction; landings, as often as not, could only be described as spirited encounters with Mother Earth.

Frances declared herself totally satisfied with the aeroplane; she would tackle the Channel immediately; it was her opinion (but not mine) that she was completely ready for the flight.

First, however, according to the terms of the contract, we had to demonstrate that the Model 21 was capable of flying thirty miles non-stop.

We telephoned Mr Duker from the Post Office. He informed us that he would be at Ashley Landing at ten o'clock the next morning to witness the test. He would bring the documents and would sign them on the spot, the moment the test was concluded.

Frances decided to do a final circuit of the field as the light began to fade.

I stood by the hangar and watched her. Engine thrashing stridently, she banked as she passed over the farm. Lord, but the machine was a sight. No wonder heads turned whenever she flew. There was simply nothing else in the air so superbly proportioned.

Now Frances angled in for her landing.

I wished that she would crash. Nothing serious. God forbid. But she could wipe off the undercarriage or wreck a wing. Something to buy time . . .

Unconsciously, oblivious to the pain, I bit my lower lip. I broke the skin as the aeroplane's wheels touched the ground. A thud. A bounce. A rising of a foot or two. Down on one wheel. Up again; then, with a convulsive shudder, both wheels made contact at last. Safe and sound, Frances taxied to the hangar with joyous little bursts of throttle.

She clambered out of the cockpit, her sturdy leather flying clothes somehow emphasizing her femininity. I held out my hand. She took it; her fingers tightened around mine as she jumped down to the grass.

'You've hurt your lip.'

'It's nothing.'

'It's bleeding.'

'Must have bumped into something.'

She smiled. Her eyes were gentle, yet they sparkled.

We helped Beresford and Eggleton push the aeroplane into the hangar. Without delay, they set about the task of overhauling her, preparing her for her test. They had much to do. Within minutes, the metal engine cowlings were rolling in a gentle see-saw motion on the hangar floor; the inspection hatches were open, like gaping wounds.

Frances said, 'If I can't be of any help, I'll go home.'

Beresford said, 'Goodnight,' without raising his eyes from the elevator hinge mechanism.

'Perhaps I'll stroll along to the station with you,' I said. 'I feel like a breath of fresh air.'

Now Beresford raised his head. 'Poor fellow,' he said. 'You've not had a breath of fresh air all day, have you?'

Frances chuckled. I blushed, conscious of the fact that I had been outside since daybreak.

'I'd love you to walk to the station with me,' said Frances. 'Thank you so much for suggesting it.'

It was dark and chilly. The air smelt sharp and clean. We huddled in our coats as we made our way across the grass and out into the street.

'It's been such a thrilling day,' said Frances. 'And you've been so patient and so considerate. I'll never forget it.'

I shrugged and mumbled something about it being nothing.

'It's frightfully exciting,' she said, 'to think that by this time tomorrow it could possibly be all over . . . if the weather's good, of course.'

I swallowed. 'Don't make the flight.'

'You know that I must,' she said softly.

'It's too dangerous.'

'I'll be careful.'

'It's not a question of being careful. You're . . . just not good enough.'

'I think I am.'

'I know you're not.'

'Now you're sounding surly again.'

I stopped. 'Dash it all . . .'

She caught my arm. 'We've talked about it before, James. You must know how important it is to me.'

'I know . . . but, you're more important than the idiotic Channel!'

She was very close to me. I could smell the freshness of her hair; her eyes were very pale, very calm, in the darkness. She still held my arm. 'It's sweet of you to say that, James.'

'I mean it.' Huskily.

'My dear, you're always so serious about everything . . .'

We drifted together, naturally, inevitably. Smiling, she inclined her head towards me. My lips touched hers. A miracle of texture and form; my head literally buzzed with the delight of her. I forgot the place and the cold. I was transported. I turned slowly, luxuriously, in space. I wanted nothing more in life, or of her . . .

Then, suddenly, she broke free.

A policeman was standing beside us, rocking on his heels.

'Evenin', sir, miss.'

'Good evening, officer,' said Frances.

'I've nothin' against affection, mind.'

'Quite.'

'But I'd be very much obliged if you'd not show so much of it on my beat.'

Grinning, blushing, we promised. He wished us a very good night indeed; we wished him the same. He thanked us and saluted us.

There was so much to say that we said practically nothing until we reached the station. Then, when the London train was in sight, there wasn't enough time.

'I'll come down with Mr Duker in the morning. I shall look forward to seeing you, James, even more than usual.'

'Yes . . . good . . .'

'And don't worry.'

'I won't . . . if you forget about the Channel.'

'I can't, James. If I did, I'd regret it for the rest of my life.'

'If you're killed, I'll regret it . . .'

'I won't be killed. I'm lucky. Didn't I tell you that?'

'Yes, but . . .'

She darted a kiss to my lips, silencing me.

'You're a dear, dear person, James Marshall . . . one might learn to grow inordinately fond of you . . .'

Six

My eyes prickled with fatigue; I had slept fitfully. After a breakfast of bread and tea, I sat in a corner of the hangar and looked out of the window. Daylight was making a reluctant appearance. A thin layer of mist covered the grass. I hoped the weather would be atrocious. I prayed for fog and high wind.

Beresford still slept soundly. His cot was directly beneath one of the Model 21's shapely wing tips. I wanted to wake him up and tell him everything. 'Beresford,' I would tell him, 'she loves me. Incredibly, unbelievably, she feels much the same sort of thing about me that I feel about her. Don't ask me why; I truly can't imagine; the important thing is that it's happened. You can therefore understand, perhaps, why I am simultaneously elated and anguished. I am incredibly happy that we have discovered one another, but I am deeply distressed that she is determined to risk her life in this stupid flight . . .'

Beresford slept on. I pressed my cheek against the cold, damp window pane and watched a bird stall neatly in for a perfect landing. Daylight crept up over the hangars; the dew on the grass looked like tiny particles of ice.

I would unquestionably do away with myself if she died

attempting the Channel flight. How could I live on, knowing that I was the cause of her death?

The decision gave me a moment of wan comfort.

I sat there, semi-comatose.

Suddenly I was awake. Mr Duker's Lanchester saloon was screeching to a halt outside the hangar. The chauffeur's head jerked forward and back. Out tumbled Messrs Duker and Fowler, closely followed by Frances. I hurried to open the door.

Mr Duker didn't waste time on good mornings.

'Well? Have you heard?'

I looked at Beresford. He was sitting up in bed, hair rumpled, eyes puffy.

'What the hell . . . ?'

I looked at Frances. Her smile was fragile; she was frowning, worried.

'Heard? Heard what?'

'We have it from an unimpeachable source that an American girl is about to make an attempt on the Channel.'

'Flying it or swimming it?' Beresford asked, yawning.

'Flying it of course!'

'Just asking.'

'Her name is Harriet Quimby. And the *Daily* bloody *Mirror* is sponsoring her.'

'The sods.'

'We've got to beat her,' Frances declared. The determination in her eyes was almost frightening. I wanted to see love and happiness in them. God, it was as if last night hadn't happened. I bit my lip. It was sore.

Beresford was asking if the American girl had actually taken off.

'We don't think so. But we're not sure. I've got people working on it. We should hear something shortly. Why the devil haven't you got a telephone?'

'Nobody wanted to say anything to us before,' Beresford replied.

Frances said, 'I'm going to make the flight today. I don't care if this Quimby woman has already taken off. I'm still going.'

My heart sank. 'But the weather . . .'

It was a dull, overcast morning; the visibility was about two miles.

'It's good enough,' she said, the fingers of her right hand busily tapping those of her left.

'We've ascertained,' said Mr Fowler in his ponderous way, blinking, 'that it's relatively quiet over the Channel this morning.'

'What the hell does "relatively quiet" mean?' I snapped at him.

'I really couldn't say . . .' He shrugged, blinked and lapsed into confused silence.

Mr Duker said, 'If we've managed to find out about the *Mirror*'s plans, you can rest assured that they know about ours. They're out to beat us at our own game.'

'We've got to win!' Frances cried. 'It's the most important thing ever!'

'I'm relieved,' said Beresford, 'that you are able to be so calm and collected about the whole thing. Might I suggest,' he added, turning to Mr Duker, 'that we fly the aeroplane to Dover. The flight – some sixty miles, I calculate – can be taken as the pre-delivery proving flight.'

Frances nodded, eager, impatient. 'Ripping idea!'

Duker approved. 'Good thinking, young man.'

Frances said to me, 'Will you fly her to Dover, James?'

'If you wish,' I replied, rather formally, I fancy.

'I do wish.'

'Very well.'

'Thank you.' She smiled, warmly.

'I wish you wouldn't . . .'

'I must.' Gently, but firmly.

Duker was quizzing Fowler. 'Did you telephone Porson?'

'Yes, sir . . . he's expecting us about noon.'

'And he's arranged for petrol supplies to be on hand?'

'Yes, sir, he assures me . . .'

'And Godbolt: is he on his way there now?'

'Yes, sir. He left ten minutes before us, sir. Saw him go personally.'

'Capital; we want plenty of pictures . . . of the take-off and heading out over the vast expanse of sea . . . in the frail little . . .'

I stepped forward, ready to throttle him. But Eggleton chose that moment to appear, wobbling on his bicycle. All attention turned to him, to his considerable surprise. Without delay, his tool box was strapped on the roof of the Lanchester and he was bundled inside. The others followed; the chauffeur jumped out and swung the starter.

Frances slid down the window. She waved.

'See you at Dover.'

'Yes.'

'Don't look so grumpy. Please.'

I managed a thin smile. For an instant, a magic scintilla of a second, she looked at me as she had the night before. Her eyes were soft and warm. But then, at once, it was today. Only the flight mattered. Everything, everyone, had to stand aside for it . . .

The Lanchester roared and rattled into motion.

I watched until it turned on to the London Road. Frances became a tiny pink spot in the window. I kept waving. The car disappeared.

Ashley Landing had suddenly become a bleak and lonely place. The wind was chilly. I shivered and went back into the hangar.

Beresford was shaving.

He said, 'You may as well resign yourself to the inevitable, old man. She's going to make the flight whether you or I or this Miss Quimby of the *Daily Mirror* or Revell's like it or not. She's absolutely determined. And it's wise never to stand in the way of express trains or determined women. Didn't Keats say that? Or was it Shaw? Possibly it was me.'

'Do shut up,' I said.

'All right.'

We opened the main doors and pushed the aeroplane out on to the grass. The wind was fresh by now; it nudged at the Model 21's wings and tail. Irritated, disturbed, her structure emitted tiny creaks and sighs of complaint.

We filled her tank to the brim. It held enough petrol for two hours of flight.

Beresford wiped his hands on a rag. 'Eggleton will give her a thorough look-over when you get to Dover. She should be running like a top.'

I examined the map that Duker had thrust into my hands. The field was clearly marked. I was assured that by the time I reached Dover, a large X would have been whitewashed on the barn so that there would be no mistake.

'Have a pleasant journey.

73

'Thank you.'

'And don't worry, old man.' His smile could be genuinely kind, at times. This was one of those times. 'She'll nip across without any trouble whatsoever. And then it will all have been worth while.'

I nodded my thanks, then I hauled myself up on to the wing and into the cockpit. I settled in the seat, touched the controls as my eyes made their automatic journey among the dials. This had always been a quietly thrilling moment: the first step in an aerial journey, travel in an element that was still largely unknown and that every day revealed hitherto unsuspected habits and characteristics. Today I felt nothing; I simply performed the function required of me because I seemed to have no choice; circumstances appeared to have outmanoeuvred me.

'All set, old man?'

I gestured with an upturned thumb. Beresford grinned and rubbed his hands together. He took a firm grip of the mahogany propeller blade.

'Everything off?'

'Yes.'

He moved the blade until he found compression.

'Ignition?'

I depressed the ignition switch and forced fuel into the cylinders by means of the hand pump.

'Right-oh!'

Beresford swung.

The Green caught. I felt the chilled air rush past my head. Beresford stepped back and regarded the whirling blades with satisfaction. He stopped and picked up the chock rope. When I had run the engine for a couple of minutes I nodded to him and he tugged at the chocks wedged in front of the wheels, first the left then the right. He dragged them clear as the aeroplane began to roll. He raised his bowler hat and half-bowed. Half a dozen men had emerged from the hangars. Mr Wardle was there; he smiled in his enthusiastic, interested way, walking along, for a few moments keeping up with me. Then I picked up speed; I felt the jarring as we travelled over the uneven ground; the bumps shivered through the aeroplane's structure and sent the controls banging against my hand. Stick back to keep the tail firmly on the ground, I steered across the grass and turned by the row of oaks bordering the farm. On the path a policeman stood watching – was it the bobby of last night? I couldn't be sure; it was too far to pick out his features. Near by, two youths also watched. From this distance they looked identical: same flat caps, same light-coloured scarfs around their necks, same dark suits, same thin, pasty faces.

The Union Jack was flapping vigorously. God, if the winds were strong here how were they on the coast? Could Frances take off in such conditions? Would she be able to react quickly enough to fight the gusts and eddies over the surface of the field? I shook my head as I thought of her, hitting a wing tip on the ground an instant after lift-off, laden with fuel . . .

Nose pointed directly into the wind. Last-minute check of oil and fuel, controls and cockpit.

Full throttle.

The Model 21 fairly bounded across Ashley Landing. Within moments, the tail was up; I felt the surge of lift from the wings, then the clatter of the wheels ceased. The grass dropped away. I banked. The row of hangars slid beneath me, angled as if built on some gigantic hill. Beresford was clearly visible, arms folded, hat balanced on his forehead. Next to him, Mr Wardle stood buttoning up the collar of his coat. Behind him, through the partially open door of his hangar, could be seen part of his multi-winged aeroplane. I felt a moment of pity for him; surely it was obvious to him that he and his labours had taken him in the wrong direction. This was the way – Beresford's way.

I levelled my wings then turned in the opposite direction. Obediently Ashley Landing pivoted. Pink faces were upturned as I sped overhead. Lord, but this was an incredible aeroplane. In a few hours' time it could be the most famous aeroplane in the world. It was a good possibility. Damn it, a probability.

I climbed higher. Ashley Landing became handkerchief-size; beside it the London Road was a black line drawn by an unsteady hand. Wispy, insubstantial gatherings of cloud whipped past. The ground vanished. Then, magically, it reappeared. I turned again. My wing tip sliced through greyness. I felt the machine wobble as the turbulent air streamed over her wings. Easily I banked the other way. I angled the nose earthward. Down, down . . . then a roaring zoom to encircle a puffy cumulus cloud. This was my privileged playground. Only a few of us were permitted entry; only we could explore the ever-changing hills and valleys. One day, it was said, the sky would be full of aeroplanes; then it would be necessary to have aerial traffic regulations, to control the movement of every machine in the sky. A dismal prospect.

The engine missed. Then picked up again, Missed again.

The rev counter needle dropped to the left.

Fuel . . . ignition . . . everything appeared to be functioning.

'Christ!' I swore at myself. This might have happened to Frances, far out of sight of land . . .

Never mind. Better to catch the trouble now.

I eased the throttle back and slipped into a gentle turn to the left. I passed between two hills of cloud; they seemed close enough to touch. The sun appeared momentarily; its rays caught the gossamer-like fringes of the cloud and created a silvery cobweb that vanished even as I looked at it.

Ashley Landing was ahead, slightly to the left.

The engine seemed to be functioning perfectly well at the moment. Possibly dirt build-up on a plug had blown away. Obviously the trouble was not of a major nature. But too many airmen had died because of minor problems.

What would Frances do if her engine conked out over the Channel?

Idiotic question. What the hell *could* she do?

Would she be able to set the machine down in the water reasonably well? Or would she hit hard and go down like a stone? I winced. The thought stung.

For me, it would present no particular danger even if the engine stopped for good now. I could easily glide to the field – or for that matter put her down almost anywhere.

Below, the world turned slowly as I angled my nose away from the field in preparation for landing. I would describe a large half-circle and come straight in, between the cemetery and the farm, directly into the wind.

I had plenty of height. I had little need of power. Throttle lever right back until the paddle-like blades of the propeller were visible as they rotated at a lazy pace . . .

I'm not sure precisely when I decided to do it. When I thought of it, it was no surprise. It was as if the notion had been active within me for some time but only now had it bothered to present itself for serious inspection.

I remember nodding to myself.

It was the correct solution to the problem.

It had to be done.

By now I could see the flag. It confirmed that the wind direction hadn't changed. I could count the windows in the houses. One roof was lacking several tiles.

Several men stood beside the hangars, watching, pointing.

I turned for the last time. A house was at my left wing-tip. The horses ignored me, but a dog looked up. A couple of crows sped beneath me, intent on their business. I could feel the jostling of the wind; I had to keep steadying the wings.

The field was directly ahead; the Ashley farmhouse to the right.

I took a deep breath. I nodded again. Yes, yes, yes. I felt so damned *good* about it; clearly it was the right decision.

I picked my spot.

A touch on the controls. Nose angled down a degree or two.

The sun appeared again, for a moment.

Below me, the blurring grass crept nearer.

'Right!' I said, loudly, just audibly. 'Now we're for it!'

For an absurdly elongated instant the oaks seemed to come no closer. They stood there, haughty, indifferent. Incredibly, I had time to examine every detail of their trunks, the muscle-like knotting of the branches. My finger flicked the ignition switch; then, smoothly, quickly, as if I had rehearsed this, I moved to turn off the fuel supply. I braced myself; instinctively I pushed my body back against the rear of the cockpit.

Oh, Christ, Frances, it's for you . . .

We hit the oaks cleanly, the Model 21 and I. To my right the wing dissolved into matchwood and ripped fabric. The machine swung. I was hurled forward. Something sharp jabbed me in the midriff. I held up my hand to protect my face. The propeller snapped with the sound of a rifle shot. I saw one of the blades spinning back at me.

Decapitation.

It was to be my well-deserved punishment.

But the blade missed me. Below me, the under-carriage buckled and smashed itself to pieces. A section of metal cowling hurtled over my head. The world became noise: crumpling, bursting, tearing, cracking noises: all combined: all assaulting my ear drums in one thundering roar . . .

Beresford, I thought, is going to be bloody furious about this . . .

Seven

I was swimming. Rapidly. Stroking like mad, going straight up from the depths. I passed all manner of fish and other denizens of the deep. I spoke to them. I apologized. Sorry; couldn't pause and chat; had to make my way to the surface while I still had time. I could see the glint of the sun and, away to the left, the bottom of a large, wooden ship. Only a few strokes more . . . I was almost there . . .

I pulled the sheet from my face. Above me, a white, terrace area. I stared at it for some moments before realizing that it was the ceiling.

'Ah, you're back with us, Mr Marshall.'

Back with us?

A nurse with a bony countenance. How on earth did she manage to make that incredibly tall cap stay put? She asked how I was feeling – but, I laboriously told myself, she really doesn't give a damn, not deep within herself . . .

'I think I'm all right . . . thank you.'

'That's good. You're a very lucky young man'.

And then I remembered everything. It all came thundering down upon me: Frances, Beresford, the aeroplane, the Channel attempt . . . the crash . . .

God, God, God.

The nurse was busy with something at the side of my bed.
Timorously I felt for my limbs.

'Am I . . . er, complete?'

'Whatever do you mean?'

'Well . . . I seem to have all my parts . . .'

'You do.'

I doubted her. Nurses would say anything to keep their patients calm. 'What time is it?'

'Half-past three. No need to worry yourself about the time.'

That was a matter of opinion. Good heavens, I had been here, unconscious, for about six hours! What on earth had happened in the meantime? Were they still waiting for me at Dover? What was Beresford doing? What of the aeroplane?

Now a man's face appeared: ruddy and sagging, topped by curly ginger hair. The face wore a cheerless, professional smile. Beefy fingers grasped my wrist. Eyes, dulled by boredom, studied a gold watch. A nod. Now an examination of my eyes. A checking of my blood pressure. Another nod. The specimen was apparently satisfactory.

'You're a singularly lucky young man, Mr Marshall.'

'So everyone keeps telling me.'

'We'll get you on your feet in a little while.'

'All right.'

'You'd best eat something first.'

'Certainly . . . have I lost any limbs . . . or anything?'

'No. All parts present and accounted for.'

The corner of a lip moved a fraction.

'Does my brother know I'm here?'

'I really couldn't say.'

'I was on my way to Dover.'

'Were you?' He was writing something on a pad.

'The engine started to miss.'

'I see.'

'I thought I'd better turn back and have it looked at.'

'Quite so.'

He didn't believe me. Neither would Frances. Neither would Beresford. I shuddered as I measured the enormity of my crime. The ramifications of it were too appalling to contemplate . . .

What was happening now? Were they still waiting for me at Dover? Or had they heard that I had crashed? Had they already abandoned the whole thing? Not likely. Surely they would be trying to beg, borrow or purchase another aeroplane, any aeroplane capable of flying twenty or thirty miles. A few hours' practice and Frances would declare herself fully competent on it . . . . and off she would go. God, she might be on her way at this very moment.

I had achieved absolutely nothing by my action – except to increase the danger to her life by forcing her to fly an unfamiliar machine . . .

Fool.

Murderous fool.

'Glad you finally woke up, mate.'

I looked to my left. The man in the next bed was sitting up, arms folded across his thin chest. He was middle-aged, with a doleful face but cheerful eyes. For the first time I saw that I was in an enormous ward. Beds seemed to stretch away to the horizon. Doctors and nurses passed between them like gardeners tending crops of vegetables.

'How do you do,' I said.

'Beginnin' to wonder if you was ever goin' to wake up.'

'I was in an accident . . . I was knocked unconscious. I don't remember much about it.' I was going to tell him about the engine missing and my turning back to have it looked at, but he wouldn't have believed me either.

' 'ow d'you feel?'

'Not too bad . . . a bit wobbly.'

'I should think so,' he said, 'after four days.'

I thought for a moment. Did I hear that correctly?

'Four days?'

' 's'right.'

'Are you sure?'

' 'course I'm sure. I bin 'ere all the time.'

Oh my God.

My teeth explored my lower lip. The cut had healed. My head buzzed. I closed my eyes tightly. I had to collect my thoughts. Four days. *Four days*! God knows what might have happened . . .

I asked the man if he had seen anything in the newspaper about a girl flying the English Channel.

He looked up at the ceiling, then held his chin. He nodded. 'Yes, there was somethin' about it, seems to me.'

'Do you . . . remember who it was?'

He shook his head. 'Don't remember the name.'

'When was it?'

'Yesterday, I think.' He snapped his finger. 'She was an American, I remember that. Yes, I'm sure she was. From California.'

An American. Miss Quimby. Oh my God.

'Did you see anything about a Miss Gray?'

'Don't think so. It was only a few lines.'

'A few lines?'

' 's'right. Stuck away in the corner.'

'You mean it wasn't on the front page?'

'No, mate. The papers have been full of the *Titanic*, nothin' else.'

I stared at him. 'The *Titanic*?' I said. 'What about it?'

Interlude

Harriet Quimby was indeed the first woman in the world to fly
the Channel. The date was 16 April 1912. Poor girl, she could
hardly have picked a less propitious day. As her little Blériot
winged its way across the water, news from another ocean
staggered the world. The *Titanic*, the largest, most magnificent
ocean liner in history, had struck an iceberg and had gone to the
bottom of the Atlantic with an appalling loss of life. Harriet's
achievement went almost unnoticed; and three months later she
was killed at Boston during an air show.

I often think of her when I pause near the Shell garage and look
at the oak trees that separate its property from that of the factory
that makes windscreen washers. There are six oak trees: half the
number that once stood there. But the one I hit with the Model
21's wing remains. The scar is still visible: it is horseshoe-shaped
and above it the tree is slightly twisted.

Not far from that spot is a park: a triangular patch of grass with
a few trees and bushes. It is rather a forlorn little area, but to me
it possesses one feature of interest: a small brick building. It is
used by the park people for storing whatever park people store.
The building in question was not, however, built for the park.
I have irrefutable evidence on that all-important fact (which no
one has yet challenged). The building predates the park by some
fifty years. It was built by the Labour Corps when the invocation
of the Defence of the Realm Act transferred Ashley Landing
to the RFC six months after the beginning of what later was
known as the Great War . . .

Part Two
Thursday 14 December 1916

One

I informed Major Lewis that I wanted to return to active service. He nodded gravely, understandingly. As usual, he almost managed to convince me that he felt as deeply about my problem as I did.

'I've been instructing for well over a year,' I pointed out.

'Has it really been that long?'

'It's time I did something more useful.'

Major Lewis's plump, smooth features kept nodding. 'I know just how you feel, m'dear fellow. I must warn you, however, that HQ considers you of the utmost value as an instructor here at Ashley Landing.'

'I'm sick to death of instructing.'

'Quite.'

'I wouldn't mind so much if we were given sufficient time to do the job properly; but we're not; the poor blighters are only half trained when they leave here.'

'True, true.'

I sighed. 'Will you process my request, sir?'

'Most certainly,' he assured me with a smile. 'Delighted to oblige.'

I gazed at him. 'But it won't do any good, will it?'

'I shouldn't think so,' he said, still smiling.

Irritated, I went back to my office. An ashen-faced cadet stood outside my door.

'Sergeant Wilcox told me to report, sir.'

'What's your name?'

'Hyde, sir.'

I remembered. 'I understand you've been having a few problems.'

'Yes, sir.'

'Your instructor tells me that you have a tendency to over-control.'

'Yes, sir.'

I tried to relax the young man. I told him that an aeroplane, by and large, is a good-natured piece of machinery. 'It will do most of the work for you if you let it. But you mustn't fight it. You have to be firm but gentle.'

'I'll remember, sir.'

But I doubted that he would. Pupils tended to be predictable, particularly the unsuccessful. I collected my gear from the battered locker in my office; we went out to the flight line and clambered into an Avro. I told Hyde to take off, climb to five hundred feet, fly twice around the perimeter of the field and then land. Poor chap, he was as nervous as a kitten. Which was hardly surprising. He knew as well as I did that this was his 'last-chance' flight; my opinion of his ability would determine whether further time and effort was to be expended in an attempt to make a service pilot of him, or whether he would be stamped 'unsuitable' and returned immediately to his regiment. He had trouble starting the engine; the wretched thing fired when the mechanic swung the prop but Hyde didn't catch it in time. The procedure, with its litany of response and counter-response, had to be repeated. At length he was successful. But while we were taxiing he came within a few inches of removing the port wing-tip of a parked Farman. His take-off was competent enough, however. He was perhaps a trifle slow in picking up a wing as we pulled away but one had to make allowances for the fact that the poor sod was carrying his Flight Commander as a passenger.

I watched the grass of Ashley Landing drop away. The High Street, bustling with morning shoppers, slipped past; then we were clattering over those rows of identical houses – among them, 43 Pogson Road: Mrs Braine's house. (She still lived there; I saw her once in the village, but to my relief she didn't recognize me.) We turned. I was about to bellow down the Gosport tube to the effect that a spot more rudder would have done inestimable good to the quality of the turn. But I remained silent. Give him time; let him settle down. Our blunt-tipped wings pointed at the hangars. The original brick sheds still stood there, mute and crumbling reminders of the days of Marshall Brothers Aeroplanes – and abject failure. Now those old buildings were surrounded by Bessoneau hangars and structures that housed offices, sleeping quarters, servicing shops, messes and stores. They were all connected by a geometric pattern of gravel paths, flanked by neat stone posts and steel chains painted white. Every path was straight; only right-angled turns were permitted. Presumably that pleased the military brain. It was idiotic. In France no one bothered with such nonsense. There wasn't time. All that mattered was getting from point A to point B with the maximum celerity.

It was more than a year since I had been in France. I spent six months there, flying artillery-spotting and reconnaissance trips for the army. It was an easy tour of duty. The airman's war hadn't yet started in earnest. In all that time I saw the grand total of a dozen enemy machines and exchanged shots with only two. As far as I know no hits were scored by either combatant. Soon after the debacle at Loos I was ordered to return to England, to train fledgling airmen. It was pleasant news. But then I learnt that, in classic military fashion, I had been posted to the very place I least wanted to go. Ashley Landing. Why, out of all the RFC fields, did they have to pick that one for me? I requested a change in posting. I was refused. Indignantly. And on a drizzly October day I returned. I had been there ever since. And there seemed every chance that I would stay there until the war ended. It was true of course that experienced instructors were in pitifully short supply (and I was, after all, one of the rare birds who had flown before the war). Only the keen-eyed young cadets seemed to be available in unlimited numbers. They arrived by train and truck, to be thrust into overworked trainers and force-fed with the elements of flying. A mass-production process. There simply wasn't time to give them more than the rudiments. The need for pilots was too acute. In France the air war had become violent. And we were losing it. The reasons: our aeroplanes were inferior and most of our pilots were only half-trained; they were easy meat for the skilled, intelligently led flyers of the German Army Air Service in their Albatros and Halberstadt scouts. Casualties mounted daily. The squadrons cried for replacements. And so, at any given moment, from dawn to dusk, a dozen or more machines might be approaching or departing from Ashley Landing. As Cadet Hyde turned to line up for his approach, I counted six other aeroplanes ahead of us. Others droned along in the rear. The ground neared. I fingered the joystick, ready to take over if necessary. Hyde was dubious material. His touch was mechanical; he pushed the Avro around the sky as if he hated it; and, Lord knows, perhaps he did. I had to remind myself, however, that some airmen were said to be late in perfecting their art; and some excellent fighter pilots were nondescript fliers. Furthermore, a great deal of precious time and effort had already been invested in Hyde. And the squadrons were still bellowing for more men.

We thumped down on the grass. Hyde taxied back to the line and switched off. He carefully avoided my eyes as he clambered out. I wondered. Decision time. I told him that he had a fortnight to cure his problems. His face lit up, his eyes moistened; for an awful moment I thought he might burst into tears and hug me.

'Thank you, sir, thank you so much . . . I'll get it right . . . I know I can do it . . .'

'I'll have a word with your instructor.'

'Thank you, sir.'

'We'll review things in a couple of weeks.'

'Yes, sir. Thank you again, sir.'

If he knew the truth, I thought, he would beg me to ground him. I should fail him the next time. As a favour, a humanitarian act. His life expectancy in France could be estimated at about eighteen hours.

The light was fading. The mechanics ('ack-emmas', we called them for some obscure reason) were pushing the machines into the hangars; students by the dozen went streaming away to their quarters for a hurried meal, followed by classes on airframes and the care and cleaning of the Lewis gun. I signed a few forms – hours flown, pupils' progress (or lack of it), damage to HM aircraft, including reason for accident, disciplinary action, if any, and repairs effected . . . As usual I wondered what was done with these forms. Were they simply filed away in batches as they were received or did some dusty clerk actually make use of these Everests of data? By the time I reached my quarters it was dark. Corby had drawn the blackout curtains. An efficient servant, Corby, but humourless. And he washed his body less frequently than I would have liked. He was gamy. I kept intending to make mention of this fact, but somehow the right moment never came along.

I put on a clean shirt and tied my tie with particular care. Even so, the damned thing emerged lopsided. I seemed to be physically incapable of tying ties properly. I inserted a dress safety pin beneath the knot. It helped. Passable. In fact, positively acceptable, although it was almost certain that Helen would straighten it. Straightening my ties had become a habit with her. I examined my reflection. Still a fairly respectable specimen, even at the advanced age of thirty-one. Little sign of sagging under the chin, only the smallest of bags under the eyes; a mere half a dozen grey hairs at last count. You'll do, I told myself. Just.

Thank God it was evening and thank God the day had been fatality-free. The only casualty of the day was a cadet who lost his footing when climbing into a cockpit; he walloped his chin on the coaming and dislodged a couple of teeth.

I was fastening the top buttons of my tunic when Bill Borthwick thrust his head into my doorway.

'All set, old chap?'

'All set.'

'There are rumours around the family that you two are going to make the big announcement tonight.'

Bill had a cherubic face with a small, upturned nose. His fair hair was brilliantined and parted in the centre. He possessed a disarming smile. I liked Bill. I liked his sister, too.

'I'm not sure I shall like calling you my brother-in-law,' he declared. 'But I suppose we must all make sacrifices in war. When's the happy day?'

'We haven't . . .'

'Well, let me know in plenty of time, there's a good fellow. I'd like to put in for some leave to attend the wedding. A good stick, Helen, in her own way. But she's got a bit of a temper at times. Had you noticed? No, probably not.' He smiled innocently.

'She's awfully good at keeping it under control when she has to And of course she's hideously extravagant. Nothing wrong with that, of course, and I'm sure you won't mind; all you've got to do is keep supplying her with enormous sums of money; she'll be as happy as a lark.'

I warned him that I would tell her what he had been saying. Pretending alarm, he ran for the door. 'Good Lord, don't do that! She'll give me a jolly good hiding. She's as strong as an ox, you know, and with that temper . . .'

An amiable fellow, Bill Borthwick. A good instructor, too; one of the few with a natural flair for imparting their knowledge to others. I had requested that he be permanently posted to Ashley Landing, but the authorities, with their sure instinct for doing the unwise thing, turned down the request. Lt Borthwick would return to his squadron later in the month to resume his duties as a scout pilot. He would fly the DH 2, an antiquated pusher biplane with which the RFC persisted in doing daily battle with the powerful German scouts which could fly at 100 mph and which mounted twin machine guns. The DH 2, with its single Lewis gun, possessed a top speed of 73 mph at 11,000 feet – and took over half an hour to climb to that altitude. A month before, the greatest British fighter pilot, Major Lanoe Hawker, VC, had died in a DH, outgunned and outperformed by Richthofen's Albatros.

'Actually,' Bill had told me, 'the DH is really quite a pleasant machine to fly as long as you avoid getting into a spin. It's the very devil to get her to stop twirling before *terra firma* is reached. And for some winsome reason of her own she has a habit of catching fire if you turn her too violently. Something to do with the way the petrol sloshes about, we think. Yes, and there's another thing: one always hopes against hope that one doesn't blow a cylinder. All too often blown cylinders seem to delight in severing tail booms. Without a tail the DH has a singularly lamentable performance.'

It was considered good British form to joke about the inadequacies of one's engine of war. But better days were supposed to be coming. Rumours persisted of new scouts with heavy armament and speed to spare. Some pilots were said to have seen prototypes; a few even insisted that they were superior to the German aeroplanes although hardly anyone believed that.

Bill had an Aviatik to his credit. 'Pressed the trigger and had two surprises. First surprise: the bloody Lewis worked. Second surprise: I hit my target. I couldn't believe my eyes. But a couple of the other lads saw it too so it had to be true. The Hun simply fell to pieces in the air. The top wing came off and then one of the lower wings, quickly followed by the second. A moment later the tail came off. The fuselage went down like a dart with the propeller still whirring away. I was so astonished I nearly collided with the C.O.'

During the balmy days of midsummer, Bill had invited me to dine with his family; they lived only half a dozen miles away. His father picked us up at the aerodrome gates. He was a doctor, a bluff individual in tweeds, emitting a faint aroma of chloroform. He drove a brown Talbot. In fifteen minutes we had been whisked to the 'old place': a large and expensively furnished establishment manned by a bevy of servants. I was impressed. I was even more impressed by Bill's sister, Helen, a *petite* creature with dark hair and immense eyes. She was twenty-three and her fiancé had been lost at sea in a destroyer (as I discovered later). She played the piano after dinner: Gilbert and Sullivan and some of the new and immensely popular songs by Ivor Novello. It was a congenial evening; I was invited to dine again a week later. I accepted. Again Helen was present. The following morning I telephoned the house and asked for her. It was Jim Marshall speaking and, yes, he was quite well and, yes, it had been a thoroughly pleasant evening, hadn't it? I cleared my throat. Would she consider popping up to Town one evening. A bite to eat at Appenrodt's followed by a couple of seats at the Hippodrome ...? I was braced for a thank-you-for-asking-but ... Helen was a pretty girl; no doubt she had suitors by the dozen. And she probably considered me quite ancient and about as glamorous as a grammar school teacher. But to my surprise she said yes. And there was no getting away from it, she sounded distinctly enthusiastic about the idea ...

Dr Borthwick was pumping my hand.
  'My dear boy, I am delighted, quite delighted.'
  I thanked him, wondering dimly whether I should start calling him 'father'.

He told me that he had had his suspicions about us for some time, so that the announcement hadn't been a total surprise. But, he assured me again, he was delighted, quite delighted.

Then I was kissing the cool cheek of Mrs Borthwick who also declared herself entirely captivated by her daughter's choice. Bill's hearty hand was pounding my shoulder; for some reason he was calling me a sly dog. Champagne was found; corks popped; a smirking maid balanced a tray of slopping glasses. There were toasts to the happy couple and future joy and the welcome new member of the family and what a truly momentous day this was and how a daughter wasn't being lost but a son was being gained. I spluttered some platitudinous response and was enthusiastically applauded. We crowded around the piano and sang carols and drank more champagne. I glowed. This was what the poets talked about; I had missed so much, for so long. I grinned down at Helen. Our fingers intertwined as we bellowed about Good King Wenceslas. I was engaged. This young woman whose eyes were moist and whose lips were smiling sweetly at me would become my wife and we would live together for the rest of our lives. I was happy. No question about it. It was, of course, quite natural for a fellow to have a qualm or two. Everyone was entitled to a qualm or two, it was said. Marriage was serious and the longer a fellow had been a bachelor the more serious a step marriage seemed to him, it was said. More cork-popping. More champagne, bubbling its easy way down the throat and warming the visceral regions. I was a lucky stiff to have found Helen. Lord knows, I was no great catch. A very temporary captain in a totally temporary occupation. And precious little in the way of long-term prospects. One day, presumably, the war would end. What then? Vaguely I had hopes of a brand new industry after the war: commercial aviation, carrying passengers and goods by air all over the country, then all over the world. Surely there would be a crying need for experienced airmen.

'Ever thought about medicine, James?' Dr Borthwick beamed at me. 'You're not too old, you know. It's a reasonably rewarding profession. I have a few chums at Guy's; be glad to talk to them about you . . .'

The next day, Martin Colman arrived.

Two

He was a slim young man. A boy, really. Twenty, according to his file. He had dark hair that was rather shaggy and was brushed to one side and left to its own devices. He was a handsome youth with regular features and alert blue eyes. But curiously enough one didn't notice his good looks first. One noticed his smile. It was a magnificent smile, generous and infectious.

'Good morning, sir. I'm Colman. I understand I'm to report to you.'

He spoke well, in a cheerful voice. But he sounded casual; like many pilots fresh from the Front, Colman seemed to find it difficult to take anything in England very seriously. This was clearly a rather tiresome interlude that had to be disposed of before he could return to his true vocation.

'Welcome to Ashley Landing,' I said. 'Do sit down.'

'Thanks awfully.'

'Just got here, did you?'

'I came from London, sir. On the nine-ten from Victoria. I believe I'm supposed to do some instructing while I'm here.'

'That is the general idea.'

'I'm not very keen on instructing, to be perfectly honest.'

'Neither am I, to be perfectly honest,' I told him. No doubt I sounded rather grumpy. I was not quite at my best, having consumed too many glasses of champagne the night before. My head felt as if it was being dismantled from within. 'But that's what I've been told to do so that's what I'm doing.'

He grinned. 'Then we're in the same boat.'

'You might say that. Have you had some leave?'

'Yes, sir, thank you.'

'Glad to be back in England?'

'Yes, I suppose so. But it's not quite what I kept imagining when I was in France.'

'Everyone says that,' I told him.

I asked him about his duties.

'I was flying BEs for some time,' he said.

'Artillery spotting?'

91

He nodded. 'Necessary work, I suppose. But not much fun.' That grin again. 'Actually I thought it was bloody awful. I was frightened to death most of the time. The old BE is far too stable. Trying to fight in one is rather like trying to play polo from a horse and cart.' He glanced out of the window; the day's flying was in full swing. 'Do you have any BEs here?'

'No,' I told him. 'Avros and Sopwiths, plus a few old Farmans and a couple of Martinsydes. You'll be instructing in Avros. They should be a pleasant change after your BEs.'

'Well actually,' he said, 'I'm not on BEs any more. I was jolly lucky. A few weeks ago they put me on Nieuports. Escorting BEs instead of flying them. Much more fun. Have you ever flown a Nieuport, sir?'

I shook my head. It hurt.

'Ripping little machine. She can get up to a hundred at ten thousand feet. Climbs very nicely indeed. And she's marvellously manoeuvrable. You can make her do practically anything.'

I said, 'I think you might enjoy instructing more than you realize. It's surprising how much we can learn by teaching others.'

It was my standard welcome-aboard phrase. Usually I gave it a little more feeling.

He shook his head regretfully. 'I don't think I'm going to be very good at instructing, sir.'

'Everyone thinks that.'

'Do they?' He appeared to consider the statement for a moment. Then he looked at me. The smile vanished. His eyes darkened; he touched my desk with his fist; not quite a pounding, but almost. 'Why the devil are chaps being sent out to France half-trained? We had a fellow a month or so ago who arrived with only about twenty hours in his log book. Meredith, his name was. Poor sod didn't have a chance. An Albatros got him on his first trip over the line. I think the Boche can sniff out the newcomers. The point is, the new boys are so busy trying to fly their aeroplanes that they don't have time to worry about the enemy. It all comes back to training, doesn't it? Surely a chap should have at least seventy-five or a hundred hours before he flies over the lines.'

I was taken aback by the almost vehement way in which he

spoke. Lt Colman was clearly a man who cared.

'Unfortunately,' I said, 'there isn't time to give students as much training as we would like.'

'But you see, they're being slaughtered before they have time to gain any experience.' He spoke in the manner of a teacher explaining an obvious truth to a not very bright pupil.

I said, 'It's out of our hands. HQ keeps insisting that we supply so many pilots this month, so many the next, and so on.'

'But if the chaps were properly trained,' said Colman, 'it wouldn't be necessary to keep replacing them. Someone should tell HQ about it, don't you think? Do they really know what's happening? Sometimes I doubt it. It's all numbers to them, isn't it? They are bastards, really.'

I told him that we did the best we could for the cadets in the time we were given. 'That's why it's so important to have fellows like you,' I added. 'You're fresh from the Front; you can give them the latest on conditions out there.'

'If I did,' he said, 'they'd all desert.'

'Where is your home?' I asked him, more to get him off the present subject than from any burning desire to know.

'Market Harborough,' he said.

'A nice place.'

'But dull.'

'What does your father do?'

'He's a bank manager, sir.'

'A responsible job.'

'Is it?' He smiled wryly. 'Yes, I suppose it is. Personally I would detest having to work in a bank. But then I don't suppose I shall ever have to.'

I wondered whether he meant that he intended never to go into banking or whether he thought it unlikely that he would live long enough to have to worry about civilian employment. Some young pilots could be incredibly matter-of-fact about death.

'Do you play any games?' I asked him. 'It's not compulsory for instructors but if you're interested, there is football and rugby . . .'

'I'm rather fond of tennis,' he said.

I perked up my ears. Not many men played tennis; for some reason it was widely considered a game suitable for females only.

Nonetheless, I was inordinately fond of it. I had had a court marked out on the floor of an abandoned hangar, making it possible to play all winter long. My problem was finding partners. I told Colman about it. He grinned. Yes, he would be delighted to have a game. This evening? Top-hole!

Two days later Major Lewis summoned me.

'Where's Colman?' he inquired, before I had had time to close the door.

Colman? I had to think a moment. 'He's flying, sir. With a pupil. Do you want to see him?'

The Major seemed flushed; he was breathing heavily.

'Is Colman the ginger-haired one?'

'No, sir; you're thinking of Bassett. He and Wardley arrived on Thursday. Colman got here a day later. Dark hair.'

'Quite so,' the Major murmured. He gazed at me for a moment. 'I just had a long chat with the Brigadier about Colman. Do you have any idea what's happened to him?'

'The Brigadier, sir?'

'No; Colman, for God's sake.'

'Sorry.'

'He's a VC,' said the Major.

I stared.

'Colman?'

'Of course!'

'Good God!'

'Just came through. Hell of a ruckus about it,' the Major declared. 'Trenchard himself has been telephoning Brigade from France. Raising the very devil of a stink because Colman isn't there, in France. Apparently had no idea he'd been posted over here. I understand that Colman has bagged twenty-four German aeroplanes in all. Just before he left France he attacked a Hun aerodrome single-handed. Got there at the crack of dawn. The Huns were all yawning and stretching. Along comes Colman and shoots the place up, wipes out half a dozen aeroplanes in the process, drops bombs on their hangars and shoots at anybody who moves. He knocked down seven more Huns in the last few days he was in France. Didn't you know *anything* about it?'

I had to admit total ignorance of these feats.

'Haven't you talked to him?'

'Yes, but only about his days on BEs . . . I had no idea . . .'

'Everyone at HQ is talking about him. He's the biggest news since the chaps who shot down the Zepps. The Brigadier wants to meet Mr Colman. He tells me that lots of things are in store for that young man. Tell me, what sort of a fellow is he? I remember him, of course,' he added hastily. 'We had a pleasant chat, he and I, but you've spent more time with him . . .'

'He's a very nice fellow,' I said. A lame description. 'I . . . er, play tennis with him. He's good. He beats me consistently. His father . . . is a bank manager at Market Harborough.'

'I'm aware of that,' said the Major. 'Anything else?'

'Good sense of humour . . . and seems to get along well with his pupils. He thinks we're sending them to France with insufficient training.'

'Does he, by George?'

'Yes, sir.'

'He should try discussing that particular matter with HQ.'

'Perhaps he will,' I said. 'He feels strongly about it.'

Major Lewis sat back in his chair, his fingers drumming on his ample stomach. 'We may as well be prepared,' he said. 'This VC for Colman is going to have its effects on us.'

'Effects, sir?'

'Effects,' said Major Lewis. He scratched the underside of his chin. 'From what the Brigadier tells me I rather think they plan to make something of a public figure of our friend Colman. The feeling is that he's just the right sort to give a bit of a lift to public *morale*. And, of course, maximum advantage is going to be taken of the fact that he is here in England rather than still in France. The Press will be involved, I imagine. Have you had any dealings with the Press, James?'

'Some dealings,' I said, 'in a small way, before the war.'

The Major lit one of his Egyptian blend cigarettes. He always kept a box of them on his desk; he bought them in lots of one hundred for four and sixpence.

'The Brigadier made it quite clear that we should cooperate with the Press . . . but unofficially. In other words, HQ wants as

much as possible about Colman to get into the Press. It's some
thing the whole British nation is going to be frightfully bucked
about . . . single-handed attack on a Hun aerodrome and all that.
The way the Brigadier expressed it was: "It's time the British
public had an ace of their own." '

'An ace, sir?'

'That's what he said.'

It was an interesting development. At last, a British ace. For
some time, the French and Germans had made national heroes of
their fighter pilots who succeeded in shooting down five or more
enemy aeroplanes. Such pilots were declared to be 'aces'; their
pictures appeared in magazines and on postcards; they were lionized by society and were never without a breathless following of
adoring females of all ages and inclinations. Officially the RFC
had always frowned upon the ace system. The argument was that
the scouts existed for the purpose of protecting the two-seaters
which performed the all-important work of reconnaissance
photography and spotting. It was felt – with some justification –
that the glorification of aces encouraged pilots to concentrate on
building up their scores of victories at the expense of protection
for the lumbering, long-suffering two-seaters. The result was that,
although some British pilots had shot down respectable numbers
of the enemy, their names were virtually unknown in their homeland.

'Mind you,' said the Major, 'don't think that this means the
RFC is going to start calling pilots "aces", at least not officially.
The Brigadier was quite definite on that point. The official HQ
attitude is unchanged.'

'They want to have their cake and eat it,' I said.

He peered at me doubtfully. 'I suppose you might put it that
way. But the whole point is, that young Colman represents Good
News, d'you follow?'

'I think so, sir.'

'The Brigadier said to me: "Young Colman will be a nice
Christmas present for the British public." '

The British public badly needed a Christmas present. To date
the year had brought only disappointment: dismal tidings of the
failure of the much-vaunted Big Push, of U-boats sending the

nation's merchant fleet to the bottom of the ocean, of the French bleeding themselves white at Verdun, of the Russians scrapping among themselves rather than with the enemy.

'Colman is going to lift a bit of the gloom on the Home Front. D'you get the idea?'

'Yes, sir. Of course, sir.'

'Personally I think they're expecting a devil of a lot from a mere lieutenant, but I suppose they know what they're doing.'

I almost asked him why he thought they knew what they were doing in this case when in practically every other case they had proved so conclusively that they hadn't the faintest; but I didn't.

'They've asked us to do everything we can . . . to help things along. In other words, cooperation.'

'I see,' I said. 'Should we give the Press free access to the field?'

He looked shocked. 'Free access? Great Scott, no.'

'I just want to get an idea of how cooperative we should be . . .'

'You'll have to use your judgement.'

'Very well, sir.'

'I'd like to have a chat with Mr Colman when he lands.'

'I'll send for him, sir.'

Major Lewis nodded. He sighed; he seemed to find the prosecution of the war quite exhausting at times.

When Martin Colman emerged from the Major's office, I called him over and congratulated him. I said, quite sincerely, that it was an honour to shake hands with a VC. He grinned. He had been uncommonly lucky, he said; that was all there was to it; sheer luck.

'Did you know the VC was in the offing?'

'I knew I had been put up for it. But of course I had no idea that it would be approved.'

'You didn't mention it when we were chatting in my office.'

He grinned again. 'You didn't ask me . . . and it's a bit much to drag something like that into the conversation.'

He had a point. 'Do your parents know about it?'

'Rather. Major Lewis telephoned them personally. Decent of him, wasn't it?'

'Very.'

'They seemed quite bucked.'

'Hardly surprising.' I found myself looking at him. Somehow, he should have been taller, his shoulders broader, his chin more determined. He looked too downright *pleasant* to have done what he had done. I said, 'May I ask you something?'

'Of course.' The dazzling grin.

'Why on earth did you decide to attack an enemy aerodrome single-handed? Didn't it strike you as downright suicidal?'

'Certainly not,' he said. 'Actually I reasoned that this was probably the most intelligent way to do it. The idea was to sneak through without exciting anyone's attention. A single machine, flying low, timed to arrive on the scene just as dawn was breaking seemed to me to have a far better chance of success than a formation. And that was the way it worked out. The worst part was finding my way in the dark. I had a horrible feeling that I might attack an Allied aerodrome by mistake! But, thank goodness, I managed to get to the right place. I arrived at first light. The poor old Huns were just getting out of bed and cooking breakfast. I suppose the last thing in the world they were thinking about at that precise moment was battle.' He shrugged, smiling. 'Which of course was the whole idea. For a few minutes I had the run of the place. I dropped my bombs – twenty-five pound Coopers – on their hangars and just buzzed up and down shooting at things. It really wasn't all that difficult. Mind you, I wouldn't want to try it again! I fancy the Boche would be ready and waiting for me!'

He sounded like a schoolboy describing the strategy that won the inter-House rugger match.

That evening, a party was held in the Mess to celebrate the great event. It lacked the frenetic drink-it-all-up-for-tomorrow-we-die quality of parties in France, but it had its moments. Ignoring threats of courts-martial, Lt Williamson poured a bottle of brandy over the bald head of Major Silverthorne. ('Brandy's awfully good for the roots, old boy'); Lt MacPhee danced the Highland Fling upon a billiard table, revealing to a disappointed world that he sported a pair of black trews beneath his kilt; Captain Cooper leap-frogged his way through a plate-glass window and escaped with only a couple of minor scratches and a drenching from the rain; Lt Walker bumped into Steward Frost and sent a trayful of drinks spinning into the piano, bringing to an abrupt end a spirited rendition of the RFC ballad which recounted the last words of the dying aviator; Lt Adams made an indecent suggestion to 2nd Lt Goddard whereupon a fist fight ensued, largely, it transpired, because of jealousy on the part of Lt Morrow; Capt Mayhew fell soundly asleep upon the sideboard; a tug-of-war was attempted, using Steward Frost as the rope.

Major Lewis appeared with an utterly elegant young captain carrying an alligator attaché case. The two of them spared only fleeting glances for the swaying, tumbling masses of khaki.

'Where's Colman?'

I found him by the fireplace drinking brandy and explaining to two fresh-faced pilots that the only way to shoot down Huns was to get in so close that you could read the time on their wrist watches. He smiled at us in a slightly glazed manner.

'Awfully nice party . . . so pleased you could come along.'

'Our pleasure, m'dear fellow.' Major Lewis positively oozed good humour. 'Having a jolly time, are you?'

'Ripping.'

'Splendid,' said Major Lewis. 'You deserve it. I'd like you to meet Captain Monnington-Browne.'

'How do you do?'

'Delighted.' The Captain was meticulously turned-out; his blond hair looked as if it had been trimmed by an expert barber only moments before. With his delicately moulded good looks, he put me in mind of something out of a cigarette advertisement.

'Captain Monnington-Browne is from HQ,' said the Major.

Colman flashed his grin. 'I rather thought he might be,' he said.

Monnington-Browne declared that it was a privilege to meet Colman. 'Please accept my personal congratulations on your richly deserved decorations . . . and indeed the congratulations and gratitude of the entire nation.' It was nicely said even though it struck one as slightly less than spontaneous.

'Don't mention it,' smiled Colman. 'Delighted to oblige.'

'I'm Press Liaison.'

'Really,' said Colman. 'I'm Church of England.' He spluttered with laughter and knocked over a glass of beer.

'Jolly good,' said the Captain with a thin smile. 'Actually we make sure the Press gets the news, and gets it in the right way, so to speak.'

'It sounds like vital work,' Colman commented, his lips twitching as his eye caught mine.

Monnington-Browne nodded. 'It has its value, we believe.' He went on to tell us at some length how important to the well-being of the entire nation it was that the news be disseminated 'in just the right balance', although he failed to inform us just what he meant by 'balance'. Certain of the larger newspapers, he declared, had their own correspondents in France and some of these had perceived various actions in what could only be described as a negative way. If it hadn't been for the keen eyes and sharp pencils of Press Liaison, a great deal of 'damaging material' might have found its way into the columns of the national Press, spreading pessimism like a plague.

'Do you mean to tell me,' said Colman, 'that the news we read could actually be *worse*?'

'Indeed it could,' declared Monnington-Browne whose sense of humour was clearly less developed than his sense of self-importance. 'In your case, however, our task is very much pleasanter. It's not to limit news but quite the reverse. The whole idea is for as many people as possible to read about you and what you have done.'

Colman shook his head. 'I don't think so, thank you.'

'I beg your pardon?'

The Captain turned his head to one side, evidently believing that he had misheard Colman. Major Lewis held a glass six inches from his lips, frozen there when Colman said no. He might have been playing Statues.

'I really don't think I want anything in the newspapers about me, if you don't mind.'

'But we do mind,' said the Captain. 'We have planned an extensive campaign on you, a great deal of work has gone into it . . .'

'Really? Awfully nice of you, but I'd rather not, thank you.'

Colman spoke in the manner of a householder turning down a door-to-door salesman.

Major Lewis's cheeks reddened. He took a quick, fortifying

swallow from his glass, then cleared his throat. 'I don't think you quite understand, Colman. All this comes from HQ.'

'Of course it does,' said Monnington-Browne.

Colman finished his brandy; someone immediately handed him another.

'But surely I have some say in the matter.'

'I'm not at all sure . . .' said the Major, 'that you do.'

'That hardly seems fair.'

'What on earth,' asked the Captain, his voice becoming a trifle tense, 'do you object to about being in the newspapers?'

'I think I'd find it rather embarrassing,' said Colman.

'But you owe it to the public.'

'Do I? Why?'

'Because you're a hero.'

'No one ever told me that I would be expected to make a spectacle of myself in the newspapers.'

'I can assure you that the treatment will be in keeping with the . . . dignity of the decoration.'

'I think,' said Colman, 'that you should write in the newspapers about all those poor sods who fly BEs over the lines every day and get shot at by Archie and the Hun scouts. Those fellows are all a damn sight braver every day than I was that one morning.'

'Most commendable of you to say so . . .' Major Lewis's face had assumed a slightly darker hue. No doubt he was conjuring up terrifying visions of irate telephone calls from HQ, demanding to know why he, Major Archibald Lewis, couldn't get a mere lieutenant to agree to having his asterisk-asterisk picture in the asterisk-asterisk newspaper. 'But it's you the public wants to know about . . . you've done something frightfully daring and exciting and it's hardly being fair on the public not telling them anything . . . you do see what we mean, don't you? We can't let the country down, can we, m'dear fellow.'

He was close to pleading. I suddenly felt sorry for him.

So, evidently, did Colman. He sighed.

Well, if it was felt absolutely necessary, he would agree. The Captain and the Major looked relieved. A meeting with the Press would be arranged.

Captain Monnington-Browne said that it had been most awfully pleasant making Lt Colman's acquaintance and he would look forward to seeing him again shortly.

When the two of them had gone, I asked Colman why he objected to being lionized in the newspapers.

He grinned. He looked like a mischievous schoolboy in khaki fancy dress.

'I don't object at all,' he confided. 'Actually I'm rather looking forward to it . . .'

'Then why . . .'

'Those chaps from HQ are so used to getting their own way in everything; I just enjoyed shaking that gorgeous captain up a bit. Fun, wasn't it?'

Three

The next morning Martin Colman was a celebrity. All the dailies carried his picture and such headings as: 'AERIAL HUN-KILLER WINS VC', 'VC IS SCOURGE OF HUN FLIERS', 'COLMAN, VC: 24 DOWN, ? TO GO?'. It was breathless stuff, concocted for a public desperate for encouraging news from the war that was supposed to have been won a couple of Christmases ago. Colman was described as 'that smiling victor of more than a score of aerial combats high above the Western Front'. According to one report, German pilots flatly refused to take to the air if they knew that 'Leutnant' Colman was in the vicinity.

'What absolute nonsense,' chuckled Colman. 'I hope nobody believes this rubbish.'

Among his fellow officers he was the object of admiration and envy, as is any individual who is suddenly elevated in rank or reputation. Among the cadets, it was a simple case of hero-worship; they gazed at him in awe; they nudged one another and pointed him out; and every one wondered if one day he too might become such a man.

I admired Colman's reaction to all this. He was genuinely modest; he accepted congratulations in the manner of someone who has drawn a lucky raffle ticket; it was all a bit of luck – and a bit of a lark. He claimed no special talent as a pilot; his successes, he said, were simply the result of getting in as close as possible and 'flailing away for all one is worth!'

It might have been supposed that the Press coverage of Colman's VC would be a one-day phenomenon. But Captain Monnington-Browne and his staff did their work well, feeding morsels of news to the papers and ensuring that the story 'stayed hot'. Their efforts were aided by the public, who evidently found Colman irresistible. They wanted to know more about this young Briton who had taken on the entire German air fleet single-handed. Here was a symbol of hope; here was proof that our side was doing something right after all. Colman was young, handsome, successful and, above all, alive.

'Lt Colman is now in England, at a large training establishment in Surrey, passing on his hard-won knowledge to fledgling airmen who will soon go to France to fight the German aviators.'

The newspapers might as well have named the training establishment in question. Ashley Landing was by far the largest in the county; thus there was never much doubt about the hero's whereabouts. A dozen telephone calls arrived the first morning; they came to my office; I promised to pass on the messages to Lt Colman personally. That afternoon there were thirty more calls. Men, women, even a few children. They wanted to tell Lt Colman how much he was admired, and how greatly the country appreciated his valiant acts. The following morning the postman brought him a couple of hundred letters. Many were surprisingly bloodthirsty. 'Keep on slaughtering Huns for dear old England', 'You must derive the greatest pleasure from seeing your foes spinning down towards the earth, wrapped in flames', 'The only language the Hun understands is death; he has to be stamped out like the vermin he indisputably is.' One man sent five pounds. A mother sent a photograph of her son, missing in action. By any chance did Lt Colman happen to see him while he was in France? Several letters came from women with distinctly predatory intent. If Lt Colman would care to call at the above address he would find that everything (underlined) would be done to ensure his total comfort and pleasure . . .

He told me that it would be impolite of him not to take some of the ladies up on their offers.

Invitations to parties and dinners poured in. He went to a 'little get-together' at Sir Roger and Lady Hatfield's place in Cadogan Square.

'Lovely place,' he said. 'Full of coronets and Staff tabs. It was good fun for a while. They made a great fuss of me. But then I realized something: I was really a bit of a freak, a sort of side-show brought in to amuse the guests. Everyone shook my hand and said what a splendid job I was doing, etcetera. But then it all dried up. They didn't know what else to ask me because they didn't know anything about flying, or much about the war, come to that. I wasn't a novelty any more. So they started talking about the things that really interested them: who's marrying whom, and who's sleeping with whom and how much Lord Fart-Pants left in his will. But it wasn't too bad in the end,' he said with a grin. 'A General's wife came over to me and said, "Would you like to pop upstairs for half an hour or so?" I was a bit dense. I asked her why she wanted to pop upstairs. And she was totally un-coy about it. "We can have sexual intercourse up there," she said. She was rather ancient – forty or so – but quite well preserved. And there was no getting away from it, she was jolly keen. I said, "Won't you be missed?" And she said, "I shouldn't think so." Incredibly casual about the whole thing. So upstairs we went. And we had an extremely pleasant time, I must say. She told me she had travelled a lot; and there was no doubt that she had picked up a great many intriguing customs on the way. Afterwards, we went downstairs again. The General was at the foot of the stairs. He said to her, "Ah, there you are, my dear. Been showing our young hero the property, have you?" I had another glass of champagne and a prawn sandwich, then I caught the bus home!' He chuckled, remembering. He said, in his frank, engaging way, 'You know, women are really quite odd.'

I observed that other men had come to much the same conclusion.

'I think the General's wife was more excited by what I'd *done* than who I *was*.'

104

I was in the middle of wishing Bill Borthwick a good trip back to France, when Major Lewis burst into my office. His face was shiny with perspiration.

'Do you have the slightest idea who is coming here today?'

'Not the slightest,' I said truthfully.

'I can hardly believe it myself,' he said. He smeared a beefy hand over his forehead. He was breathing heavily. 'The CO just telephoned; he heard it from the Brigadier . . . so it's true . . .' He glanced at Bill as if noticing him for the first time. 'The Prince of Wales,' he said.

'Good Lord,' I said.

'Apparently he's visiting some Army unit near by . . . and he's expressed a desire to meet Colman. And so it's been arranged that he'll nip over here for lunch. As if we couldn't easily have taken Colman over *there* . . . But you know how very *democratic* HRH is . . . and apparently frightfully keen on aeroplanes . . .'

He plumped himself down in my chair. There was so much to do and so little time . . . and everything had to be *right*; it was the very devil of a thing to dump in a fellow's lap . . .

I sympathized with him – but wondered precisely what great load Major Lewis was bearing; presumably Radshaw, the Catering Officer, had most of the worries.

'Where is Colman?'

'Flying, sir, with a pupil.'

'Right, well, get hold of him the minute he's down and bring him to my office. He probably needs a haircut and a clean shirt. You'll look after that, won't you, m'dear fellow?'

'Yes, of course . . .'

'HRH is supposed to be here sharp at thirteen hundred hours. It's an informal visit, the Brigadier tells me; the work of the aerodrome has to continue as usual.'

'Right, sir.'

'I want the aeroplanes washed down and the cadets in their best uniforms; HRH might decide to look at the Flight Line. And make sure the hangar floors are swabbed with petrol . . . and I don't want any of those beastly pictures from *La Vie Parisienne* left hanging on the wall . . . oh yes, and there's a chap – an equerry or something – on his way here now to brief Colman on how to address the Prince. Is that all? Yes, I think so. I hope so.'

Muttering to himself, he headed for the door.

'By the way, sir,' I said.

'Yes?'

'Lt Borthwick is leaving today.'

'Who?'

'Lt Borthwick, sir.' I indicated Bill. 'He's going back to France.'

Major Lewis nodded. 'Ah yes. Of course. Thanks so much for all your help, m'dear fellow. Good hunting over there.'

It was with considerable relief that everyone observed how well HRH and Colman got along. There were no awkward pauses in the conversation, no mumbling and stumbling on the part of the commoner. The two young men – of almost identical ages – might have been school chums. HRH was keenly interested in Colman's exploits and in flying in general; he said that he wanted to learn to pilot an aeroplane, but 'the family' wouldn't let him. 'Bad luck, sir,' said Colman. He was mid-way through his third brandy. 'Do you enjoy flying?' the Prince inquired. He was short and fair with delicate, almost girlish features. He wore the uniform of a Colonel of the Grenadier Guards.

'Yes I do enjoy flying, sir . . . particularly if no one is shooting at me.'

HRH chuckled. And so the coterie of generals and colonels chuckled too.

'It's hard to imagine how it must feel,' said the Prince, 'thousands of feet in the air, diving and turning and firing at the enemy. Is it extraordinarily exciting?'

'Actually,' said Colman, gulping down the remains of his third brandy, 'it's exciting but it's also thoroughly uncomfortable. You see, sir, it's terribly cold, particularly at this time of the year, of course. The whole idea in dog-fighting is to get on top of your opponent. That means going higher, always higher. And the higher it is, the colder it is. And of course there's the constant danger of messing one's trousers.'

'Trousers?'

'Yes, sir. The point is that our engines are rotaries which means that the cylinders rotate around a fixed crankshaft. On rotary engines petroleum oils aren't much good because they get diluted by the petrol. So we use castor oil which, as I'm sure you know, is insoluble in petrol . . .'

'Oh quite.'

A red-tabbed figure stepped forward.

'I don't really think his Royal Highness is interested in *technicalities* . . .'

He made the word sound like an obscenity.

'But I am,' declared the Prince. 'Please do go on, Mr Colman.'

'Well, the trouble with castor oil,' said Colman, 'is that we have to breathe the fumes of the stuff for hours a day. There isn't a pilot who flies a rotary and who suffers from constipation!'

The Prince nodded, smiling thoughtfully. Behind him, a purple-cheeked General scowled at the mere slip of a lieutenant who dared to offend the royal ear with such subjects. He seemed about to say something, but there the Prince asked:

'What about the German aviators? What is your opinion of them?'

'They're good, sir.'

'But surely not as good as our men.'

'As a matter of fact,' said Colman, 'most of them are a damned sight better.'

Someone spluttered in his whisky.

'Really?' said the Prince.

'Absolutely, sir. Generally speaking, they're better trained, more experienced, and they fly superior aeroplanes. A year ago they brought out their Fokker monoplane with the synchronized gun. It was far better than anything we had. The mystery was why they didn't build hundreds of the things and shoot us all out of the sky. But they didn't; they left it too long and gave us time to bring out the DH. It didn't have a synchronized gun but it could fight the Fokker on more or less equal terms. The trouble is, we're *still* flying the DH while the Huns have brought out the Albatros and the Halberstadt. Awfully good aeroplanes, I can assure you, from personal experience.'

'How can we make all our pilots as successful as you?'

'They need more training, sir. They're being sent out to France before they're ready. They're brave and eager but they're being shot down in droves simply because they don't know enough about their profession.'

The Prince murmured something to an aide, who nodded and made notes with a gold pen.

'Tell me, Mr Colman, what are your thoughts at the moment of victory, when you shoot your enemy down?'

Colman reflected for a moment. 'I'm thrilled . . . and relieved . . . and a little sickened . . . usually all at once. The first aeroplane I shot down was a two-seater, a Rumpler, I think. It caught fire. I think the pilot must have been killed. He just sat there while the flames roared over him. But the poor sod of an observer was still very much alive. He was frantic. You see, the aeroplane wasn't diving. It was going down in a gentle, banked turn. I imagine the pilot was still holding on to the stick. The machine went around in a couple of great circles, trailing smoke and flame. I followed. And I could see the observer, trying to reach into the front cockpit to get his hands on the controls. But he couldn't of course. In a moment his clothes were alight. He tried to beat the flames out but an open cockpit isn't the best place in the world to try and do that. In the end he jumped. He was still about five thousand feet up. Certain death. But it was preferable to being roasted alive in the cockpit. Over the side he went. He looked straight at me as he fell. He moved his legs and arms in a funny, mechanical sort of way, as if he was trying to walk in the air. I lost sight of him. A moment later the Rumpler's wing folded up and everything went straight into the ground. I felt very sick for a long time. I couldn't sleep because I kept seeing that poor devil, looking at me. And I've thought of him every time I've shot down a Hun.'

'Are you married? Engaged?'

'No, sir.'

'I imagine half the unattached women in England are after you. Lucky fellow! I envy you!'

Colman grinned. 'I shall do my very best to accommodate them! The more the merrier!'

Then the ubiquitous Captain Monnington-Browne materialized, with two photographers. They busied themselves as the Prince took his leave of Ashley Landing. He shook hands with Colman.

'I've enjoyed our meeting, Mr Colman. I wish you every future success – in the air and in the boudoir.'

After the Prince's departure there were more photographs to be taken: Colman clambering into the cockpit of an Avro (a picture that was later said to depict him boarding his machine in France in preparation for an offensive patrol); Colman demonstrating to a group of pupils the relative positions of victor and victim in a dog-fight; Colman playing the piano in the Mess; Colman enjoying a game of billiards 'with a pal' (a 2nd lieutenant whose name he didn't know). I even managed to involve myself in the proceedings. I am the officer on Colman's right in the widely published photograph that is invariably said to show him and his squadron-mates at their evening meal 'somewhere behind the lines in France after a hard day's dog-fighting'.

'I had a feeling about you, Colman,' declared Captain Monnington-Browne. 'The timing was obviously right. But I didn't know quite *how* right! I had no idea the GBP would respond with such heartfelt enthusiasm.'

'GBP?' grunted Major Lewis, who seemed to have been physically exhausted by the proximity of royalty.

'Great British Public, sir. Excuse the esoteric jargon.'

'Quite so.' The Major peered at Colman. 'Don't you think you were rather familiar with His Royal Highness?'

Colman looked suitably innocent. 'Was I, sir? It wasn't intentional. He asked me some questions and I did my best to answer them . . .'

Beresford helped himself to more turkey. 'Do you realize,' he said, 'that this idiotic war is costing us sixty-six pounds per second. Per *second*, mark you. Not per hour or even per minute. No; per bloody second. The retail price of food has gone up forty-eight per cent since the outbreak of war. No wonder they've had to put income tax up to five bob in the pound.'

'Oh, do shut up, dear,' said Miriam, his wife. She was a handsome woman with jet black hair and deep blue eyes. She and Beresford had been married six months; according to him he was her fourth husband. She had neither confirmed nor denied the statement. 'It's Christmas Day. Helen and James don't want to listen to your twaddle.'

'A simple little calculation will tell you that sixty-six pounds works out to three thousand nine hundred and sixty pounds per minute. And that means two hundred and thirty seven thousand six hundred pounds per hour. Of your money! How much do you suppose that means per day?'

'Christ only knows,' said Miriam disdainfully. She gave us a long-suffering smile. 'And he isn't saying.'

I glanced at Helen. I could see that Mirian and Beresford were a new species to her. In her experience, nice ladies didn't say 'Christ only knows'.

'Per diem,' said Beresford, 'this lunacy is costing us seven million seven hundred and two thousand four hundred pounds. And that, if you happen to be interested . . .'

'We're not,' said Miriam.

'. . . adds to the tidy little sum of fifty three million nine hundred and sixteen thousand eight hundred pounds per week. Fifty three million pounds, up in smoke. Literally. I've no doubt we shall win the war . . .'

'Thank God,' yawned Miriam.

'. . . but at what cost? How on earth can a country of forty million people afford to keep spending fifty-four million pounds a week and get nothing in return? We can't, of course. It's impossible. But the government keeps printing more and more paper money and we keep pretending that it represents what it says it represents. But it doesn't. It bloody well can't.' Detail by bleak detail he went on to paint a picture of post-war Britain: idle factories, useless paper money, endless lines of unemployed ex-soldiers and their hollow-cheeked children.

'Beresford really does talk a lot of bilge at times,' Miriam told us, 'but he's a dear in other ways. Although at the moment I'm damned if I can think of one.' She beamed at Helen. 'I was tickled pink to hear about you and James. Marriage will be good for James. All men should be married.'

'It's a goal,' said Beresford, 'to which Miriam has devoted her entire life.'

The flat in which we were enjoying Christmas dinner was

decorated in violently contrasting colours: dark browns and bright yellows, reds and white. Miriam subscribed to several thoroughly voguish decorator magazines that were sent to her from America. 'Dreary, safe colours,' she told us, 'are definitely *passé*. It's essential to excite the senses with the colours of your rooms.' Personally I thought the effect quite revolting but Beresford didn't seem to mind. I doubt that he even noticed. He had recently been engaged as the head of the Design Department of a large motor company that was for the moment involved in the manufacture of RE8 two-seater biplanes under licence. The company had its corporate eye on the development of entirely original designs which could be produced for sale to HM Government at an attractive return. The possibilities were enticing, but first Beresford and his team had to create an aeroplane that the Air Board wanted to buy.

He told me that a new and very exciting machine was nearing completion in the experimental shop.

'All we have to do now,' he said, 'is convince those morons at the War Office of its qualities. By the way,' he added, 'how is dear old Ashley Landing these days?'

'Actually,' I said, 'it's quite exciting. We have a celebrity there. Martin Colman, the VC. Perhaps you've read about him.'

Beresford stopped chewing. 'That's extremely interesting. Do you know this Colman chap?'

'James knows him very well,' said Helen with some pride. 'The two of them play tennis regularly.'

'Really? What sort of a person is he?'

I shrugged. 'Very young. Modest. Awfully pleasant really. Has a wicked back-hand.'

Miriam said, 'I saw his picture in the paper. I thought he was absolutely delicious.'

'Try to contain your lust,' Beresford told her. To me he said, 'I'd like to meet him.'

'I suppose it could be arranged.'

'Good,' said Beresford, resuming his chewing, 'then be a good chap and arrange it.'

'Why?'

'He might be of some use to me.'

'To you? How?'

'I'd like to obtain his opinion on something.'

'May I ask what?'

'Yes,' said Beresford. 'I'd like his opinion on the Swift.'

'The Swift?'

'The new scout I was telling you about. It might be worth while to get this Colman fellow to fly the Swift. And then I'd like his opinions about certain of the cockpit details and the controls. After that, he'll be full of enthusiasm for the machine and he can nip up to the War Office and tell the cretins the facts. He's a VC. They'll listen to him. You'll arrange it, won't you?'

I told him that I should do no such thing.

He peered at me. He was getting a little short-sighted but vanity wouldn't permit him to wear glasses. 'Why, pray, would you do no such thing?'

All my life he seemed to have been asking me such questions. And all my life I had stammered replies that sounded cogent and rational in my mind but which became vacuous warblings by the time I uttered them. But now I was older; I was a captain; I could stand my ground. I explained that my relationship with Martin Colman was purely professional: he was an instructor; I was his Flight Commander; that was all there was to it and I hadn't the slightest intention of creating an invidious position for myself by putting myself in his debt ... I was rather pleased with myself. But Beresford seemed not to have absorbed a word.

'All you have to say to him is that an aeroplane manufacturer wants him to try out a new machine. Flattering as hell for a lieutenant, I'd say.'

'There are channels,' I replied, 'through which aeroplane manufacturers sell their wares to the government. I think it's a bit thick to expect a lieutenant who is not yet twenty-one years of age to do your company's dirty work.'

Again I pleased myself. My words had emerged strongly and my tone was firm. From the corner of my eye I could see Helen nodding her approval.

But I could also see Beresford shaking his head.

'What an extraordinary set of values you have, James, Incredible, really, when you've had the priceless advantage of several years' close contact with me. Did it not occur to you while you were mouthing your platitudes that assisting us might be a thoroughly good thing for your not-yet-twenty-one-year-old lieutenant? No one would expect him to perform this sort of service for nothing.'

'He can't possibly accept payment . . .'

'Who said anything about payment? There are other ways to repay people. Hotels for the weekend. A girl or two . . . or three . . .'

'Beresford . . . !'

'Merely a business arrangement,' he said, unruffled. 'It's not important. What is important is that the end result can be enormously important to him, to you, to us, to every British airman and indeed to the whole idiotic war effort. All we want to do is get the bloody aeroplane into production so that our airmen can use it to defeat the enemy. And that, I believe, is the whole idea, isn't it?'

'Yes, but . . .'

'But nothing. Our airmen are being killed daily because fat-headed bureaucrats decide what shall be built and what shall not. That criminally incompetent government design office keeps producing useless aeroplanes that are batted out of the air like flies. But this doesn't seem to matter as long as production promises are being met. The right numbers of machines are coming off the production lines. The right numbers of squadrons are being equipped. All is therefore well. God only knows how many men they've killed in that abortion of a BE. Now the bloody criminals have given birth to a replacement that's worse! We're making them in our factories at this very moment. And we're aiding and abetting the bloody enemy by so doing! All I want to do is help *our* side, for Christ's sake!'

'Your brother is a persuasive man,' said Helen as we waited for a bus. 'I like him, of course. But he's a bit frightening in his own way. Do you think he's right about all the things he says?'

'When he talks about aeroplanes he's usually right,' I told her.

'I'm glad you're going to arrange for Martin Colman to meet him.'

I shrugged. 'It might be a good thing.'

'Do you think after the war it will be as bad as Beresford says?'

'Of course not. We won't allow it.'

'We?'

'The chaps who were in the war. Do you realize that after the war there will be millions, literally millions of fellows who were in the army and navy and RFC. All of them will have shared a common experience. There will be a bond between them. What that means is, there'll be an entirely new voice in politics. And the politicians will have to listen. We simply won't allow them to do what they did in the old days. They'll have to toe the line.'

'It sounds exciting.' She smiled up at me. I felt tall and masculine and confident of the future that we were building. No doubt the gin and brandy contributed to my euphoria. The war, with all its horror and degradation, would have created something important and worth while. Madness would have given birth to a new and permanent sanity. I believed it fervently. It was beyond comprehension that it had all been for naught.

'Do you think we will be happy, James?'

'After we're married? Yes. Ecstatically.'

'I'm serious.'

'So'm I.'

'Do you think we're well suited?'

'Perfectly. You're female and I'm male.'

'Wretch.'

'I must warn you, young lady, that it is a heinous crime to call a holder of the King's Commission a wretch. Or even a cad.'

'What is the punishment?'

'A dirty weekend at the Florence Hotel.'

'Very well,' she said. 'I plead guilty.'

I looked at her. She was grinning in a self-satisfied way.

'You mean . . . you will?'

'Yes,' she said. 'I deserve the punishment . . . don't you think?'

'Good Lord, yes,' I said. Her response caught me off balance. I was unprepared. 'Jolly good,' I mumbled. 'Jolly, jolly good.'

She held my arm tighter. Our relationship to date had been warm and affectionate, but unconsummated. And our 'understanding' was that it would remain so until our wedding. The decision was prompted as much by ignorance of effective contraceptive methods as by moral fortitude. In this, we were like many of our contemporaries. Continence was frustrating but it was also foolproof. Only the very rich and decadent seemed able to indulge in sexual games without a qualm. For the rest of us, the dangers loomed too large. It was all right to invest a few francs or shillings on a prostitute but the girl next door was better left unsullied unless one was prepared to pay for the consequences.

'You mean it?' I asked, idiotically.

'Of course. I want to. I want you.'

She snuggled against me. What a wonderful creature! How lucky I was.

Four

That week, the last full week of the year, was a kaleidoscope of Christmas parties and presents (Helen gave me a solid silver cigarette case from J. C. Vickery; her parents' gift was silver-backed military hairbrushes from Mappin & Webb), of meeting royalty (or, at least, of being in close proximity thereto), of tennis with a national hero (who usually won), of fending off newspaper men, of industriously copying down admiring telephone messages for the valiant Lt Colman. Saturday evening found us at the Gaiety Theatre. The management had sent Colman a complimentary ticket for the Royal Box which accommodated half a dozen people with ease. ('Decent of them,' he said. 'Although to be honest I wish it had been the Hippodrome; *Chu Chin Chow*'s on there . . . but beggars can't be choosers, what?') He was taking his parents to the show; he asked me if I wished to join the party; I was most welcome to bring my fiancée. I accepted with pleasure; everything was working out marvellously, for this was the very weekend that Helen and I had planned to spend in town, at the Florence Hotel.

We sat in a corner of the box, holding hands in the darkness. She was at her prettiest; she wore the gold and enamel RFC brooch that I had purchased from the Goldsmiths and Silversmiths Company, for the sum of four pounds fifteen shillings. She kept glancing at me, her lips wearing a tiny, secret smile. This was our night. And it was perfect. The show was *Theodore & Co.* starring Leslie Henson with Madge Saunders, Julia James and Peggy Kurton: amusing, fast-paced musical nonsense; ideal for the occasion. Mr and Mrs Colman sat beside us. They were decent, unassuming people, wearing their Sunday best and, apparently, feeling slightly dazed by events. It was hard to realize that these two had produced Martin Colman; he should have had a buccaneer for a father and an aerialist for a mother. Mr Colman insisted on calling me 'sir'; I wanted to ask him to refrain but I wasn't sure how. I compromised by addressing him as 'sir' too.

Martin Colman was an attentive and considerate son. He bought a large box of chocolates for his mother and he ordered a tray of tea and biscuits for the interval between the acts. It was interesting to observe that he was far more formal with them than he had been with the Prince of Wales.

The show ended. The cast took their bows.

Leslie Henson stepped forward and raised his hands for silence.

'Ladies and gentlemen, I have a most pleasant duty to perform. For the past few days you have all been reading in the newspapers about a British war hero of the air, a gallant airman who will shortly be presented to his King to receive the highest of all awards for bravery, the Victoria Cross!'

'Oh God,' groaned Colman quietly. 'I was afraid they'd do this.'

'That young man is here in this theatre tonight.'

He swung his arm in our direction.

'Good gracious,' said Mr Colman.

'May I have the house lights, if you please! And would you, ladies and gentlemen, join with me in honouring that splendid, splendid hero of the hour, Lieutenant Martin Colman!'

The applause exploded – and, for an instant, it was frightening because the audience had vanished; the world had become a dazzling, deafening glare. We blinked owlishly; only when one stepped back, out of the direct light, was it possible to catch a

116

glimpse of row upon row of people, all standing, all clapping with the greatest enthusiasm, their eyes glued upon us. I glanced at Colman. He was smiling modestly and nodding hesitantly, as if unsure what all the fuss was about.

Helen squeezed my hand.

'Isn't this fun. What a lovely, lovely evening, James.'

With the Florence Hotel in mind, I murmured something about it getting better and better before long.

An usher appeared at the box door. Would we all be so kind as to step backstage? It would be so deeply appreciated by the members of the cast and the stage hands . . . only a few minutes of our valuable time . . . if we would all kindly step this way.

Backstage we plunged into an orgy of handshakes and smiles from faces still caked with sweaty make-up. Gins and ginger beer were pressed upon us. Someone asked if we would pop along to the 400 Club in Bond Street for a spot of supper afterwards. We would? Ripping! I had the uneasy feeling that the man who asked thought I was Colman. The man with the notebook and the inch of cigarette definitely thought so. When did I shoot down my first Hun? Did he go down in flames? I explained that I had never shot down a Hun; I wasn't Martin Colman, merely a friend. Without a word, the man moved away. A portly man asked me why we didn't drop bombs on Zeppelins. I made the mistake of saying that I would pass the idea on to the appropriate quarter. The portly man felt that he should be rewarded for the idea. I escaped and found Helen telling Leslie Henson that he was much funnier than Harry Tate. He informed her that such exquisite taste and perspicacity were rare in anyone of her tender years. I glimpsed Martin Colman, talking to half a dozen pretty actresses, his hands describing the zoomings and divings of aerial combat. The girls looked suitably impressed.

Then Mr and Mrs Colman were thanking me for my kindness to their son.

'It was nothing,' I said, wondering when I had been kind to him.

'I can hardly believe what has happened,' said Mrs Colman.

'You should be very proud of him.'

'We are, we are.'

I heard a voice behind me.

117

'Which one is Martin Colman, if you don't mind my asking.'

Good God. I felt my mouth drop open.

I turned.

'Good God,' said Frances.

Beside me, a man with a high-pitched voice was describing the rigours of pantomime in Manchester: 'Slavery, dear boy, no other word could possibly hope to describe it. Three shows a day, four on matinees . . . and the *people* . . .'

'Hullo.'

'A surprise, James . . .'

'Yes.' Lord, I looked at her and the years dissolved. We were back at Ashley Landing and I was teaching her to fly and she was scribbling her notes and writing articles and hoping that another woman wouldn't fly the Channel before her . . . 'Your hair is different,' I blurted. 'Shorter . . . but nice, of course.' I apologized. 'I'm sorry. It's an idiotic thing to talk about after all this time. I can't think why I said it.'

She smiled. 'You look just the same, James.' She glanced at the pilot's wings on my tunic. 'Are you home on leave?'

'No. I'm based in England. At Ashley Landing, oddly enough.'

'At Ashley Landing . . .' She nodded, slowly. 'What a curious coincidence. How are you?'

'Very well. And . . . you?'

'Very well too, thank you.'

'You look marvellous.'

'Do I? Thank you. How is Beresford?'

'He's well. He married again, you know. He lives in Richmond. He's designing aeroplanes still . . .'

'I'm glad.'

Then Helen was at my side. She had edged close to me, in the possessive way of women when they sense competition.

'Helen Borthwick . . . Frances Gray.'

'How do you do?'

'How do you do?' said Frances. 'But actually my name isn't Gray any more. It's Russell.'

I swallowed. I knew it . . .

'James and I are old friends,' Frances told Helen. 'He taught me to fly, years before the war.'

'How very interesting.'

'Have you ever flown?'

'Not yet,' said Helen. 'But I will. James and I are engaged to be married.'

Frances glanced at me. 'I do hope you'll both be very happy.'

Helen thanked her. 'Are you connected with the theatre, Mrs Russell?'

Frances shook her head; now her eyes were avoiding mine. 'As a matter of fact I'm here on business. I'm a part-time journalist. I used to be in journalism before the war. When my husband went to France I was doing nothing very much, so I offered my services to the *Telegraph*. Much to my surprise they accepted me. They sent me down here tonight to do a little feature on Martin Colman.'

I offered to introduce her. She thanked me, but declined. 'I'll just push in with the other reporters. I see they've beaten me to the post . . . as per usual. But perhaps I can steal some of their stuff.' She smiled. 'Awfully nice to have seen you again, James. All the best to you both.'

'I shall only be a few minutes,' said Helen. She kissed me; then she was gone in a swirl of gossamery night attire.

I sat on the bed. Desperate, I reached for a cigarette. When I lit the thing I found that my hands were unsteady.

Christ, this was awful! What on earth could I do? I thought fleetingly of running. No, dash it, I couldn't. Oh damn, damn, damn!

The patterns on the carpet were shifting, edging close to one another. I turned away and looked at myself, without enthusiasm, in the dressing-table mirror.

Why tonight, of all nights, for God's sake? How bloody cruel of Fate!

I thought of Frances. I told her that I was just now, after all these years, recovering from her. I could go for days sometimes without thinking of her. The wound was healing nicely. But now . . .

The extraordinary thing was that Helen had noticed nothing wrong. Affectionately she had clung to my arm as I had registered as 'Capt. and Mrs James Marshall'. A 'boy' of perhaps sixty-eight had carried Helen's small case and had shown us to our room on the fourth floor. He had accepted the sixpenny tip with a courteous enough nod; but there was something about the way he smiled his thanks. The old devil knew we weren't married. It was obvious to him why we were here. When he closed the door behind him I had the strongest conviction that he had some means of watching as we kissed and clung to one another. My embrace was fierce because I wanted to lose myself in Helen, to obliterate Frances from my mind. I tried, damn it. But I failed. Helen had suggested, smiling shyly, that we might as well prepare for bed; I had agreed. While she changed I had walked to the bathroom at the end of the corridor. It reminded me of a hospital with its great white tiles and metal pipes. The decent thing, I had decided, was to return to the room, tell Helen that meeting Frances again had . . . had what? Robbed me of my sexual desire for Helen? That was the truth of it. And wasn't it kinder to put the cards on the table? Helen, I kept telling myself, was making a great sacrifice for me tonight; I couldn't take her virginity under false pretences, so to speak . . .

But when I had returned to the room it was impossible to say anything of the sort. Helen was beautiful in her flimsy things. And, damn it, it was obvious that she was *looking forward* to our love-making! This was no long-suffering surrender. This was a healthy young female eager to get to grips with her mate.

The door knob turned.

'Hullo, darling.'

'Hullo.'

'I thought you'd be in bed by now.'

'Just having a quick smoke.'

'Shall I sleep on . . . this side?'

'Yes . . . rather.'

'You don't have a preference?'

'No. Not at all.'

'Are you going to turn the light out? Do you think we should pull the black-out curtain? Then we can look out over London.'

'Capital idea,' I said.

'Darling.'

'Yes?' She had noticed something amiss; she was suspicious, jealous . . .

'I'm very happy.'

'Good . . . good.'

I stumbled across the darkened room, loathing myself, cursing life for always managing to outmanoeuvre me. This was un-questionably the meanest blow yet . . . As I tugged on the curtain pulls, I knew that what I had to say was something about regret-ting the decision to anticipate the wedding night. She should go to the altar unsullied; she would be happier in herself . . .

I made my way back to the bed. Her small hands took mine.

'It's lovely and comfortable in here,' she said with a giggle.

I clambered in beside her. Instantly she was pressed close to me, nuzzling me under the chin. It was remarkably pleasant. I held her tightly; I could feel her breasts pressing insistently against my chest; my hand slid easily down the back of her nightdress. God, she was a delicious little creature. I kissed her.

'It's delightful in bed,' she said. 'It'll be even more delightful if I take this thing off, don't you think?'

'Well . . . I . . .'

Before I could organize a sensible reply, she had whisked it off and tossed it aside. In the semi-darkness I could see her teeth as she grinned happily.

God, the only thing to do was to get out of the bed this instant and tell her . . .

'It was a marvellous evening, darling. Thank you so much.'

'My . . . pleasure.'

'You looked so handsome.'

'Thank you. And you looked very beautiful.'

'Darling . . . were you engaged to her?'

I swallowed. 'Her?'

'You know who I mean. The one at the theatre. Mrs Russell.'

'Oh, her.'

Oh, her. Forgive me, Frances.

'No . . . I just taught her to fly.'

'That's all?'

'Yes . . .'

'She seemed very fond of you.'

'Fond of me?'

'The way she looked at you.'

'She's rather short-sighted,' I said. My mind had become

paralysed. 'As a matter of fact, she was jolly nearly the first woman in the world to fly the English Channel. Beresford built an aeroplane for her and ... oh, never mind; it's ancient history now.'

'Did you know she was married?'

'No, of course not. I haven't seen or heard of her for years.'

God knows how or why the mind responds the way it does. For some incredible reason this talk of Frances acted as a stimulant. I was physically excited and I couldn't conceal the fact. It should have had the opposite effect. I found myself caressing this lovely girl, revelling in the closeness of her, the feel of her supple young body, the scent of her hair. It was hopeless when she began to run her hand up and down my back; then she undid my pyjamas ...

Five

The morning papers carried photographs of Colman arriving for breakfast with Mr Lloyd George and members of the Cabinet. ('Really quite pleasant chaps – but a bit dull; they reminded me of the fellows in Father's bank.') A few days later there were more photographs; this time the location was the pavement outside Buckingham Palace. It was raining heavily but Colman's grin was as bright as ever. His cap set at a jaunty angle, he held the arms of his parents, apparently obeying the photographer's request to bring them in closer. His parents still seemed to be having difficulty believing it all. His father held a folded umbrella, apparently oblivious of the downpour that had already soaked his bowler. An hour earlier, Colman had received the Victoria Cross from the hands of King George V. ('A thoroughly nice old stick,' Colman told me. 'He said that he had heard all about me from his son and was looking forward to meeting me. "Keep up the good work, but don't take any unnecessary risks." Good of him, wasn't it, to put it that way. Considerate.')

122

After that the newspapers abruptly lost interest in Martin Colman. He had ceased to be news. In a way, it was a relief. Life at Ashley Landing could now return to its normal pace.

When bad weather prevented flying, Colman conducted informal lectures on the tactics of dog-fighting. They were immensely popular, not only because of his fame and reputation but because he taught well, with the fervour of one who feels deeply the importance of conveying the truth to his pupils. With the aid of wooden model aeroplanes and diagrams on the blackboard, he described the tactics that produced victory. He told the cadets to ignore the nonsense that the magazines published. 'Only suicidal idiots perform loop-the-loops during dog-fights. In a loop you're defenceless; as you go over the top you're a perfect target. And don't listen to people who talk about dog-fights going on for half an hour or more, with aeroplanes manoeuvring around to get on their opponents' tails. It's hardly ever like that. The whole idea is to get higher than the other fellow, always higher. Height means speed. You see your target. Put your nose down. And go after him, preferably with the sun behind you so that he can't see you coming. You have to keep on boring in until you're really close. Fifty, thirty . . . even twenty yards. You can't possibly miss! Fire! Then get out of the way. Fast as you can, or one of his chums is liable to be doing the same thing to you. The art of staying alive over there is being observant. Always keeping looking around. And above. The Hun that will get you is usually the Hun you don't see. So train your eyes to pick out aeroplanes miles away. Learn to scan the sky, and keep on scanning it. You've got to see the Hun before he sees you. And if a Hun does get on your tail, don't help him to anticipate your moves by giving him nicely coordinated turns. He can see your rudder and ailerons move an instant before they take effect. The answer is to skid. Rudder only; no ailerons. Your job is to get to hell out of the way, not to please a flying instructor with your coordination . . .'

The cadets listened, wide-eyed. No one stirred; no one whispered. This was too important; these words from the oracle might mean the difference between life and death.

'You're a flying gun platform,' Colman told them. Your whole purpose in life is getting those guns to bear on the enemy. And hitting him! And that means that you have to be able to shoot.

Keep practising your gunnery. You can never be good enough. Learn as much as you possibly can about your weapon. The Lewis weighs 26 pounds; it is 50½ inches long, it has right-hand rifling; it can fire at 500 rounds per minute and it has a muzzle velocity of 2440 feet per second. Practise releasing a jam. On the ground and in the air. Do it at night, blindfolded. Repair it yourself; know what can go wrong with it. In fact, find out everything you possibly can about your weapon and its ammunition. Examine your rounds. Look for cracks around the indent which joins the case to the cannelure of the bullet. It doesn't look like much of a problem but it could kill you, because it could cause a jam at the crucial moment. Look carefully at every round that goes into your magazines. It's a damned nuisance. But worth the trouble! Look for bulged bullets, caps set too deep, bullets that are loose in their cases. Too many pilots spend their time learning the fine points of flying: making beautifully coordinated turns and touching down without a bump. That's all very nice, but it isn't important in fighting. All that matters is shooting down the enemy – and staying alive, so that you can fly again tomorrow and shoot down some more!'

Invariably the cadets burst into spontaneous applause at the conclusion of his lectures, then crowded around him to ask him a hundred more questions. He was patient with them because he knew how desperately they needed to absorb every morsel of information if they were to survive more than a few hours of combat on the Western Front.

Major Lewis informed me of new orders from HQ: henceforth all student pilots were to be given an average ten hours more per man.

'They seem to feel,' he said, 'that we've been passing them out too soon.'

'That *we've* been . . . ?'

'HQ is never worng,' he murmured.

'I wonder if what Colman said to the Prince of Wales had anything to do with this.'

'They'd never admit it,' said the Major. 'Particularly if it's true.'

*

Colman sat beside me at lunch.

'I got a letter this morning,' he said, 'from a Mr Beresford Marshall. He says he's your brother.'

Good God! I'd forgotten.

'He seems to want me to fly an aeroplane of his.'

'Yes, he told me about it.'

'Jolly nice of him.'

'Do you think so?'

'Rather! He says he wrote to me because you were reluctant to mention that matter to me personally.'

'That's so.'

'I'm very flattered that he wants me to fly the plane. The Swift. Is it good? I've never heard of it.'

'My brother is a good designer. The trouble is that he's always a few years ahead of everyone else.'

'He sounds interesting.'

'He's never dull,' I agreed.

Colman said, 'But I don't quite see why he wants me to fly the Swift. Surely his firm has its own test pilot.'

'The idea,' I told him, 'is that you will fly it, then be so impressed that you'll put in a good word for the machine in high places.'

Martin laughed. 'Me?'

'Yes. Beresford thinks that because of your . . . fame, the powers-that-be will listen to what you have to say about the sort of machines that we send to France.'

'I think your brother is exaggerating my influence.'

'Possibly.'

'But I do feel very strongly about the quality of our machines.'

'It's Beresford's case that the wrong machines are going to the Front because of bureaucratic incompetence.'

'I think he's right,' said Colman with a shrug. 'All right, I'd be delighted to fly the Swift. But, honestly, I don't think it will do any good.' He grinned. 'Mind you, I could have mentioned it to the King the other day.'

'That would have made Beresford very happy, I'm sure.'

When I returned to my office I telephoned Beresford and told him that his ploy had worked. Never one to say, 'I told you so,' he merely murmured, 'Now, isn't that good of him. I'll have the

125

car sent down. Thursday afternoon all right? About two? Can you arrange it? Good fellow. My regards to Helen.'

Why, I wondered, did things always manage to work perfectly for Beresford?

I pulled a trayful of paper towards me. As my fingers touched the tray the building shook; the windows rattled. There was a deep-throated bang that seemed to emerge from the floor beneath my feet.

I sprang to my feet and rushed to the window.

The Avro was recognizable by its rear section: its square tailplane and circular rudder. The rest of the machine was smashed to pieces: a twisted heap of lumber, metal and fabric twenty yards from 'B' Flight hangar. And already the hungry flames were at work, dancing from strut to strut, feeding on the fuel-soaked carcass.

I threw open my window.

'What happned?'

A corporal yelled back at me:

'A cadet spun in from five hundred feet. Name of Hyde, sir.'

Six

We buried Cadet Hyde. His coffin had been filled with earth and blackened bones and other odds and ends that might have been bits of him or the aeroplane.

'Why did it have to happen to him?' Hyde's mother asked the question insistently, her face ugly and twisted with grief. 'Why? What was the point of it all?'

'There, there,' said the father, a stooped man in his sixties. 'It doesn't help matters, dwelling on them. It was quick. He didn't feel anything.' He looked at me; he had cut himself shaving; a spot of blood marred the crisp whiteness of his collar. 'Isn't that true, sir? It was a very quick death for our boy, wasn't it?'

'I'm confident,' I said, 'that he felt nothing. Death was instantaneous.' But, I wondered, what did the poor bastard feel as Ashley Landing spun beneath him: the hangars, the fields, the roads, the upturned faces, whirling around like a picture gone mad, growing bigger and bigger, until they smashed right into him. How did Cadet Hyde manage to cope with those last few moments?

'It was a blessing,' declared his father. 'The speed of it, I mean.'

'Such a waste,' moaned Hyde's mother. 'My boy . . . my poor boy . . .'

'What was it that went wrong, sir?'

'Pardon?'

Hyde's father wanted to know the details. Was it a mechanical failure that killed his son? Had someone done something wrong?

'No,' I said. 'It was an error of judgement on his part. Apparently he turned too tightly; he lost flying speed; he stalled; the machine snapped into a spin. He couldn't right it in time.'

'Wasn't he told how to turn?'

'Yes, of course.'

'You mean, he disobeyed his instructions.'

I shook my head; I felt the sweat under my armpits. 'No, sir, you see, it's simply not that easy to judge when you're flying. Sometimes things happen suddenly; a gust of wind, too abrupt a movement of the controls . . . it's hard sometimes for a pupil to know what to do.'

His mother snapped, 'You shouldn't have let him up there by himself.'

'He had to learn . . . very quickly . . . the war, you see.'

'He was so young.' Her eyes were fierce; she seemed about to fight to defend her offspring even after death.

'I'm terribly sorry,' I said. 'I mean it. I liked your son. He was keen . . . on flying. I wanted him to succeed.'

'Then why weren't you up there, helping him to learn?'

'He had to learn to fly alone . . .'

'There, there,' murmured the father. 'It's over now, Madge. I'm sure this gentleman did everything that could be done for Brian . . .'

'They killed him,' she intoned. She glared at me. I tried to meet

127

her eyes but I couldn't. Then, mercifully, her husband led her away. Thank God. I thought she was going to accuse me personally of killing her son. I wondered if I looked as guilty as I felt. Why the hell didn't I ground Hyde and send him to the infantry? But no, I had to take a chance. And he lost.

At last the ceremony was over. The guard of honour, chilled and bored, sloped arms and marched away across the boot-flattened grass to hand their rifles in at the guard room and have a late lunch. They agreed that it was hard luck about Hyde. But it was expected that some chaps would be unlucky during training. He was quickly forgotten.

The Rolls tourer was parked outside the guard room, a chauffeur, in grey livery, standing beside the door. The scene looked like an advertisement in *The Tatler*.

Beresford waved to us from the back seat.

I introduced him to Colman.

'Awfully good of you to come and have a look at our aeroplane.'

'I'm looking forward to it.'

'I think you'll find it of interest.'

We discussed the Swift as the Rolls whisked us towards London.

'She's at least twenty-five miles an hour faster than the Albatros at ground level,' said Beresford. 'Which of course is excellent. The obvious penalty is in a high landing speed.'

'We operate out of very small fields in France,' said Colman.

'Quite so. The problem vexed for us some time. And then we decided on a solution to the problem that I think will intrigue you. What we have installed on the Swift is, literally, an extra wing – a winglet, we call it – that the pilot can wind out as he is approaching to land. What this does, of course, is to increase the overall wing area considerably, thus lower the wing loading and increase the induced drag . . . and slow the aeroplane down.'

'What an ingenious idea!' Colman responded in his ebullient way.

Beresford smiled. 'Thus the Swift is perfectly capable of operating out of small fields. Touch-down has been clocked at forty-six miles per hour – not too frightening, in my opinion.'

'Certainly not, sir.'

'We've marked out a section of the field to correspond roughly to the size of a typical front-line aerodrome. I think you will have little trouble in putting the Swift down in that area.'

In less than an hour we were at the field on the outskirts of London. The managing director, a Mr Corfield, met us at the gate. He was a lean man with colourless eyes. He was professionally charming, heaping praise on Colman, saying how honoured everyone was that he was here. We shook hands with a platoon of managers, superintendents and supervisors. And then, as if we had run a gauntlet, we were free and walking across turf to a brick hangar. We entered through a side door, held open by a smiling man in freshly laundered overalls; a handful of workers stood nearby; they applauded as Colman passed. He waved and grinned.

The Swift stood in the centre of the empty hangar.

I ran my eye over her. I found myself smiling. Beresford had a touch, a style. With the exception of old Bessy, his designs embodied a striking look of balance and *rightness*. They gave the impression of not only being capable of flight but actually *wanting* to take to the air.

'There's a lot of the Model 21 in her,' I told him.

'It's better, much better.'

To Beresford, an aeroplane was always a 'thing', to be referred to as 'it', never as 'she'.

We met the firm's test pilot and some of the design staff.

I followed Colman as he walked slowly around the Swift, his eyes never leaving her. He seemed to want to absorb as much of her as possible in the shortest possible time. He spent several minutes admiring the neat installation of the engine.

'It's one of the new Hispano-Suiza motors,' Beresford explained. 'Magnificent little unit. Water-cooled, eight cylinders; each bank of cylinders cast as a one-piece block of aluminium. Hundred and fifty horsepower for only four hundred odd pounds.'

Colman whistled appreciatively. He said he had heard of the motor but this was the first example he had seen. He ducked beneath the Swift and examined the auxiliary wings that were tucked beneath the trailing edges of the main planes.

Finally he stood back, so that his gaze could embrace the entire aeroplane. He crossed his arms; he looked as if he was hugging himself with delight.

'She's magnificent, Mr Marshall.'

Beresford nodded. 'Yes, it is.'

'And you say the Air Board has turned her down?'

'Not in this form,' Beresford told him. 'A slightly older version; it was turned down flat. Two reasons: one, it was a monoplane and those imbeciles have somehow absorbed the notion that monoplanes are unsafe; two, the landing speed was about fifty-five. Too fast for France, they said. So we got to work on the winglet idea and an assortment of other little improvements and this is the result. We think it's a good aeroplane, probably far better than anything the Germans have. But is it as good as we think? Should we improve it in certain details? We want your opinion, you see.'

'It's awfully good of you, Mr Marshall. I'm flattered that you want my opinion. But I'm really not sure what it's worth.'

'Let us worry about that,' smiled Mr Corfield. 'Our aim is simply to produce the best possible aeroplane. We value your opinion because you are, after all, just about the most successful airman in the world today.'

'I wouldn't say that . . .'

'But we would,' said Beresford. 'We'd like you to fly the Swift, if you will.'

Colman grinned. 'Delighted, but I'm no test pilot ... and I can't pay for anything I bend.'

'We'll risk it,' said Beresford.

The hangar doors were wheeled open. Half a dozen men in overalls pushed the Swift out on to the grass. The sun was peeping gingerly through the 'overcast. Flying clothes were produced for Colman; he declined a helmet; he said that he preferred to fly bare-headed, particularly on a new machine. He clambered on to the wing and swung himself into the cockpit. Beresford and the test pilot stood on either side of the fuselage, pointing to switches and controls and making him privy to the secrets of the aeroplane. His dark head kept nodding as each morsel of information was absorbed. Plenty of left rudder during the take-off run to correct the swing; keep the speed up during turns . . .

More nods; a pat on the shoulder; the advisers withdrew; Colman was alone: a small, dark head, semi-enclosed by the cockpit coaming. The engine burst into life. Colman's hair was caught by the slipstream. A gloved hand appeared over the rim of the cockpit, waving the chocks away. The Swift's tail bounced lightly on the uneven turf as Colman applied power. He taxied out to the edge of the field and turned into the wind. We heard his engine roaring as he ran it up, testing the magnetos. Then he was bounding past us, tail already off the ground. The wheels broke free of the turf. Easily, the aeroplane lifted away, banking.

We stood there and watched Colman turn and dive, climb and swoop for thirty minutes. Then, carefully, because no pilot is contemptuous of bring a new aeroplane back to the earth, he turned in to land.

'All right . . .' Beresford snapped his fingers. 'Apply your winglets now . . . easily . . . no need to leave it to the last bloody minute.'

We caught our breaths as the Swift wobbled in flight.

'Oh, Christ . . .' said the managing director.

'It's all right,' grunted the test pilot.

The Swift righted herself as she approached; the wings became level with the ground. Gently she skimmed over the grass. Her wheels touched; she bounced lightly then settled.

'Absolutely splendid,' grinned Colman as he scrambled out of the cockpit. 'Lovely aeroplane . . . she'll be a marvellous fighter in France.'

'We're delighted to hear you say that,' said the managing director.

'You felt uneasy with the winglets when you first applied them,' said Beresford.

Colman nodded. 'It affected the aeroplane's attitude in the air. But after a moment it was tophole, I found her very pleasant to land. I didn't look at the airspeed; I was too busy but it didn't feel too fast.'

He had touched down easily within the area marked by brightly coloured stakes.

131

Colman ran his hand through his hair. He stood back to look at the Swift. 'Of course the lads will have to get used to operating the winglets, but it's not hard; it's rather like handling the trim-wheel for the tailplane.'

Mr Corfield suggested a brief tour of the factory. 'I know our people would be honoured to see you; and I think you might find it interesting.'

'The most interesting part,' said Beresford, 'will be after the tour is over.'

'Pardon?' I said.

'Never mind.' He smiled in his enigmatic way.

We bundled ourselves back into the Rolls and were transported to the factory buildings on the other side of the aerodrome. There, several hundreds workers were busy constructing RE8s.

'We're building this monstrosity under licence,' Beresford told us. 'The Air Board has ordered God only knows how many thousands of them; I understand half a dozen different factories are turning them out. They're being foisted upon our unsuspecting airmen in France as replacements for their dreadful BEs. The point is, that in their innocence, our airmen have the idea that the replacements are going to be superior to the abortions being replaced. Unhappily, they are totally mistaken. This thing,' he declared, pointing at the line of RE8s under construction, 'is totally unsuitable for aerial combat. It's horribly unmanoeuvrable, yet the designers have managed, with great ingenuity, to build in the most vicious spinning characteristics. And when it spins the top wing usually breaks away. The first models went to France a week ago and so many poor sods of pilots were killed that they replaced these things with old BEs! I ask you, is it any wonder that we are going to any lengths to try and get decent designs to our airmen?'

Colman peered dubiously at a newly completed RE8 at the end of the production line.

'I heard something about this machine,' he said. '52 Squadron got them and almost every pilot crashed; half of them were killed.'

It was late afternoon when we completed the tour. We were led to the Board Room – all oak panelling and leather chairs – where a dozen men awaited us. They were the firm's directors: middle-aged individuals with well-bred accents and expensively tailored suits in sombre blues and greys. Colman charmed them. 'So typically British,' I heard one of them say. 'Not a hint of bombast. Can't imagine a bloody Prussian being so modest after batting down a score of enemy aeroplanes, can you?'

Three remarkably attractive young ladies glided among the men with trays of champagne. I saw one of them whisper something in Colman's ear. He blushed, grinned and nodded.

I cornered Beresford.

'Do you really think this is going to sell your wretched aeroplane for you?'

He shrugged. 'I hope so.'

'But all this . . .'

'Business, old chap. It's the way things are done. It may all be a total waste of time and effort. On the other hand, your Colman may come into contact with just the right individual and he may say just the right thing about the Swift.'

A peculiar world, where decisions concerning equipment for the nation's fighting men should be influenced by champagne and well-displayed breasts.

Beresford told me to relax and enjoy myself. The firm was doing nothing more than being hospitable to a hero: paying him a spot of tasty homage, so to speak.

Half an hour later we were ushered into an adjoining room. The party had magically shrunk to four. We sat down to a table laden with delicacies. Pre-war quality and variety. Anything was available if you had sufficient influence and cash. Thank God Hyde's parents couldn't see me.

I undid the top buttons of my tunic and listened as Colman promised to do anything he could to convince the powers-that-be of the Swift's qualities.

'That's all we ask, dear boy,' purred Mr Corfield.

Now the girls were serving us, bending low as they brought the food, revealing delicious glimpses of cleavage.

'This is topping!' grinned Colman across the table.

The food was superb and the drink plentiful. My brain began to feel fuzzy. I rubbed my eyes; they seemed to be a little reluctant to focus. During the coffee and cognac I got up and wobbled along a corridor to a lavatory. I washed my face in icy water. My face looked spotty and pasty in the mirror. I regarded it without enthusiasm. I almost resented Frances. Dash it all, I had adapted myself to life without her. Now she was back, in the guise of Mrs Russell . . .

I saw the telephone as I made my way back to the Board Room. It stood on a polished desk in a darkened office. I stared at it for a moment. Then I went into the office and sat down at the desk. There was a telephone directory in the top right-hand drawer.

'Number, please.'

'City 6850.'

The lines clicked and buzzed. Someone had drawn a horse on the blotting pad. The body wasn't bad, but the legs looked peculiar. Difficult, horses' legs . . .

'*Daily Telegraph.*'

'Mrs Russell, please.'

'Editorial, isn't she, sir?'

'I believe so.'

'Just a moment, please.'

Another voice announced that I was connected to the Editorial Department. Mrs Russell? The voice wasn't sure whether she was in just at the moment.

'Ah, yes . . . hang on a sec, will you?'

My heart thumped; my rib cage seemed to vibrate; I wondered if I was about to have a heart attack.

'Hullo, Mrs Russell here.'

I swallowed. A stab of pain along my breastbone. 'It's James.'

'Hullo, James.' Her voice was level; she evinced no surprise.

'I . . . I got through to you quite easily.'

'I'm glad.'

'I suppose I shouldn't have rung you.'

'Why did you, then?'

'I wanted to. Are you annoyed that I rang you?'

'No. I'm not annoyed, James.'

'That's good.'

'But your fiancée might be.'

134

'I had to talk to you.'

'About what?'

I wasn't sure. 'It's been such a long time. I simply couldn't just meet and then . . . nothing.' When you looked at the horse upside down it looked like a castle. 'Is it . . . er, all right, my ringing you at the office?'

'Actually it's against the rules to receive personal telephone calls on the office telephone.'

'Sorry . . .'

'It's all right. Everyone does it.'

I said, 'I want to talk to you; it's been so long . . .'

'But, James,' she said – and I thought of her patiently explaining why it was so essential that she risk her life trying to fly the Channel – 'under the circumstances it really isn't such a good idea, is it?'

'I don't see why not.'

'Yes, you do. You're engaged.'

'I know. And I'm honestly not forgetting it.' I laboured to unearth the right words. 'It's nothing to do with . . . my being engaged, if you see what I mean.'

'I'm not really certain that I do,' she said gently. Tiny pause. The intonation of the last words created the feeling of indecision, of a glimmer of hope . . . 'But I suppose we could chat over tea one afternoon, if you wish.'

'I do wish,' I said.

She laughed. For the first time.

I hung up the receiver and wrote 'Thank you,' on the blotting pad.

I walked back along the corridor to the Board Room. Now there was the scrapy sound of gramophone music trickling through the door. I entered. The lights had been lowered. Beresford and Colman were dancing with two of the girls. Mr Corfield and the third girl were on a settee, drinking champagne, and giggling, their arms linked.

'Where on earth have you been?' Beresford asked.

'We were getting worried about you,' said Colman, chuckling.

Obviously, the girls were well briefed. As soon as I was in the room, the girl dancing with Beresford disentangled herself from his arms and came to me. Would I care for a drink? A bite of food? A bite of her? A cuddle? She smiled sweetly. She was a pretty thing and she possessed charm. Obviously someone in the firm went to some trouble to find the right types to entertain valued customers and those who could do the firm some good.

'Can you do the Turkey Trot?'

I shook my head. She said she would be pleased to teach me.

'It's awfully good fun,' said Colman.

'I imagine it is,' I said, observing that his partner's right breast had popped free of her dress. I accepted another drink, knowing that I shouldn't.

We danced and kissed and drank. The sequence of events is blurred in my memory. I seem to recall the girls dancing in the near-nude for our benefit; I also recall a discreet little room adjoining the main room, a cosy place with couch and roaring fire; there was a framed photograph of Windsor Castle and leather-bound copies of *Punch* and the leather chair was cold to the bare bottom. One of the girls had a tiny, heart-shaped mole beneath her left breast; another had quite the most prominent and splendidly shaped nipples I had ever seen . . .

Seven

'When were you married?'

'About six months after the war started,' Frances told me.

(I thought: somehow I should have known; I should have felt something.)

'He was the editor of an engineering magazine. He joined the Royal Artillery.'

I nodded mechanically. We looked at one another. We didn't know what to say.

'This is an awfully nice restaurant,' she said, at last.

It was the Wigmore; they did afternoon tea at one shilling per person.

I said that I was glad she liked it.

'You're looking very well, James.'

I thanked her. I made no mention of the excesses of a few nights before. Shame still stung me. God knows when I had fallen asleep. All I know is that I dimly recall being driven through darkened streets; and there were curt military voices and hard hands heaving me into my bed. I stayed there for a day and a half. What made it worse was that Colman appeared to be in the best of spirits the following morning.

'Do you still take flying so seriously?'

She inclined her head a few degrees. I saw her once more in front of the Marshall Brothers' hangar at Ashley Landing, about to clamber into Bessy's precarious cockpit, asking a question about the controls, ready to jot down the answer in her ever-present notebook.

'Flying,' I said, 'has become very serious business.'

'And you're back at Ashley Landing.'

'It's changed a great deal. All very military. You'd hardly recognize it.'

'And you're training airmen?'

'By the gross.'

'Fred – my husband – wanted to fly. But they wouldn't pass him because he wore glasses.'

Wore? Past tense? 'Is he in France now?'

She nodded.

'Where?'

She looked at me. 'He's dead,' she said.

I lied. I said how deeply sorry I was.

'You would have liked him.'

'I'm sure I would.'

'He was killed on the first of July.'

'The Somme.'

She nodded. 'We all called it The Big Push. It was supposed to end the war.'

'Where do you live now?'

'I'm at my sister's place . . . in St John's Wood.'

'I thought your sister lived in Reading.'

'She did. They've sold their place there. Jack is something to do

137

with the Advocate-General's office. Is there such a thing? Have I got the name right?'

'I think so.' I gazed at her; she had known tragedy and I hadn't shared it with her. Again I felt that I had failed her in some way. 'Did you stay at Revell's for long after . . . ?'

'I went to Canada,' she said. 'Toronto. I wanted to get away. My father's brother has a clothes shop on Yonge Street. A very nice place. I worked there until the outbreak of war. Then I came back to England. I telephoned Mr Duker one day; they told me that he had retired. I think Mr Fowler is still there, though.'

I apologized for ruining her chance at the cross-Channel flight.

She smiled. 'I was furious for a long time. I used to wake up at night with my fists clenched and my teeth grinding away. "If it wasn't for that wretched man, I would have been the first woman across!" It used to be hours before I could relax enough to go back to sleep!'

'I'm awfully sorry.'

'It seemed so important then; now, when I think back it all seems so trivial. How could it matter so much to us? Who remembers poor Harriet Quimby now? Who even read about her then? She timed things dreadfully, didn't she? And it might have been me.'

'I'm relieved that you've forgiven me.'

'You did a very noble thing, James. When I cooled down, I realized just how noble it was. But by then I was in Toronto and I hadn't the faintest where you were. I wrote to you, you know. At Ashley Landing. But after months and months the letter came back "Addressee Unknown".'

'We moved,' I told her. 'The firm broke up quite quickly. In fact, by the time I was out of hospital it had ceased to exist. Beresford went to work for Vickers. I got a job as an instructor with Graham-White at Hendon. I stayed there until the war.' I lit a Kenilworth cigarette and took a deep drag. 'I'm not going to let you go again.'

'You mustn't say that, James.'

'But I do say it. It happens to be the truth.'

'You're engaged.'

'I know. But when I got engaged it never entered my mind that I would ever see you again.'

The statement sounded crude and mechanical, but it was the truth.

'Would you have said that if my husband had still been alive?'

'I don't know . . . yes, perhaps . . . I'm not sure. I think so.'

The waitress wanted to know if we had had enough tea. Did we require more cakes? I shook my head.

'I think they want us to leave,' said Frances.

At the door, grim-faced ladies and gentlemen waited, eyeing the tables meaningfully. In wartime London there was never enough room.

I paid the bill. It was dark when we got outside; dark and raining heavily. The street looked like glass; one wondered how the Maudslay vans and the Austin taxis could stop without skidding. We stood in the doorway while we buttoned up our coats.

Suddenly the words tumbled out.

'The fact of the matter,' I told her, 'is that I love you. I've loved you since those days at Ashley Landing. I love you now. I thought I was going to have to manage to lead my life without you, but now it's all different. I know that I shall never ever love anyone in quite the same way.'

Oddly enough, she was still fastening her top buttons as I said these things; she was listening to me and her hand seemed to be acting on its own.

'What about your . . . fiancée?' she said.

'I'm extremely sorry about Helen,' I said. 'But it's quite clear to me that I can't possibly marry her now. Even if you walk away now and I never see you again, it won't make any difference as far as Helen is concerned. It's over.'

Passers-by looked at me curiously. I suppose I was making something of a spectacle of myself. I didn't care.

Frances touched my arm, in a tentative way, as if she was unsure how I might react. 'I don't think I know quite what to say.'

'You don't have to say anything.'

'James, this is so important . . .'

'I'm going to tell Helen that it's off.'

'No . . .'

'I must. It is off. That's the simple fact of the matter. It's off because I've found you again.'

'How can you be so sure? We've not seen each other for so long . . .'

'My mind is made up.'

'Think about it, James. For a week or a month.'

'*Think* about it? What on earth do you think I have been doing?'

'She will be terribly hurt . . .'

Eight

Colman spent several days visiting factories and telling workers what a splendid job they were doing and how much the lads in France appreciated their efforts. It was during one of these visits that he met a General who was involved with the procurement of aircraft for the RFC. In his direct, ebullient way, Colman told the General about the Swift. The General professed complete ignorance of the machine, but if Lt Colman, VC, thought highly of it, then clearly it was possessed of special merit. A telephone call was placed immediately to Mr Corfield. Yes, a visit could indeed be arranged. And was. Colman flew the Swift again. The General was impressed. Why had he not been informed of the existence of this splendid machine? He would, he said, have to look into the matter without delay.

There was no right moment. The fact had simply to be stated.

Helen said nothing in reply. She nodded, her eyes dry but puzzled, as if she didn't understand what she had done to deserve this.

'I'm frightfully sorry,' I said inadequately. Still she said nothing. The silence was agonizing. I wished she would attack me or scream or cry . . . anything but this silence. I mumbled, 'I know this must come as a . . . dreadful shock. But . . . in a way, it was a shock to me too, if you see what I mean. I had no idea that . . . I would ever see her again. So I thought it best just to . . . say what was on my mind.'

I distinctly heard the ticking of the grandfather clock in the hall; someone was scraping a bowl in the scullery.

At last she spoke. 'I don't know what to say to you, James. I think I shall soon hate you. But at the moment I feel nothing. I feel numb about everything.'

'I'm frightfully sorry,' I said again.

'Are you?'

'Yes . . . really.'

'I would have thought you'd be rather pleased with yourself. You've found your real lady love after many years . . . in the nick of time, so to speak. Imagine how awkward it would have been if she had reappeared after we were married.'

'You're the last person in the world I want to hurt. But I have to hurt you. And I'm terribly sorry.'

'You keep saying that, James.'

'Yes . . .' I stared past her. I hadn't the faintest idea what to say next. I had an absurd inclination to reach out my hand to shake hers; the gesture symbolizing the conclusion of a business deal. We stared past one another. In the kitchen a tap ran, then stopped.

I said that I had to leave. I swallowed. At any moment her mother or father might walk in. It was a petrifying thought; I had declared myself an enemy; from this moment the people who had accepted me as one of theirs would detest me, and rightly so.

She shrugged; now her eyes began to glisten.

'Will you keep the ring?'

The question had an unintended tone. It sounded calculating; I hadn't meant it that way. My thought had been that she should keep the ring as a sort of compensation, I suppose, for what I had done.

At once she tugged the ring off her finger. 'You can have the rotten thing back,' she snapped. She threw it at me. It missed and hit the wall; I heard it tumble lightly to the hardwood floor.

Once more I apologized. Helen shook her head as if refusing to listen to me. I fled into the hall. Thank God it was empty. I took my cap and Burberry from the stand and hurried outside. Thankfully weak with relief, I breathed the chilly air. A frightful ordeal was over. (Later, I had the sense to realize that, for Helen, it was just beginning.) I was free. I had a vague notion that Helen might be able to sue me. Breach of promise, wasn't it called? But I couldn't worry about that now. I had to telephone Frances. Poor Helen; poor Mr Russell: they lost; we won.

I caught the bus back to Ashley Landing. .

Major Lewis saw me as I made my way to my quarters.

'Have you heard the news?'

'News, sir?'

'Bill Borthwick. You remember him, don't you? Nice fellow. Got himself killed this morning in France. Shot down in flames. Bad luck, what? Don't you know his sister?'

Nine

I told myself that Bill's death had nothing whatever to do with the fact that I had broken my engagement to Helen. I couldn't be blamed for the timing; it was outside my control. But then I remembered what a first-rate instructor Bill was. Why didn't I fight harder to keep him at Ashley Landing? Why did I so readily accept the decision of the powers-that-be? I despised myself, just as the Borthwicks must have despised me. Why, they must have asked, should Marshall remain in the comparative safety of Ashley Landing while their son goes to his death over the lines ... ? I wrote a letter to the family. It was appallingly difficult, but it had to be done. I attempted to say how deeply and sincerely I felt about Bill's death; and I hoped, that under the circumstances, my condolences would not be considered an impertinence . . .

I was surprised, a few days later, to receive a printed card stating that Dr and Mrs Borthwick wished to express their appreciation of my kind wishes at their time of loss. The envelope had been hand-written; I wondered who had penned my name. Helen? Her parents? Dr Borthwick's nurse? For some reason, it mattered to me.

Oddly enough, the arrival of that card seemed to cauterize my feelings of guilt. I had been, in some subtle way, forgiven my transgressions. I was free to go.

Frances and I decided to marry on the 10th March, her birthday.

I asked Martin Colman if he would consent to be my best man.

'I'd be honoured,' he said, 'but I'm not sure that I shall still be here at Ashley Landing. I've been making myself tiresome about going back to France. I think it's working; I've heard a rumour or two.'

We agreed to proceed upon the assumption that he would still be available. I explained the situation to Beresford and he agreed, with suitably long-suffering sighs, to be deputy best man.

'Mind you,' he said, 'I can quite understand your desire to have a national hero as your best man rather than your aging and infirm brother. Quite understandable.'

He was in a sanguine frame of mind because the Air Board had ordered two prototype Swifts, to be constructed as rapidly as possible and shipped to Martlesham Heath for official testing. 'Marvellous, isn't it, what a spot of influence will do. The biggest job a chap has in this world is to get people to listen. If you're a PM or a VC everyone listens. And believes.'

During the last week of January Colman was promoted to the rank of Captain. I didn't see him for several days; he had been spirited away by Monnington-Browne's people to visit factories and show his famous smile to the populace. Frances told me that she saw him on a Pathé News film, chatting to Lord French; the venerable warrior looked slightly bemused, she reported. Colman arrived back at Ashley Landing in a Staff car; a Brigadier had given him a lift from Woolwich. Colman was the first to admit that being a VC had its advantages.

I asked him if he had an enjoyable trip.

'Not too dusty,' he said. 'I had two very accomplished ladies in London and an Honourable-Somebody-Or-Other in Luton, who was a bit too angular for my liking but a jolly sight better than nothing!' 'By the way,' he added, 'I rather gather that my posting will be through in a few days. But don't worry, it looks as though I shall still be in England for the wedding.' He grinned, obviously

143

delighted with developments. 'I'm going to 56 Squadron as a Flight Commander. We're going to be the first squadron to be equipped with the new SE5s. Topping, what?'

I agreed that it was indeed topping.

A week later he left for Gosport. He telephoned me the following afternoon to inform me that only two of the new SE5s had been delivered. It looked as if it might be several weeks or even months before the squadron was ready for France. He had already applied for leave 'to do his stuff at the wedding'.

'Tell Beresford that the SE is a fine machine – but no match for the Swift.'

I promised to tell Beresford.

Frances and I spent a weekend at Basingstoke. Mr Gray was a charmingly vague individual who was more interested in grand opera than the timber business; his success in commerce seemed to be one of the minor miracles of our time. His wife kept calling me 'Frederick', but apart from that we got along famously.

On the way back to London Frances told me that her parents thought highly of me. 'And they're terribly impressed that you're going to have the famous Martin Colman as your best man.'

Ten

The SE5 circled. We watched, open-mouthed. Nothing so speedy and powerful had ever been seen in the air above Ashley Landing. It turned over the village and slid in to a neat landing. As it taxied between the rows of trainers you could see the Vickers gun on the fuselage and the movable Lewis on a Foster mounting attached to the centre section of the top wing. At last the RFC had a scout that looked capable of tackling the Hun Albatros.

A crowd quickly gathered around the new arrival; everyone knew that the pilot was none other than Colman, VC. Mechanics hurried forward to secure his wheels with chocks.

I thanked him for coming.

'Delighted,' he assured me. 'Didn't fancy the train, so I borrowed one of the new SEs. Ripping, isn't she? She'll do very nicely – until the Swift comes along, of course. We're having a bit of trouble with the big windscreen.' He pointed out that the canopy-like structure swept back and partially enclosed the pilot. 'It keeps the wind off awfully well, but it obscures a chap's view rather too much. There's talk of replacing them with much smaller jobs. I think I'll take the head-rest off my machine later on. I like to be able to see as much as possible in every direction. The motors are still a bit unreliable. They're Hispanos, you know. We've had a few conk out at inopportune moments, but the experts are working away, so I suppose they'll have it all sorted out in due course.'

He was in the best of spirits. Clearly he found the work of training his Flight for combat in France far more stimulating than teaching neophyte pilots how to land and take-off. I asked him about his parents. He said they were in fine form and that he planned to spend a few days with them after the wedding.

'By the way,' he said, 'you will brief me on what I'm supposed to do, won't you? I'm a bit nervous about it. I've never been to a wedding before.'

Frances and I were married at precisely fourteen minutes past twelve on Saturday, the tenth of March, 1917. I know the time because I glanced at my watch just as dear old Captain the Reverend Albert Petrie declared us man and wife. (Afterwards I wondered if he thought I was concerned about the ceremony taking too long.)

Frances gave me the tiniest of nods and a gentle, totally sweet smile. Then she blurred as my eyes filled with tears of sheer, unalloyed happiness.

After the photograph-taking by Ignatius Porson of Ashley Landing village (and some two hundred airmen and cadets who wanted snaps of the famous Martin Colman), we repaired to the Feathers for the reception. There were the usual speeches (Beresford spoke well – almost totally on the subject of himself) and toasts (Major Lewis rambled on for ten minutes before getting to the point and promptly spilling the contents of his glass down the front of his uniform). Various relatives mumbled stock platitudes and were enthusiastically applauded for their efforts. It was thoroughly pleasant and of interest only to those who were directly involved.

Frances and I caught the seven-fourteen to London. We spent the night at the Park Lane Hotel. At nine on Sunday we travelled to Devon. We had a minute cottage there. It was ours, totally ours, for a week. Our first home. We revelled in it. We made love and slept and ate and drank and walked for miles along the springy turf and listened to the pounding of the waves and told each other that no other couple in the history of mankind had ever cared so deeply. For seven magical days we lived only for ourselves; we forgot the war and the rest of the world; we avoided newspapers and read Dickens and Tolstoy aloud in the evenings.

Thus, we knew nothing of the accident until we returned to Ashley Landing.

It had happened the day after the wedding. At ten o'clock in the morning, while Frances and I were on our way to Devon, Colman had climbed into the cockpit of his SE. Ten minutes later he had taken off. At least a hundred men saw him go; several had snapped photographs. Some men say they saw him waving as he left the ground.

Then the SE's motor cut. No warning. It simply stopped.

It was awkward but not particularly dangerous. Colman could have eased his nose down a few degrees and kept flying in the same direction, gliding over the road and landing in the ploughed fields beyond.

But he did what every student is told never, under any circumstances, to do: he tried to get back to the field. He banked. His speed fell away. The wings lost their ability to support the nineteen hundred pounds of aeroplane and pilot.

The SE hit the ground almost vertically. An instant later, the still-tumbling, bouncing, disintegrating wreckage erupted in flame. The trim little fighter had become a pyre, from which black, oily smoke bubbled. By the time the first men came panting on the scene it was too late to do anything for Colman. In fact, of course, it was too late the moment he attempted that turn. Which was why, Beresford told me later, he hadn't sent a telegram to

Devon. It was kind of him, yet, in a way, I felt we should have been told. The memories of our honeymoon were clouded.

That evening I trudged across the field to the spot where it had happened. The ground was battered and disfigured; the engine had carved an ugly wound. The grass was blackened; my boots grated on the sand that had been thrown in a vain attempt to quell the flames. Of the machine and its pilot nothing was left. The maintenance squad had cleared away the charred remains; the souvenir hunters had claimed the rest. Genuine bits of wreckage from the fatal crash of the famous ace, Martin Colman, VC. Conversation pieces. Family heirlooms.

Why had it happened? Every pilot knows that it is suicidal lunacy to attempt a 180-degree turn with a dead engine and only three hundred feet of altitude. The air is a jealous mistress. Treat her with respect and caution and she will be tender; take her for granted and she will be utterly merciless.

So died Martin Colman. He made a mistake. Possibly he had read too many newspaper stories about himself; perhaps, slowly, insidiously, the belief had taken root that he was indeed a wizard in the air and that the rules that mere mortals had to follow no longer applied to him. Ironically, it was because of him that Frances and I were now married; it was because of our marriage that he had died. I promised his memory that I would do everything in my power to make the marriage worthy of his sacrifice.

Interlude

Number 37 Howard Close stands upon the spot where Martin Colman died. It is a pleasant house, with white brick and blue trim. A family of five lives there, plus a ginger cat named Wilhelmina. A red Hillman is usually parked in the drive. Although I know the members of the family by sight, I have only said 'good day'. I have never mentioned Martin Colman. The family might not welcome the knowledge that a man's life ended on the place where they made their home.

A mile from Howard Close is a supermarket. The building itself is as characterless as others of the ilk. Only the car park is of interest to the indefatigable trivia-hunter; it is part of what was once the tarmac in front of the famous Terminus, built when the aerodrome became London's main airport, and the name became simply Ashley . . .

Part Three
Monday 21 May 1928

One

I always liked Wilfred Forsyth. He was invariably cheerful, courteous and punctual. What more could one ask of an airline steward? Only honesty. A smallish, sleek-haired individual, Wilfred seemed to have been born for service. He possessed a kind of pert obsequiousness, managing always to impart the impression that there was nothing in the world he would rather be doing than absorbing orders and then scurrying to carry them out. He was a familiar figure on the London-to-Paris run. Resplendent in peaked cap, white jacket, winged collar and black bow tie, he would prance along the narrow aisle of the Handley Page, trays of drinks and sandwiches deftly balanced on splayed fingers. To my knowledge he never stumbled, never spilt a drink or dropped a morsel of food. It was a commendable record, for our aeroplanes, of necessity, flew slowly and at modest altitudes; they were prey to every current and eddy the sky had to offer.

We took off from Ashley every morning (weather permitting) at nine o'clock, arriving at Le Bourget, Paris, at half past eleven. The return flight left Paris at three and (with luck) touched down at Ashley some two and a half hours later. If the elements were indulgent and if the equipment functioned properly it constituted a good day's flying and a remarkably pleasant way of earning one's living. I was most fortunate to be employed as an airline pilot. And I knew it. Jobs in aviation were few and far between for the simple reason that only a minute fraction of the population seemed to have the slightest desire to go anywhere by air. And only a tiny fraction of that fraction could afford it.

When (in such agonizing detail and neurotic secrecy) the Corporation investigated the whole affair, there was a suggestion that I should have reacted to Chief Steward Forsyth's preoccupation with the social and financial standing of our passengers. I pointed out (with some heat) that it was the man's *job* to be interested in the passengers. He existed to cater to them; the more he knew about them the better he was able to do that job. The Corporation man murmured something about *degree*; surely I would admit that it was hardly usual for a steward to display such *intense* interest. I fumed. But it was hopeless, of course. The captain of an airliner is in much the same position as the captain of a ship. He is responsible for everything that takes place aboard his craft. According to the rules of the game, I should have known what was going on and I should have taken the appropriate action. No matter that I spent every flight in the open cockpit in the nose of the aircraft, unable to stir from my seat for a moment and completely cut off from the passenger cabin, I was expected to know.

The fact is, in all the months we flew together I can recall only one occasion on which Forsyth made more than a passing reference to the passengers. It was one Tuesday, in January; we were delayed at Le Bourget because snow showers had moved into the area. While we sat in the lounge waiting for the weather to clear, Forsyth observed, in the somewhat orotund manner he sometimes adopted when speaking to me:

'I'm more and more impressed, Captain, by the quality of our passengers. A hopeful sign, I call it, an indication of the growing acceptance of aerial travel. Think of it, today we transported a duke, an international banker, a leading Hollywood film director, a couple of company chairmen and the heir to a brewery fortune. We picked them up at London and whisked them across the Channel, then put them down, gentle as a feather, in France.'

I said how glad I was that he was impressed.

'*Grème de la crème*,' he declared, his Cockney twang adding a peculiar flavour to the expression. 'You might say that we've got a veritable Who's Who on every flight.'

He was right. It couldn't be denied that the majority of our passengers were affluent. They had to be. They were required to pay a return fare to Paris that was about four times the weekly wage of the average working man. Ironically, that diligent average working man was helping his more fortunate neighbours take to the air, for the government, through taxes, subsidized every seat sold to the tune of two pounds ten shillings.

On the afternoon of the 21st of May a lively headwind made us seventeen minutes late at Ashley. I taxied to the tarmac area in front of the brand new Terminus, turned so that the aeroplane's door would be parallel to the Terminus entrance and switched off the motors. Abruptly the world stopped vibrating. This was always a delicious moment, savouring the stillness. I tugged off my helmet and unbuttoned the collar of my leather flying suit. Forsyth was shepherding his passengers to the Terminus. He darted from one to the other, answering a question here, acknowledging a comment there. His cap bobbed as he nodded, smiling, always smiling. He put one in mind of a particularly ebullient sparrow.

Behind me, Pettigrew, the Mechanic/Wireless Operator, emerged from his narrow compartment beneath the cockpit. A pale, withdrawn young man, Pettigrew. He informed me in his hushed voice that the port motor was still showing a slightly low oil pressure. He would take the matter up with Mr Semple, the Chief Mechanic.

It occurred to me that I had never seen Pettigrew smile. A singular fellow.

I went into the Flight Office. Butterworth, the Dispatch Officer, was there, purse-lipped and self-important as ever, surrounded by his bits of paper and clutching his clip-board.

'Aha,' he exclaimed on seeing me.

'Aha yourself,' I returned with lightning wit.

'I've been wanting to have a word with you, Captain Marshall.' He accorded me a toothy smile. 'You have a *particularly* distinguished passenger list for tomorrow's flight.'

I looked the list over. Sir Jonathan Bennington, the Corporation's Chairman of the Board, was about to make one of his infrequent voyages with us, to demonstrate yet again to the world that he believed in air travel.

'This time,' said Butterworth breathlessly, 'Lady Bennington will accompany Sir Jonathan. It will be the first time she has ever flown!'

'A milestone in aviation history,' I declared.

The rest of the names meant little to me: Carton, Levy, Mallett, James, McKay, Bagley, Pasquale, de Madon. I gave the list to Forsyth who had just entered with Pettigrew. It was the steward's job to determine if any special arrangements had to be made for the next day's flight. My concern was limited to the weight of the passengers and their baggage.

I remember how wide Forsyth's eyes became as he read the list.

'A bumper crop of *la crème*, Captain.'

Pettigrew reported that Mr Semple was personally examining the port engine; it would be in perfect working order for the morning run.

'It had better be,' said Butterworth.

'A precious cargo tomorrow,' Forsyth informed Pettigrew. 'Particularly big names, Mr P.'

Pettigrew's mouth opened. He seemed about to say something. Then he closed his mouth. He looked awful. Was he ill? One heard of men failing to report illness in order to keep working and earning. Perhaps this was the case with Pettigrew. I would keep an eye on him.

I rode home on my 350 cc BSA. Turn left at the entrance. Left again at the High Street. Right at Coventry Lane, left at Harvest Road. It took only a few minutes, hardly enough time to warm up the BSA's motor. Frances and I had bought number 47 at a bargain price during the slump immediately after the war. It was a pleasant home; all it lacked was a garage. I was obliged to leave the family Morris parked on the street.

Mr Roseberry, the accountant who lived next door, was working in his front garden. He wished me a very good evening.

'Been flying off to exotic parts, have you, Mr Marshall?'

He made it sound slightly naughty.

I told him we had been to Paris.

'Amazing.' He clicked his tongue. 'I saw you leave this morning. And here you are, back again, from France. It's a marvellous age we live in, old man. But sometimes I wonder if we're not

152

moving too rapidly for our own good. Something to think about, wouldn't you say?'

'Absolutely,' I said. I always agreed with Mr Roseberry. Disagreement meant earnest, interminable discussion.

When I got inside the house I found Beresford in the drawing-room with Frances.

'Curses,' he said, 'I was just beginning to make some headway.'

He was as slim as ever; but now his hair was vanishing rapidly and what was left had turned grey. He sported flannels, a loud jacket, a bright blue shirt with a polka dot cravat at the neck. He had recently married a young lady of Spanish extraction by the name of Carlotta (Miriam and he having parted shortly after the war). They lived at Richmond and seemed happy enough.

Frances kissed me. 'Had a good trip, darling?'

'Very pleasant,' I said.

'How,' said Beresford, 'could it possibly be pleasant in that absurd aeroplane you fly? It has occurred to me that perhaps the Handley Page organization was at one time involved in the design and manufacture of stage coaches. Your cockpit is remarkably similar to the driver's perch on a coach; you are stuck up in the front, exposed to the elements, out of touch with your passengers . . .'

I told him that we airline pilots preferred to feel fresh air on our cheeks; a man couldn't do a proper job of flying cooped up in a cage.

'Bilge,' he said. 'You'll learn.' He glanced at his watch and announced that he had to be on his way.

We invited him to stay for dinner.

'Thank you, no. Carlotta is making something special. Something embodying an aphrodisiac or two, I fancy, to whip up a spot of enthusiasm in the old fellow, you know.'

'I hope it works,' said Frances.

'I expect it will; it often does.'

To change the subject (although I was the only one who seemed to feel that it needed changing) I asked Beresford about business.

'It's bloody awful,' told me. 'We need a damned good war. No

153

one wants to buy aeroplanes in peacetime.'

He wished us goodnight. Poor Beresford. Fortune had still not smiled upon his endeavours. The Swift should have made him world-famous. Unfortunately, Martin Colman's death had signalled the termination of official interest in the design. The prototypes languished for months at Martlesham Heath. Despite enthusiastic reports from test pilots, no more Swifts were manufactured. Eventually the prototypes became hulks on which trainee riggers and mechanics learnt their trades. Beresford worked for Vickers for a couple of years; recently he had become a partner in a small company that had exciting, adventurous ideas but very few orders.

'What was Beresford doing here?'

'He popped in to seduce me,' said Frances.

'Be serious.'

'Is it so unlikely?'

'For him, yes. He's getting past it but he won't admit it.'

'He was in the vicinity, so he dropped in.'

I suspected that there was more to it than that but I didn't pursue the subject. I would find out in good time.

The children were playing in the back garden: Martin, ten, and Georgina, eight. Nice, healthy offspring with straight limbs and good eyesight. I was inordinately proud of them.

During dinner, Frances said:

'Guess where I was today.'

'Shanghai?'

'No.'

'Where, then?'

'At the aerodrome.'

'Doing what?'

'Flying.' She beamed. 'Two hours on the Flying Club's Avian. Mr Lofthouse thinks I did awfully well considering I haven't flown for years.'

'And who is Mr Lofthouse?'

'The CFI at the club. Very nice man. Flew with the RNAS during the war.'

'Good for him,' I muttered. I was less than delighted by the news. In my thoroughly subjective opinion, Frances simply didn't

154

possess the makings of a safe pilot. It had been bad enough when I had attempted to teach her; I squirmed at the thought of some-one else shouldering that awesome responsibility. 'Why did you decide to fly again?'

'I thought it might be fun.'

'And was it?'

'Rather!' She grinned in her wholehearted way. Bobbed hair suited her. It gave her face a mischievous frame.

When she had served the jam roll and custard she said:

'I think we should have a go at the Atlantic.'

I choked on my jam roll. The room turned red. Martin leapt from his chair with the greatest of enthusiasm and slapped me on the back. Georgina followed suit; a moment later the two of them were squabbling about what sector of my back each should thump. I recovered and shoo'd them back to their seats.

Then I pointed an accusatory finger at Frances. 'Now I know why Beresford was here. You were talking to him about using that new twin-engined machine they've designed . . .'

'You'd have to do most of the work,' said Frances, unabashed. 'After all, you're much better at it than I am. But I could so some of the flying and navigation. And I'd be the first woman to fly the Atlantic . . .'

I informed Frances that it was not seemly for housewives and mothers to think of such things.

'I detest that word "housewife",' she said. 'And I'm not particularly fond of "seemly" either.'

I turned to the children. 'You wouldn't want to see your mother in an aeroplane trying to fly across the Atlantic Ocean, would you?'

Martin frowned, indicating the seriousness with which he was considering the matter. Finally: 'I'm not sure. No one else in the class has a mother who wants to fly the Atlantic.'

'There,' said Frances.

Georgina said it wasn't fair; she and Martin should be allowed to come along.

'What you don't understand,' I told them, 'is that it is a very dangerous business. Very dangerous indeed. A lot of people have tried to fly the Atlantic and they have vanished.'

'Vanished?'

'Vanished. No one knows what happened to them. You see, the Atlantic is well known for its violent storms and fogs.'

'In that case,' said Martin, 'wouldn't it be sensible to fly in a seaplane? It would float if you had to come down.'

'Good point,' I said approvingly. 'The trouble is that the waves are usually so enormous in the Atlantic that a seaplane would almost certainly be broken up in a very short space of time. So what chances do you think your mother and I would have?'

I rather expected tears from Georgina and a firm rejection of the idea from Martin. But children are invariably unpredictable. They both considered the matter gravely, then exchanged a few words. Nods. They informed us that they had agreed that we were both far too old for such an undertaking.

Frances glared. 'You wait,' she said to me.

I left the table in high good humour. Another crisis successfully averted – at least temporarily.

My humour would have been considerably lower-pitched had I been aware of the conversation between Chief Steward Wilfred Forsyth and Mechanic/Wireless Operator Malcolm Pettigrew. It took place shortly after I left the aerodrome. The two of them strolled across the High Street and took a corner table in the Aero Café. The proprietor of the establishment later testified that the two men ordered cups of tea. The gentleman did not overhear their conversation but it might reasonably be assumed to have proceeded on the following lines:

Forsyth: It's tomorrow, then, Mr P. Agreed?

Pettigrew (even paler than usual, his voice little more than a whisper): Are you sure . . . I mean, d'you think it's the right . . . day?'

Forsyth: No question about it. That ruddy passenger list wouldn't be much better if we'd made it up ourselves. I suppose we could have added Henry Ford and the Aga Bloody Khan, but that's about all. We've got *la crème*, Mr P. Big dollops of it.'

Pettigrew (with a nervous swallow): All right, if you say so . . .

Forsyth: There's Sir Jonathan and Lady Bennington, Foster McKay, the American oil millionaire, Angela Carton, the film star . . .

Pettigrew: I don't want to know anything about them, their names or anything.

Forsyth: Why not?

Pettigrew: I'd just rather not.

Forsyth: Your privilege, Mr P. So you'll take my word for it that we've got the right passenger list at last.

Pettigrew: Yes . . . yes, of course.

Forsyth: And the weather forecast is perfect. Don't see how we could improve things much, do you?

Pettigrew: No . . . Have you talked to Moody?

Forsyth: I will. Soon as we've had our tea.

Pettigrew (biting his lip): God, I dunno . . . are you sure?

Forsyth (firmly): It's going to work. Everything is going to be all right. We've thought about it long enough, haven't we?

Pettigrew: Yes . . . yes, I suppose so.

Forsyth: No supposing about it. Remember, Mr P, we're the ones with the big advantage. *Initiative*. We're doing something no one else has ever done before, so no one will know how to react. Right, Mr P?

Pettigrew (with a sigh and a nervous nod): All right. Tomorrow it is, then.

Forsyth: Good man.

The two of them are then believed to have proceeded to the telephone box at the corner of the High Street and London Road. An eleven-year old lad named Percival Trotter declared that he saw two men in uniform enter the box at about half-past six. The boy had a reputation in the neighbourhood as a congenital liar; in this instance, however, it would appear that he may have been telling the truth.

The telephone call was made to Clement Moody, twenty-nine, who resided in a boarding house in Ealing. Moody was employed by a shipping company in Leadenhall Street; he was a junior clerk. Three years before, he had left the Royal Air Force rather hurriedly after a disagreement about Mess funds.

The conversation between Forsyth and Moody was brief.

'It's me.'

'Christ . . . it's been six months. I thought you were dead. Or inside.'

'It's on tomorrow.'

'Well.' Moody's tone brightened. 'That's better. Got a good load, have you?'

'A lovely load, mate.'

'About time.'

'Can you get the aeroplane as we discussed?'

'Of course.'

'You know what to do then.'

'Is Butterworth still the bloke to call at the aerodrome?'

'Yes. And if he's not around, one of his flunkies will tell you what time we took off.'

'Tomorrow it is then.'

Forsyth hung up. He nodded meaningfully to the perspiring Pettigrew.

'Everything under control?' Pettigrew inquired, his voice husky and low as if he was about to come down with a bad cold. 'He's going to show up all right?'

'No doubt about it, Mr P.'

There was a question about it, of course. There was always a question. Things could go wrong. But there was no point in worrying about it; such worrying contributed absolutely nothing to the enterprise, therefore should not be indulged in . . .

They stood for a moment, as if considering further points to discuss. But it had all been said. Again and again.

Forsyth advised Pettigrew to get a good night's sleep.

'*Sleep*?' Hollow croak. 'I won't sleep a wink.'

'Never mind. Catch up on your shut-eye later on.'

'I can't think beyond tomorrow . . . I can't; it's a sort of mental brick wall.'

'Don't worry, mate. After tomorrow all your problems'll be over. It'll be a new life. Think about it. And don't forget your . . . implement.'

'I won't.'

The two men parted. Forsyth headed for the bus stop. He felt marvellous. A giant among these poor sad little folk who thronged the pavement. Humdrum *hoi polloi*. No turning back now. He was committed. Countless hours of diligent planning were about to be rewarded. There was a gentle fluttering somewhere in the visceral region; not fright but a subtle stirring, a rousing of the senses in preparation for the grand command performance. Him against Them. He would be the victor. Confidence filled his narrow chest like heady mountain air. Really, when you got right down to it, the only question marks were the confederates. Complete opposites, the two of them. Pettigrew, a bundle of jangling nerves; Moody, six feet of thick skin. But one couldn't be too choosy in an enterprise of this nature. One had to use the people who were qualified and suitably motivated. And, above all, available. Both Pettigrew and Moody craved for escape. Pettigrew from a mountain of debts and a pretty spendthrift wife who had succeeded in reducing him to near-bankruptcy in two years of singularly unidyllic marriage; Moody from a society that had labelled him (accurately) as less than totally honest and therefore worthy of only menial employment.

On the way to the bus stop Forsyth paid his penny for an *Evening Standard*. The news was unspectacular. The Socialists were gaining ground in the German election; during the weekend there had been a jolly little get-together at Marsden Manor, near Cirencester; all the guests had flown in aboard their private aeroplanes. He smiled. Once upon a time he would have smarted with the sting of jealousy upon reading such a story about the antics of the privileged classes. No more. He was almost one of them.

It was nearly an hour's journey to Hounslow, necessitating two changes of bus and a ten-minute walk at the other end. Forsyth had for several years wanted to move nearer to Ashley, but Norah had resisted. Her mother lived only two streets away; she wanted to be near her. All very understandable and heart-warming, of course, except for the fact that mother and daughter gave every impression of hating the sight of one another; they could rarely exchange more than half a dozen sentences before engaging in quite savage mouth-to-mouth combat. The strange thing was that they insisted on seeing each other daily.

The Forsyths occupied a four-room flat above Messrs Herrington and Nott, Ironmongers. The place was supposed to have been a temporary home: somewhere to live until they purchased a house, preferably semi-detached. But ten years had gone by; the house fund amounted to precisely seven pounds fourteen shillings.

Norah had gained weight recently. She was on the point of starting to sag, like snow that has piled too heavily on the edge of a hill. He asked her what she had been doing all day.

'What d'you think I've been doing?'

As usual, her voice had a little snap to it.

'I don't know what you've been doing,' he said. 'That's why I asked.'

'Nothing,' she said. 'Same as I do every other day.'

She served fish cakes with white sauce followed by tinned peaches and custard. She had a habit of emitting a tiny sigh whenever she placed a plate upon the table. It was as if the act of feeding him caused her pain. For years it had irritated Wilfred. In spite of himself he had listened for the sighs, nerve ends a-jangle, and invariably she had managed to sigh an instant earlier or later than he had anticipated. Her timing was uncanny. He had mentioned the sighs but he could have saved himself the trouble. She had ignored the remarks; she had the capacity for ignoring practically anything that displeased her. Extraordinary, thought Wilfred, that the young female I married could have become this. He found himself remembering the merry times and the tender times. Something had once existed between them: a spark, a chemical reaction ... something. But it had gone ... died, evaporated, shrivelled up. And yet the pretence was maintained; perhaps it had to be; honesty was merciless; it would destroy whatever was left, utterly and finally.

'Enjoy it?'

Her tone dared him to say no.

'A treat. Nice and tasty, that.'

'I s'pose you want some more tea.'

'Ta.'

'I thought you would,' she sighed. 'It needs more hot water.'

The fact of the matter was that Norah had become a horribly dull person. Possibly she had always been horribly dull; but in the early days sexuality had artfully concealed the fact. Now it was exposed for all the world to see. Was there a single reason (other than pity and habit) why he should continue to share his earthly existence with her? He couldn't think of one. Perhaps he should be ashamed of the fact; perhaps she should be ashamed. It didn't

160

matter. What did matter was that he intended to do something about it.

Two

I awoke to the sound of bare feet thumping along corridors. Giggle. Then another giggle. A door slammed.

'Little bastards,' Frances muttered.

'Sods,' I said. I opened an eye in the general direction of the alarm clock.

Quarter to six. The offspring had robbed me of fifteen minutes' sleep. Somewhere below, another door slammed. No bloody consideration. It was the basic characteristic of the younger generation.

Frances sat up.

'If they're going to persist in getting up so early I should teach them to put the kettle on.'

I said I thought it unwise; they would probably burn the place down in the process.

'Typical,' said Frances.

'Typical?'

'Of your opinion of others.'

God. So early.

'I was merely pointing out . . .'

'I know. But it is an accurate indication of your general distrust of the capabilities of others. In your opinion there is only one person who is able to do everything under the sun.'

'And who, pray, are you referring to?' I had an idea.

'And as far as a mere *woman* attempting to do anything . . . well . . .'

'Now we're discussing that idiotic idea you have of tackling the Atlantic.'

'Idiotic, is it?'

'Only if you consider suicide idiotic. I do.'

She got out of bed and slipped into her dressing-gown.

'Sometimes,' she said, 'you manage to be remarkably pompous for a man of your years.' She banged the bedroom door on her way out.

I glanced out of the window. It was sunny out there, if not in here.

Wilfred Forsyth had slept surprisingly well. He smiled at the sight of the sun streaming over the window sill and across the wall. A brand new day. *The* day. From this day on, his life would never be the same again. Probably much, much better; possibly much worse. But different. Totally different.

Norah gazed at him without apparent recognition. Her sleep-dulled gaze failed to focus; he might have been invisible.

'Good morning,' he said.

Grunt.

He inhaled enthusiastically at the open window. The air tasted fresh and clean.

'A grand morning,' he reported.

A grand morning, he thought, for grand larceny. Bright, clear; not a trace of that early-morning mist that so often delayed flights and infuriated passengers and pilots alike. This morning the visibility was superb; the Met. man had been dead right for once.

As he washed he ruminated. Had he planned for every eventuality? Would the authorities be as surprised and confused as he suspected?

Norah's slippers slapped past the bathroom door.

'I suppose you want an egg for your breakfast.'

'No; just a bit of toast and marmalade this morning, thanks.'

Grunt.

He shaved with care, paying particular attention to the tricky areas beneath the nostrils and at the corner of the mouth. He was thirty-eight – but he would be thirty-five, or perhaps even thirty-four, in his new life. Ah, the new life. His blood stirred when he thought of it. Luscious ladies by the score. He would taste every pleasure that life had to offer. The females would be more than willing. Females were always willing when there was sufficient lolly on hand. It was the way of the world. Anything could be bought. Love? Yes, love too. Lots of girls would be delighted to love him. For a fee. Not for ever, perhaps. But what, he asked himself as he shaved his jutting chin, is for ever in this life? It was a truth known to the corpulent gentlemen who took the afternoon flight to London, regularly, to be met by sweet young things good enough to eat. And it was known to the powdered and corseted old biddies who dragged their lithe young men around like championship hounds . . .

He dried his face. Not bad. Not bad at all. No Valentino; on the other hand, no Lon Chaney either. A face with a bit of character. Pity about the height, though. Another couple of inches might have made a lot of difference in life . . .

Norah was already seated at the breakfast table, her jaws working rhythmically, as she gazed at the golliwog on the marmalade jar. God, but she was unappetizing. He wondered if she would ever, for an instant, entertain the thought that she might in some small way have contributed to the whole thing. No. Not a bloody chance. Norah simply wasn't the sort to want to know unpleasant things about herself. When she weighed herself on the machine at the railway station, she resolutely refused to believe it. Obviously it was broken. It lied. It wasn't that she had put on weight, it was that the mechanism of the thing had gone wrong.

He buttered a piece of toast.

The fact of it is, he thought, that people like me marry people like Norah because of the system. For the *hoi polloi*, life is a grand procession of compromises. He remembered that he had had his eye on Gloria Swanson. Ideal, was Gloria. Beautiful, intelligent, rich. And witty, according to *Silver Screen*. But Gloria was out of reach. Norah was the compromise. He couldn't have what he wanted, so he made do with what was available. It was the same with his job. He should have been a surgeon, or Prime Minister, or even King. But what chance did lowly little Wilfred Forsyth have? None; the system saw to that. So he became a steward. Compromise again. Who in his right mind would *want* to be a steward? But you did it because you had to do it or something just as dreary.

But now the compromising was over. Cross-roads. Either he would live life just as he wanted to, without ever again having to accept second-best, or he would be languishing in prison for the next few decades. Fair enough. Glory or misery. Nothing in between . . .

'Bognor this year?'

'What? Yes . . . yes, why not?'

'You said you hated the sight of the place.'

'What place?'

'Bognor. Wash your ears out. Mrs Hill heard you.'

'What I meant,' he said carefully, 'was that I was sick of Mrs Hill's boarding house. Not Bognor. I like Bognor.'

'You'd better write away, then.'

'Right.'

'Tonight.'

'Yes. Tonight.'

'I s'pose I'll have to remind you,' she said with a sigh.

I don't think you will be reminding me, he thought. How much, he wondered, will you remember of this silly little conversation? How many people will you bore to tears with your memories of the notorious Wilfred Forsyth? Perhaps you will think it important that we spent so much time talking about summer holidays. And perhaps you will offer it as proof that I had no intention of doing what everyone will say I did.

Perhaps, he thought, to your dying day you will think that I was a victim of gangsters.

He finished his tea. The last cup in this rotten little flat. Cup back in slightly cracked saucer for the Christ-knows-how-many-millionth-time. Click. Never again, not here. He stood up.

'Must be off.'

He had the odd feeling that he was acting, performing on a stage; he half expected laughter and applause and a curtain signifying the end of this Act. It would have seemed perfectly natural to turn to an invisible audience and declaim:

'And so Wilfred set out to prune Norah and the flat and the job so that, metaphorically speaking, he might grow taller and stronger.'

Norah was still at the table, drinking more tea and glaring short-sightedly at the *Daily Sketch*.

'Cheerio, then.'

She nodded, her eye still on the last paragraph of a story about a parson with peculiar tastes. She raised a pasty cheek.

He kissed it. No last-minute regrets. No sadness. I suppose I just don't give a damn about you, he told her silently. He looked back at her as he passed through the doorway, but she was already deep in the paper again.

He closed the door.

Three

The Corporation owned four Handley Pages. They were large, angular aeroplanes, constructed of wood and covered with fabric and plywood. Developed from a wartime bomber, they were powered by two 450-horsepower Napier Lion engines – reasonably lusty units but sadly inadequate when coupled to the ungainly Handley. If one of the two engines failed in flight, the fully-loaded Handley was quite incapable of staying up. The Corporation's publicity department had cleverly diverted attention from this fact by publishing photographs of the machine flying along with one engine stopped. No one seemed to notice the empty cabin windows. The machine being photographed was in fact carrying only the pilot and about half of the normal fuel load. An earlier version of the Handley had a third engine mounted on the nose. While this motor provided more power, it also meant much more weight – and mind-numbing noise and vibration for the passenger cabin. The design rapidly reverted to the twin-engined layout. The Handley was a biplane; its 75-foot span wings were strutted and braced with wires that had to be adjusted, aligned and tightened repeatedly. Within its box-like fuselage the Handley accommodated fourteen passengers in moderately comfortable wicker chairs, without seatbelts. Each passenger had his own window because the seats were positioned on either side of the fuselage with an aisle down the middle. The windows were curtained and could be partially opened. A small vase beside each window contained a fresh flower every day. Luggage racks ran the length of the cabin, above the windows, almost identical to those equipping the carriages of the LMS railway. The Handley was an advance on its predecessors in that cabin heat was furnished (albeit somewhat erratically) by means of hot air taken from muffs around the exhaust pipes of the engines. On the ceiling of the cabin a diagram showed the route to Paris, naming the towns over which the machine would pass. The designers of the machine's interior had attempted to create a feeling of solidity and safety in the cabin; hefty-looking (but hollow) black beams criss-crossed the ceiling (prompting Beresford to dub the Corporation 'Tudor Airway'). One beam bore the legend: 'Ripping Panel. In Case of Emergency Pull Ring Sharply.' The crews called it the 'Dripping Panel' for, if any rain was encountered in flight, much of it was certain to find its way into the aeroplane by means of this device.

When the Handleys were first delivered, the Corporation had proudly advertised them as the very latest aerial luxury, capable of speeding passengers to their destinations at more than one hundred miles per hour . . . 'yet, within the spacious cabin only a faint drone can be heard from the aircraft's powerful engines'. The truth was that the Handley could rarely manage more than ninety without a stiff tail-wind; and the din within the cabin was appalling. Stewards became adept lip-readers.

Not only did passengers have to be wealthy and adventurous, they had to be monumentally patient. Delays and cancellations were everyday occurrences, often because of weather, just as often because of mechanical problems or inadequate loads. When bookings for flights were particularly disappointing there were usually 'technical reasons' for cancelling the trips altogether. Sometimes Corporation staff members flew as passengers simply to make the whole enterprise look more firmly established than it really was. The Corporation offered two classes on the London-to-Paris run: a Standard Fare of eight pounds and the Golden Wing Fare at nine guineas. The difference? The Golden Wing Flight carried a steward and provided light refreshments but, far more important, its passengers were the *elite* of air travellers.

You stood a good chance of seeing *somebody* on the Golden Wing flight.

I arrived at Ashley a few minutes before eight.

Pettigrew was in the Flight Office. He seemed to be on edge. When I said good morning he jumped as if I had stuck a pin in him. He looked waxy. I wondered anew about Mr Pettigrew.

'Are you quite certain you're all right?'

'Yes, sir . . . yes . . . quite all right.'

I wondered about that. Bundle of nerves, Mr Pettigrew. Perhaps he should be given a ground job. Again I reminded myself to keep an eye on Mr Pettigrew.

Together we strolled out on the tarmac to inspect the aeroplane. We kicked tyres and squinted at aileron hinges, tugged at bracing wires and drummed our fingers on fabric to test its tautness and freedom from rot. I cast a critical eye around the passengers' quarters. Everything had to be particularly spick and span this morning. It was. I was unable to find a speck of dust or finger marks on the silver flower holders or the altimeter and airspeed indicator on the front bulkhead. In the magazine rack nestled the very latest issues of *The Tatler* and *The Sphere*. Surely there was nothing for the Chairman to complain about. But no doubt he would find something. He usually did.

I went forward and clambered up into my seat. It was a lofty perch (perhaps Beresford had a point about the similarity with the coachman's chair); one's head stuck out of the top of the fuselage with only a small windscreen for protection against the elements. Even in summer the warmest of garb was necessary. I glanced behind and below. I could see Pettigrew wedged into the wireless operator's compartment, checking over his knobs and dials. I ran up the engines. Mr Semple and his cohorts had done their job well. Oil pressure on the port engine was now slightly higher than that of the starboard engine.

I signed for the aeroplane and went for a cup of tea.

Wilfred Forsyth hung his sports jacket in the locker. Soon, he thought, someone will be going through these pockets, looking for clues. What you'll find, he told the unknown searcher, is a pocket book on conversational Danish which I hope will put everyone on the wrong track for a little while, a letter from someone who signs himself 'Roger' saying I had better do what I'm told or else it will be my wife who pays, which also, with luck, might help to cause confusion. (The letter had been typed in the Flight Office, on Mr Butterworth's machine.) In addition, the searcher would find two tickets for 'Lumber Love' at the Lyceum (discovered under Seat F on the afternoon of the 18th of May) and a penknife minus the imitation tortoise-shell grip panels. He took his steward's jacket from its hook, automatically dusting the shoulders with his free hand. He loathed that jacket. It was a symbol of his servitude, a gleaming badge denoting his lowly rank. He held it at arm's length. The rotten thing had been cut with all the flair and style of a prison uniform.

He put it on and fastened its four brass buttons. Then he crossed to the mirror. Collar and tie neat, crisp and straight; trousers well creased; shoes gleaming. You're a regular credit to the profession, he told his reflection with a smile.

Outside on the tarmac they were warming up the Handley. Its broad wings shivered as the engines roared; the poor old thing looked as if it had palsy. A mechanic leant against the lower wing, yawning. In the cockpit sat Captain Marshall. Not a bad bloke, in his way. A bit stuffy, of course, like all the pilots. But better than most. Fairly steady type. And that was important. No good having the sort who'd refuse to cooperate out of sheer bloody stubbornness.

With a bang and a puff, the engines rumbled to a halt. Silence. Marshall's head disappeared into the fuselage. A couple of jiffs later he appeared at the passenger door. Pettigrew wasn't with him. Three hearty cheers for Mr P. Had a small job of work to do, what might be termed a minor adjustment of the Handley's equipment . . .

Forsyth waited and watched until, eleven minutes and forty-two seconds later, Pettigrew emerged. He paused on the steps and adjusted his tie. Forsyth breathed a sigh of relief. Everything was set.

The recently completed Terminus at Ashley was widely publicized as 'the most modern airline facility in the world, with every imaginable convenience for the air traveller'. Arriving passengers entered the reception hall . . . 'in which is prominently displayed the latest information concerning the movement of airliners departing from and approaching Ashley. In addition, details of meteorological conditions over Britain and the Continent are provided.' The walls of the hall were liberally decorated with pictures (some in colour) of British airliners 'from the modest de Havillands of the immediate post-war period to the gigantic multi-motored Handley Pages of today' and their pilots . . . 'without question the most experienced and skilled aviators in the world, hand-picked to ensure the utmost safety, speed and comfort'. Porters took passengers' luggage and conveyed it to airline clerks and their scales. Officially (and usually only for Standard Fare passengers) there was a forty-pound limit per person, although lighter-than-average passengers were often permitted a rather more generous allowance. Unlike a number of Continental airlines, the Corporation did not subject passengers to the indignity of a weighing of their persons. Instead, clerks made calculated guesses – and remarkably accurate they were.

When the data had been compiled they were passed to the Captain whose job it was to calculate the weight and balance of the aeroplane.

I heartily disliked the business of meeting passengers, but it was a Corporation rule. I knew why. The captain was a sort of father figure, a symbol of security for the expedition into the mysterious sky. Fair enough. Why not then, I once suggested, engage an individual with just the right sort of rugged, reliable features and warm, comforting manner; let him spend his time greeting passengers at the Terminus and pretending to be their pilot. Frosty glares were my reward.

My dislike of meeting passengers was partly due to the fact that many of them took me for a porter and handed me cases to carry, and partly to the fact that I was usually at a loss for something to say. After 'Good morning, I'm Captain Marshall, your pilot' I tended to dry up. Unfortunately, all too many of my passengers didn't. Some were nervous and wanted reassurance (and I invariably found it hard to lie and say that there were absolutely *no* dangers); others fancied themselves as experts on matters aeronautical and wanted to discuss several dozen aircraft and airmen. Still others (many of them female) seemed to believe that airline captains were authorities on everything. At times I found myself embroiled in conversation on such topics as free love, Isadora Duncan, Pablo Picasso, Bix Beiderbecke, communism, the Sitwells, prohibition and the wonderful new gramophone that could automatically change up to twenty records. The fact that I knew practically nothing about any of these things made no difference; my opinion mattered because I was the captain.

The Malletts arrived first: bronzed, wealthy South Africans on their way to do some shopping in Paris. A dark-complexioned business man and his fussy, middle-aged secretary arrived next: Mr Pasquale and Miss Cuthbertson. Ten minutes later the Corporation limousine purred to a halt at the Terminus entrance. The glistening door – bearing the legend AIRLINE SERVICE – opened and out stepped Herbert Bagley, the phenomenally successful playwright, current darling of the West End. He wore white flannels and a striped blazer and carried a novel and a notebook. Rumour had it that he was travelling with us in order to research a play set aboard an airliner. When I wished him good morning he peered at me for a moment as though my words were only just beginning to force their way through his wall of concentration.

'I think I want to go to the lavatory.'

I indicated the direction.

Foster McKay strode in. An American. Boisterously friendly. He took my shoulder in a vice-like grip. He was, he assured me, downright tickled to make my acquaintance. He was, he told me, a close personal friend of Charles Lindbergh. 'Helluva guy. You'll like him.' He made me promise that if I ever found myself flying over Houston, Texas, I would land and call at 1347 Parker Street West. I promised. A moment later I was shaking hands with Sir Jonathan Bennington. He instructed me to treat himself and Lady Bennington like any other passengers. Lady Bennington kept dabbing her forehead with a fringed lace handkerchief. When I said that I hoped she would enjoy her flight she looked at me as if I had said something absurd.

A bright blue Rolls-Royce arrived. A uniformed chauffeur stepped out and opened the door for Angela Carton, the film actress. She was followed, rather breathlessly, by a Mr Levy, her business manager. Miss Carton, I was informed, was a star of the first rank. *The Bystander* had described her as 'vivacious, audacious and orchidaceous!' A Corporation publicity photographer materialized and clicked away industriously. Miss Carton smiled. Quite beautifully. Then the smile vanished. She looked around the reception hall. Her eyes hardened; she saw no one of the slightest interest. Ah, wait! Wasn't that What's-his-name, the playwright? A few discreet words with Mr Levy confirmed the fact. The smile reappeared. Mr Levy was left with the bags. Five minutes later the Baroness de Madon arrived. Stout, eighty or so and a bit dotty. The Baroness spoke English well; her voice was strident enough to serve a sergeant-major. She told me to bring her case from her taxi. While I was conveying this instruction to a porter, the Gordon Jameses arrived, Mr and Mrs Late as usual. Madcap types. Incredibly wealthy, according to rumour; he was the heir to the newspaper empire.

Butterworth informed me self-importantly that my passengers had arrived and would shortly be processed ready for boarding. He held his clip-board as a courtier might hold a royal proclamation.

'An excellent complement of passengers today, Captain.'

'Are we full up?'

'Almost,' he told me. 'You have thirteen passengers.'

Four

The roof of the Terminus was the observation deck. If you paid a penny you were permitted to go up there and watch the airliners come and go. As a rule you had a good deal of waiting to do, for flights were infrequent. It was a rare day at Ashley when two or more aeroplanes were in motion at the same time.

From my cockpit I could see the ground staff tugging the steps away from the door. It was time to prepare for flight. The great silver bird would, if everything worked properly, take to the air.

I twisted around and glanced down behind me as the forward bulkhead door opened. I had a glimpse of a passenger's legs. Forsyth, the steward, poked his head in and looked up at me.

'Passengers all aboard, sir. Door is closed and latched.'

I told Pettigrew to stand by for starting engines. He gave me a pale nod in reply.

'Fuel cocks on, sir.'

I raised a thumb to the ground crew.

Crack . . . splutter . . . roar.

The Lions thundered into life. Everything began to tremble. Below, the mechanics looked self-satisfied as they always did when the engines started the first time. A quick check of ignition and pressures. In my earphones I heard a crackling and buzzing as the wireless warmed up. The control tower gave me permission to taxi and wished me a good flight. And, because no one really trusted the wireless, they flashed a green light as well.

The ground crew dragged the chocks from the main wheels. The Handley began to move in the sulky way of any large, unwieldly structure being pulled along from somewhere about its middle. I felt the wheels leave the tarmac and trundle on to the grass of the field proper. How many times had I bounced and jolted over this grass? Presumably if I took the trouble to wade through the countless pages of my log book I would find the answer.

The windsock fluttered lethargically. There wasn't much wind to assist us into the air, so it would be necessary to make the take-off run as long as possible. I taxied the Handley to the north-east corner of the field, next to the London Road, turned and aimed the nose at the south-west corner.

Another quick check of pressures and temperatures. I listened to the engines. Healthy sounds, thank God. With a full load like this, a splutter from an engine during take-off would send us all into the cemetery.

I opened the throttles. The din became horrendous; the floor beneath my feet was alive, bouncing, quaking, apparently in imminent danger of parting company with the rest of the machine. Then we were moving. We banged along for a few yards with the tail skid scraping along the turf. Then, with a heave, the tail rose. We picked up a few more miles per hour. The wing swayed and flexed; still the air wasn't passing quickly enough over their surfaces. The wind shrieked past my head; I could feel it pulling at my helmet. Now we were fairly bounding along. The corner of the cemetery property went sailing past on the right. The trees at the end of the field were clearly visible. But now, ugly duckling that she was, she wanted to fly. I eased back on the controls. Up she went, with dignity if not celerity. Behind me, Pettigrew would be dutifully noting the time of departure from Mother Earth; this would be recorded in the Flight Record, for what purpose I had not the slightest idea. A touch of rudder to keep the Handley straight. The trees slid below. At five hundred feet I banked gently. The Handley's blunt nose edged around until it was pointing towards the coast. Soon I saw the Sevenoaks tunnel and the Southern Railway line. My first navigational check point. It was a gorgeous day.

I relaxed. This was the way flying was intended to be.

Forsyth watched the ground recede. Right, he said, time for David and Goliath. He grinned in spite of himself. They had the power. But he had the imagination and initiative. And audacity. Priceless advantages. He was defying them all. And they didn't know it. But they soon would. Within a few hours his name would be on everyone's lips. What would the papers say about him? How would they describe him? Handsome? Urbane? Daring? Cool? It was delicious to contemplate friends and relatives. They would be agog. Young Wilfred? No, surely there was nothing of the criminal about him. But on second thoughts perhaps there was something about the set of his eyes or the curve of his mouth. Some might even say they had always thought there was something odd about him . . .

The passengers were relaxing. Every trip it was the same: take-off meant a bracing of shoulders and a stiffening of the neck; when the aeroplane successfully dragged itself off the ground the breathing started again. Forsyth was as relieved as anyone; it had always been a mystery to him how those flimsy-looking wings could support the weight of the aeroplane and all the passengers. He stood, folding his seat back into the rear bulkhead.

He walked forward, smiling at the passengers: the mechanical, everything's-absolutely-all-right airline smile. 'Always keep smiling' they had told him before that first trip in the funny little one-engined biplane with six passengers. 'Doesn't matter how bumpy it is; doesn't matter if bits start to fall off the aeroplane. Keep smiling. It'll make the passengers feel better even if it doesn't do anything for you.'

The front bulkhead accommodated a large altimeter and a somewhat optimistic airspeed indicator to inform the passengers how high and how fast the aeroplane was flying. Beside these two dials was the hatch leading into the cockpit compartment.

The passengers all looked healthy enough; the take-off hadn't been too traumatic for the poor dears. Still smiling, Wilfred Forsyth retraced his steps, between Angela Carton and Mr Levy. (As she had entered the machine, Miss Carton had loudly inquired whether 'this thing' would be getting to Paris on time. 'Maurice' was waiting at Le Bourget. And, interjected Mr Levy, Mr Chevalier didn't like to be kept waiting.) He passed between Mr and Mrs Mallett (gold mines ran in their family); between Mr and Mrs Gordon James (grinning, giggling idiots; Gordon James had insisted on having a gin before the Handley had even begun to move, yet he knew perfectly well that drinking was illegal on the ground); between Foster McKay on the port side (ol' buddy, like most rich Americans, but quick to freeze you out if you responded in kind) and Herbert Bagley on the starboard side (he looked as if he was sizing up the interior of the Handley as a possible stage setting); between Mr Pasquale and Miss Cuthbert-son (already working furiously out of bulging briefcases); between Sir Jonathan and Lady Bennington (sour-looking sods, both of them, yet they were bowed and scraped at as if they were some higher form of life). And, in Seat M, the Baroness de Madon who, it was said, owned half of Algeria.

You are all my prisoners, Forsyth told them silently as he smiled. You are in my power. And there isn't a bloody thing you can do about it.

An extra smile for the Baroness as he opened the pantry door. The microphone and ear-piece were hanging neatly on the hook. Good old Mr P!

There was no need to keep one's voice low, not in this din.

'Is that you?'

'Yes . . . yes . . . you?'

No mistaking Mr P's tortured tones. The reception was remarkably good. Just like a telephone call around the corner.

'It's me,' said Forsyth. 'And it's time to get things going.'

My head-set suddenly went dead. I tapped the earphones. Nothing. Blast! I slipped the set off my helmet and passed it down to Pettigrew. Idiotic thing. Always going wrong. A moment later, Pettigrew's hand appeared clutching a note. YOUR HEAD-SET DEAD. I STILL HAVE CONTACT WITH GROUND. I looked down at him and nodded. Let him worry about talking to the ground. It was pleasant to fly along without having that static and those frenzied-sounding voices babbling away in your ear all the time. I relaxed again.

'Young man.' A dry, withered hand.

'Can I do something for you, Baroness?'

'I wish a cup of coffee. With cream, not milk.'

Silly old bitch. Where did she think he was hiding his stove?

'Sorry, Baroness, only cold drinks.'

'What?'

Age had stamped a perpetual grimace on her leathery face. She took the cotton wool out of her ears. Forsyth repeated the statement.

'I don't like cold drinks so early in the day. They give me constipation.'

Finally she settled for some lemonade.

'But don't put any ice in it. They do that in America, you know; whatever you drink it has great icebergs floating about in it . . .'

Gordon James said, 'I think a couple of gins, steward. We're off the bally ground, now, what? Toss in a spot of the old Italian, will you, old sport?'

'Certainly, sir.'

Angela Carton wanted something to eat; she hadn't had time for breakfast; Forsyth promised to provide her with sandwiches in a matter of moments. A whisky for Sir Jonathan, a lemonade for Lady Bennington; a glass of water for Mr Bagley . . . Smile, nod, smile, nod. Forsyth had an almost overpowering desire to burst out laughing. The whole lot of them were being kidnapped – and they didn't know it!

Five

According to the Wireless Room log, the message was received at Ashley at 9:15 am GMT.

'This is the Golden Wing flight to Paris. Are you receiving me? Over.'

Dundas, the operator, flipped the switch on his microphone. 'This is Ashley, Golden Wing. We are receiving you loudly and clearly. Proceed. Over.'

'You'd better get a pencil and write this down. Over.'

'I have a pencil. Over.'

'All right . . . er, this aeroplane has been commandeered by anarchists. Did you get that? Over.'

The wireless operator frowned. Damned static. He cleared his throat. 'Repeat that message, please, Golden Wing.'

'I said that the aeroplane has been commandeered by anarchists. They are holding guns on us. They are threatening to destroy the aeroplane and kill all the passengers. Over.'

Dundas's spine felt as if it had turned to ice.

'Hey God . . . er, over.'

'I am instructed to pass on the holding demand to you. Do you have a pencil? Over.'

'Yes. Over.'

But the pencil was trembling like a flag pole in a gale. Frantically, Dundas yelled for someone, anyone, to notify the Chief Aerodrome Officer.

Pettigrew's voice – understandably tremulous and tense under the circumstances – came through once more.

'Please write the name "Angela Carton". And then put fifty thousand against it. Have you got that? Over.'

'Yes, Golden Wing, yes. Carton. Fifty thousand. Over.'

'Next, "Levy". Write five thousand. Over.'

'Levy, five thousand. Right, Golden Wing. I have it.' A thought suddenly struck the wireless operator. 'Good heavens, Golden Wing, you have Sir Jonathan and Lady Bennington on board.'

'Yes . . . and you'd better put one hundred and fifty thousand against their names.'

George H. Wheeler was worried. The King and Queen were due for an official visit in ten days and the plumbing in the new Terminus was still acting in the most peculiar manner. He said he was doing his best to correct the problem, but he was only human . . .

The *Illustrated London News* had, a few weeks earlier, done a four-page display on the wonders of the new aerial Terminus at Ashley. 'The man in charge of this remarkable new facility is Mr George H. Wheeler, the Chief Aerodrome Officer. Mr Wheeler might be described as a station master of the aerial age. He is responsible for the entire operation of the Terminus, the comings and goings of the aeroplanes and the smooth passage of passengers.'

A ghastly commentary, if this individual couldn't maintain efficient toilets! Imagine if one of their Majesties used the facilities and . . .

A rap on the door. A freckled, worried face. Would Mr Wheeler come immediately to the Wireless Room. Cold sweat.

'A crash? Trouble?'

'No, sir. I don't think so. I'm not sure what it is. But I was told to ask you to come up, sir, if you will.'

When Mr Wheeler reached the Wireless Room, the pencilled list of ransom demands was complete. Dundas was staring at it as if doubting its existence. He told Mr Wheeler the story. Anarchists had taken over the flight. They knew the identities of the passengers. They were demanding enormous ransoms.

'Here's the list, sir.'

Mr Wheeler's eyes widened as he digested the names. Good grief, it was like a page out of *Who's Who*! And the ransoms, the staggering, incredible ransoms the swine were demanding . . . !

'Who . . . is the pilot of that aircraft?'

'Captain Marshall, sir.'

'Have you spoken to him?'

'No, sir. I spoke to Mr Pettigrew, the wireless operator. He sounded very nervous.'

'I don't wonder. Poor devil.'

Mr Wheeler sat down. He had to collect his thoughts. It was vital that this monstrous thing be handled the right way.

'I'd better speak to them.'

'Certainly, sir.' Dundas tuned in the Golden Wing flight and, with obvious relief, handed the headset to Mr Wheeler.

'This is Wheeler. What the devil is going on? Over.'

Pettigrew's voice crackled through the ether. He sounded nervous, poor fellow. 'The aeroplane has been taken over, sir. By anarchists. Over.'

'Tell the . . . er, anarchists, that we are not to be threatened in this disgusting way. Tell them to . . . er, put down their arms immediately or the most awful punishment will await them. Over.'

'I don't think that will do much good, sir. In fact,' added Pettigrew, his voice shaking audibly, 'I know it won't, sir. The lives of the passengers are at stake . . . and the crew too. Over.'

A fine sweat had broken out on Mr Wheeler's forehead. His mouth had gone dry; he felt a little sick.

'Let me speak to Captain Marshall. Over.'

'Can't, sir. Sorry. There are men covering him with a pistol. They say that all messages have to be transmitted and received through me. Over.'

'Well . . .' God, God. 'Let me speak to the . . . er, anarchists themselves.'

'Yes, sir. I can do that. Hold on, will you?'

'Of course I will!'

Lord no, mustn't break, not now.

There was a crackle and a buzz. Then a new voice came on the

178

air. A curt, businesslike voice, a marked contrast to Pettigrew's tremulous tone. 'We're not playing games; we mean business. You got your instructions. Follow 'em. If you don't we'll come back and fly over Ashley and we'll toss out one passenger every five minutes until you do. Got that? Over and bloody well out, mate.'

Mr Wheeler stared at the microphone.

Had he heard the man correctly? Could anyone even suggest anything so unspeakable? He wanted to bellow his outrage to the world. No; he had to be calm. He had to act rationally. This was his moment of trial. He had to think. But his brain seemed to be momentarily paralysed. He was mentally trapped by this room and these faces, all riveted upon him. God, the responsibility! One's entire career could depend upon the next few moments. He turned to Dundas.

'Get Mr Butterworth up here. But don't tell him what's happened. Next, ring Scotland Yard. Ask for Inspector Harlow.'

Nods. Hurrying feet.

Mr Wheeler clutched the paper bearing those fantastic, unthinkable demands. The names, God, the names! Such influence! If only the anarchists had a bunch of steerage passengers . . .

The money was to be collected in two hours . . .

Two *hours*?

They were mad, quite mad. It simply wasn't possible . . .

The telephone numbers were all listed there, written in an infuriatingly neat hand. Ring this number in regard to Mr Bagley, this number in regard to the Carton, Levy party . . . Get the money, so much to a suitcase . . . bring the suitcases to Ashley . . . place them neatly in the very centre of the field. Close the field to all other traffic.

Of course they were mad, of course, of course . . .

The Southern Railway line slid below. All one had to do was to keep an eye on it and it would take one to the coast and point the way across the Channel to Boulogne. After that, the idea was to raise Le Bourget on the wireless and advise them of the position and ETA at the aerodrome.

The sun was warm now; it promised a hot summer. I scanned

the horizon. It was as well to keep one's eyes peeled. Poor old Robin Duke had been so busy looking down at a highway in France that he had flown straight into a French airliner whose pilot was doing the same thing. Although there were few aeroplanes about, they all tended to fly the same routes. The traffic experts at Ashley and Le Bourget were supposed to ensure that airliners didn't simultaneously occupy one chunk of sky, but no one had yet told them how to do it. Channel ahead. In view of the dubious single-engined performance of the Handley we invariably selected the shortest routes: Folkestone to Cap Gris Nez or Dungeness to Boulogne.

Thinking of the Channel made me think of Frances. One had to hand it to her; she was the most remarkable of wives. But she was also foolhardy. No thought of failure. She felt she could cross the Atlantic by simply climbing into an aeroplane and heading west. Absolutely absurd! I shook my head as if to reinforce the thought to myself. What was a wife and mother thinking of such things?

Then I frowned. Was I being hypocritical? Would I resent her accomplishing such a feat? Would she put me in the shade? Was that the root of my objections? I hoped not. I hoped that I was big enough to share honestly in my wife's accomplishments.

A remarkable woman, Frances. I was lucky to have her as a wife. I reminded myself to tell her so one day.

I yawned. Peaceful, the verdant field of England sliding gently past my left shoulder, the sun warming the top of my helmet, the wind massaging my cheeks. What a pleasant life, flying airliners, when conditions were so tranquil.

'It's absolutely out of the bloody question!' snapped Mr Milton, the Corporation's Chief of Operations, from his desk in the City. 'Sir Jonathan would never submit to the demands of such people!'

Mr Wheeler nodded into the telephone. 'I know he wouldn't, under normal circumstances ... but do bear in mind that he is one of those being held.'

'What ...? Yes. True.' It was possible to hear Mr Milton's anguished fingers drumming on his desk. He was breathing heavily. 'They're bluffing,' he said, but he didn't sound sure.

'I hope so.'

'Do you think they might actually . . . er, throw out the passengers . . . over the field?'

'I don't know. All I can do is tell you what they said they would do.'

'God, if they did that . . .'

'Unthinkable.'

'But . . . one hundred and fifty thousand *pounds* . . .!'

'In two hours.'

Mr Milton sounded a little smaller. 'I've got to talk to the directors . . . that's obvious. Christ, one can't decide such a thing by oneself . . . Have you talked to the police?'

'Yes, Inspector Harlow is on his way here now.'

'What did he say when you told him what had happened?'

'He advised me to follow their instructions.'

'What?'

'In his opinion there is little point in bringing the situation to a head at this juncture. Far better to agree to the demands for the moment and let . . . well, let nature run its course, was the way he put it.'

'What the bloody hell does that mean?'

'I'm not sure, Mr Milton.'

'Ye gods, the Golden Wing service is the very last word in air travel! Can you imagine what would happen if those wretched . . . No! No, it's too bloody awful to contemplate. I can't think about it. I mustn't.' He breathed heavily for a moment. 'What we're dealing with,' he said, 'is piracy.'

'Quite.'

'I suppose the same rules of piracy apply to the air as to the sea.'

'I don't know,' said Mr Wheeler apologetically. He rubbed his forehead as if attempting to create the knowledge by friction. 'No one has ever done this before, so there are no rules, so to speak.'

'Someone should have bloody well thought about it,' snapped Mr Milton. 'If those maniacs so much as harm a hair . . . How many of the swine are there?'

'Two or three, we think.'

'You don't know?'

'No.'

'How the blazes did they get aboard the machine?'

'I'm not certain. Possibly they bought tickets.'

'What?' For an instant Mr Milton sounded as if he thought Mr Wheeler was being funny at his expense. Then: 'Yes, I suppose it is possible. What are you doing about the other passengers?'

'We're not doing anything, sir. The passengers are in an aeroplane belonging to the Corporation, not to this aerodrome or the Ministry of Works. While we are, of course, only too pleased to make every facility available to you, any decision pertaining to the passengers must be yours.'

Mr Milton was silent for a moment. He sighed. 'I suppose you're right.'

'The aeroplane is now outside our jurisdiction, so to speak.'

'I must talk to my directors.'

'I think that would be wise.'

'Our first concern must be the safety of the passengers.'

'Of course.'

Mr Milton sounded near to tears. 'Christ, this is awful, isn't it?'

Wilfred Forsyth smiled his airline smile at the passengers as he made his way forward. Another gin for Mr James? Certainly. A cushion for the aristocratic head of Baroness de Madon? *Mais certainement.* More sandwiches for Miss Carton? With the greatest of pleasure.

'What is that, steward?' Sir Jonathan Bennington pointed an overfed finger towards the ground.

'That'll be Tunbridge Wells, sir.'

'So it is. How far to the coast?'

'A few minutes, sir.'

'Fifty thousand *pounds*?'

The man sounded incredulous; there was a rasp in his throat, as if the mere passage of the sum caused him pain.

'That's the sum that was suggested, sir.'

'But, Christ, man, I can't lay my hands on that sort of money at short notice . . . what the hell do you think this is, a bank? This is Paramount Pictures, for God's sake.'

'I know that, sir. And this is Ashley aerodrome. And I am

182

merely advising you of a situation that has arisen involving one of your . . . er, performers. The demand is for fifty thousand pounds to guarantee Miss Carton's safe return.'

'We can't possibly pay that sort of dough.'

'Very well, sir, shall I say that Paramount Pictures refuses to accede to the demand?'

'You bet your life. Sure, you go ahead and say that.'

'Very well, sir.'

'Call their bluff.'

'Right, sir. I think I should point out, though, that they are threatening to drop one passenger out over the aerodrome every five minutes.'

'What?'

'We have no way of knowing whether this is an empty threat or not, sir. We do think we should point out, though, that these men are obviously dangerous . . . and desperate. They have already committed an act of aerial piracy . . . which is a crime punishable by death . . . we, er, believe. The fact of the matter is that they have nothing to lose. We have to take the position that they mean what they say.'

'But . . . fifty thousand pounds. How the hell am I to get it?'

'I don't know, sir.'

'Christ, it's your bloody airline she's flying on. You get the dough.'

'We are already committed to providing a substantial part of the money, sir. Sir Jonathan Bennington and Lady Bennington are among the passengers. The anarchists are demanding no less than one hundred and fifty thousand pounds to guarantee their safety.'

'One hundred and fifty?'

'That is correct, sir. We are instructed to put the money, in bank notes of small denominations, in a suitcase and place it in the centre of the aerodrome. In two hours the airliner will return to Ashley; it will land and the money will be picked up . . . somehow; I don't know how. All we know is what we have been told. At the moment we don't see any option but to obey these instructions.'

'Yes, but listen, if these anarchists are told that everyone has coughed up the dough and it's all in the suitcases, then they'll come down. And the passengers can get away, right?'

'No, sir. They inform us that if the money is not provided as per their instructions, the aircraft will be blown up on the ground.'

'What?'

'That is what they claim, sir. Again, I can't say whether they are bluffing or not. But we see no alternative at this point but to accede to their demands. That is the advice that Scotland Yard has given us.'

'Let me get this straight. Are you saying that if the guys don't get the money exactly as they want it, then the plane will be blown up, with the passengers inside?'

'That's right, sir, as far as we can ascertain.'

'So if someone doesn't cough up, then everyone gets it?'

'That appears to be the pattern, sir.'

'Jesus Christ.'

'Yes, sir.'

'I've got to get on the phone to California.'

'Of course.'

'When does the money have to be at Ashley?'

'At approximately half past eleven.'

'Good grief.'

'I'm sorry to have to convey this message to you, sir.'

'Christ, if Angela Carton was killed ... she's big box office, that girl.'

'So I've heard.'

'My God.'

'What's wrong?'

'I just realized something. It's the middle of the bloody night in Hollywood!'

Six

Inspector Harlow sat down at the conference table. He was a slim man with cavernous cheeks and a pencil-line moustache. He scratched the bridge of his nose as he took a notebook from his coat and slapped it on the table before him.

'Where is the aeroplane at this moment?'

'Almost at the coast,' said Butterworth, still clasping his clipboard. His eyes seemed to have become larger in the last thirty minutes. 'Near Dungeness, by now, I'd say. That's where they start their crossing.'

'And have you been in touch with the various parties, as per your instructions?'

Mr Wheeler nodded damply.

'With what results? Are the moneys being gathered?'

'Yes . . . although I don't know how it's being done at such short notice . . .'

'In my experience,' said Inspector Harlow, 'money in almost any quantity can be obtained if it's needed badly enough and if the people concerned are influential enough. And in this case they most certainly are.' He scratched the bridge of his nose again. 'It may of course be necessary to let these desperadoes have the money.'

'What?' The word emerged from Butterworth as a squeak.

Inspector Harlow shrugged. 'Look at the situation objectively. This is a case of extortion. Pay the money or something extremely nasty will happen to some important people. At the moment the only way we can retaliate is to ask the RAF if they would be good enough to shoot the airliner down. That course of action has some obvious disadvantages, however.'

'My God,' said Mr Wheeler, paling, as if seeing the airliner plunging in flames, taking its cargo of luminaries to eternity.

'But I've asked the air force people to look out for the airliner and see what there is to see.' He turned to Butterworth.

'What do you know about the crew of the airliner?'

'The pilot is Captain Marshall. A very experienced man, sir.

He's been with the Corporation since it was formed.'

'Age?'

'Early forties.'

'Married?'

'Yes. Lives in the village here. Two children, I think.'

'Anything untoward about him?'

'Untoward? No . . . of course not. He wouldn't be flying with the Corporation if there was anything . . . er, untoward about him.'

'Quite so. Tell me about the others.'

'The wireless operator is Mr Pettigrew.'

'What about him? Married? Children? Odd political affiliations?'

'No . . . I don't think so. He lives in Maida Vale.'

'Bit pricey for a wireless operator, isn't it?'

'I couldn't say.'

'I could,' said Inspector Harlow. 'Anyone else?'

'Just the steward,' Butterworth cleared his throat. 'Mr Forsyth. He's been with the Corporation almost as long as Captain Marshall. I know him well . . . poor soul. He lives in Hounslow. I can get the address if you like.'

Harlow nodded. He flicked a finger at an aide. 'Get someone on to looking into these three birds right away, will you? Good man.'

Mr Wheeler sighed. 'What can we do?'

'Not a great deal,' said Inspector Harlow. 'Just wait. Tell me, when you talked to the wireless operator, this man Pettigrew, did you tell me that he described the intruders as anarchists?'

'Yes. Anarchists. That was the word he used.'

'Odd.'

'Odd?'

'Yes. If you were holding a gun on a man, would you bother to waste breath telling him you were an anarchist?'

'I haven't the faintest idea, Inspector.'

'Makes you wonder, though.'

I told Pettigrew to inform Ashley that we had crossed the coastline and were heading for France. It was another morsel of information for some diligent clerk to note.

Below, the waves sparkled like cascading jewels. A small black steamer chugged purposefully towards Folkestone. Gulls circled with indolent ease, ignoring the clumsy, noisy monster buzzing overhead.

I flew on. The minutes drifted by.

The French coast would be visible shortly: a slender strip of solidity. I felt the Handley rock. The wind was fresher. I had to crab a few degrees to keep the compass needle on the correct number.

It was then that I became aware of the Siskins: RAF interceptors: little silver biplanes with funny, perambulator-like undercarriages: They were flying in formation with me, two of them. The pilot of the nearest machine was studying me with interest. I frowned. He was getting too ruddy close for comfort. Blast him! I waved a gloved hand, shooing him away, telling him to keep his distance. I was on the point of telling Pettigrew to inform Ashley. But, dash it all, I didn't want to get the young lads into trouble. No doubt they wanted to show off to the passengers. Angela Carton perhaps. But now it was all over. The Siskins were peeling off, buzzing back towards the coast.

I concentrated upon my compass course once more.

'The RAF pilots state that everything appears to be normal on the airliner. The pilot, Captain Marshall, waved; so did some of the passengers.'

'Poor devils,' murmured Inspector Harlow. 'Help so damned near and yet so far away.'

Mr Wheeler said, 'There was a conversation by wireless between the RAF and the airliner. Apparently the wireless operator thought it would be better if the fighters kept their distance; their presence made the anarchists nervous.'

'I don't wonder. Have you informed Paris?'

Mr Wheeler nodded. 'As soon as the aeroplane reaches Boulogne it becomes the responsibility of the controller at Le Bourget. He will direct the machine to Paris.'

Harlow sighed. 'If it goes to Paris, that is. But I doubt that it will.'

'Is there nothing we can do?' inquired Butterworth.

'I can't think of anything,' said Inspector Harlow frankly.

'But . . .' Butterworth evidently thought Inspector Harlow should be able to think of something.

Mr Milton burst into the conference room, having rushed by Daimler from the Corporation's head office in the City.

'Well?'

'Well what?'

'What's happened?'

'Not very much. The airliner is at the moment over the Channel. Presumably it will turn around and return to Ashley when the ransom has been collected. By the way, how do you suppose the so-called anarchists knew who would be on this morning's flight?'

Mr Milton shrugged. 'It's no secret. Any number of people within the company have access to passenger lists.' He peered at Harlow. 'Do you think Corporation people are involved in this?'

'It's possible,' said Harlow.

Mr Wheeler shook his head miserably. 'Do you realize that this could be the death of the airline industry. Who do you think will travel on airliners knowing that this sort of thing can happen?'

'Perhaps,' said Inspector Harlow, 'it will be necessary to search each passenger before he or she boards an aeroplane to make sure that no arms are being carried.'

Mr Wheeler looked shocked. 'No passenger will ever put up with that sort of treatment,' he declared.

Wilfred Forsyth glanced at his watch. Another five minutes. Nothing to gain by hurrying things. It takes time to collect the best part of three quarters of a million pounds. He grinned to himself. What a haul! A quarter of a million each. Clear. Tax-free. Courtesy of the privileged class. Never have to worry about money again, ever. Nice feeling. Lord, but the old heart gave a bounce or two when those RAF fighters came nosing around. Presumably they had been sent by the authorities to see what there was to see. But there wasn't much to see. Good old resourceful Mr P had handled himself quite well, as soon as he was told what to say. Now it was all peaceful. Just droning along, as smoothly as a Handley could drone.

He observed with some pride the calm that had overtaken him. Clearly fate had intended him to be a man of action and had equipped him accordingly. He was in complete control of himself, thinking clearly, without a qualm. You can handle yourself, Wilfred my lad, he told himself. He had always known it, but it was good to have the fact confirmed.

Had the news leaked out yet? It was a possibility. The newspaper boys had a way of sniffing out good stories, and the wireless messages could have been intercepted by anyone with the right equipment. At this very moment the newsboys could be yelling, 'Airliner pirated over Channel! Famous passengers held for ransom!' That would sell a few newspapers for Fleet Street. The funny thing was, people would be thinking of ropes and gags and guns held to temples. But the funnier thing was, not one of the passengers had the slightest idea that anything was the tiniest bit wrong!

Except Lady Bennington.

She was slightly green.

'This horrid thing is making me feel sick. I didn't want to come,' she told Sir Jonathan, 'but you made me.'

'You'll be all right, m'dear.'

'I will not! I shall be sick . . . quite soon, I think. Tell the driver to go back.'

'Out of the question.'

'*Quite* soon.'

'Mind over matter, m'dear.'

Forsyth handed her a greaseproof paper bag, provided by the Corporation for just such emergencies.

'What's this beastly thing for?'

'If you do feel upset, my lady, perhaps you would be kind enough to . . . er, project into this bag.'

'What, *here*?'

'If you would be so kind.'

Silly old bitch.

Gordon James had fallen asleep. Snoring. A peculiarly cutting snore, audible above the din of the engines. In the opposite seat, Mrs James was reading *Vogue*, her tiny mouth in pouty repose. Utterly spoilt, of course. But beautifully constructed. She and

189

Angela Carton. Simultaneously. Now there would be a treat. And why not? With money, everything was possible. All doors opened. You entered a bright new world ... welcome, rich Mr Forsyth, is there anything your little heart desires?

Another glance at the watch.

It was time for stage two.

The sunny sky was beginning to make me feel more sanguine about the possibility of a husband-and-wife flight across the Atlantic. The more one thought about it the more the idea appealed. A first. And if Frances and I pulled it off we would be the toast of the country! Of the world! She would be the first woman ever to make the crossing by air – and who deserved the honour more? Of course it would be necessary to talk to Beresford about that machine of his ...

' 'Scuse me, sir.'

Pettigrew thrust a note into my hand.

'Message from Ashley, sir.'

I read it.

Then I reread it.

I read it a third time.

POLITICAL UNREST AND GENERAL STRIKE IN FRANCE AND BELGIUM. LE BOURGET CLOSED. RETURN IMMEDIATELY TO ASHLEY.

I yelled at Pettigrew.

'Where did this message come from?'

'The Wireless Room at Ashley, sir.'

I read the message yet again. It was nonsense. Of course it was nonsense. There had been nothing in the morning paper about political problems in France. Or Belgium, for that matter. No one mentioned anything at the aerodrome before the flight. I told Pettigrew to hand me his head-set. I would talk personally to Ashley.

'I'll tune you in, sir,' he shouted, then ducked down into his cubby hole.

I slipped the head-set over my helmet.

Crackle, spit, clatter.

'Is that Ashley? Over.'

'This is Ashley. Proceed. Over.'

'This is the Golden Wing Flight.'

'Have you received our message, Golden Wing?'

'Affirmative,' I replied. 'But what is all this nonsense about a revolution in France? Over.'

'It's confirmed, Golden Wing. We have been advised that there was a *coup* this morning. Just before dawn. A left-wing uprising. There are reports of awful bloodshed. The Foreign Office has advised us to cancel all flights to France and Belgium until further notice. Some RAF fighters were sent to try and head you off but we understand they experienced wireless troubles and couldn't communicate. Over.'

So that was why the Siskins were buzzing about. Evidently this thing in France was serious. The voice wanted to know my present position.

'I'm half-way across the Channel. Over.'

'Please confirm that you are turning back. Over.'

I shrugged helplessly. 'Very well. I am returning. Over.'

'Thank you, Golden Wing. Over and out.'

Pettigrew regarded me with his gloomy eyes. I handed him his head-set.

'We're turning back!' I yelled at him. 'See if you can raise Le Bourget!'

He nodded and disappeared below. A moment later he returned. Le Bourget, he announced, wasn't responding. I shook my head. What a world! One day, gay Paris; the next, a Bolshevik outpost. What next, for God's sake?

It was a tight squeeze for Chief Steward Forsyth. The pantry at the rear of the cabin had been designed to accommodate sandwiches and drinks. It was therefore a tribute to Pettigrew's ingenuity that he had managed to install the wireless hook-up in there and to Forsyth's litheness that he had managed to insert his person into the limited space. Good lad, Mr P, thought Forsyth as he backed out, and nice to chat to you, Captain. Now please don't get the idea of talking to Butterworth or Wheeler personally . . .

Marshall would be bloody furious.

And you could hardly blame him. Rather embarrassing for him to find out the truth. He had turned completely around after a nice, long, cosy chat with the steward on his own aeroplane! Old Wheeler, too, when he found out the identity of the 'anarchist' he had been chatting with! It all went to lend weight to the theory that people are far more likely to be taken in by gigantic whoppers than by pathetic little falsifications.

He locked the pantry door behind him, then strode forward, his seasoned limbs compensating for the pitching and swaying of the Handley.

Beyond the front bulkhead Pettigrew was sitting at his wireless set, his face pale, his lips set. He jumped as Forsyth entered. Nervous, was Mr P. But everything was working out exactly as planned. Forsyth winked. Pettigrew had already printed the message twice, on two official radiotelephone forms:

MUCH REGRET MUST RETURN TO LONDON DUE TO POLITICAL UPSET IN FRANCE. CAPTAIN MARSHALL.

Forsyth gave Pettigrew's shoulder a confident pat, then he took the forms and returned to the cabin. The passengers were gazing expectantly at him: latter-day aristocrats in their aerial tumbril. What was going on? Why all this conflab with the cockpit? And why was the aeroplane starting to turn?

Without pausing, Forsyth handed one note to Angela Carton in Seat A, the second to Mr Levy in Seat B. Would they be kind enough to pass the notes back to the passengers in the seats to the rear when they had read them?

The hands shot up, the mouths projected irate questions. What the devil was this all about? Didn't the bally airline understand that a fellow's time was deuced important? *Maurice* waiting, for God's sake! In reply, shrugs and apologetic gestures. Orders straight from London. From the top; probably from the Prime Minister himself . . .

Sir Jonathan was less trouble than Forsyth anticipated. There was no insistence on talking to Ashley, no conferences with the Captain. He was, thank God, much too busy with the greenish Lady Bennington who seemed to be under the impression that the aeroplane was turning around because of her indisposition.

'What is the world coming to?' The Baroness de Madon was

shaking her Marcelled head and staring at the sea.

Never mind, old girl, Forsyth thought, you'll find in good time that you haven't lost France, just a hundred thousand quid.

Wilfred watched the broad wing dipping towards the sea. Soon the coast of Britain was ahead once more.

Seven

Inspector Harlow pointed to a diagram of the aerodrome, indicating a spot half-way down the field. In line with the southern-most boundary of the cemetery property.

'We suggest, gentlemen, that the suitcases be placed here. We will put a squad of twenty men here, at the corner of the field bordering on the cemetery, another here, at the south-west corner, a third concealed in the old sheds here, immediately south of the main building. The money will therefore be under surveillance from three directions at all times.'

'Until they take it away,' said the man from Paramount Pictures.

The man from James newspapers demanded to know what was being done to ensure the safety of the passengers.

'All we can do at the moment,' said Inspector Harlow, 'is to follow the instructions and await developments.'

'Are you going to rush the plane when it lands?'

'The anarchists have threatened to blow it up if we do.'

'So what the hell are you going to do?'

'We are going to await developments.'

'For God's sake.'

'The aeroplane,' said the Inspector, 'will descend over the village of Ashley and will land pointing almost directly south. Isn't that correct, Mr Milton?'

Milton nodded curtly. 'That's the wind direction and unless it changes it's almost certain that he'll land directly into it.'

'Then what?' snapped the man from Power Petroleum.

'The anarchists have not let us into their confidence. You must appreciate, however, that this will be a critical time for them. So far their plan will have worked perfectly. Now comes the difficult part: getting away with the spoils. They have several choices. First, they may use the airliner that they are presently holding. Their only problem is a shortage of petrol. They have to refuel to get any distance; and so far they have made no such demands. Which leads us to believe that they will be as good as their word and release the passengers and the aircraft and make off by some other means. Now what options are open to them? A fast car? Possibly. But the centre of an aerodrome is hardly the best place to make an escape by car. No; our guess is that they have made arrangements for another aeroplane to arrive at Ashley at just the right moment and whisk them away with the money to wherever it is that they intend to go.'

'What can we do to stop them?'

'Perfectly simple,' said Inspector Harlow. 'The Royal Air Force. I have already been in contact with the appropriate officials. A flight of fighter aeroplanes is standing by at Biggin Hill ready to take off and pursue the villains at a moment's notice!'

Nods and smiles of approval. At last! Positive action!

But Inspector Harlow felt less confident than he sounded. He had already discussed the matter with the air force; they said they would do their best, but the sky was enormous and aeroplanes were tiny; they could provide no guarantee that a successful interception would be made, since no one knew in what direction the machine was to fly . . .

Dungeness slipped below the wing. I told Pettigrew to report that we had returned safely to the coast and were proceeding directly to Ashley.

What a turn-up for the books, this *coup* in France. God knows how long it would be until London–Paris air travel was resumed. If ever. It was a cheerless thought.

The Southern Railway line hove into view.

All I had to do was fly along it and it would bring me back to Ashley.

*

Solemnly the men in dark business suits placed the cases upon the turf. Each gazed for a moment at his case as if taking a last look at a recently departed friend.

They returned to the Terminus and hurried immediately to the observation lounge which had been temporarily closed to the public. From that vantage point, with the aid of binoculars, they could keep their eyes on the precious cases and their contents. Grim-faced, they waited.

Forsyth watched the coastline slip beneath the Handley's wings. Not far to go. His heart pounded. If the passengers were a trifle narked now, imagine them when they realized the truth! Something to look forward to.

'Got any Otard's brandy, Steward?'

'Certainly, sir. With pleasure.'

'What time will we be back at Ashley?'

'Approximately fifteen minutes, sir.'

'Bally waste of time, this.'

'Awfully sorry, sir.'

That, thought Forsyth, may be the very last apology I have to make. Ever. No more bowing and scraping; no more grinning like a hyena, even though your feet hurt and your back is sore. I will be one of you, he told them silently: a charter member of the indolent, self-indulgent club.

Below there were green fields, neat and rectangular; softly waving trees, healthy and plump in the spring sunlight.

The Sevenoaks tunnel slid into view.

I decided to have another look at the machine Beresford had designed. With a mod or two, it might be just the job for the transatlantic trip; and possibly some arrangement could be worked out with his firm about paying for it . . . after all, I would surely rate as a top-notch candidate – considerably more experienced than Lindbergh himself, as a matter of fact. At negotiation time it would be a good idea to have Frances along to help do the talking. I recalled how splendidly she had waded into old Duker, getting him to put up the money for her Channel attempt. Frances could sell brilliantly; she had that fervour, that conviction of the absolute rightness of what she was saying. I smiled to myself as I conjured up the headlines: 'HUSBAND AND WIFE TEAM FLY THE ATLANTIC, SMASH LINDY'S TIME.' 'MR AND MRS FLY TO AMERICA NONSTOP AT RECORD SPEED.' I snapped my fingers and apologized to Beresford; I added: 'IN AEROPLANE DESIGNED BY BERESFORD MARSHALL.'

I noticed a small aeroplane flying a parallel course, about a mile away. Probably heading for Ashley too.

'Excuse me, sir.'

Pettigrew was bellowing in my ear.

'What is it?'

'We are clear to land, sir.'

I nodded.

'Wind five knots from one-ninety, sir.'

I nodded again. Conditions hadn't changed since our departure.

The small aeroplane had fallen behind. It wasn't going to pull the common small-aeroplane stunt of attempting to overtake the big airliner and land first. Sensible fellow at the controls.

A train was puffing industriously along the Southern Railway line, the sun sparkling on the engine's brass fittings. We were overtaking it. But only just. I hoped the passengers didn't notice the train. It always embarrassed me, our bare margin of speed over the wretched locomotives.

Ashley emerged: the clusters of buildings, the L-shaped expanse of grass. Dear old Ashley; I kept coming home to her and today I was coming home a little earlier than expected.

Pettigrew was standing behind me, ready to help with the throttles or switches if necessary. But today he wasn't necessary. Conditions were sublime.

An easing back of the throttle levers to begin the descent. The object of the exercise was to time everything so that one's rate of descent brought one to the required height by the time the aerodrome was reached.

I joined the London Road just south of the field and kept it running beneath the centre of my port lower wing. Heavy traffic . . . perhaps a Pickford's van or two . . .

It was then that I noticed the black objects in the middle of the field.

I pointed at them.

'What the hell are they?'

'No idea, sir,' yelled Pettigrew. Odd, the high wind was making his lips wobble.

'Ask the tower, will you?'

'Yes, sir.'

A moment later he was back. Pale, still wobbling.

'Something to do with the drainage, sir.'

'The what?'

'The tower said not to concern yourself, sir.'

Good God, what was the bloody place coming to? *Objects* left lying around in the middle of the blasted field . . .

The green light was winking from the window of the control tower. I glanced at it as I reduced power another notch.

The windsock pointed the right way.

I turned over the houses – straightening on to my final approach almost directly over Pogson Road (Mrs Braine still lived there).

The little roofs paraded beneath my wheels. Then came High Street.

Now the grass of Ashley was swishing past my wheels. A touch of rudder and aileron to hold her steady. A squeak from the tyres, a rumble . . . the tail scraped down and slowed the pace.

The Handley rumbled to a halt near the mysterious objects. They looked like cases. I applied a spot of throttle on the right side to swing her around to face the Terminus.

Pettigrew said something in my right ear, He mumbled; I couldn't understand him.

I started to tell him to repeat himself, but then I became aware of the automatic pistol that he was holding against my neck.

'Awfully sorry, sir,' he said, withdrawing the thing a few inches. He had gone a ghastly grey tone.

'I should bloody well think so,' I said. My throat tickled.

'P . . . p . . . please taxi in that direction, sir.'

'Why the blazes should I?'

'Because . . .' The barrel of the pistol wobbled in concert with his lips. '. . . I've got . . . this.'

It seemed a good enough reason. The trouble was, he sounded so bloody nervous he might pull the trigger accidentally. I tried a bit of bluster. I asked what he thought he was up to. The words sounded ridiculously inadequate: they were for a child caught stealing a chocolate biscuit out of the larder, not for a man holding a gun on one. A Colt; I could see the name stamped on the side of the barrel. Surely he wouldn't actually *pull* that trigger . . .

'P . . . p . . . please do as I say, sir.'

Where were the authorities? What the hell was *happening*?

'I'm sorry, sir, but we do mean business. Honestly.'

We. More than one of them. Brilliant deduction.

I taxied to the middle of the field.

There he made me leave the engine ticking over; he told me to put my hands behind the seat.

'What the devil for?' I demanded to know.

I soon found out. I heard the snap of metal. My wrists were in a steel grasp. I was handcuffed. To my own aeroplane! And then, to make matters worse, a sticky bandage was pressed firmly over my mouth.

From that moment on, things seemed to happen at once. I saw a light aeroplane of the Moth type touch down, bounce lightly and pull up beside us.

Behind me I heard the bulkhead door opening: voices of the passengers demanding to know what the blazes was going on: Forsyth, the steward, assuring them that everything was under control and that the delay would be momentary and would everyone please stay firmly glued to their seats.

I thought I was going to burst a blood vessel in my efforts to blow the bandage away from my mouth so that I could inform the passengers that something was most definitely wrong and would someone please apprehend Pettigrew and, presumably, Forsyth too.

Perhaps it was as well that I couldn't dislodge the bandage.

Unreality. It was all an upside-down dream. First the Le Bourget thing, now this. Was there some connection? Were the working classes revolting in both countries? Was it some gigantic plot against the Establishment?

Then I saw a man jump out of the light aeroplane. Quickly he heaved the cases, one by one, into the rear cockpit, snapping open the lids and glancing at the contents as he did so. It was done in a few moments: time enough for Pettigrew and Forsyth to sprint across the grass to join him. Simultaneously I saw men in blue haring towards us from three directions, helmets bobbing as if they were on springs. Somebody was yelling something through a megaphone; someone else was yelling immediately behind me, demanding to know what the bloody hell I thought I was doing, sitting there, letting them get away with it . . .

With what? Suitcases?

Now the little aeroplane was in motion again. The rear cockpit looked perilously over-crowded; the two occupants, Forsyth and Pettigrew, were sitting on top of the cases, hanging on for dear life, being blasted by the slipstream. . . .

A hand ripped the bandage from my mouth. It stung.

'What the devil is all this about?'

I glared at Sir Jonathan Bennington.

'How the hell do you think I should know?'

'Well, you're the bloody Captain, aren't you?'

It was undeniable. I pointed to the ignition switch and asked him to turn it.

The policemen were near, puffing and red-faced. But the little biplane was already moving rapidly, bouncing and bounding on the uneven turf, its wings swaying from side to side. A couple of the policemen dashed gallantly in pursuit but it was hopeless. The tail was up; the motor was roaring away at full throttle. In a moment the machine would be airborne, with my crew and a large supply of suitcases. Presumably filled with something. But what? I began to feel thoroughly uneasy about Le Bourget and about the RAF fighters and my obedient return to Ashley . . .

'Are you all right, sir?'

A perspiring constable stood beneath the Handley's nose.

I nodded. 'What was in the suitcases?'

'Best part of three quarters of a million pounds, sir. Are the passengers all right?'

'Christ,' I whistled. 'As far as I know,' I said.

Forsyth and Pettigrew. Rogues. And what rogues! The mind reeled.

Suddenly humanity was swarming around and within the Handley: uniformed constables, plain-clothed men and passengers: all babbling, asking questions and uttering exclamations. Feet thumped up and down the cabin behind me; everything was swaying and creaking and in imminent danger of collapsing under the weight.

I yelled for someone to come and get the handcuffs off; several people came clattering up behind me; I felt them pulling at the cuffs and examining them, then going away again. Why the hell didn't policemen carry hacksaws?

I looked in the direction of the small aeroplane, expecting to see it climbing out of sight.

But it was still on the ground. It had turned. Now it was barrelling along the grass again, tail up, wheels spinning furiously. As it whistled by, I saw Forsyth and Pettigrew, still clinging tightly to the cockpit, their hair sticking out horizontally behind them.

'Bastards!'

Angela Carton was dark with fury. She mumbled something about Paramount deducting fifty thousand from her future earnings . . .

Sir Jonathan was talking earnestly with someone about one hundred and fifty thousand. My addled brain began to comprehend the truth. The pieces fitted. I had been duped, the Corporation had been duped, Paramount Pictures, Power Petroleum, the Jameses . . . Three quarters of a million pounds! In cash! And those wretches were getting away with it, nipping away into the sky . . .

But they weren't.

The little aeroplane was still on the ground. Now it had reached the southern boundary and was dashing back again.

I started to smile. It was suddenly quite clear. The poor little thing simply couldn't make it. Three full-sized men – and two or three hundred pounds of paper money was too great a load.

We watched. And as we watched, we started to relax. Everything took on the atmosphere of an outdoor show. A spectacle, for our benefit. All we had to do was wait. Cigarettes were lit: someone found his way into Forsyth's pantry and poured gins and tonic. Our heads moved in concert as we followed the little machine; it dashed across the field, striving to get up sufficient speed to make the wings take the load. Downwind, upwind, crosswind. North to south, south-west to north-east, north-west to south-east: the pilot tried them all; and failed. His frustration seemed to be echoed in the frantic, high-pitched wail of the biplane's engine. From time to time the machine would rise a foot or two – and it was hard not to raise a cheer in response to such a brave effort – but, inevitably, wearily, the biplane would settle again.

The end came abruptly. The ups and downs were too much for the slender undercarriage. Suddenly a wheel broke off and went bouncing across the grass. With a skid and a clatter, the biplane spun around and came to an untidy halt, one wing crumpled against the ground.

The police rushed to the spot and collared the dazed villains before they had a chance to run.

Twenty minutes later, someone found a hacksaw and released me.

Mr Roseberry was digging up his front garden.

'Ah, Captain Marshall. Paris again today?'

'No,' I told him, 'we didn't get to Paris today.'

I was grounded 'pending a full investigation'. Every day I went to Head Office and sat through interminable conferences at which the whole affair was examined, analysed, reconstructed, rationalized and synthesized. No direct blame came my way but everyone seemed to have their turn at saying, 'And this completely escaped your notice, did it, Captain?' and 'You were quite unaware that this was going on, were you, Captain?' plus an occasional 'Odd that it didn't occur to you, wouldn't you say, Captain?'

The only thing that everyone agreed on was that the whole story had to be suppressed. If the general public ever got wind of what had transpired, it might mean the end of air travel for ever.

They had reorganized the schedules while I was grounded. I was to fly the London-to-Belfast route. I decided to take a fortnight's holiday and let the whole thing cool down. Besides, by now I was thinking seriously of the Atlantic trip. A husband and wife effort. It had never been done before. Frances would be the first woman in the world to make the flight; it would enhance my prestige at the Corporation (and it badly needed some enhancing) – and we would make Beresford's aeroplane famous in the process.

We went to Brighton with Beresford and Carlotta to discuss the project further and sort out our plans.

One wet morning after breakfast we sat in the lounge and discussed suitable wireless equipment for the Atlantic attempt. Beresford came in with *The Times*. He sat down and rubbed his chin.

'Have any of you,' he asked 'ever heard of a young lady by the name of Earhart?'

We shook our heads.

'Well, I'm sorry to inform you that she landed this morning at Burry Port, in Wales. She's just flown the bloody Atlantic!'

Interlude

Twelve years later, during the Blitz, I bumped into Wilfred
Forsyth on Shaftesbury Avenue. He looked thinner but very
cheerful. He wished me a very good afternoon and told me that he
had just 'got out'. He was considering the question of
employment.

'Can't go back to stewarding, Captain, not when you've done a
spot of time.'

'I suppose not,' I said. 'What are you thinking of doing?'

'Conjuring, for entertaining the troops, like,' he said, 'I've been
practising.'

And diligently. Five minutes after parting company with him, I
discovered that he had my wallet.

Part Four
Wednesday 18 November 1942

One

They got the news precisely eleven days after the wedding. They had spent a week at Bournemouth and they had just started to fix up the back bedroom; then Donald was told that he was posted.

'They say the Yanks are going to take over the place.'

'What, Ashley?'

'Yes. Bind, isn't it?'

'Hell's bloody bells,' said Georgina.

'*Darling*,' murmured Frances in her automatically shocked voice.

'I knew it was too good to last,' said Donald with a wry grin. A likeable young fellow, Donald Forbes, a Cornishman. He flew Beaufighters and spent most of his nights roaming the sky looking for Dorniers and Heinkels.

I asked Donald if he knew where he would be going.

'Norfolk, I think, sir. That's what a chap in the Orderly Room told me. Those OR wallahs usually know everything, don't they?'

Frances wanted to know whether Georgina intended to stay here at Ashley or go to Norfolk with Donald.

'I'm going,' was the unhesitating reply. 'Donald is my husband and my place is at his side for as long as it's possible.'

'But what will you do about accommodation?'

'I don't know yet. But we'll manage something.'

'But wouldn't it be better if you stayed here, dear? You could travel up to Norfolk at the weekends and Donald could come here . . .'

'Definitely not,' Georgina replied. She was twenty-two and she had her mother's good looks – and obstinacy. 'We've talked about this. Donald may well have to go abroad at some point in the future. I hope he doesn't, of course, but we have to face the fact that it's a very real possibility. If it happens, then we shall at least not have wasted a moment more than we had to while he was in England.'

'I'm sure we'll be able to find something,' said Donald. 'It's fortunate that the C.O. is quite good about chaps living off the station.'

I didn't like the idea of her stuck in some pub or dreary boarding house. I was on the point of voicing my view, but I decided against it. They would do what they wanted to do and if things didn't work out, they would presumably do something else. In wartime people have to make their own life styles.

'It was inevitable of course,' said Donald. 'I've been here almost a year. By RAF standards that's a jolly long time.'

Georgina said she resented the coming of the Yanks. 'Ashley is a British aerodrome. It always has been, for donkey's years.'

'I agree,' said Donald. 'Unfortunately, however, I wasn't consulted.'

'Norfolk can be quite pleasant,' Frances observed. 'I think I have a cousin in Norwich . . .'

'I am not staying with any cousins,' said Georgina.

'But . . .'

'No, Mother, thank you. Please don't start writing letters. We'll sort something out.'

'On second thoughts,' said Frances, 'I rather think they moved to Middlesbrough. He was a surveyor . . . or a scientist, or something. I never could keep my cousins sorted out. No; I fancy he was the chap in the electrical business . . .'

'It doesn't matter,' said Georgina. 'I'm not going to stay with him.'

Donald grinned. 'He'll never know what a narrow squeak he had.'

They went to the pictures, to see the new Betty Grable film at the Lido.

*

Ten days later Donald's squadron departed for Norfolk. Georgina followed a few days after that. She telephoned the following morning. They were nicely settled, she said, in furnished rooms in a village a couple of miles from the airfield. She said the rooms were pleasant and clean. We said how glad we were, but we didn't believe what she told us. I doubt that she expected us to believe it.

At Ashley it was eerily quiet. Since the outbreak of war the field had echoed to the din of military aircraft. First, Battles and Blenheims that flew to France and were shot to pieces over Liège and the Albert Canal. A Wellington squadron moved in; it lost more than half its number on an ill-conceived daylight raid on the German fleet. At once the word came down from HQ: No more daylight raids. From then on the war was to be carried to the enemy by night. It sounded fine in theory; the problem was that the Bomber Command had neither the equipment nor the trained crews to do the job. Doughtily, they took off night after night; in the mornings, the newspapers rang with their exploits. Large sections of major German cities had been wiped off the face of the earth, said the *Mail*, the *Express*, the *Sketch*, the *Mirror*. Only later did the Air Ministry learn that in a distressingly high percentage of the raids the crews had failed even to find the cities in question, let alone blast them off the face of the earth. It was perhaps as well that no one, including the crews themselves, knew the truth. Back at Ashley and at a score of other fields, numbed, weary airmen had poured out enthusiastic reports on their missions to Intelligence Officers who were only too anxious to believe every word. The harsh truth was at last revealed by daylight aerial photographs. It was promptly suppressed. Bad for morale. Late in 1940 Ashley waved goodbye to the Wellingtons. The night fighters arrived, just in time. The Germans were busy demonstrating how efficient they were at finding and bombing targets in the dark. To counter them the RAF sent off all-black Defiants, single-engined, two-man fighters that had proved woefully inadequate in the daylight tussling of the Battle of Britain. Just the job for night-fighting, was the official opinion. But the task of locating aeroplanes in the blackness was almost insuperable. There was simply too much sky. Hunter and hunted could

207

pass within a hundred yards of one another without either being aware of the fact. The Defiants chalked up few successes. Then the first airborne radar sets became available. There wasn't room for them in the Defiants, so Blenheims were used. Initially, civilian technicians flew as crew-members to operate the mysterious machinery. Usually it failed; occasionally it worked. And gradually, as the gremlins were routed one by one, the list of victories grew longer. The Blenheims were replaced by Beaufighters, lean, powerful machines packing a fearsome wallop; a couple of seconds of fire from their four 20 mm cannon and six .303-inch machine-guns could rip a Heinkel and its unfortunate crew to shreds. But the Beaufighters were tricky aeroplanes to fly. Soon after they arrived at Ashley, one spun into a house; the pilot was said to have made a minute error in his approach speed during landing; the aeroplane simply fell out of the sky. Pilots had to work hard to handle their spirited machines. And their navigators had to work just as hard to interpret the flickering green lights on their radar screens. Slowly but steadily they mastered it. No longer did the darkness mean virtual safety for the German bombers. Again and again the night was illuminated by the fiery plunges of enemy intruders. Radar was brilliantly successful. But it wasn't our secret alone. The Germans too were working diligently to improve their night fighter defence, mounting equipment and antler-like antennae on twin-engined Messerschmitts and Junkers. Soon, the Luftwaffe had more targets at night than the RAF. The decision had been made to attack the enemy's cities with all our might; bombing was one of the few ways in which the Western Allies could carry the war to the Germans and so aid the hard-pressed Russians.

My son, Martin, was in Bomber Command, flying Halifaxes from an airfield in East Yorkshire.

One might have supposed that the American occupation of Ashley would be a fairly gradual business, with a few officers and men arriving first to reconnoitre the place and set up facilities; the remainder coming along in dribs and drabs. Nothing of the sort. It all happened overnight. One day the village was its usual, rather dull self; the next morning it was full of young men in smooth, olive drab uniforms who wore sunglasses and chewed

208

gum and peered at us and our shops and houses with the same sort of genial interest that tourists everywhere regard the odd institutions and customs of exotic peoples. It struck us as peculiar that we should be so regarded. Our village and our way of life was *normal*; it was others who were foreign. I suppose we resented the young men; I hope that resentment wasn't too obvious.

Their high-sprung trucks rumbled along the High Street, a never-ending convoy bringing in men and stores and supplies.

'The girls will love having them, if no one else does,' observed Frances. We were walking back from a visit to Sainsbury's; the family's rations of bacon, butter and margarine lay in minute packets in her shopping bag.

She smiled as a truck driver whistled at her.

'Saucy blighter,' I said.

'I've always rather liked Americans,' she said.

'I didn't know you knew any.'

'I don't really. But I feel I've come to know them rather well, through the films.' She turned to me. 'You know they represent opportunity?'

'Who? The Yanks?'

'Yes.' She had that alert, alive look that I had come to know only too well. 'The Trimbles' shop is still empty, isn't it?'

'As far as I know.' The Trimbles had a small pet shop at the corner of the High Street and Patrick Road: they had packed up and gone to live in Somerset soon after war was declared.

Frances nodded. 'It suddenly occurred to me that in the entire village of Ashley there isn't a gift shop.'

'A what shop?'

'A gift shop. The sort of place where you can buy good quality English leather items, stationery, framed hunting prints, nice china . . . all those things one hardly ever buys for oneself. You buy them for other people, for Christmas and birthdays and so on.'

I pointed out that Ashley had managed to get along without such a shop for many years.

'True,' she said, her eyes sparkling and keen. 'But Ashley didn't have the Americans until now. They're all frightfully overpaid; I read it somewhere. They've got to spend their money somewhere. Why not in my shop?'

'You've no idea how to run a shop.'

'I can soon learn the tricks of the trade,' She grinned; she looked twenty years younger; I could see her in her nautical hat and business dress. 'This is a real opportunity, James. The Americans will be dying to buy all sorts of gifts to send home, English things, and they'll want to get little odds and ends for their girl friends. Don't look so dubious. It's a splendid idea.'

'It's not bad,' I admitted. 'But are you sure you want to tie yourself down with a thing like this? It would take up all your time.'

'Good,' she said. 'My time badly needs taking up, now that the children have gone.'

'And there's the cost of it . . .'

'I still have the two thousand Uncle Reginald left me. And you might want to invest a little, don't you think? This will be a real moneymaker, James. I know it. I can feel it in my bones.'

Secretly I rather hoped that over the next few days she would forget about the gift shop and leather and prints and odds and ends. I lacked Frances's initiative; to me things were generally best left as they were. But I should have known Frances by now. When an idea appealed to her, she could not rest until she saw it put into operation. Without a word to me, she went around to see Lawrence Bootle, our solicitor. A couple of hours later she returned, triumphant.

'Lawrence thinks it's a first-class idea.'

'Lawrence was never particularly bright.'

'You're jealous that you didn't think of it first.'

'Quite correct.'

'He's going to talk to the owners of the property. Do you think I should ask for a five-year lease?'

'I haven't the faintest idea.' Five years would take us to the end of 1947. It seemed impossibly distant.

Frances said, 'Good Lord, it just occurred to me. If I make a lot of money I shall become a wartime profiteer.'

'Never mind,' I said, 'I'll put in a good word for you with the revolutionary tribunal.'

While Frances was busy making arrangements for her new shop (Gifts Galore was the name she currently favoured – after rejecting Ideas Unlimited, Frances's Gift Shop and Ye Olde English Gift Shoppe) the Americans were just as busy on the airfield, setting up their ordnance, quartermaster's stores, military police establishment, finance, weather, medical and service units, bomb dumps, ammunition storage, mess halls, motor transport yard and all the assorted organizations that are needed to run a bomber base. The first American aircraft to land at Ashley were twin-engined C-47s; one of the Oxfords on loan from the RAF dropped in a few times, sporting the US white star on the blue circle. In the middle of January the Flying Fortresses arrived. Four-engined bombers, B-17F models, in official parlance, they roared out of a dour overcast, shaking the village with the sound of their Wright Cyclone motors. They were impressive-looking machines, with their cigar-shaped fuselages and their enormous vertical tail surfaces. Guns seemed to be sticking out of the Fortresses at every conceivable angle; big .50-inch calibre things, too, not the rifle-calibre guns that our fellows had to use to fight off cannon-firing fighters. Rumour had it that the German pilots were scared stiff of tackling Fortress formations, so fierce and multi-directional was the defensive fire. Since the late summer the Americans had been raiding targets in France and Belgium; their numbers had been relatively modest, but it was a taste for the enemy of what was to come; with the still-secret Norden bombsight, the Americans were said to be able to drop a bomb in a pickle barrel from 30,000 feet. Their plan was to attack the Germans by day, leaving the hours of darkness for the RAF. 'Round-the-clock' bombing was the term that was enthusiastically bandied about. It sounded marvellous: a twenty-four-hours-a-day assault on the enemy, destroying his factories and his homes, giving his population a taste of the medicine they had been handing out too liberally since the war began. If the Allies couldn't yet mount a full-scale invasion of Europe to aid the Russians, non-stop, round-the-clock bombing was the next best thing.

I watched the Fortresses land. There is something enormously satisfying about the return of an aeroplane to earth. No pilot can resist the sight. He smiles if a 'greaser' is pulled off; he winces if the aircraft bounces and cavorts about the runway like a drunken

211

elephant. That day at Ashley the Fortresses were using the run-way running more or less parallel to the High Street. Thus, if one strolled along past the waterworks office and walked up to the first level of the pedestrian bridge over the Southern Railway line, one had an excellent view of the proceedings. It was chilly up there; there was a raw easterly wind; had Frances been present she would have scolded me for not wearing my winter coat and a scarf. But I didn't notice the chill; an air show was being presented for my benefit. The Fortresses were describing great circles around the field, each awaiting its turn to land. I wondered what those airmen thought as they glimpsed Ashley for the first time. An airman looks an aerodrome over thoroughly when he sees it for the first time – particularly if he knows the place is to be his home for the next few months. He scans the surrounding terrain. Flat? Hills to hit in the dark? Gasometers in line with the run-ways? Power lines skirting the boundary? Surely, I felt, Ashley would stand up well under such scrutiny.

The B-17s were camouflaged in green and grey. I wished them luck and I felt glad they were on our side. They looked formidable. I thought about their crews: young men, sent thousands of miles from home to risk (and some would inevitably lose) their lives for a cause that must have seemed a little remote upon occasion. One of them was talking about it in The Lion the other evening. He was mystified. 'Why did Roosevelt declare war on the Germans? I don't get it. The Germans didn't attack Pearl Harbour; it was the goddam Japs.'

He had a point. Presumably Long Island didn't feel itself in danger of invasion by the *Wehrmacht*.

Bang!

I saw the puff of smoke from the aircraft's tyres.

'God!'

The Fortress, some twenty tons of aluminium, steel, rubber, plastic and aviation fuel, a weapon of war costing the American taxpayers a quarter of a million dollars, slewed off its bituminous path. Chunks of earth flew as it bounded on to the grass. An instant later the undercarriage collapsed. I seemed to feel the ground shudder as it took the falling weight. A propeller blade snapped and soared through the air.

The odd thing was, from my vantage point on the pedestrian bridge I could also see the people in the High Street, ambling along, going about their business as if nothing untoward had taken place. A fence prevented them seeing that a great bomber was slithering and sliding over the sodden grass, heading straight for the Sugdens' fish and chip shop.

I watched, pop-eyed, frozen. The Fort described a great semi-circle, tearing a gaping trench in its wake. By the time it reached the fence it had lost much of its momentum. It had just enough urge left to thrust its plexiglass nose through the wood and steel bars.

I hurried down the steps and across the road.

No sign of fire, thank goodness.

A stocky young man was struggling out of the nose compartment. He stumbled and fell. I helped him to his feet. He muttered his thanks, then hurriedly joined his crew-mates who, shapeless in their flying gear and harness, were energetically placing as many feet as possible between themselves and their aeroplane. I didn't blame them; I knew just how they felt; crashed aircraft are unpredictable creatures.

Slightly bewildered, the airmen found themselves among shoppers and buses on the pavement of the High Street.

One of them, a tall fellow with dark hair and a lean, angular face, thanked me for my help. He seemed to be the skipper. He asked the stocky man if he was all right.

'Sure, sir . . . I guess so.'

He sounded a trifle dubious.

'Did your tyre bust?' I asked the captain.

But he wasn't listening. He was calling to the other members of the crew. Was everyone out? Everyone OK?

He turned to the civilians who were materializing by the dozen.

'Keep back, folks . . . please . . . she could go up!'

The swarm retreated a few paces.

'Should we call the police?' a woman asked.

The American nodded. 'That's a great idea, ma'am. Will you do that?'

A few minutes later, the MPs arrived, to the accompaniment of sirens and flashing lights. Rifles and revolvers at the ready, they swarmed out of their jeeps. Simultaneously, crash wagons and ambulances came bouncing over the grass. The aircrew relaxed.

'Apologies, guys,' said the captain. 'A tyre blew.'

The stocky fellow said, 'Forget it, lootenant. I always liked dramatic entrances.'

A flat-cheeked soldier in a white tin hat spied me.

'Let's go, mac. This is restricted.'

I suggested that he might make his request a little more acceptable by the addition of a 'please' or possibly an 'if you don't mind'.

'Cut it out,' he snapped. 'This here's military property.'

'On the contrary,' I said, 'it belongs to the village of Ashley.'

'Not now it doesn't. This here airplane landed on it, therefore it's US Government property and if you don't move your ass, mister, I'm goin' to have to move it for you.'

And then the captain, the lean-faced pilot, was between us.

'There's no need for that kind of talk, soldier.'

'Sir, this guy . . .'

'He isn't a "guy", soldier.'

'Uh?'

'This gentleman is a citizen of this town. You call him "sir". You understand?'

'Why yes . . . sure, sir.'

'Go ahead, then.'

'What, now?' said the soldier with the white helmet and the flat cheeks.

'Now,' said the pilot.

The soldier directed a fierce gaze upon me as he said, 'Sir, would you kindly move your . . . yourself off the sidewalk while we clear away this mess.'

'Delighted,' I said. I nodded to the pilot. He grinned.

Two

'It is my pleasure,' said Malcom Fleece, who ran the iron-monger's for his father-in-law, 'to welcome you to the business community of Ashley.' He beamed, and produced a vase of flowers from behind his back. 'Your fellow merchants along the High Street want to wish you a long and prosperous career.' He placed the flowers on the counter in front of Frances.

'As long as you're not so prosperous as to make us unprosperous,' added Ernest Hobday, the butcher.

'Speech, speech!' bellowed Sid Freemont, the estate agent.

'I don't know what to say,' Frances declared. She looked down at the flowers, blue and white daisies and red carnations. 'They're so pretty . . . and you're all so very kind. I had no idea you were going to do this.'

'Nor me,' said Archie Broadbent, the proprietor of The Lion, ''till they asked me for a shilling.'

'Pipe down, Archie,' said Malcolm, 'let the lady have her say.'

'I . . . I feel that I'm very fortunate to be going into business among such generous and hospitable gentlemen. I'm touched by the way you have accepted me and my little shop into your business community. I hope . . . I shall be worthy of you.'

'Hear, hear!'

Applause.

Stuck away in the corner, I smiled. Frances was having the time of her life. And, Lord knows, she deserved it. She had worked so hard for the past couple of months, making all this happen. Now Gifts Galore – was a reality. And a trim, lively little place it was. Somehow she had secured stock – no mean feat in January, 1943. The shelves were packed with attractive items; and they had been packed with style, for Frances had revealed a keen eye for display. She had made a point of supporting local talent; she carried the water colours of an Ashley artist; a lady in near-by Sudby made leather purses and wallets by hand; collections of photographs of the area were available taken by local photographers. Astonishingly, she had secured a large stock of souvenir items – all made in Japan. They had, the wholesaler assured her, arrived on the last boat 'before the Far East went pop' and were available 'at the most attractive of terms'. All in all, it was a thoroughly appealing little shop, even if I said so myself.

'A credit to the High Street,' said Mr Hobday, 'that's what this shop is, a regular credit.'

I thanked him.

He said, 'Your wife has a businessman's mind, Mr M. Very astute thinking, opening up a place like this now that the foreigners have arrived in force.'

Mr Broadbent said, 'I don't think you should refer to them as foreigners, Mr Hobday.'

'Really? Well, what else would you call them, if you don't mind my asking? They're Americans, aren't they? Therefore they're foreigners.'

'You miss my point,' said Mr Broadbent, but he didn't elucidate.

'If they can't beat the Germans,' said Mr Fleece, 'they can buy them up. They came in the other day. Tools and screws and nails and dustbins and ladders and anything else they spied. Chap pulled out a great wad of pound notes and paid spot cash for everything. They'll be good for trade, if nothing else.'

'The officers are looking for houses already,' said Mr Freemont, the estate agent. 'Some pretty fancy prices could be found for the right properties, unless I miss my guess.'

'How many of them are there?'

'A hundred and thirty million or so, I believe.'

'Not *there*. I mean, *here*. Ashley.'

'Couple of thousand, they say.'

'They've got some black ones among 'em.'

'Funny smell they've got, in the warm weather.'

'Who?'

'The black ones.'

'How do you know?'

'I know. I've smelt 'em.'

'When?'

'Last night, in The Lion.'

'Everyone in The Lion has a funny smell.'

216

'Well,' proclaimed Mr Fleece, 'I do believe we should be moving along, gentlemen, to attend to our own businesses and to let this charming lady get down to the running of hers. Again, dear lady, our warmest wishes.'

It took another ten minutes, but at last they were all gone.

I closed the door. The little bell rang, the spring quivering eagerly.

'I was going to replace that bell,' Frances said. 'But it's too sweet. It must have been up there a hundred years.' She looked out of the window. 'Blast, it's raining. Isn't that rotten of the weather. It might at least have stayed fine for my first day in business.'

I wished her luck. We kissed.

'Wouldn't it be frightful,' said Frances, 'if no one came in.'

'Don't be silly.'

'It's not silly. I could spend the rest of my life standing behind this counter . . . and nothing would happen.'

'Nonsense,' I said, 'you'd have to go to the lavatory sooner or later.'

She patted her cheeks with both hands, she always did it when she was nervous; I remembered that she had patted her cheeks just before clambering aboard old Bessy for the first time. A lifetime ago; lots of lifetimes ago.

'At times like this,' she said, 'one can quite easily be convinced that one has made a dreadful mistake . . . spent all that money on stock and decorating and fixtures . . . Perhaps I'm wrong; perhaps no one has time for any of this trivial stuff in the middle of a war. It's worthless. I should be stocking cigarettes or Spam or French letters. Something useful. I'll never sell any of this stuff, James. Why ever did you let me do it . . . ?'

At that moment the bell clattered. The door opened. A man entered. An American, an officer; he wore a plastic cover on his cap to protect it from the rain. I thought: What a thoroughly sensible idea; why don't our men wear something similar?

Then I recognized him.

'Hullo, again.'

He frowned, then smiled. 'Well, hullo again, sir. Nice to see you.'

'I hope you haven't blown any more tyres.'

His smile became wry. 'No, sir, that's one thing I haven't done.'

I told Frances that this was the pilot of the machine that had trouble landing and ended up in the High Street.

'I hope you weren't hurt,' said Frances.

He shook his head; he had a deliberate, measured way of doing things. 'No, ma'am, we were lucky; just kind of shaken up.'

'Rather an unfortunate introduction to Ashley,' I said.

'That's true,' he said.

'Is there something I can show you?' Frances enquired.

He looked around. 'I'd like to get something for my mother. Nothing too big, you know; just a sort of little gift, something English, that's not too big otherwise it'll be tough to mail . . .' He shrugged.

Frances pondered the matter. In the end she suggested a calendar, featuring a series of coloured pictures of English country scenes. The American pilot was enthusiastic; it was just what he was looking for.

While she was ringing up the sale, Frances said, 'Did my husband tell you that he once crashed not far from where you ended up?'

'No, ma'am.' He turned to me. 'Is that right, sir?' His wanting to know seemed genuine enough.

'I had an engine catch fire,' I told him. 'I came down rather hurriedly. It all happened a long, long time ago. Before the Great War.'

He whistled. 'The field goes back that far?'

'To 1910.'

'Holy cow.'

'Ashley was one of the first fields in Europe to be used only for aviating,' said Frances. 'But it was called Ashley Landing then.'

'It was quite famous in its time,' I added.

'And you've been flying that long.' He smiled thoughtfully. 'What was it like, sir?'

'Dangerous,' I said. 'But we didn't have the sense to realize it. We did everything by trial and error. Mostly error. My wife flew too. As a matter of fact she was one of Britain's first woman pilots.'

218

Grinning, Frances said, 'I was never much good at it but I loved it. Do you love flying, Lieutenant?'

He scratched his chin. 'To be honest I liked flying a whole lot more when I was learning, on J-3s. Now it's all become too serious for my taste. I think I'm just a Sunday flier at heart. It'd be great to get back on that J-3,' he added wistfully. Then he asked me if I was still flying.

I told him that I did some ferry work for the Air Ministry. A Maintenance Unit still occupied the south-east corner of the aerodrome. Damaged Lancasters were brought there for repairs. I was one of the civilian pilots who flew them when the work was done.

'That's very interesting,' said the American. He was a kind and courteous young man.

Frances handed the calendar to him.

'I hope your mother likes it.'

'I'm sure she will, ma'am. And thanks for all your help. A pleasure to meet both of you. See you again, maybe.'

We said we hoped so.

He waved; the little bell rang triumphantly as he departed.

'My first customer,' chortled Frances. 'And such a nice fellow. I don't think I could possibly have had a nicer one, do you?'

'Girls,' I said, 'are always sentimental about their first.'

On Saturday night there was a fight in The Lion. Half a dozen American airmen – privates and corporals: 'enlisted men' in GI terminology – encountered a similar number of RASC men from nearby Manby Barracks. There was a difference of opinion concerning the merits of British and American beer. Inevitably this led to impassioned words on the qualities of British and American cigarettes, motor cars, tanks, aeroplanes, weapons, generals, troops, railway stations, lavatories, coffee and, finally, females. Despite the energetic efforts of Archie Broadbent and his twelve-stone wife, Felicity, words became blows. No one was sure who struck first. Some said it was the curly-haired Yank with the Italian name, others declared the culprit to be the red-haired Liverpudlian with the lance-corporal's stripes. In any event, damage amounted to thirty-nine pounds, twelve shillings and fourpence. The following morning Mr Broadbent found a tooth embedded in his counter.

A USAAF major called at The Lion to deliver the personal apologies of the Base Commander. He was, the major said, prepared to place The Lion off limits to US service personnel, if Mr Broadbent so desired.

'Well,' Archie told me later, 'I wasn't entirely in favour of that notion. The Yanks may be a bit troublesome, but they spend. You've got to say that about them. They spend. So we left it that they would make sure the MPs are in the vicinity near closing time every night. But I told him: I'm not going to put up with some slip of a twenty-year-old banging his glass on *my* counter and demanding a fill-up. "You'd better tell them that," I said. "That's not the way we do things at Ashley." '

There was little doubt, however, of the economic advantages of having our American allies stationed at the aerodrome. The Americans seemed determined to spend every penny of their impressive pay packets as rapidly as possible. As far as the aircrews were concerned, this was understandable. Casualties among the bombers of the Eighth Air Force were mounting. According to some, a crew had only one chance in five of completing the twenty-five mission tour.

Frances's shop flourished. As she had predicted, a large proportion of her customers were Americans. They had the cash – and they seemed to delight in spending it on others. Frances had decided to convert the back room into a tea shop. 'It's planned sales strategy,' she said (she had been reading an erudite tome entitled 'Secrets of Successful Retail Merchandising'). 'People will have to go through the shop to get to the tea room. They will see lots of things that they never before realized they wanted; and then they'll never be able to live with themselves until they get it.' I told her she was cold-blooded; she shrugged and said it was total war. The big problem in those days was obtaining the right materials and paints to do a decent job. That was why we finished up with a pink and grey tea room. It was the last combination either of us would have selected; but, oddly enough, it worked very well. Frances was of the opinion that it gave the place a vaguely decadent look. 'And decadence is good for business.'

Soon the tea shop became a popular meeting place for the

Americans and the local belles. Frances employed two girls to work there, one of whom spent part of the day in the gift department.

I was deeply impressed by her initiative and industry. And I was glad that she had an interest in life significant enough to take her mind off the children, at least part of the time. Martin was nearing the end of his first tour of ops; Georgina was still living in furnished rooms near Donald's airfield. At any moment dread news might arrive from Yorkshire or Norfolk. It was best not to think about it; and not thinking about it was possible only if the mind hadn't the time.

One grey Thursday afternoon I delivered a Lanc to a depot near Lincoln. I was supposed to get a lift back in an Anson going to Hendon, but it didn't materialize. In the end I took the train home arriving, grubby and unshaven, early Friday morning. I telephoned Frances then set out to walk home.

Halfway across the pedestrian bridge to the High Street I encountered a uniformed figure, hands thrust deep in his greatcoat pockets.

I recognized him first. He gave me two looks, one right after the other.

'Mr Marshall. How are you?'

'Dishevelled,' I said. 'And you?'

'Surviving,' he replied. 'So far. How's Mrs Marshall?'

'Very well, thank you.'

'Say, would you mind telling her that my mother is crazy about the calendar. She's showing it off to all her friends and neighbours.'

I said I was glad to hear it. Then I asked him how Ashley was treating him.

Obviously it was the wrong way to phrase the question.

He frowned; for an instant he looked as if I had struck him.

'What do you mean?'

I assured him that I didn't *mean* anything. The poor fellow was badly down in the dumps. Was he lonely and homesick? I thought about my son. Martin said he found it bad enough, living two hundred miles away, in Yorkshire. This young man was a continent away from his family.

'I don't know your name.'

'Sorry, sir. It's Deane. Everett Deane.'

We shook hands. We were, we said, pleased to make each other's acquaintance.

On an impulse I asked him to dinner.

Immediately I added, 'Look, don't feel that you have to say yes . . . I hope you do, of course, but you don't have to. There's just the two of us, my wife and myself. And I'll probably want to talk aeroplanes the whole time and bore you to death. But if you've got nothing better to do . . . on Sunday, say, you'll be very welcome.'

He nodded thoughtfully. 'That's nice of you, sir.'

I scribbled the address and telephone number on the back of a Gas, Light and Coke Company envelope. 'Sunday all right? About seven?'

'Why yes, sir. But your rations . . .'

'Don't worry about the rations. We'll manage something. Remember, if for any reason you can't come, don't worry. It'll be all right.' I waved and started to walk away.

'Thanks again, sir,' he called.

I waved again but didn't look behind. Best to let the poor fellow decide for himself. Possibly he was grimacing back there, thoroughly overwhelmed by the prospect of dining with the Marshalls. And who could blame him? Why would a young fellow want to go and spend a valuable evening with a couple of old fogies? (We *weren't* old fogies, of course, but I felt sure that he must have classified us so.)

When I told Frances she was pleased. But she shared my doubt that he would take us up on the invitation.

Thus we were hardly astonished when he failed to turn up the following Sunday. We shrugged and grinned at each other, as people who have made a *faux pas* often do. We both agreed that the poor chap could hardly be blamed for his decision. The arrangements *had* been thoroughly casual; nothing the least bit binding on either side. No doubt the young man was looking for livelier diversions than could be found at 47 Harvest Road.

He telephoned the following morning.

'Mr Marshall?'

'Speaking.'

222

'This is Everett Deane, sir. I've got to apologize about last night.'

'Don't mention it.'

'I couldn't help it, sir. I was all set to come. I was looking forward to it. But I spent the night in Durham some place. We were doing a cross-country. Of all the ships to have engine trouble, ours had to be the one. We landed at an RAF field. They had a mission in progress; they wouldn't let us make any outside phone calls. Or send a wire ... or any damn thing. Please tell Mrs Marshall that I'm real sorry about it. I'd like to take a rain-check on that invitation, sir, if it's OK with you.'

'Rain-check?' The term was unfamiliar to me.

'What I mean, sir, is I hope I can take you up on the invitation some other time.'

'Some other time? Yes, of course.' I was delighted. 'What about next Sunday?'

'Great.'

'Same time?'

'I'll be there.'

But he wasn't. He flew to Ostend. He brought back two dead gunners; the starboard undercarriage leg collapsed upon landing; his machine ground-looped and was completely wrecked. He spent the rest of Sunday in the Base sanitarium.

'Checking us over,' he explained the next day on the telephone. 'But we're OK ... except for Myers and Luskic, of course. Hell of a thing to lose men ... you get to know them well. I guess you know how I feel.'

'I think so,' I told him.

We decided upon Saturday evening. He telephoned during the afternoon.

'I'm going to have to let you down again, sir. Some dumb Congressman is coming to visit us. No one leaves the place.'

On Sunday he telephoned again.

'Sir, this is Ev Deane. If you're still talking to me I'd like to take you up on that invitation.'

I told him to come over at once. An hour later he arrived, burdened by tins of Spam, dried eggs, tongue and butter, as well as packets of cigarettes and chewing gum.

Frances stared at him. 'Whatever did you bring all this stuff for?'

'I thought you might be able to make use of it, ma'am.'

'Well yes, but you shouldn't have . . .'

'I've put you folks to enough trouble. I'm just glad I can bring you a couple of things. I hope you don't mind.'

We looked at the treasures and then at each other. No, we had to admit that we really didn't mind at all.

I learnt that Everett Deane was twenty-four and that he hailed from a place called Bedford, Massachusetts. His father was an engineer, working for a large manufacturer in Boston; his mother came from Sarasota, Florida, and was proud of something she called her Southern heritage. Everett Deane had been attending North-Eastern University.

'I could have stayed there until I graduated,' he said. 'No problem. But, oh no, I had to enlist. Dumb,' he added with a twisted smile.

'But understandable,' I said. 'A young man finds it hard to resist a call to arms. Unfortunately, the reality of military service is quite unlike what he imagines it will be. But by then it's too late.'

He snapped his fingers. 'That's for sure. Boy, if I'd known what I know now.' He shrugged, grinning and sipped at the whisky I had poured him. He was beginning to relax. 'This is a nice home, sir, warm and friendly. A lot like ours back home except that we have fly-screens on our windows. Sir, why don't the British have fly-screens on their windows? It's been bugging me ever since I got here!' He chuckled as he got to his feet to examine the photographs on the mantel-shelf.

'That's my son, Martin,' I told him. 'He's a Flight Lieutenant. He's based in East Yorkshire and he flies a Halifax bomber.'

'He looks a lot like your wife, sir.'

'That's what everyone says. The other young man is Donald Forbes. He's a Beaufighter pilot and he's married to my daughter, Georgina, the girl in the centre.'

'Very pretty,' he murmured. 'She looks a lot like Mrs Marshall too.'

'So I'm told.'

Everett Deane knew how to be a welcome guest. He asked the host about himself.

'Tell me some more about your crash, sir.'

I filled up our glasses and told him that for years I was known as the Luckiest Man at Ashley Landing. 'I was flying a new aeroplane. My brother had designed it – he's retired now and lives in Somerset with his fourth or fifth wife; I never can remember which. At any rate it was a fine machine – except for the fact that it burst into flames five minutes after I had taken off. A fuel line, we decided later. Of course this took place before the days of parachutes, so I had no choice but to go down with the aeroplane. Naturally I thought my number was up. But the machine came to pieces about a hundred feet up. I fell out and landed on a van full of birdcages. I was bruised but unhurt. Hence my title, the Luckiest Man at Ashley.'

'And the aeroplane was destroyed?'

'Completely. We started to build another one. And the roof fell in on it. And then . . . but it's ancient history.'

'Interesting, though,' said Everett. 'I've always had a lot of respect for guys who flew in those old stick-and-wire aeroplanes.'

I told him that I had a lot of respect for those who flew daylight bombing missions.

He smiled wryly. 'It's nice of you to say so. But don't get the idea I'm any hero. I'm not, believe me.'

It was a remarkably pleasant evening. We enjoyed Everett Deane's company and he appeared to enjoy ours. We told him to come back whenever he felt like it. He took us at our word. A week later he returned. A few days after that he turned up again, always bearing supplies of Spam and Chesterfields, corned beef and canned chicken. Tirelessly we discussed flying and fliers, the war, England, America, Ashley . . .

'You've been here all these years, at this one field?'

I nodded. 'Fate seems to have decided that here is where I shall make my living.'

We talked about Ashley. Everett wanted to know about it in the Great War days and before. He had another whisky. And another. Then, when Frances went into the kitchen to make coffee, he told me the truth. How he hated Ashley. How the place

225

had meant the most appalling luck for him and his crew . . .

'The fact of the matter is,' he said, 'I'm going to get killed here.'

'No . . .'

'I just know it,' he said. 'I've gotten the message.'

Three

The instant he saw Ashley (Everett Deane told me) he knew he would die there. There wasn't a shadow of doubt about it.

The field and the village appeared simultaneously through a haze of cloud.

Breithaupt, the co-pilot, nodded in the direction of the field. 'There she is, right on the goddam button.' He grinned across the cockpit.

Everett managed to nod in reply. He rubbed his eyes with a gloved hand. He shivered. What the hell . . . It was warm in his electrically heated flying suit but icy fingers seemed to be touching his nerves. He pushed back in his seat as if trying to squash the chill.

He stared at the field again. Just another field. Sort of L-shaped. Three runways: one long, two shorter. Village to the north; main road to the east.

Kill him? That place?

He took a deep breath. It must have been a day-dream. How could a field convey a message, for God's sake? And even if it could, why the hell would it want to? That field, he told himself, doesn't give a damn about you.

But still the feeling wouldn't go away. The *certainty* . . . a glimpse into the future . . .

No. He wouldn't think about it. He had to attend to the business of getting the B-17 and its crew back to earth.

'Pilot to Engineer. Crew in landing positions?'

'Yes sir. Crew standing by for landing.'

DeNiza, the engineer, always sounded as if he couldn't take all this seriously.

Greene, the radio man, reported that the antenna had been wound in.

Everett and Breithaupt checked the automatic pilot, the booster pumps, mixture controls, intercoolers, filters and turbos.

'One-third flap,' said Breithaupt. 'Speed one-forty.'

A heave on the control wheel and hard pressure on the rudder pedal brought the runway swinging into line.

'One-twenty. Full flap.'

He angled one wing slightly to compensate for the stiff cross-wind. Opposite rudder kept the nose aimed straight at the ribbon of concrete ahead. Another B-17 was turning off the runway after completing its landing run. Back with the cluster of throttles. The hedge slipped below. Column back to kill the speed; as usual, the Boeing floated along the runway, her nose held high, her wheels reaching down for the ground. The stylish thing was to put her down on her two main wheels and her tailwheel at precisely the same instant.

He did. And at the same instant one main wheel and the tail-wheel burst.

As the big machine swung off the runway, he thrust forward on the inside throttles. But it was too late. With a grinding and snapping, the undercarriage crumpled.

'Holy cow!' Breithaupt's hands were clutching for support.

Already . . . my God, it's happening already . . .

Voices, scared and disbelieving, were jabbering in his ear-phones. Strained tones blended with the tearing and ripping beneath him as the airplane slithered across the grass. It was shaking itself to pieces with a kind of deliberate fury.

It slowed.

At last, with a final crunch, it stopped.

The village street was suddenly in full view. Surprised pedes-trians, their shopping baskets still over their arms, were looking at him, just a few feet away. A car, a little boxy thing, stopped dead in its tracks; the driver wound down his window. A bus nearly ran into the back of him.

*

The Colonel did his best to be sympathetic, but he was clearly upset by being obliged to report major damage to an aircraft the first day at Ashley.

'Your crew are OK?'

'Yes, sir,' Everett affirmed.

'That's something. Major Crawley says the ship may be salvageable.'

'I hope so, sir.'

'But it'll be out of action at least a couple of weeks. We'll assign another ship to you.'

'Yes, sir.'

'You're all right, are you?'

'Fine, sir.'

'That's good. Get some flying time in tomorrow.'

'I will, sir.'

The Colonel's lip broke into a thin smile.

'It was just bad luck, Lieutenant. And no one's blaming you.'

'Thank you.'

'Hit the sack early. Get a good night's sleep.'

'I will, sir.'

He followed the Colonel's advice but he slept poorly. The bed (an ex-RAF item) was hard and unfamiliar. The hut creaked in the wind like an old boat. The blackout curtain just above his head kept tapping against the window. It sent garbled messages in Morse. S-N-O-X-W-J-P-U. The guy in the next bed, a Californian named Dingle, would occasionally murmur something about a girl named Betty and her boobs. He kept sighing; he sounded deeply contented.

A silly line from a song kept occurring to Everett: 'Little man, you've had a busy day.'

That was for goddam sure.

A crash-landing and a premonition of death. It was enough for any one day.

The premonition was crap, of course. Of course.

His father would say, 'Premonition of death? Forget it. You created it. It came out of your brain because you were tired and scared and didn't know what the hell tomorrow would bring. Your brain created it so your brain can destroy it.'

QED.

How many guys had similar premonitions? Lots, probably. Perhaps everyone. Everyone, but no one admitted it. Like self-abuse. A common, awful secret.

He wondered about combat. It was the moment of truth. At last you found out for sure about your Gut Quotient. What if you failed? Some guys said they had special places in the country for airplane commanders who broke under fire. They had to be kept away from the other members of the Eighth because their problem could be contagious.

Already the Eighth had hit targets in Germany. It was, said the newspapers, the first blow of a battle that would knock Germany out. But at what cost? Rumour had it that some Groups had lost half their number in a couple of missions. An unusually high incidence of colds in the nose and mysterious back-aches were reported by those Groups . . .

Some experts said that the B-17s of the Eighth would get their asses shot off, flying daylight bombing missions over Germany. The Luftwaffe was just too damned good and bombers flying in formation made Grade A targets.

It was hard to argue the point.

The advocates of daylight bombing placed all their faith in formations. They had developed elaborate charts showing, from above, below, front and back, how the B-17s should be stacked to provide mutual protection and present a devastating curtain of fire to attacking fires.

But what happened when some bombers got shot down? Did the holes they left in the formation make much difference? And how about flak? What did it care how great the formation was? All a formation did was to create a better target.

Over the sun-baked plains of Texas they had practised formation flying hour after hour. 'A good formation is a safe formation,' said the handbook. 'An air collision is the result of carelessness or lack of clear understanding between members of the formation. If the simple rules, as outlined, are followed explicitly, there is no excuse for mistakes in the air. A mistake in formation flying may result in costly, irreparable loss of lives and equipment.'

He wondered about the crew. How much confidence did they still have in him? Poor bastards. Hellish, to have to rely totally on the skill (or lack of it) of other guys.

'Aw, let me,' muttered Dingle.

Everett fell asleep. He dreamt of Cape Cod and Martha's Vineyard and a girl named Kitty to whom he had once declared his undying love in order to persuade her to have sex with him. Afterwards, he had realized that, as an individual, Kitty was of not the slightest interest to him. It was a realization that saddened him; he wondered if he would always feel that way. Perhaps he was incapable of loving in the usual sense.

In the morning he awoke. He remembered the premonition. It jabbed momentarily, but then it had little sting. He had a good breakfast.

The weather had improved. A front of high pressure had moved across the southern counties; the many-layered ceiling of grey cloud had, reluctantly, shifted and broken. The sun splashed on the damp runways and warmed the metal skins of the B-17s on their hard-standings around Ashley's perimeter. Appreciatively, the mechanics squinted up at the sun as they worked on recalcitrant cylinders and malfunctioning elevators. The aircraft were new: B-17Fs, straight from the factory in Washington. Virgins, they had still to be tested in combat; although some already bore defiant names – *Goering Buster*, *May Hem*, *Dinah Might* – none yet wore the painted bomb symbols indicating missions successfully completed.

'My personal feeling,' said Myers, the ball-turret gunner, 'is that we should call her *Adolf*. What Jerry pilot is going to shoot down a ship with a name like that?'

'What the hell kind of a name is *Adolf*?' sneered Greene, the radio man. 'A ship's a she, for Chrissake. *Daisy Mae*, *She Loves To Lay*: that's the kind of name I'd like to see.'

'You've got it on the brain, buster,' said Delaney, one of the waist gunners.

Greene shrugged. 'Tell me sump'n better to have on your brain.'

Everett silenced them. 'It's academic, fellers. This isn't our ship. We may get 028 back in a few days. No use giving this one a name until we know whether we're going to keep her.'

They nodded; there was no arguing with that fact. They tossed their parachutes and gear aboard the new aircraft, plugged in their heating systems, their oxygen, their intercom jacks, adjusted their helmets and settled in their seats. Those in the centre of the machine could hear the two pilots mumbling their pre-start check-list mumbo-jumbo: intercoolers, generators, cowl flaps, hydraulic brake pressure, brakes, turbos, boost pumps, fuel . . . Then the clatter and bang of the engine start-up; at once the machine was alive with a million tiny nudges and vibrations, fretting to be away. Bumping, swaying, creaking, the big ship waddled along the taxi-way.

'OK . . . here we go!'

The noise became deafening, as always. The gunners, looking back, could see the blast from the propellers making the tail surfaces wobble. A guy sure hoped those designers knew what the hell they were doing. Maybe they should have beefed it up a little bit here and there . . .

At one hundred and ten miles per hour the clattering of the main wheels ceased. The runway dropped. The little black and white checkerboard hut slipped by signifying the end of the runway.

And all at once all hell broke loose.

A screaming from the motors. Frantic yells over the intercom. Suddenly, a pitching, a rolling. The ground tilting, rushing up at one side . . . a blurring, a rushing . . .

A bang. The machine shuddered. A hedge appeared, vanished.

Another shattering, eyeball-shaking impact with something.

Another.

Breath was punched out of frightened bodies as harnesses took sudden, fearful loads. A crumpling, collapsing cacophony. And then it was quiet.

'Get the hell outa this thing!'

'Move it!'

'Jeez, she's liable to go up!'

Gasping, bewildered, they threw themselves out of hatches; they fell on sodden ploughed earth; they stumbled and fell and cursed.

'What the . . . hell was all that about?'

'Jesus Christ, I . . .'

'Is everyone out?'

Dazed, they looked at their aircraft. It was bent and torn; mud-spattered, its propellers turned back like umbrella handles.

'Nice work,' gasped Breithaupt.

'Thanks,' said Everett, white-faced.

'Nice work?' snapped Maxted, the navigator. 'What the Christ was so nice about that?'

'We lost two engines, buddy.'

'Uh?'

'Two engines, just as we came off the goddam deck,' declared Breithaupt. 'You're goddam lucky you're still breathing, mister. If it wasn't for . . .'

'We were all lucky,' said Everett.

DeNiza said, 'Is there sump'n about this field you don't like, Lieutenant?'

'Both engines?' said the Colonel.

'Yes, sir; one right after the other. I'm . . . sorry about the airplane, sir, but I couldn't straighten her out to go around again . . . She just wouldn't fly any more. She sort of mushed into the ground . . . it was a break that she was the right way up.'

The Colonel rubbed his forehead and sighed. 'I'm glad you're OK, Lieutenant.'

'Thank you, sir.'

'You've had one hell of a lot of bad luck since you got here . . . and, Jesus, you haven't been here a day yet!'

'Yes, I'm sorry . . .'

'Nothing to be sorry about. No one's blaming you for . . . what's happened. I'm just damned glad the results weren't one hell of a lot worse! Believe me! Seems to me you handled things just fine to keep that ship from cartwheeling all over the airfield.'

'Nice of you to say, sir . . .'

'I mean it. These things happen. Occupational hazards, right? Only you've had your share all together. Chances are, you'll have plain sailing from now on.'

But it was not to be.

Two days later, Everett's B-17 collided head-on with a seagull.

The bird's body smashed through the plexiglass nose, showering Maxted with fragments and feathers. His face was badly lacerated. After landing, he reported a partial loss of vision in one eye.

'It keeps coming and going,' he told Everett. 'Sorry . . . I may be out of the crew for a little while. The MO says I have to go up to London to see a specialist.'

'Bullshit,' declared Joe DeNiza when he heard the news. 'He can see as good as you or me. But he wants out of the crew; that's all there is to it. He wants out. He thinks we're bad luck. Christ knows why,' he added stoutly.

Maxted's replacement was a Texan named Johnstone, a lean, smooth-faced young man whose father, it was said, was a fundamentalist preacher and a millionaire.

One week to the day after his arrival at Ashley, Everett was obliged to land his aircraft wheels-up, after the gear resolutely refused to descend from its compartment in the inner engine nacelles. Fortuitously, the B-17's design had had such emergencies in mind and had left a portion of the retracted main wheels protruding beneath the nacelles. The aircraft could be brought to earth in such a condition with very little damage. And Everett did an excellent job. The B-17 slithered to a halt with only a few dents and scrapes to tell the story. But it was yet another incident to add to the Deane legend. Already the mechanics tended to look askance at him and his crew. The stories were beginning to circulate. The Base Library was said to have advised members of the Deane crew to borrow only books of short stories; all mail for the Deane crew was supposedly being directed automatically to the Sick Quarters; the Luftwaffe was considering Lt Deane and his crew for a decoration in recognition of their toll of American aircraft.

'In a few days' time,' the Colonel told his crews, 'we'll be joining the rest of the Eighth Air Force in combat. And I'm going to be proud of you, gentlemen, of that I have no doubt whatsoever. I know you will conduct yourselves with the pride and devotion to duty that befits any member of this outfit.'

The Colonel paused, as if daring any man to disagree. His grey eyes scanned the ranks of pale-faced young airmen in their leather and fur flying clothes.

233

'Some of you,' he declared, 'are going to get killed. It's certain. Let's not have any misunderstanding. This is one hell of a rough game we're getting into. The *Luftwaffe* is good. And experienced. And it sure as hell isn't beaten yet, no matter what the newspapers say. We're going to take casualties. But we're going to take fewer casualties *if we do our jobs*! And that means good, solid formation flying, the best in the Eighth! Our Group is going to be the solid Group! Tight as hell! And you know why! Because those Jerry fighter pilots aren't so dumb. They'll keep away from a Group that's flying a great formation!'

But what about the flak? Everett thought. The tighter the formation the better the target for the gunners . . .

'We're going to have the best goddam reliability record in the Eighth!' declared the Colonel. 'We're going to have the lowest record of aborted missions. And we're going to have the best record of ships available for missions! And we're going to have the lowest sickness rate in the Eighth! Do you read me, gentlemen?'

Yes, they told him; they read him; they understood.

A brave man, the Colonel, but a pain in the ass at times.

Glumly Everett considered his chances of living to a ripe old age.

The aircrews were given a three-day pass. Everett spent the first morning in the village of Ashley. A funny little place. The towns of Concord and Lexington, near his home, looked more English than Ashley. He went to a gift shop and bought a calendar which he mailed to his mother. He wrote his parents a long letter, enclosing a couple of recent pictures: 'Me in the main street of the village here. Building on left is a genuine English pub. The beer is warm but tasty. The washroom smells. This is my crew. Milt Breithaupt, my co-pilot, on the left. Joe DeNiza next to him.' He didn't know what else to tell them. There was no point in mentioning that he would soon be going into combat. It would serve only to worry them. He asked about relatives and friends and said that he hoped they were well and prosperous. It was a lie. He didn't care one way or the other. They were just names. They belonged to another life, a life that had become extraordinarily remote. Only this business of uniforms and airplanes and bomb-loads and formations was real.

For lunch he had a plateful of greasy sausages and French fries (they called them 'chips') in the station restaurant. He caught the train to London. He arrived at Victoria shortly before dark. A Technical Sergeant directed him from there. 'You wanna get downtown, Lootenant? Take the subway – only they call it the Underground. Get out at Oxford Circus. Take a walk down Regent to Piccadilly. Real nice stores. Piccadilly is where the action is, Lootenant.'

He followed the sergeant's advice. He was looking for action. A woman. Possibly two: One white, one black, perhaps. Hell, maybe a yellow one too, for good measure. The idea was to absorb as much pleasure as possible in the shortest possible time. This was most likely the last chance.

The London subway system was rapid and efficient. But desperately overcrowded. He had to stand wedged between a soldier loaded with rifle and full equipment, a family of three with five suitcases and a plump lady with two shopping bags. It was a relief to get out at Oxford Circus and be carried by the throng up to street level. The sergeant's directions were sound. He strolled down Regent Street, admiring the fine stores and their expensive merchandise. All very classy. This was the kind of England he had been waiting to see ever since he landed. C. Aubrey Smith would have been right at home here.

Piccadilly was solid humanity. You had to push your way through forests of elbows. Lots of chatter; lots of laughter. No despondency here, he thought, smiling as he imagined himself to be Edward R. Murrow, reporting on the embattled capital of the British Empire. Goodnight from London. He looked up at the starless sky. Were the Germans coming that night? Would they succeed in getting him on the ground instead of waiting until he got into the air? One felt very vulnerable, waiting to be bombed. Presumably there were people across the Channel feeling much the same.

He called at the USO club to organize accommodation. He was scolded for not seeing to the matter before. London, he was told, was busier than hell. But they found him a place on Brompton Road. ('Not the Waldorf, Lootenant, but OK.')

He went into a pub and had a plateful of shepherd's pie and a pint of brown ale. The food was tasty. He listened to a man talking about the criminally insane way the Ministry of Food was being run.

A blowsy blonde woman rapped him on the shoulder.

'Feel like a bit, darlin'?'

Her voice was pitched low – but not low enough to avoid being overheard by the portly man behind the bar. 'For Gawd's sake, Greta! I told you before! I won't 'ave none o' that in 'ere!'

'None of what, I'd like to know?'

She managed to sound suitably indignant.

'You was propositionin' the Yank.' He wagged a grubby forefinger at her. 'What sort of a place d'you think this is?'

'I wouldn't know, I'm bloody sure.'

'I'm sorry, mate,' the portly man said to Everett.

'It's OK. I didn't catch what she said.'

The man winked. 'You don't want to catch anythin' from 'er, mate.'

Everett grinned as he paid and went out into the street again. He liked the Londoners. They were earthy and crude, but very much alive. They reminded him of the fast-talking taxi drivers in New York and Boston; there must be something about living in the heart of a major city that affected people and gave them an edge to their personalities.

The theatres were lined up along Shaftesbury Avenue: farces, naughty but nice, reviews, topical and spicy, drama, musicals; you took your pick and lined up ('queued', according to the British) to secure whatever tickets might still be available to that night's performance. The pickings were slim, but he had the advantage of requiring only one ticket. He found himself at the side of the stalls in a small, ill-ventilated theatre watching a play that the audience seemed to find uproarious but which struck him as supremely silly. From the thunderous applause that greeted a small man in a bright check suit, he gathered that he was witnessing the performance of a star of stature. He found the man boring; his gestures were outrageous and his accent made him hard to understand.

He left in the middle of the last act and crossed the street to the nearest pub. He had a brandy this time; it was that or gin, according to the grim-faced barmaid. The pub was packed; the smoke was thick enough to conceal the identities of patrons on the other side of the bar. Everyone seemed to be talking at full volume; laughter was explosive and somehow frantic, as if it all had to be out by closing time.

'Packed, what?'

Everett turned. A British army captain with a ginger moustache was beaming at him. Everett agreed that the place was indeed well patronized.

'Stupid drinking laws in this country; I suppose you've noticed.'

'I'm from Massachusetts; the laws are pretty dumb there too.'

'Really? How extremely interesting. I had no idea.' The captain had a ready smile. He spoke well, in the clipped, precise way of Englishmen of better education. 'Is this your first visit to London?'

'How can you guess?'

The captain smiled. 'Shot in the dark, old boy. You looked a bit forlorn.'

'I wasn't feeling forlorn.'

'Of course not. Birds of a feather, what?'

'I guess so.' The captain seemed a pleasant enough individual and it was good to have someone to talk to. 'Is London your home town?'

'Great heavens, no. I'm in your boat, old boy. Thrust into this fiendish place by the exigencies of total bloody war.' He looked around. 'Hate the place. Too crowded, too noisy.' He shrugged. 'But what can one do? Have to make the best of it. The only thing about London,' he said matter-of-factly, 'is that one can get just about anything one fancies in the way of entertainment provided one knows where to look. You know what I mean, old boy?'

'Well . . . yes, I . . .'

'I've made it my business to know where and how and at what price. After all, I said to myself, if I've got to spend an inordinate time in this madhouse I might as well derive the maximum benefit therefrom. You know what I mean?'

237

Again Everett assured the captain that he knew what he meant.

'Are you here overnight? Or a few days?'

'A couple of nights.'

'Hope you have an awfully good time,' said the captain.

'Thanks very much.'

'See all the sights . . . and everything.'

'I'll sure try. Care for a drink?'

The captain shook his head regretfully. He picked up his cap. 'Have to shove off.'

'Too bad.'

'Good luck, old boy.'

'Thanks.'

With a cheerful 'Chin-chin!' the captain vanished into the throng of pub patrons. Everett held up his glass in the hope of getting it refilled. Pity the guy had to take off. He seemed to know his way around. Could have been useful . . .

'I say, old boy.'

The captain had returned. Beaming.

'Look, absolutely none of my business. But on the way out it struck me that you might be looking for a bit of . . . well, fun. And it just so happens that I know a rather special place not too far from here that might be just the ticket . . . if that sort of thing appeals to you, of course. If it doesn't, well, no harm done, what?'

'No, of course not . . .'

'Lots of lovely girls there. All frightfully willing. Any colour, shape or size you fancy . . . and adept at all the specialities, if you get my meaning.'

'I think so.'

'Mind you, it's a bit on the costly side.'

'How costly?'

'Ten to twenty pounds, depends on what you buy.'

'Jesus!'

'Too much, old boy?'

'No, not if it's . . . really worth it.'

'Worth every penny, in my experience. After all, these are artists in their chosen field,' he added with a chuckle.

'OK,' said Everett. Anticipation darted through him, setting nerves a-quiver. 'Sounds great.'

'I knew you were a sportsman, old chap.' He glanced at his wrist watch. 'Look, I'm going that way now. Only five minutes from here. I'll show you there.'

'That's very kind of you.'

'Pleasure, old boy. Delighted to be of service. Ready?'

'Sure . . .'

'Good. Let's go. I'm in a bit of a hurry, so you won't mind if I move a bit smartish, will you?'

They crossed several narrow streets, stepping through alleys. It was an area of foreign restaurants and dark windows. Women in doorways called out to the two officers as they hurried by; the captain kept shaking his head.

'Sorry, old girl. Next time, perhaps.'

Everett panted after the Englishman. They were in a sort of passage. Where on earth was the guy going? And why would he go so far out of his way to . . .

Everett stopped. Hell no; this was stupid. How dumb could you be.

It was too late.

A hand grabbed his shoulder from behind. Turning him. Another pushed him. He stumbled against a damp wall. He saw the captain stop and face him, hands on hips.

'What . . .'

The world exploded.

'You got a nasty bang on the head,' the police sergeant observed.

Everett nodded. It hurt. His head had been X-rayed at a near-by hospital; a thin-lipped doctor had told him that everything appeared to be in order.

'Did they take everything, sir?'

'Yes.'

'How much in cash?'

'Thirty pounds . . . maybe thirty-five. I forget.'

'Anything else?'

'My watch . . . and an identity bracelet.'

'What make of watch, sir?'

'A Bulova. Gold case.'

'Dear me,' said the sergeant, writing the facts in a ledger. 'Tell me about the captain, if you feel up to it.'

239

'Ginger moustache . . . fair hair . . . well spoken . . . hundred and sixty-five pounds . . . mid-twenties . . .'

'Did you notice anything about his uniform? Anything unusual?'

'No. It looked like a regular British army uniform.'

'What regiment, sir, did you notice?'

'No. Sorry.'

'He's been working this little trick for a couple of weeks. All Americans and Canadians and the like; all officers, all by themselves . . .'

'I'd like to meet that son-of-a-bitch again.'

'I'm sure you would, sir. We would also like to meet him. And in all probability we will. We usually do. These chaps always make a mistake in the end. How are you feeling now, sir?'

'OK,' said Everett. His head ached and he felt rather sick. That limey bastard, so goddam *natural*, so *believable*. One hell of a fine actor, when you got right down to it.

'If it's any comfort,' said the police sergeant, 'we had seven last night. Two Americans, a South African, three Canadians and a New Zealander. All of them were carrying a fair bit of cash on them. He seems to avoid British servicemen. Too poor, I suppose. Or possibly it's his idea of patriotism.'

'Same routine every time?'

'More or less. He seems to be able to sniff out people who are strangers to London. Not very difficult these days, I suppose. We'll get him in the end, sir.'

'Let me know when you do.'

'Rather.'

'Can I get one of the lads to drop you off somewhere, sir?'

Everett shook his head. 'Thanks, but I feel like a walk.'

'Sure you're up to it?'

'I'm sure. Thanks again.'

'Glad to be of service.'

After signing half a dozen forms and answering a score of questions, Everett was permitted to cash a cheque to pay for his hotel, purchase a couple of meals and a train ticket back to Ashley. The USO man was a lip-clicker, a righteous creep; what an unfortunate experience for poor Lt Deane; how careful one had to be in big cities these days. Too many temptations. No doubt the USO man believed that Everett had been rolled in some whore's room. It would have been preferable, in Everett's opinion; at least there might have been a little action for his money.

Breakfast was tea and dry toast. He spent the morning walking. It was Sunday. The streets were quiet. The sun shone first thing but within the hour it had begun to drizzle. The bruise on his head ached; his mouth tasted vile. He felt foolish and ashamed. A prize boob, a perfect mark for the con man in the pub. There he was, the innocent from across the water, overpaid, but not overbright. All it took was a few words, a vague promise or two. His own dirty mind did the rest; it created all the pictures, positioned all the players and equipped them with superbly proportioned breasts and slinky hips, sensuous mouths and daring eyes. For a given sum (gladly given!) they would perform. A little stroke here, sir? Application of tongue here, sir? Possibly a touch here and a tickle there.

He wandered down a narrow street and found himself beside the river. The water was turgid and murky. Bits of paper and wood floated wearily by. Something that looked vaguely like a dead cat soon followed. God knows what lay beneath the surface. How many hopeless lives had ended at this very spot? Sad as hell. But sadder than meeting your end over Germany? Or at an airfield called Ashley, in the County of Surrey, England? His vision blurred; he blinked a tear away. No; he had to fight self-pity; he daren't let it near . . .

I'm not going to die at Ashley, he told himself. I'm going to survive twenty-five missions and live to a ripe old age.

Damn this country. This cheerless place. He hated it. He wanted to go home.

He sat down on a bench. It was damp and cold; he could feel its chill through his clothes. Everything about England was chilly. Why did men fight so passionately to protect it? Let the Germans have it; then they could be sitting here, shivering their guts out, instead of him.

Two small, grubby boys approached.

'Got any gum, Yank?'

'What?... No, I'm sorry; I don't have any...'

'Mean sod.'

'No, you don't understand...'

But the boys had already hurried on.

Jesus, he thought, I'm going to get killed for you little creeps. Isn't that enough? You want gum too?

He got up. Now the rain was falling heavily. He fastened his trench coat about his neck. His train was due to leave in an hour, thank God. It would be pleasant to get back to Ashley and be among his own kind.

He ate a tasteless meal at a restaurant on Vauxhall Bridge Road. The *Sunday Express* informed him that Mahatma Gandhi had just concluded a 21-day fast; 'In Which We Serve' was breaking attendance records in the West End and the RAF had pulverized most of Berlin in its heaviest raid to date. Civilian morale was (according to 'reliable sources') crumbling rapidly; the Reich's leaders were said to be deeply concerned about the situation. 'Hitler and his henchmen know it will worsen', the article reported. 'The Americans are now producing bombers at gigantic factories all over the country. Flying Fortresses and Liberators are pouring off the mass-production lines like Ford cars. Soon they will join the RAF in darkening the skies over Germany.'

Too damned soon, Everett thought.

His stomach churned when he thought of combat, of flying through flak-torn sky and maintaining formation discipline while Messerschmitts and FWs screamed in to attack from every angle. There is a very real possibility, he thought, that I simply don't have the guts. But the people who had selected and trained him seemed to be of the opinion that he was made of what they liked to call 'the right stuff'. They had written 'competent' and 'reliable' in his official records, his 66-1. They were the experts; they were supposed to know. But what about the stories of B-17s that had broken formation under attack? Of pilots that simply couldn't take it? Ironically, they were the first to die because the fighters always pounced upon single aircraft; they were easy meat compared with entire formations.

242

The orders were explicit: stick to the formation through thick and thin. If you see your brother or your best friend damaged and falling behind, let him go.

'In my book,' the Colonel had declared, 'any man who breaks formation to go to the aid of another is guilty of desertion in the face of the goddam enemy. And in the unlikely event that the son-of-a-bitch survives to return to base there'll be a court-martial waiting for him! Your first responsibility is to your Group formation!'

Odd, how some men had responded to the Colonel's words, clenching their fists and scowling, already hating the sons-of-bitches who might one day jeopardize the Group formation.

It wasn't hard to start fearing the Colonel more than the enemy.

The case for daylight precision bombing still had to be proved. The British had declared it to be impossible; according to them, losses would be prohibitive; they said the Eighth should be dedicated to aiding in the night attacks. But the USAAF Generals didn't agree; they said they knew better. And they were quite prepared to back their arguments with a few hundred bombers and crews. If they were all shot down, presumably the Generals would admit to guessing wrong. Back to the drawing board.

He drank some abominable stuff they had the nerve to call coffee.

It was time to catch the train back to Ashley.

Four

The fighters seemed to be concentrating on the B-17 called *Boomerang*. From every point of the compass they darted in, lean Messerschmitts, spitting cannon fire from their noses; the Focke-Wulfs with their distinctive radial engines; twin-engined 110s and 88s, all as easy as hell to recognize, all looking just as the aircraft recognition manuals said they would look.

'Two o'clock . . . low!'

'A pair of Me's. Six o'clock! Got that, ball gunner ?'

'Yeah, I see 'em, for Crissake!'

Voices were harsh with strain. Fear broke sweat out on men's bodies; it froze in the sub-zero temperatures five miles above the earth. The metal hull of the B-17 became ankle deep in brass cartridge cases from the 0.50-inch machine guns.

The aircraft shuddered. For an instant Everett thought he had collided with another machine. Then he realized that they had taken a hit in the nose compartment.

A 20 mm shell had decapitated Johnstone, the navigator. His blood exploded about the cabin; in a moment it became an icy, glutinous mass that hung in ghastly shrouds from bulkheads and longerons. A fiendishly cold blast of air scythed through the compartment. Breithaupt ducked down to see what had happened. White-faced, he told Everett:

'Christ, he's still twitching! He's got no goddam head and he's still twitching!'

It was of only passing importance. A second later Breithaupt was hit in the right shoulder. The arm was almost severed. Breithaupt's eyes rolled back in their sockets; his head lolled to one side.

'Joe. Get up here! Milt's been hit!'

'OK, sir. Be right there.'

DeNiza sounded as unperturbed as ever.

Everett ducked as an FW hurtled in for a flank attack. He felt the thud of missiles hitting the fuselage behind him. The dark shape flashed by, only a few feet away, suicidally close.

Crazy bastard, Everett thought, as if the German were a reckless driver on Route 19. The air was acrid with the stink of cordite.

To the right, a B-17 reared up, banking steeply. Flames streamed from numbers two and three engines. Then a wing folded up, neatly, firmly. The airplane ceased flying. It became a lunatic monster bent on self-destruction. Spinning furiously, trailing flaming debris, it vanished into clouds far below.

In a minute, Everett thought, that'll be us. There was no way to keep surviving this. No way the shells and bullets could keep missing vital parts.

'I hope there isn't a guy called Custer leading this formation,' said Joe.

Everett smiled in spite of himself. A character, that Joe.

Automatically his eyes kept darting over the instrument panel, checking speed, pressures, temperatures; he glanced at the ball in the glass tube: part of the oxygen system; as long as it kept bobbing up and down, the oxygen was flowing correctly. When it stopped, you had a problem and the amount of time you had to correct that problem depended strictly upon your altitude. Incredible that the ball should keep bobbing through all this.

The prop wash of the aircraft ahead kept shoving *Boomerang* aside.

'Keep it in tight, for God's sake! It's getting goddam sloppy!'

The Group Leader's voice rasped in his earphones. He was talking to the entire formation but it was easy to believe that the message was just for you. How could you concentrate on flying formation with the air full of Fritz fighters . . . ?

The tail gunner yelled:

'I got him! I got . . . I did! I got the bastard . . . !'

'What?'

'An Me! He's goin' down . . . burning to beat hell!'

'Keep your eyes peeled, gunners. We're not through the woods yet.'

Why the hell didn't they laugh right back at him? Stupid, obvious statement.

A lull. An intermission between acts. For several minutes the formation flew unchallenged in clear, untroubled skies. The burning aeroplanes and swaying parachutes were left far behind. You could almost make believe that you were touring Surrey by air.

Joe DeNiza appeared beside the pilot's seat, a portable oxygen bottle in one hand. His flying suit was dark with blood. He shook his head.

'I think Milt's gone. He bled . . . I tried to give him morphine but it . . . froze; the thing wouldn't work. Sorry.'

Everett nodded. 'OK. Thanks a lot.'

The crew reported in. Everyone but Johnstone and Breithaupt

was alive and kicking. No navigator, no co-pilot. The gunners were concerned about their ammo. Joe took belts from the front guns, looped them over his shoulders and, looking like a Mexican brigand, made his way aft to the section of the airplane known as Arctic Alley, where the two waist gunners stood beside open hatches, manipulating their heavy guns.

The formation closed ranks. The target was only five minutes away.

Then came the flak. Black puffs dotting the sky ahead: countless puffs, all at the same height, all signifying the detonation of enough high explosive to blow the B-17 and its crew to Kingdom Come.

And suddenly the black puffs were all around. You could hear the snap and bang of the explosions; you could smell the stink of them. Something glanced off the right windshield panel, tearing a deep scar in the plexiglass.

'Jesus, *Cutie Pie* got it!'

A hurried glance to the left. Yes; the B-17 with the indecent nude on the nose . . . only it had no nose now, and no indecent nude. The fuselage ended at the pilots' cabin; forward there was nothing but tangled metal.

'She's still going!'

'Like hell . . . there she goes.'

'Poor bastards . . . any chutes?'

'OK, let's close it up, for Chrissake,' came the Group Leader's voice.

Obediently the remaining bombers edged closer together. Did the German pilots recognize the Group as a bunch of first-timers? Was this the reason for the attention?

The flak had no favourites.

You stared ahead. You waited. You concentrated on your job which was to fly this airplane to the target and drop the bombs and then, in the unlikely event that you were still alive and breathing, you flew the airplane home in order that it might be refuelled and rearmed and generally readied for another expedition over the enemy's homeland.

'Sir . . . Delaney's hit!'

God, no. What the hell can I do about it? I'm flying the

goddam airplane by myself . . . no co-pilot . . .

'How bad?'

'Jesus . . . bad, real bad.'

'OK . . . see what you can do for him.'

'Yeah . . . sure.'

Vaguely disgruntled. Did he think there were half a dozen Red Cross nurses sitting at midships, ready to go to Delaney's aid? Who the hell did he think could be spared, for God's sake . . . ?

'Bomb doors open.'

Target dead ahead. The flak looked thick enough to land on. How did any aircraft manage to survive for more than a few seconds? The fighters were diving through their own flak in their eagerness to get at the bombers. The dry rattle of their guns was audible above the din of the Cyclones.

The red bomb door light blinked on the instrument panel.

Ignore the flak and the fighters. Just fly straight and level because these few moments are what it's all about; they are the reason for all the preparations and all the planning and the briefing and the phenomenal expenditure of effort and money and blood and guts . . .

Concentrate, for Christ's sake!

A sort of dazed calm had come over him. He had lost the capacity to be shocked or scared any more. He knew the outcome of all this; it was simply a question of the moment that was to be decided . . . It was strange, how calm a man could be, once he was resigned to death, once he had finally abandoned hope . . .

A twin-engined Messerschmitt sped across *Boomerang*'s nose. Gunners bellowed in the interphone. Their guns hosed the surrounding air with lead. Someone reported a hit. Someone was always reporting a hit,

Everett's head ached from the rumble and clatter in his earphones.

A hatch door spun past. No time to wonder from which aircraft it had fallen.

Luksic reported that Delaney was still breathing.

'Roger. Thanks.'

Christ, how many of the crew were left? He had lost count. He couldn't remember. He had to think. Johnstone, Delaney, Milt Breithaupt . . . three, seven left . . .

'Bombs away!'

Suddenly lighter by six thousand pounds, *Boomerang* bounded upward.

Two more B-17s went down during the turn-out from the target. A wing tip came within inches of hitting *Boomerang*. The offending Fort skidded away; a gunner sat at the waist hatch watching the near collision without apparent emotion.

'Keep your distance, buster,' said someone on the interphone.

'Cut the chatter, you guys.'

His mouth was dry from breathing pure oxygen too long. His arms ached; the throttles had to be worked ceaselessly to keep the aircraft tightly in formation. You couldn't relax for a moment; you were always travelling too rapidly or too slowly. Spend too many seconds admiring the scenery and your propellers would be chewing someone's tail off. With Milt dead there was no one to spell him. Joe? No; he had been learning the rudiments of flying but he sure as hell didn't know enough to handle a B-17 in formation in combat . . .

Now the fighters came swarming in again. Hornets spitting lead. They loved to roll, these Jerry FWs and Messerschmitts. Did they think it made them tougher targets for the Fort gunners? Maybe they were right.

'Two FWs; six o'clock low!'

'Yeah . . . got 'em in sight!'

'No; they've turned!'

'Don't waste your ammo.'

'I think I hit him.'

'Jesus . . .'

'Eleven o'clock . . . an Me.'

'OK. I see the bastard.'

The B-17 trembled as the machine guns blazed away.

'I hit him! I saw it!'

'Where is he?'

'Dived away . . . smoking.'

'Exhaust smoke.'

'For Christ's sake it wasn't no exhaust smoke.'

'Let's argue about it later, uh?'

'I'm getting low on ammo again. How much longer, sir?'

'I don't know. We haven't got a navigator any more. We're just following everyone else. Make your ammo last.'

'OK, sir.'

Problem solved.

Minutes passed; minutes lost utterly because time had no meaning in the daze of battle. The mind could cope only with the sights of enemy fighters skidding by, firing, always firing; it had to cope with the business of flying this monster in the prop-wash of Christ knows how many other monsters.

'Coast ahead, sir.'

'What?'

Good God, it was the coast. Good God, the airplane was still in the air. Good God, some of the occupants were still alive. Good God, Good God . . .

Over the coast the flak became spiteful again. *Boomerang* bucked in the blast of a near-miss. The hull shook as steel fragments collided at eight hundred miles per hour.

'Everyone OK. Check in.'

It was done by numbers, from the tail, from number one to number nine. Three numbers absent, three numbers representing Johnstone, Delaney and Breithaupt. Everyone absent accounted for.

The crew members were silent during the trip across the Channel. There was much to think about, but little to say.

As the English coast slid into view, the formation began its let-down. No longer was it necessary to fly in tight; you could relax a little and occupy twice as much sky. And you could rip off your oxygen mask and breath real air.

Heaven.

Joe asked if he could be of help during landing.

'Sure. You can read the speed and operate the flaps. OK?'

'You bet.'

From the tail came a plaintive voice: 'Lieutenant, please be sure he pulls the right goddam lever.'

There was such an imploring note in the voice that it set everyone laughing. The laughter died as each man suddenly remembered that he was flying in an aluminium charnel-house; the bodies of crew-mates were only a few feet away.

The English fields were soft and green. Pale sunlight brushed them; the shadows of the lowering Forts were light and grey; they bounded playfully across hedges and ponds, vanishing into trees, re-emerging a little larger, a little bolder.

Ashley.

Neat, straight runways; orderly groups of buildings, clusters of ground crews at every hard-standing, waiting to see who was coming back. At this moment the control tower balcony would be crammed with officers, binoculars at the ready, counting the dots in the sky.

I wonder, thought Everett, if I'll get it this time. The airplane might fall apart when I turn in to land. It might blow up. These things happen.

'Should we fire a red flare, sir?'

Flare? Hell, yes, he had forgotten. A red flare signified the presence of wounded aboard an aircraft; it secured landing priority.

'Right – fire a flare now.'

A green light winked on the control tower. *Boomerang* was clear to land. At the far end of the runway the meat wagon waited, its big red cross visible a mile away.

A gentle turn over the village. No point in stressing a structure full of holes. Little boxy Austins and Standards chugged along the High Street. People stood on the sidewalks, some looking up, pointing, some ignoring the racket overhead. It was the same world of every day; and he had returned to it.

God, but he was tired. He had to fight to keep his eyes from closing. Maybe, he thought, I'll fall asleep and fly the ship into the ground. Maybe that'll be the way Ashley will get me.

'Stand by for landing.'

Incredibly, all the aircraft's systems were in working order. The gear came down; so did the flaps.

'Full flap.'

The runway floated below. Column back. Throttles closed. Patience while she lets her airspeed die. Hold her off; keep her nose up; nudge her rudder to keep her straight; wings level.

Now. Bang – thud.

Not the greatest landing of all time, but they were down. Mission completed. A touch of brake to counter the cross-wind against the huge vertical tail surface. Her speed slackened. She was docile. He let her roll to the end of the strip then turned off to the right where the ambulance waited. Before the propellers had milled to a halt, the medics were running for the tail door, hanging on to their little bags, the prop-blast flattening their fatigues against their bodies.

Everett dragged the helmet off his head. The silence seemed to rush in upon his ear drums, like some strange weight. Behind, the medics were making a hell of a clatter, banging doors and clattering about inside the fuselage.

Joe hauled on the parking brake. He sighed.

'We made it,' he said.

Everett nodded, wearily. He unfastened his harness. I'm alive, he thought. This time I made it. Nice . . . to have made it once at least. I know I won't make it back every time, but I'm glad I did it this time . . .

Major Cohen, the Group Flight Surgeon, scrambled forward to the flight deck. He opened the hatch and disappeared into the nose.

'My God,' he muttered as he returned.

'His name was Johnstone,' said Everett. He wondered why the fact seemed important.

Cohen shook his head. 'Can't do a hell of a lot for him.'

'What about the others?'

'Breithaupt's dead.'

'We figured.'

'Delaney's badly cut up. But he could pull through.'

'Thanks.'

'You OK, Lieutenant?'

Everett nodded. The engines were crackling as they cooled.

'You'd maybe better drop in and see me after debriefing. OK?'

'OK,' said Everett. And promptly forgot all about it.

He and Joe taxied *Boomerang* back to her hard-standing, using only the inboard engines. The ground crew waited, their faces grey with cold.

After shutting down the engines Everett filled out the Form One. Then he dragged his parachute pack back along the length of the fuselage, ignoring the dark blood stains on the torn sides.

'Rough, uh, Lieutenant?' The crew chief sounded sympathetic.

'Rough enough.'

'Glad you made it.'

'Thanks.'

As Everett slumped into the back seat of the jeep he heard one of the ground crew say to another:

'I wouldn't fly with that guy for all the tea in China.'

Joe acted as if the remark hadn't been made. He started talking about going down to The Lion for a few beers after debriefing.

'Terrific,' said Everett, but all he wanted to do was sleep.

The next day, number three engine caught fire during the final approach to landing. A new co-pilot occupied the right-hand seat, a thin young man from New Jersey by the name of Newton. There were frantic moments of opening cowl flaps and closing fuel shut-off valves, feathering and firing the extinguisher. A moment later the aircraft thumped down on the runway. A week later was the Ostend mission. Luksic and Myers were picked off by the fighters. *Boomerang* made it back to Ashley with half the rudder shot away. On touchdown, the starboard undercarriage leg collapsed. The wing slapped the runway, bounced, shed its flap and aileron and buckled like a sheet of paper. The aircraft skidded off the runway and spun to a stop in the middle of the field. The surviving crew members hurled themselves out. But there was no fire. *Boomerang* was a write-off, however, her main spar gone.

Doc Cohen insisted that Everett spend the night in Sick Quarters.

'I've got a dinner date.'

'Cancel it.'

'I'm OK, Major.'

'You are like hell. You've been through a lot in the last couple of weeks.'

'I'm having dinner with some people in Ashley.'

'Call them.'

'OK.' Everett telephoned. In a way it was a relief. He was stupid with fatigue. All that really mattered was sleep.

In the morning Major Cohen examined him. Nothing appeared to be amiss. The surgeon was of the opinion, however, that Lt Deane should be relieved of flying duties for the period of one week.

Everett found himself arguing vehemently. Even as he spoke he wondered why. What was the big hurry to get himself killed? Was it some subconscious desire to get it over and done with as rapidly as possible?

'I'm OK, Major.'

Cohen sighed. He had an ugly, kind face. 'Suit yourself, Lieutenant – but I'm going to keep my eye on you.'

Five

Everett seemed to adopt us as his second family. He would arrive at odd times, usually without warning, almost invariably bearing tins of this and cartons of that. We could offer him nothing in the way of entertainment, but it didn't seem to matter; he told me that it was enough simply to be in our home, with us. I was glad. He was a personable young man. I received a letter from his father, thanking me for the warm hospitality that we had extended to his son; he said that he hoped we would come to Bedford, Massachusetts, after the war; the Deanes would be honoured to have Frances and me as guests. I was touched – and a little embarrassed. We had done nothing more than provide Everett with a few meals and the company of civilians; for this we had been more than adequately recompensed.

Martin came home on leave early in April. He looked half a dozen years older than when I had last seen him. He had done nineteen ops and had collected a DFC which he dismissed with a shrug. ('They send them out by the trainload. I just happened to be around when ours arrived.') Everett came to the house the day after Martin's arrival. The two airmen seemed to hit it off well, comparing notes on the idiocies of their respective military organizations and decimating my supplies of whisky and pale ale. I left them yarning and laughing; it was three o'clock in the morning; I couldn't keep my eyes open any longer. At his noon-time breakfast Martin was complimentary about Everett. 'Jolly good type,' he said. It was the highest of praise. I told Martin some of Everett's bad luck: several crewmen and aeroplanes written off in only a handful of missions. But I didn't tell him about Everett's conviction that he would get killed at Ashley. It was privileged information. I often wondered if Everett regretted telling me; he had never made mention of it since that evening.

In the next few weeks he flew half a dozen missions. His second co-pilot, Newton, was badly injured and shipped back to the United States. His replacement was a Southerner from Georgia, by the name of Fawcett. A frank, likeable young Second Lieutenant of twenty-two, he told Everett: 'Look, sir, I'll be real honest. I get scared shitless when I contemplate flying with you. You've got a reputation, sir. I'll do my best, sir, but please bear in mind that I'm scared shitless at all times.'

They flew three missions without incident. Then they staggered back from Kiel on two engines, the rear-gunner, Priddle, near death and Wolonsky, the new left waist gunner, nursing flak in his shoulder. *Boomerang II* was written off. A new B-17F was assigned to Lt Deane; the crew decided to retain the appellation *Boomerang*; the earlier machines had managed to live up to the name, albeit in sad condition. *Boomerang III* was brand new, undented, unmarked; her hatches fitted tightly; her window panels slid properly; her controls were firm; her plexiglass unmarred.

There were bets among the ground staff on *Boomerang III's* life expectancy. A corporal in the Adjutant's office was offering three to one that it would be lost on either of the next two missions. There were remarkably few takers.

But the new machine seemed to bring the crew luck. They flew to Lorient, to Flensburg, to Wilhelmshaven, to La Pallice, to Rennes, to Hüls, to Cologne, to Hamburg, to Le Mans and to

Nantes: they didn't suffer a scratch. *Boomerang III* acquired a respectable array of swastikas on her nose, each signifying a successful mission.

Then came the Emden mission. Greene, the radio man, was killed over the target; a cannon shell ripped open the B-17's fuselage and almost cut him in half. Ten minutes later, Grogan, the waist gunner who had replaced Luksic, was killed instantly by four 7·9 mm machine gun bullets. Freiburg, the navigator, took a chunk of shrapnel in the left leg; he fainted. Joe DeNiza applied a tourniquet which saved his life. The aircraft's hydraulics were shot away. Everett landed on the emergency runway at Manston. *Boomerang III* was consigned to the scrap heap.

The survivors of the crew were given ten days' leave.

Everett spent three of those days at 47 Harvest Road. He slept in Martin's room, twelve and fourteen hours at a stretch. It seemed to be his greatest need. By the third day, however, he had had his fill of sleep. He was relaxed and cheerful. In the evening we went to the Lido to see a film called 'I Thank You', after which we repaired to The Lion.

It was a pleasant night. We took our time strolling home. Everett told us that he intended to go to Scotland for a few days. His mother's grandfather had emigrated to America from Dundee; he wanted to see something of the city and its environs.

We turned in at the house. I frowned when I saw that the garden gate was unfastened. I always fastened it; I was particular about that sort of thing . . .

The front door opened. Light split out along the path, shattering the blackout.

Georgina stood in the doorway.

'It's Donald,' she said slowly and flatly. 'He's missing.'

There wasn't much to tell about Donald's fate. He had flown to France on an intruder mission. Low-level stuff: a formation of half a dozen Beaufighters. A fellow pilot had seen Donald's aircraft turn away, suddenly, streaming flame. Ground fire had found its mark. He hadn't seen the crash. But nothing more had been heard since then. Nothing from the Germans, nothing from the Red Cross.

'No news is good news,' I murmured, taking her coat and hanging it up by the door.

'Donald's CO came to see me,' said Georgina. 'He was still wearing his flying boots. He said that Donald could have put the machine down safely . . . it's possible.'

'Of course it's possible.'

'But I don't think he believed it had happened.' She looked up at Everett. 'I suppose you're the American mother told me about.'

'Yes,' said Everett. 'I'm very sorry about your husband.'

Georgina nodded. Her face was expressionless. 'So am I,' she said. 'I telephoned here,' she told me, 'but there was no answer. So I got on the first train . . .'

'What time did you get here?'

'Half past seven.'

Frances looked at me, her eyes full of tears.

Our consciences stung as we thought of the poor girl, pacing away the hours while we watched Arthur Askey and chatted in The Lion. We should have known.

Everett packed his bag and returned to his base for the night. We told him it wasn't necessary, but he insisted.

He telephoned the following afternoon. Was there any news about Flying Officer Forbes? I told him no, not yet.

'I'm sure he'll be OK.'

'Of course,' I said.

Everett said he would check again in a few days. He thanked me for everything.

'It was nothing,' I said. I meant it.

I went to Norfolk with Georgina. We talked to Donald's CO, a soft-cheeked boy of about twenty-five. There was still no word, but every effort was being made to find out what had happened. Donald, said the CO, was a good type. I thought of Martin. We picked up Georgina's things from her furnished rooms; the landlady seemed offended that the room was being vacated at such short notice. I explained the circumstances. The landlady said, 'Very unfortunate, I'm sure, but it still makes a difficult situation for me, doesn't it?'

'You're a heartless and evil person,' I informed her.

She was dumbfounded. She gaped at me; she seemed to shrink

physically. But I could take no pleasure in the fact. Georgina and I left.

Five days later the telegram arrived. Donald was alive. A prisoner. The war was over for him. No more flying; no more combat. Georgina cried for an hour. Relief, she said: sheer relief. She felt as if a ton weight had been lifted from her shoulders. I broke out the whisky and rang Beresford.

In the middle of the celebrations, Everett telephoned. He had just returned from Scotland. I told him the good news. He hooted with delight.

'Come on over,' I ordered him. 'Join the fun.'

'Gee, I don't know; it's kind of a family thing, isn't it?'

'We insist.'

'All right,' he said. 'Thanks a lot.'

And that, I suppose, was the beginning.

Thinking back, it's hard to remember when I first realized what was happening. Perhaps Frances knew or guessed; if so she didn't mention it to me.

Georgina expressed some thoughts about going to London and getting a job; but it never seemed to happen. She started helping Frances at Gifts Galore, for a couple of hours a day at first, then for mornings or afternoons, then more or less on a full-time basis. She became the manageress of the tea shop; and very efficient and smart at it she was. She was, after all, an extremely good-looking girl with an excellent clothes sense. She would have been a striking asset to any business of the type; she was responsible for turning the tea shop from a modest success to a veritable gold mine. The American Air Force men were the principal source of revenue. Many of them knew about Georgina's marital situation and asked about Donald. There was, predictably, a certain amount of flirting but she knew how to handle them without offence.

Perhaps I was rather obtuse. Only gradually did I become aware that we hadn't seen anything of Everett for some time. I knew he was still alive because I had heard the girls mention seeing him at the tea room. I supposed that he had at last realized what a dull pair we were at 47 Harvest Road and had found better things to do with his leisure time.

By the middle of Summer, the Eighth was dispatching larger and larger formations against the Third Reich. The B-17s from Ashley were going out almost daily, thundering over the village, making the taped window glass rattle. Sometimes they fired red flares as they returned; sometimes stationary propellers and torn fuselages and wings were mute testimony to the vigour of the defences. Two Fortresses collided and exploded one day in July, spraying the village with burning fuel and fragments of aircraft and crew. Miraculously, no one on the ground was hurt; but twenty airmen had been blown to smithereens by the detonation of their bomb loads. Frances told me that evening that neither of the machines was Everett's. He had telephoned the shop upon his return from the mission. At the time I wondered briefly why he had telephoned the shop and not the house but I hadn't pursued the point.

The next day was Sunday. Georgina went out shortly after breakfast. I sat down at the desk in the drawing room and started a letter to Martin. Frances sat beside me.

'There's something that I think we should talk about.'

I put down my pen, having accomplished nothing more than hoping that Martin was enjoying good health and good weather.

'It's about Georgina.'

'Yes?'

'And Everett.'

'Everett? What about him?'

'She's going to meet him this morning. She's been seeing a great deal of him recently.'

'Who? Everett?'

'Yes. And I'm concerned.'

I reacted in the instinctive way of a man: resenting having to absorb yet another problem and attempting without any real hope of success to dismiss the whole thing as unimportant.

'Well . . . she knows him . . . I mean . . . they met here in this very house.'

'What has that got to do with it?'

I wasn't sure. 'But you don't mean . . .'

Frances sighed. 'Yes, I do, James,' she said in that matter of fact voice that women use to explain basic truths to mere men.

'*Georgina*?'

'Yes, James.'

'But . . . she's a married woman.'

'I'm aware of that fact.'

'You must be wrong.'

She shook her head.

'How do you know?'

'He's been coming into the shop.'

'What proof is that?'

'I've overheard . . . certain things . . .'

'What things?'

'It doesn't matter. Besides, I also heard two of his friends talking.'

'Georgina wouldn't do anything like that.' I said it loudly. But not firmly. I wanted to prove Frances wrong. But in my heart I knew it was hopeless. Frances would never have breathed a word unless she was absolutely certain.

'Have you talked to her about . . . it?'

'Not yet.'

I looked about the desk as if expecting to find the answer among the notepaper and envelopes.

'What are we going to do about it?'

'I don't know,' said Frances.

'Christ almighty . . . Donald a prisoner . . .' I wanted to kick something. 'I still can't believe one of my children would behave so . . . so badly.'

'We did,' said Frances.

I glared at her. 'We weren't married.'

'Would it have made any difference?'

I didn't answer. I didn't have to. I mumbled something about it not being the point; but it was, of course.

Georgina came home shortly after eleven that evening. The news was still on; Alvar Liddell was talking about the turn of the tide in Russia.

Georgina looked in the drawing room; she grinned as if she didn't have a care in the world. She started to wish us goodnight, but Frances cut her short.

259

'We'd like you to come in here.'

'Now?' I suppose she knew what was coming.

'Yes, please.'

I was on the point of saying that it was late and we may as well leave it until the morning; but Frances was right; we had to face the problem sooner or later.

'I'll just hang up my coat.'

'Very well.'

We heard her moving about in the hall. We looked at one another; we shuddered. Family rows could bo so horribly destructive, tearing away the fabric of love and respect that has been so painstakingly created over the years.

Georgina returned. Her lips were tightly set. She sat down beside the empty fireplace.

'I think I know what you want to talk about.'

'It's Everett,' I said.

She nodded.

'I'm very sorry, Daddy,' she said.

'I ... can't believe that you would ... actually be seeing another man when your husband is ... a prisoner.'

'I couldn't have believed it if you had told me about it six months ago.'

'It's true, then.'

'Yes.' She held her head high but her eyes had fallen on the dials of the Cossor wireless set; she seemed mesmerized by them.

'I'm ashamed of you,' said Frances.

Georgina nodded, still gazing at the wireless knobs. 'I understand how you feel. I am awfully sorry to have ... burdened you with it.' At last she looked at us. 'I'll leave the first thing in the morning. I'll get a room somewhere.'

'That won't solve anything,' said Frances.

'Of course it won't,' I added.

Georgina spread her hands. 'Look,' she said, 'I didn't want this to happen. I mean, I didn't look for someone to while away the hours until Donald came home. It wasn't like that. I'm not even sure I know just how it did happen. But what I do know now is that I love Everett far more deeply than I ever loved Donald. Don't ask me why. I don't know. I'm not proud of what has

260

happened; but it's a fact and I'm prepared to take my medicine.'

'But Donald's a prisoner . . .'

'I know. And he must hate me. He must think me despicable. But it doesn't change anything.'

'That wretched American,' Frances muttered. 'After everything we've done for him; what a way to repay us . . .'

'It has nothing to do with you or Daddy or what you did for him. Don't you see that?'

'No,' said Frances, 'I most certainly don't.'

'We both tried,' said Georgina. 'I know you probably don't believe me, but it's true. Because of Donald and you . . . we both tried.'

Something Georgina said earlier suddenly triggered a thought in my befuddled brain. 'You say that Donald must hate you? You mean you've told him?'

'Yes. I wrote to him more than a fortnight ago.'

'Why?'

'Don't you think he deserves to know the truth?'

'Yes, but . . .'

'This isn't a foolish flirtation, Daddy. This isn't something that will blow away in a couple of weeks. Something terribly important has happened to me, something that has changed my whole life. I had to tell Donald. He had to know.'

'He must have enjoyed reading your letter.'

'Would it have been better not to mention anything about it? Would it have been better to have pretended that everything was just as he left it?'

'Yes,' I muttered. 'I think so.'

'I'm not very good at pretending,' said Georgina.

By midnight all the acrimony had been aired. Gradually it stopped being us against Georgina; the three of us found ourselves talking about the subject as if it was an illness or a financial matter, a family problem which between us we wanted to solve. In a way I suppose it was a credit to our family that it went that way; at least, I like to think so. Soon I had the sense to realize that there really wasn't anything more for me to say. In a way, it was none of my business. It was a matter between the youngsters. Everything in the entire world seemed to be the concern of youngsters.

I went to bed.

Everett telephoned the next morning.

'Sir,' he said, 'I know you must be as mad as hell at me. And I'm sorry. Really. Georgina said she had told you.'

'Yes,' I said.

'I'm glad ... in a way. Look sir, we've talked it all out. I've got five more missions to fly ...'

'Five?' I didn't know he had completed so many.

'Yes, sir. If I get to finish my tour I'll go back to the States. With a bit of luck, I'll make it through the war. Georgina says if I finish my tour, she will institute divorce proceedings.'

'What if you don't make it to twenty-five?'

'Georgina has told her husband about ... us. She says he's most likely to want to divorce her; and of course she won't stand in his way.'

'I see.' They talked so casually about divorce.

'I'm very sorry about this, sir. I've hurt you and your wife ... after you've been so good to me. I want you to know that ...' I could hear voices at the other end of the line: someone asking for Charlie Veltkamp, someone else complaining about the bus service to London. 'I want you to know that this isn't something we've gotten into ... lightly.'

'I should hope not,' I said. 'It's a dangerous game, taking up with another man's wife.'

'I know, sir. And under the circumstances – his being a POW and everything – it seems even worse. We feel badly about it.'

'Everyone seems to feel badly about it,' I said.

'Yes, sir. I guess they do. And it's understandable. I know I've done the ... wrong thing ... and yet I'm not sorry about it; I'm glad. Do you know what I mean, sir?'

'I suppose so.'

'Georgina and I want to marry.'

'So she's told us.'

'I'll make her a good husband, sir.'

'Good,' I said. Frostily. I wondered whether he would live long enough to marry her.

'My family isn't rich, sir, but I guess you could say they're

262

comfortable. I can provide for her, sir. I only have one year of College left.'

They had worked everything out between them. And they seemed to feel that they owed us all the facts. No secrets. Complete plan out on the table for everyone to see. Plan A if Everett survived his tour, Plan B if he didn't.

Sometimes I think there's a great deal to be said for subterfuge and deceit.

The adaptability of the well-balanced family is the sum of the adaptability of the individuals comprising the family. We absorbed the problem of Georgina, Everett and Donald. We had our respective says. Then we avoided the subject like the plague. We went about our daily business pretending it didn't exist. We pretended superbly. Perhaps it was that our love for one another was of far more importance to us than the problem at hand; perhaps it was simply the instinctive British dislike of making a fuss. In any event, we seemed to be able to convince ourselves that our earnest, well-meaning discussions had solved it all. They hadn't of course. All we could do was to wait and see whether Everett survived his twenty-five missions. Plan A or Plan B. We heard the Forts go out. We heard them return. The telephone would ring. He was back. Relief combined with the beginnings of fear for the next trip. Although he kept returning, Everett had more bad luck in a score of missions than most crews experienced in a hundred. So far he had earned only an Air Medal. His fellow airmen at Ashley were of the opinion that the members of his crew should each receive the Congessional Medal of Honour just for going up in an airplane with him. It was unfair, because Everett was the most painstakingly by-the-book pilot on the base. He kept doing everything correctly but circumstances kept outmanoeuvring him.

I saw nothing of Everett for most of that rather peculiar period in our lives, although Frances encountered him in the shop from time to time. She reported that he looked well enough but rather tired and strained. I said, huffily, that I didn't wish to know anything about him or his state of health. It wasn't true, but there seem to be times in life when one is compelled to make what one thinks of as the right sort of response. It's more for one's own benefit, I fancy, than anyone else's. The weeks passed. In spite of myself I began to talk about Georgina-and-Everett rather than Donald-and-Georgina-and-Everett. Donald, poor chap, was being shunted out of the picture without being able to lift a finger on his own behalf. It was unfair as hell; damn it, it was monstrous. Which is precisely the way war should be described. Donald's marriage was one of the casualties.

The 19th of July was Georgina's birthday. At dinner we had a bottle of wine and a somewhat tasteless birthday cake (courtesy of the Ministry of Food). Shortly after the meal, Georgina went out. She returned half an hour later with Everett. There were a few awkward moments, but not many. The fact of the matter is, only a totally soulless individual could fail to respond to two young people who are deeply in love and to whom time is the most precious commodity. By the end of the evening Frances and I had surrendered, unconditionally. I remember how warmly I shook Everett's hand.

'Thanks, Mr Marshall,' he said simply.

'Don't mention it,' I responded in automatic British fashion, as if acknowledging thanks for a glass of beer.

On the 24th of July the Group flew to Norway to bomb the nitrate factory just completed by the Germans at Heroya. Flak punched a dozen small holes in *Boomerang IV*'s wings and tail. It was minor battle damage. But *Boomerang* was the only aircraft in the Group that was touched. The following day it was Hamburg. The city was still ablaze from the RAF raid of the previous night (in which Martin participated); smoke towered fifteen thousand feet above the city. Angered by the appalling destruction, the German fighter pilots were fearless. They swarmed in to attack the Fortresses from every angle. *Boomerang IV* lost part of her rudder and hydraulic system, but she got home and her crew was unharmed. The next day the target was Hanover: the Continental Gummi-Werke. Everett and his crew flew a borrowed aircraft because *Boomerang* was in the repair shop. The borrowed machine was almost cut in half by a blazing Messerschmitt's wing. On touch-down, the fuselage folded and broke. Another mission was scheduled for the next day but bad weather caused it to be scrubbed. Exhausted, the crews slept through most of the daylight hours. They were called in the early morning, for a dawn take-off. The target was Kassel. Everett and his crew were assigned to a B-17 named *Duchess*. They returned on two engines, with both waist gunners wounded.

Number twenty-four had been completed.

Six

The mist clung to the ground longer than expected. Take-off was postponed two hours. Then another hour.

'My personal opinion,' said Joe DeNiza, 'is that they're trying to make me lose interest in this mission.'

Everett smiled. He was fond of Joe: one of the few survivors of the original crew. The New Yorker was as unperturbable now as he had been on the first trip. Nothing fazed Joe.

Everett had slept badly. His dreams were jagged fragments of past missions: screaming, skidding fighters, the stink of cordite, the thud of flak: helplessness, waiting for the inevitable. Voices mocking him and his hopes of finishing twenty-five. And Ashley. God, how the place had implanted itself on his consciousness. It was just another airfield with runways and hangars; a small village nearby. And yet it had changed his life. His whole existence, all his hopes and fears revolved around it. And only a few months ago he hadn't heard of it.

The coffee wagon called at the dispersals. Everyone was dry, but no one dared drink much; a full bladder is agonizing at 30,000 feet.

The Air Exec's jeep came bounding around the peri track. Start engines in forty-five minutes; take-off in one hour. On the nose.

'For sure?'

'For sure.' The jeep roared to the next dispersal.

Everett had visually inspected *Boomerang IV* hours ago; when the first light was creeping over the horizon. But he went through the motions again, partly to use up a few more minutes, partly to reassure himself that she was really sound in wind and limb after her major work in the hangars. He had learnt the sequence so long ago; he seemed to have spent most of his life looking at the various components of B-17s. Ball turrets; locked position, guns stowed, door locked; main wheels: tyres sound, no cracks along the flanges in the rim; hydraulic lines, drag links, drag struts, oleo cylinders and axle knuckles, wheel nacelles, pulleys, electrical wiring, turbo wheels, waste gates, cowl flaps, inspection plates, drain plugs, de-icer boots, fuel caps and gaskets, air ducts, governor cables, cooling fins, pitot tubes, antennae, bomb bay tank vent, marker beacon, tailwheel shear pin and slot . . .

Fawcett was settled in the right-hand seat on the flight deck, clutching his check-list as if it had religious significance. He took his duties as co-pilot seriously.

'Gear switch.'

'Gear switch neutral,' Everett responded, placing his hand upon the lever that activated the undercarriage mechanism, in the manner prescribed by the manual.

'Intercoolers.'

'Intercoolers cold.'

Fifteen minutes later, *Boomerang IV* rumbled and swayed off her hard-standing.

Her ground crew watched her, hands in pockets, caps thrust forward or back. They wore dirty coveralls, the uniform of their trade. They were tired, having worked most of the night to ready the machine. They shook their heads as the big aeroplane taxied away. Would it get back? Would it make the magic twenty-five? No one would bet on it. That Lt Deane had had all the stinking luck that a pilot could have – except that he kept on coming back. If he held true to form, it would be him who made it back, with all the crew dead and the airplane shot to hell. No wonder the crew looked tense; poor guys, who could blame them? Only that crazy engineer, DeNiza, didn't seem to give a goddam about anything.

The sun broke through the hazy cloud as the B-17s queued up, nose to tail, nose to tail, engines rumbling, propellers churning the humid air, as they waited their turn to take off.

Everett's eyes darted among the instruments. Oil pressure OK at 70 pounds, oil temperature 68 degrees, cylinder head temperature 170 degrees, fuel pressure 18 pounds, carburettor air temperature 38 degrees, tachometers steady, manifold pressures steady, hydraulic pressures 800 pounds. Trim tabs set at zero. Turbo controls off; propellers from low rpm to high; tachometer drop 350 rpm. Voltage output OK. Pilot heaters OK. Turbos to take-off setting.

Prince Pete turned on to the runway and began her roll.

'Unlock brakes.'

'Brakes unlocked.'

Engines idling at 900 rpm, *Boomerang IV* moved forward; her nose swung to face the two thousand yards of runway.

'All windows closed and locked?'

Affirmative.

'Take-off check.'

'Booster pumps.'

'Lock tailwheel.'

'Stand by for take-off.'

'Tailwheel locked. Lights out. Gyros.'

'Gyros set.'

'Generators.'

During the take-off run Fawcett's hands were on the controls, ready to take over in an emergency; his eyes scanned the engine's instruments: the manifold pressure, tachometers, pressure gauges and temperature gauges.

'Sixty . . . sixty-five . . . seventy . . .'

The paved road unrolled beneath *Boomerang*'s nose. She was accelerating well, but she was still a creature of the ground. In the distance, the oak trees could be seen – the trees that old man Marshall crashed into a hundred years ago.

'Ninety . . . ninety-five . . .'

Now she had the right idea. Her wings were shaping the air that streamed over them, forcing it to work, to create lift, to accept the fifty thousand pounds of aeroplane, crew and bomb load.

267

'One hundred . . . one-o-five . . .'

Just in time. The end of the runway was clearly visible. School-boys in grey caps leant against the fence, watching the Forts take off.

The book said the B-17 had to leave the ground from a tail-down position.

That fact alone was enough to ensure that some pilots would invariably put their machines up on to their main wheels before lifting off. Everett had never attempted a two-wheel take-off. Un-adventurous of him, perhaps; but he had never felt any desire to prove the manual wrong.

The ground fell away. Everett eased the column forward. The boys with grey caps had pink faces that were upturned as the Fort sped over their heads. Airspeed one twenty, one thirty, one thirty-five . . . He nodded to Fawcett, who applied brakes, then retracted the gear. Everett glanced out of his window.

'Landing gear up left.'

'Landing gear up right,' Fawcett responded.

Joe reported that the tailwheel was locked away correctly.

Fawcett shifted the gear switch to neutral. It wouldn't be needed again until the magic twenty-fifth was over.

Speed one-forty, cylinder-head temperatures two-o-five, twenty-three hundred rpm . . .

It seemed to take an age to organize the group that day. B-17s were wheeling around the sky for many more minutes than the planners had anticipated. One machine had an engine failure soon after take-off and had to return to Ashley. Another experienced a failure of the interphone system; it too returned to Ashley whereupon the interphone operated perfectly.

The sky cleared completely as the formation climbed over the Channel. It looked blue and inviting down there, the tiny ships looking like insects with little white tails.

A B-17 from the lead group passed below, heading back to England. Presumably it was suffering from some malady, but from *Boomerang* it looked in good shape. The crew would un-doubtedly be enduring that familiar feeling of relief mixed with frustration endured by all crews whose missions are cancelled or aborted. Although there is some gratification in knowing that your chances of being alive tomorrow were now much better than those of the crews that had gone ahead, it solved nothing. The war wouldn't end. You'd still have to do your twenty-five.

Everett prayed that nothing would go wrong with *Boomerang*. He wanted to get this ride over more than anything he had ever wanted.

You've got to get back, he told himself, you've got to. Only one more mission. Take off, fly to the target, release the bombs, fly back to Ashley.

That's all. A milk run. Let the Germans be caught off-guard, let it be a national holiday there or a general strike of fighter pilots and flak gunners. Just let me get there and get back. Please.

The sun was dazzling. Not a cloud to be seen. Picture book weather. The sort of weather the planners had in mind when they conceived the idea of a great fleet of Flying Fortresses utilizing the incredible Norden bombsight to pinpoint and annihilate targets twenty thousand feet below. All too often the great scheme had been frustrated by clouds and rain. Europe wasn't precision bombing country.

The coast was plainly visible. Some of the gunners were testing and warming their guns. Snatches of smoke were whipped by the wind from the muzzles of the point-fifties. One of the gunners in the 100th Bomb Group was said to have killed the co-pilot of a friendly machine while testing his guns; the other Fort wandered into his line of fire just as he pressed the trigger. According to rumour, he was charged with murder in a full-scale court-martial. But no one seemed to have heard what happened after that.

Oxygen check every ten minutes.

Everyone still alive and kicking.

If they recalled missions after the enemy coast had been crossed, they usually counted the trip as a mission flown . . . But there would be no recall today.

Ahead flak was already staining the clear sky. The gunners were on the ball as far as altitude was concerned. Incredible that they hadn't hit anyone yet. The level was perfect but the shells kept exploding in the cubic foot of sky which had just been vacated by a Fort or which was about to be occupied by same . . .

'Gunners, watch for fighters.'

Officially it was Fawcett's job to coordinate the defensive fire of the aircraft. In practice, it was usually a question of every gunner blazing away at anything that came within range.

The fighters had to leave; their fuel supplies were getting low. They waggled their wings in farewell. A hundred fingers aboard the B-17s were raised in derisive reply. Nice deal, the fighter boys had. Just a quick flip over the Channel, then buzz home to the broads and booze at base while the Forts slogged on alone. It was said that the P-47s would soon be equipped with drop tanks beneath their bellies, enabling them to fly escort missions deep into the Continent. But when?

Meade, the navigator, reported that the winds were becoming far stronger than Met had predicted. Everett winced as he felt the sting of fear deep within him. Strong winds could add many minutes, perhaps even an hour, to the mission. They might make all the difference between the formation getting back in daylight or after dark. No one liked night returns. There wasn't enough night-flying experience among the crews; the danger of collision was tripled or quadrupled.

'Fighters! Two o'clock high!'

Yes, there they were, climbing for altitude. God only knows how many of them.

'OK,' said Fawcett to his gunners, 'now let's keep our eyes *peeled*, uh?'

He sounded like a Southern football coach. Perhaps the tone had been borrowed from some high school game. It had worked then; the home town team had won; maybe it would again.

'Bastards are getting against the sun.'

Predictable.

Oxygen check. Everyone still alive and kicking.

'Anyone see those goddam fighters now?'

'No! The sun . . .'

'Yeah, I see one!'

'Where?'

'One o'clock. High . . . high!'

A moment later, the mechanical rap-rap-rap of their guns. And out of the sun they came, skidding, sliding across the flight path of the formation, half-rolling between the Forts while every

270

gunner sprayed lead in wild arcs, screaming invective over the interphone. A moment's respite. The first pass was done. No one hurt. *Boomerang* had not, apparently, been a target. Everyone responded; everyone still alive and kicking.

'Two o'clock high!'

'Dead ahead!'

The Fort trembled with the vibration of the defending machine guns.

Ahead, a Fort suddenly turned to the right: vertical bank. Almost certainly the pilot had been hit; you would tear a Fort's wings off doing that. The first B-17 slammed into a second. The explosion shook the sky. The formation was shaken, its elements scattered as burning fragments spun and twisted, then fell. One B-17 got into the prop-wash of the machine ahead. It reared like a frightened horse. It almost stalled. The machine behind nearly ran into its tail. Incredibly the formation sorted itself out. Ranks were closed. Before the last fragment had hit the ground the formation was again serene; neat and organized, presenting a well organized battery of guns against attackers.

The fighters kept swarming in. One suddenly streamed smoke and spun away towards the earth. A dozen gunners claimed him as theirs. Another Fort went down, turning slowly on to its back and remaining in this position as it plunged. No one saw any chutes.

Tough.

An FW came crabbing at colossal speed across *Boomerang*'s nose. You could see the flames darting from his wings and cowling. He had a bright red spinner. His canopy glinted in the sun; the pilot was hunched in his seat, his shoulder harness taut. His flight jacket was white.

He had gone. Somewhere.

Another took his place, diving almost straight through the formation. They were brave, the Kraut fliers. But so were American fighter pilots. And wouldn't they be just as tenacious if they were defending Cleveland ... or would they? Was Cleveland worth dying for?

'I got that son-of-a-bitch! I did! For Crissake, I got him!'

'OK, let's cut out the chatter. Stick to essentials.'

'But I got him. I'm claiming him.'

Everyone still alive and kicking? Yes. Yes. Yes. Yes. Yes. Yes. Yes. Yes. Yes.

He had a curious feeling of being a spectator. He could do nothing to influence events; it was all out of his hands. Luck would be the decider. In an odd sort of way it removed the tension. Why worry about something when it will do no good? He watched. The good guys and the bad guys. It was like the Saturday matinee back home. A dime for the ticket; a nickel for the popcorn. One good guy down: trailing black, oily smoke that described a gentle descending curve. One chute, two, three . . .

The twin-engined jobs tended to stay out of range and lob rockets into the formation. Their accuracy was poor. But when the rockets struck home, the effects were devastating. A smooth, powerful, well-proportioned bomber became an ugly carcass of metal, burning and exploding until there was nothing left of it or the ten men who flew it.

The fighters seemed always to be skidding across the sky. At times they appeared to be out of control but it was simply the odd illusion created by the converging lines of flight.

Strained, frightened voices kept barking in his head set. They became one voice, wailing at the plight of the men who hurled missiles at one another in the sky, who risked awful death, who laid cities to waste and slaughtered innocents by the thousand and who were praised and admired for their work . . .

Another Fort.

One wing ablaze from tip to root. Incredibly, the machine maintained its place in the formation. The flames streamed back, apparently endangering the machines immediately behind. But they didn't appear to adjust their positions.

'Jump!' yelled someone, urgently, as if the men aboard the doomed Fort could hear. 'Now, for Crissake!'

Too late. The blazing wing folded. The Fort vanished earthward, plummeting like a stone.

'Why the hell didn't you jump . . . ?'

The voice had an oddly bad-tempered tone.

An Me sped by to the left. Everett eased *Boomerang* down in order to give the gunners an extra fraction of a second of target . . . The aircraft trembled as the guns blazed away. But no one claimed the Me.

'Two minutes to IP.'

The 8:45 from Hartford will be pulling into Grand Central in two minutes.

When the formation reached the Initial Point, the bombardiers would take control of the individual aircraft. Until the bombs were released, the airplane commanders were virtual passengers.

Crew check. Everyone still alive and kicking.

'Any damage to report, anyone?'

Negative.

So far – although one hardly dared mention the fact even to oneself – dear old *Boomerang* was untouched. Luck, please hold. Please let the fighters choose other targets. Please let the flak miss. Please let me get back to . . . being alive and loving Georgina.

'IP coming up.'

'OK, she's all yours.'

'Bomb doors open.'

The red light winked on the instrument panel. Next to it, still dark, was the indicator light that would indicate the release of the load of thousand-pound general purpose bombs stacked neatly immediately behind the pilots' cabin.

An FW streaked past, half-rolling away from the formation. Did he fire at *Boomerang*? If so, he missed. How did the German pilots select their targets? Did some Forts look more appetizing than others? Or did they just hurl themselves at the formation and did one target simply loom larger than the others? Luck again. Blind, stinking luck. You sat and you felt the drumming of the engines and the shivering of the airplane as the guns fired. All you could do was to hope for the best. Russian roulette five miles above the earth. Next time, next pass, the fighter might select you. The more chances you took, the fewer you had left.

Suddenly someone was screaming – but with laughter. The noise hurt.

'What the hell . . . ?'

'Did you see that, for Crissake?'

'No, what?'

'That goddam FW ... it got hit by his own flak! He did! I swear to God he did! Took his whole right wing off! Funny as hell!'

Funny. You had to hand it to the Kraut fighter pilots. They had guts. They ran the same risks from flak as did the bombers, but they kept on coming.

'Bombs away.'

Thank Christ. Red light.

'Bomb doors closed.' Red light out.

Tiny black dots, hundreds of them, plunged towards the city below.

A Fort followed its bombs. It had been blown in two by a direct flak hit. The nose and wings went first, then the tail section. As the torn aft fuselage spun, Everett caught a glimpse of one of the waist gunners struggling on the floor. Was he injured? Trapped by torn metal? No one reported any chutes.

Tough.

Flak bursts created a line of black smudges, like drops from a leaky pen. Nearby, Forts wobbled and swayed, but kept on flying.

'You know,' said the bombardier, 'that wasn't a half bad drop.'

Everett felt himself grinning into his oxygen mask. A good drop. Great. There was nothing in the world more infuriating than flying halfway across Europe and being shot at all the time and at the end of it all missing the goddam target. Three cheers for a good drop that may contribute to the shortening of the war by a millisecond or two.

The flak eased as the formation left their target, a pillar of smoke in the sparkling sky. But the fighters kept up their assaults, wave after wave of them, diving, soaring, rolling – and *skidding*, always *skidding* – in to savage the bombers. They attacked, used up their ammunition and fuel, buzzed back to the nearest base for re-armament and refuelling, then it was back into the air again to try and knock out a few more Forts on their way home. They hated the bombers. And, presumably, their crews. *Terrorflieger*, they called them.

Wryly, Everett thought: There's an RAF prisoner somewhere down there who probably hates me more than any of them.

I'm genuinely sorry, he said silently to Donald Forbes.

Hypocrite. If you felt so goddam sorry about it you'd tell Georgina that it was all over. And you won't do that because you want her . . .

If I get killed on this mission, he thought, *she's going to be in a hell of a situation. Poor kid, she'll have lost two men . . .*

He wondered if it was love, thinking only of her problem, not his own.

A Ju 88 banked in close to the formation and fired its load of rockets. One streaked beneath *Boomerang*'s belly. Plant, the ball turret gunner, said that he felt its heat through his plexiglass shell.

The fighters were still coming out of the sun. But now the sun seemed to be on the formation's level, and it was steadily sinking. Soon the shadows would be long and beautiful on the ground . . . the blessed, solid ground that he would never, ever leave again, willingly. He had had enough of flying to last him the rest of his life. He never wanted to see another airplane. Let some other guys be the heroes. All he wanted to do was live . . .

Christ, he was day-dreaming! Was his brain going sour on him? A crew depended on him, for God's sake! Damn, he should have shaved again before take-off; his stubble was rubbing against the oxygen mask; it would be sore in the morning.

If there was a morning.

A Fort was hit. Streaming burning fuel, it turned out of the formation. One wheel hung limply from its nacelle; the tyre was aflame. The crew jumped, one after the other: nine chutes opened. But not the tenth. The Fort snapped into a spin and took the pilot to his death. It was an oft-told story. The pilot held the crippled bomber in more or less level flight so that the crew could jump, but crippled airplanes won't fly by themselves. When it came to his turn there was no one left to fly the airplane. The moment he left his seat to jump, the plane plunged. Centrifugal force probably pinned the poor bastard to the floor; all he could do was count the seconds until impact. How many seconds? And how long did each one seem? But then, *finis*. No lingering. No wondering whether the doctor would say that the tests were positive or negative.

Damage check. None.

Unbelievable. No hits. And everyone *still* alive and kicking.

According to Meade, the ETA at Ashley would be forty-three minutes after sunset. Meade had all the times, Double British Summer Time, Greenwich Mean, Daylight Saving, and all the rest of them. He was the only man in the world who could explain them and what they meant. So if he said it was going to be a night landing, there was no point in arguing the point.

A grey FW zoomed down through the formation. Crazy swine. He was liable to hit someone doing a damn fool trick like that . . .

God knows how many Forts had gone down. This must have been the worst day in the Eighth's history. The formation looked slight now; and it was badly spread, elongated, stretched out of shape. The Group Leader kept snapping at the pilots to close it up, but it was tough to fly a great formation when you were ducking FWs and Messerschmitts. Far below a couple of stragglers could be seen. Fighters buzzed about them like flies at a dying carcass.

He squinted ahead. Yes, it was the coast! The Channel, the No-Man's Land between enemy territory and the friendly skies of Britain. Where the hell were the P-47s? Where was the rendezvous? Almost instantly he saw them. The whole formation was crabbing, just like the Kraut fighters. Someone was chortling happily about the US Cavalry, arriving in the nick of time. Fawcett told him to can it.

The P-47s had waded into the Kraut fighters and they were all miles away, scrapping and shooting the hell out of each other. The Forts were left in relative peace. Only the occasional German fighter was able to tear loose from the dog-fights to continue the attacks on the Forts. After the mass assaults, the single fighters were relegated in men's minds to minor irritations. Which wasn't so clever; one fighter could shoot you down as rapidly as one hundred.

Flak got one last Fort over the coastline. A direct hit blew most of its tail off. Like a wounded beast, it tried to keep going. Erratically, awkwardly, it staggered. Four of the crew jumped. Then gravity would be denied no longer. The Fort tumbled, forlorn bits of debris fluttering in its wake.

How many Forts had been lost? Everett shook his head. It was better not to attempt a calculation; the mission wasn't yet completed. But the crew was relaxing now. As far as they were concerned it was as good as over. They had beaten the odds once more. No doubt they were all wondering at the whimsy of fate: *Boomerang* was the hard luck ship and yet on the day when the Eighth got itself slaughtered, not a single bullet or shell had hit it,

The P-47s had tucked themselves around the Forts – well out of range, for they were only too conscious of the B-17's gunners' propensity for blazing away at anything that flew within a quarter of a mile, whether it bore the white star of the United States, the red, white and blue RAF roundel or the black cross of the Third Reich.

Cylinder head temperature two-twenty; oil temperature a whisker over seventy-five; oil pressure seventy-five; fuel pressure sixteen.

Everything fine and dandy. *Boomerang* was in perfect working order. She might have gone for a half-hour check ride down to Brighton and back instead of ploughing through an aerial battlefield on which God only knows how many men, Americans and Germans, were killed and maimed. Who could ever calculate the misery the day's mission had caused?

'Coast ahead!'

'You're sure it's the British coast?'

'Of course,' said the navigator. A good navigator, but no sense of humour.

It was almost dark as the airmen tugged off their oxygen masks and gratefully breathed in crisp, clear air. Below them, the land was shrouded in purples and blues. The air was calm now, except where the Forts were carving furrows. But it was desirable to stay well away from the other aircraft in the formation. With darkness closing in, collisions were an ever-present danger.

The formation began to break up as the Groups – what was left of them – headed away to their individual bases. By now the ground was invisible, but there was still light in the sky. The undersides of the Forts caught the last glimmers; their fuselages were deep in shadow. Joe assembled his camera and clicked away happily.

'Nice tones,' he said. 'Great shot. I'll send it to *Yank*. They'll print it and maybe pay me a hundred bucks.'

'Like hell,' said someone.

Wing tip navigation lights, tiny dots of red and green, swayed in the semi-darkness.

Everett settled himself in his seat and prepared for the business of getting *Boomerang* safely back to earth. Fawcett called for the crew to take their landing positions.

'And gunners, make sure your guns are properly stowed for landing.'

None of the gunners responded. No doubt they were irritated by the reminder.

In the distance a ribbon of light suddenly appeared. Everett smiled. A welcome sight: the Ashley runway, all lit up, ready to receive the birds home.

'Auto pilot off.'

'Booster pumps on.'

'Mixture controls auto-rich.'

'Intercoolers off.'

'Carburettor filters on.'

A red flare shot through the darkness ahead. Someone had wounded aboard and requested priority for landing. Another flare, from a different direction. A moment later, a third. The boys had had a rough day.

Down there Georgina was waiting. Chances are, she was out there, trying to count the ships as they returned. She knew what the red flares meant. Poor kid, she was probably sick with apprehension; a hell of a lot depended on *Boomerang*'s safe return . . .

He flew parallel to the runway at one thousand feet. It looked cosy and inviting down there; the landing lights imparted a silvery look to the runway surface. One B-17 was turning off the runway at the end of its landing run; another was just touching down on the patch of rubber smears.

'Gear down. And locked.'

Speed one-fifty.

He had started his cross-wind turn, when the warning crackled through on VHF:

'Enemy aircraft in the vicinity! Repeat: enemy aircraft in the vicinity! Kill your lights!'

An instant later the air became alive with streams of streaking flashes.

'Christ, there's one on our tail!'

Everett winced as he felt the bullets thudding into *Boomerang*'s wings and body.

Bastards! The Krauts had followed the formation home, hungry for easy victories over vulnerable Forts in the landing pattern with gear down, and displaying more lights than a Christmas tree, their crews half asleep . . .

At once number three engine burst into flames. In the darkness the fire was almost blinding in its intensity. Fawcett's mouth had dropped open; he seemed to be stunned. Everett yelled at him.

'Feather three! I've got the valve!'

Fawcett snapped to. He punched the feathering button and simultaneously cut the mixture control and ignition.

The interphone crackled.

'Son-of-a-bitch is still on us!'

Full power. No time for the niceties of the normal go-around.

'Jesus . . . my ammo!'

Confused, frightened voices. Everyone hitting their jackboxes at once, trying to convey what they could of the sudden attack.

Inside that blazing cowling, carbon dioxide was being discharged over the engine. But it wasn't having any effect.

'Look out . . .!'

Boomerang shuddered as missiles ripped through her fragile metal skin and tore holes in her structure.

'Number four, for Crissake . . .!'

God, the whole wing seemed to be ablaze!

Despair clutched Everett's heart. This was where his luck ran out. This was where it all would end. So bloody near . . .

'Prepare to bale out! I'm climbing!'

The wing was a frightful smear of flame. Incredibly it was still doing its job of converting the speeding air into lift. But in a moment it would fold or tear away . . . or the entire ship would blow up . . .

'Fifteen hundred feet.'

'OK, go! Get out! Pull your cords the instant you're clear of the ship.'

He gesticulated impatiently at Fawcett. Go! You're not contributing anything but weight!

Someone's voice came over the interphone: 'Good luck, Lieutenant.'

Then the awkward, bulky forms were scrambling for the emergency exits. A blast of cold air assaulted Everett's ankles. Fawcett disappeared through the bomb bay hatch.

Mercifully, the Kraut seemed to have gone looking for other game. He had to fight *Boomerang*'s controls; she was lurching, wobbling. The wind-battered flames threw weird patterns on the window. He was alone.

OK. Time to leave. A glance at the compass. The nose was pointed south. Away from the city. God knows what difference it made; she would probably spin in the instant he let go of her controls . . .

Hell, the hatch was only a few feet away. A push to get himself out of the seat. Another heave to cover the tiny distance to safety . . .

Even as he moved he felt the aircraft go. The floor revolved. He was pinned. His fingers grasped the edge of the hatch but he couldn't move. He weighed fifty tons. Hopeless . . . stupid to keep trying . . . but he had to . . .

Empty cartridge cases rained on him and went bouncing away against the lacerated hull; one of Meade's navigation books tumbled on his hand; it stung. Then it was gone, tossed by the wild gyrations of the aircraft as it plunged. This was unquestionably it. Any instant now. He wasn't afraid of death but the thought of it saddened him; living would have been good . . .

He *saw* the detonation. Brightness. He felt the heat of it. Simultaneously he heard the B-17's structure snapping: a succession of reports like a fantastically rapid machine gun. A wave of heat swept over him. He was spinning.

Seven

From the ground it was a weird display of winking, streaking lights, of bangs, of flames, of the frenzied tones of engines at full power.

We had run out into the street. Mr Roseberry announced that the Yanks were shooting at one another.

'They've gone bloody mad,' he said. 'I'm going inside.'

Georgina's white face looked upward.

'What's happening, Dad?'

I didn't know, but it had to be the Jerries. A raid of some sort. We ducked as an aeroplane roared overhead. In the darkness it seemed to have missed us by only a foot or two, but no doubt it was much higher. A stream of tracer streaked by. Odd, how slowly it appeared to be moving; the pace looked almost leisurely.

Frances begged us to go back inside the house.

We turned as flames streamed across the sky.

'It's hit! Look!'

You could glimpse its shape as it went by. A B-17. An instant later we heard another machine. We saw the lights streaking between the two machines. And then they were out of sight.

Of course we had no idea that it was Everett's aircraft that was on fire. But we all knew that it might be. And because it was as important as hell to all of us, we made no mention of it.

Frances was clutching my arm, pulling me back towards the house. Sensible of her. Guns seemed to be going off in every direction. Something hit the chimney; a bullet perhaps; part of a brick slithered off the roof and fell at my feet.

Then we saw the blazing Fort again. It had turned back towards the field; now the whole of one wing seemed to be a mass of flames. I expected the machine to plunge, but it kept staggering on. I thought the pilot was trying to attempt a landing, then I realized he was climbing. We watched, horrified yet fascinated. Flames marked the agonizing path through the sky. Then, suddenly, the flames changed direction.

'James . . .!'

The explosion was spectacular. A great ball of fire erupted. Blazing fragments spewed out like rockets. There was a boom that shook the ground beneath us.

'My God . . .' breathed Frances at my side. 'Those poor boys . . .'

A piece of wing, its engine mounting, ribs and spars clearly visible through its wrapping of fire, came tumbling: a huge flare that illuminated the street and the white-faced people who watched.

And in its light we saw the figure of a man, plunging, a half-opened parachute fluttering above him. Arms and legs splayed, he described a somersault before disappearing from our view.

Appalled, we could only look at one another.

Malcolm Fleece was inside the pub. He thought a bomb had hit the place.

Everett's descent demolished or did critical damage to: sixteen panes of skylight glass, one double bed belonging to Archie and Felicity Broadbent, one attic floor, one bedroom floor, most of one wall, three pictures, four electric light fixtures, three mirrors, twenty-seven half-pint glasses, forty-one pint glasses, thirty-six bottles of light ale, twelve of brown ale, seven of port and fifty-five of Scotch.

He burst through the ceiling of the Saloon Bar, preceded by the Broadbents' bed, a shower of glass, plaster, timber and electric wiring.

'For a moment,' Malcolm reported later, 'I thought the whole bleedin' place was going.'

An old chap named Joe Plumb stood there, holding his pint of bitter, gaping at the mountain of debris that had abruptly materialized before him.

As for Everett, he had stopped falling midway between the ceiling and the floor, entangled in his parachute harness, his flying suit singed, caked in plaster and festooned with wooden slats.

Joe Plumb claimed that he muttered, 'You'll have to excuse me, barging in like this,' before passing out.

He had, fortuitously, encountered the one tree that stood in The Lion's back garden. His half-opened parachute had snagged the branches, breaking his fall. Meanwhile, he had entered the pub through the skylight in the attic, landing on a spare bed. The old, tinder-dry floor of the attic had instantly collapsed under the shock, tumbling into the Broadbent's bedroom which also gave way. An Engineer Officer from the base examined the structure and, confirming Malcolm's observation, declared it incredible that the whole building hadn't fallen down.

We visited Everett in the Base Infirmary. He had a broken leg, a dislocated shoulder, a few minor burns and an impressive collection of bruises and cuts.

'The other guys jumped just before the ship blew up,' he told us. 'I remember the bang. After that, nothing. I guess I was blown out. And I must have pulled the ripcord or maybe the explosion did it for me. I don't know. The next thing I recall is an old guy holding a pint of beer and looking at me as if I was a prize exhibit at the zoo.'

I told him that he had officially inherited my title of the Luckiest Man at Ashley. He grinned. He was a happy man. He had completed his twenty-fifth mission.

They sent him back to the United States. A year and a half later he was shipped out to the Far East to fly B-29s against Japan. He completed fifteen more missions by war's end without a scratch.

In May of 1946 he returned to Ashley and stayed until Georgina's divorce from Donald was final. Then the four of us went to Bedford, Massachusetts, for the wedding. Everett and Georgina lived in Bedford for several years. They had two daughters, Linette and Lisette. Then, in 1963, they all returned. After nearly demolishing The Lion, Everett became its proprietor. He still is. It is an occupation that seems to afford him endless pleasure. Georgina and he now live above the pub; there is room enough since both the girls have married and set up homes of their own.

Perhaps there really are signs. And perhaps they really were communicating with Everett. If so, it looks as if they may have been correct. Perhaps Everett will die in Ashley after all.

*

One day in March, a couple of years ago, an odd thing happened. A snappily dressed man of middle age entered The Lion. He ordered a brandy and soda. According to Georgina, who witnessed the whole thing, Everett and the man talked for ten minutes or more. Then the man said goodnight and left. A moment later Everett followed him out to the car park.

He returned after a few minutes. He was dishevelled and his fists were bleeding. But he was smiling. Beatifically.

When questioned, he would only say that the man was someone whom he had met in London, once, years and years ago.

Epilogue

I invariably look skyward when I hear an aeroplane. It is the automatic, instinctive reaction of the old aviator. Usually I am disappointed. The sound emanates from some speck of a jet God knows how many thousands of feet up in the sky. Who can relate to anything so remote? But one hot day last week I saw an Antoinette circling. Nonsense, you say; Antoinettes date from the early 1900s and none exists outside museums. You are correct, of course. Undoubtedly it was a trick of the light or a touch of sun stroke or the onset of senility. No matter, the Antoinette clattered overhead and turned. Again it flew over me, lower this time. I waved. In reply, a gauntleted hand fluttered. Suddenly I realized what was wrong. The pilot was searching for the aerodrome and all he could see was houses! Endless rows of them! Where was the field? I could have told him, that moustachio'd gallant in his draughty cockpit. The field has ceased to be. It is nothing now but a fragment of the past. It exists only in memories and on the pages of history books.

But if the field has gone, the people haven't. They are still here, every one of them. I see them daily. We exchange a few words. We reminisce. We have an endless store of memories. Every day we produce them, like trophies from the cabinet, to be examined and re-examined for the umpteenth time.

Sometimes passers-by glance twice at me, probably thinking I am mumbling to myself. I'm not of course. I'm chatting to Eggleton or to Martin Colman or Bill Borthwick.

They are kind, my friends from the past; they tell me that I am looking fit and haven't changed at all.

Only Beresford tells me the truth.

'You're a blithering old idiot who has lived far too long.'

I have a feeling he is correct. As usual.

I assure Frances that the children are in good health and prospering: Georgina and Everett here at Ashley, Martin and his family in London.

She puts her head to one side, smiles and asks, 'When are you coming to join me?'

I tell her it can't be long now.